Camping in the Backyard

Camping in the Backyard

Home on Leave

Anthony J. Zatti

Writers Club Press
New York   Lincoln   Shanghai

Camping in the Backyard
Home on Leave

Writers Club Press
an imprint of iUniverse, Inc.

For information address:
iUniverse
2021 Pine Lake Road, Suite 100
Lincoln, NE 68512
www.iuniverse.com

ISBN: 0-595-17408-6

This book is a work of fiction. It is the product of the author's imagination. None of the characters have ever existed outside the author's mind and any resemblance to actual persons, living or dead, is entirely unintentional and coincidental. Most locations and businesses are entirely fictitious, however, New York City and Radio City Music Hall existed in 1960 and are still in existence.

Printed in the United States of America

Dedicated to Brother Stephen, one of the nicest people anyone could have as a friend, and to the best editor in the world, Robert Marchesani, who helped me correct hundreds of errors in my original manuscript.

Prologue

Much of Michael's childhood was happy, full of warm memories of life in the little bungalow in Mellon, a small village outside of Poughkeepsie. Michael and his sister, Rosa, moved to the house on Maiden Lane with his mother and father in 1943.

Rosa was two years older than Michael and was going to go to school in the fall. Michael wasn't sure what that meant, but his mother and father mentioned it all the time. Somehow he could sense that it wasn't going to be a good thing for him. After all, the only other little person he knew was Rosa. Mellon was a tiny village and no children lived within walking distance, and the Manganaros didn't have a car.

The radio in the kitchen was playing a song by the Andrews Sisters on *The Make-Believe Ballroom*. Michael's mother listened to that program every day, particularly when she was busy in the kitchen. The kitchen was the largest room in the house with four windows overlooking a flower and vegetable garden, a garden of which his mother, Louisa Manganaro, was quietly proud. It was August now, and the garden was continuing to yield its fragrance and bear all kinds of vegetables. There were beans and tomatoes ready for picking, and there was an abundance of squash that would be ready at the end of September, probably after Rosa went to school.

The kitchen was his favorite room. The walls were covered with yellow wallpaper with dark green ivy on it. It covered all the walls except the one behind the large, black, coal stove which was used during the winter to heat the house, more often than for cooking. For cooking there was a gas stove with a large oven that was above Michael's head. He couldn't see into it when his mother was baking or roasting something unless he stood on a chair. The oven fascinated him. Stuff went in one way and came out another, delicious, wonderfully delicious stuff. He loved roasted meats and baked goods of all kinds.

Today was a good day to go outside and play, he thought.

"Michael, let's go out. I'll help you get your bike out of the cellar," Rosa said as she tugged on his undershirt and opened the screen door.

"Don't go too far. Lunch'll be ready in ten minutes," Louisa said as the screen door slammed behind them.

It was hot and humid outside, and the sounds of crickets confirmed that summer would soon be over. The sun was almost overhead and made Michael's curly, golden blond hair sparkle. Michael was a good-looking boy, more pretty than handsome, with delicate features, fair skin and big blue eyes. Michael resembled his mother. Rosa on the other hand had strong features, a prominent nose, a large, full mouth, olive skin and dark brown eyes. Her shoulder length, straight hair was dark brown. She looked older than she was. Rosa was her father's daughter; not only did she look like him, but she possessed many of his character traits as well.

Michael didn't want to ride his bike because it was so hot, but chose instead to ride the swing. There were two swings that his father had built for them. Anthony Manganaro was handy with tools and liked to work on projects in and around the bungalow. He built the swings, the chicken coop, and kitchen cabinets and was forever doing something in the basement. Since the family's income was limited, his being handy around the house was a blessing. Both Michael and Rosa rode the swings, enjoying the cooling breeze the motion created and the shade of the sour cherry tree overhead. The swings were right next to the flower garden, and Michael loved looking at the flowers. The blue and pink hydrangeas were in full boom. He enjoyed the flowers, and the way they smelled and wanted to pick a bouquet for his mother.

Michael asked his sister, "Can we get some flowers for mommy?"

"We better ask her first, and if she says, 'yes,' we can do it after lunch."

From inside the kitchen, Louisa hollered loudly in a Wagnerian mezzo-soprano, "Michael, Rosa, come and get it. Soup's on!"

Fall, unfortunately for Michael, came. He would always be able to remember the sadness he was feeling at that moment every fall of his life. His best friend was gone. His companion gone. His teacher gone. His protector gone. He did not believe when she walked out the front door of the house on Maiden Lane that she would ever return. She got on that yellow bus and disappeared. Rosa was gone. She had never left him before.

He stood in the bay windows after she left. Would that yellow bus come back? His mother brought his lunch to him, so he could continue his watch. She made Campbell's vegetable soup and a half of a tuna sandwich. She put the soup, sandwich and glass of Ovaltine on the small table in front of the window. She was distressed to see her son in such a state of sorrow, grieving for his loss. He waited and waited. Mrs. Manganaro tried to keep busy in other parts of the bungalow, as she could not bear to see her sad, little boy holding his Teddy.

When 2:45 p.m. came around, Michael heard a vehicle with a noisy engine coming down Maiden Lane. It was the big, yellow school bus, and it stopped in front of his house. The door opened. No one came out, but then there she was. Rosa was getting off.

Michael, who had not done so for six months, wet his pants.

"Mommy," he screamed, "Rosa's home."

Michael didn't leave Rosa's side until it was his bedtime. He was so glad she had returned to him.

During the months ahead, after Rosa went to school, Michael spent most of his waking hours watching his mother doing things around the house. He followed her everywhere with his Teddy in tow. Slowly, he began to help. He learned to dust and to fold laundry. He also learned how to look for coins in the living room chair under the cushions. He didn't know that his father left the coins on purpose.

He only left his mother alone when she was vacuuming. He hated that vacuum cleaner. It made too much noise. He hated noise.

His mother spent a lot of the day in the kitchen, and since it was his favorite room, so did he.

There was an old Victrola in the corner of the kitchen near the pantry where it was cooler than the rest of the room. Michael loved to crank up the machine, so he could play the hundreds of records, mostly operas, that his mother had accumulated. Sometimes Louisa would sing along with the arias.

He learned many things over the next two years from his mother. Louisa drew the letters of the alphabet on colored paper and put them up on the refrigerator and walls. She taught Michael to read ingredients in her *Woman's Home Companion Cookbook*.

The first word he recognized in print was milk. She had taught him how the 'M' should sound and one day when he was looking in the cookbook he pointed to the word "milk" and asked what the word was.

She said, "How does the first letter sound?"

He sounded, "Mmm."

"That's right," she affirmed and told him he could find it in the refrigerator.

He brought back a bottle of milk and said, "I know what that word is, Mommy. It's milk."

In the next few weeks, Michael began to learn many words: flour, sugar, butter, Crisco, baking powder, pan, cup, teaspoon, tablespoon, sift, and more. He learned what the abbreviations were for many things found in the kitchen.

He loved looking at the pictures in the cookbook. There were beautiful, colorful pictures of prepared food, table settings, all kinds of cakes and pies and many how-to insets. He never tired of looking at the pictures in the cookbook, and he never tired of learning new words.

He learned how to measure ingredients, sift flour, mix things, and to help his mother with her kitchen activities. He enjoyed shaping the rolls from the yeast dough that she made every Friday. As he got more and more fascinated with helping in the kitchen, he grew less and less anxious about Rosa's homecomings. Rosa was making new friends and gradually played less with her little brother after school.

Before Michael went to school, he could read. Louisa was proud of that. He could read from Rosa's second grade *See and Say* easily.

He could also open and close the door on the black stove and add wood to keep the fire going.

He listened attentively to Rosa's stories about school, and he was looking forward to going at the end of the summer, but he would miss his mother and the time they spend together in the kitchen. He would also miss the hours he had spent reading the cookbook in the garden. But, he was ready for the adventure.

One afternoon late in August 1945, Mrs. Manganaro went out on the back porch to summon Michael. He was riding the swing.

"Michael, I'm going to make a peach pie. Do you want to help?"

"Sure. I'll be right there.

She went back inside, and Michael came in a minute later. She noticed that he didn't have Teddy. "Where's Teddy?"

"Oh, Ma. He's outside playing on the swing. He didn't want to help, and he doesn't want to go to school in a couple weeks. He wants to stay home with you. Do you mind?"

"No, Michael."

"What's wrong, Ma?"

"Nothing. I was just cutting an onion."

Michael was going to miss the few chickens they raised behind the garden. But he planned to feed them in the mornings before school and in the afternoons after school. He could still collect the eggs, too. He liked that.

Chapter 1

It was November, 1960. He had had his twentieth birthday while in boot camp. Michael was on the plane with his friend, Jonathan. They were headed home, home from Chicago to New York. Michael had said a good Act of Contrition to himself, just in case the Church was right about a number of things that Michael disagreed with. And since this was only his fourth airplane ride, he figured he'd better give them the benefit of the doubt. They had taken off a few minutes ago. When the No Smoking sign was turned off, he offered a Lucky Strike to Jonathan, who took one. Jonathan ignited his sterling silver lighter and lit Michael's cigarette and then his own.

"Thanks, Jonathan. Can you believe we're going home?"

"Pinch me," Jonathan said and Michael obliged pinching Jonathan's thigh. "Ouch!"

"Sorry. Just trying to be accommodating."

They laughed. Michael was sitting next to the window, and Jonathan had the aisle seat. A stewardess stood in the aisle next to Jonathan. She was pushing a cart. "Would you like a beverage? Champagne, cocktails, soft drinks?"

"Yes, thank you. I'd like a screwdriver. Michael, what would you like?"

"Do you have a Manhattan?"

"Yes, sir. I have two."

"I'll take them," Michael said.

She gave Jonathan his screwdriver in a crystal glass with ice and two small, chilled bottles of Manhattans to Michael with a tall stemmed cocktail glass with the airline's logo on it.

Michael noticed a pronounced southern drawl as she said, "If you need anything, please press the call button and I'll come right back. It's about a four-hour flight. We'll be serving your meal in about an hour. We have a choice today of roasted rack of lamb, roasted prime rib of beef *au jus* or roasted capon stuffed with hickory-smoked ham and Swiss cheese. You can let me know whenever you're ready, and I'll place your order with the galley."

"We'll let you know in a few minutes," Jonathan cooed. "See you later."

She pushed her cart forward.

"I'm glad you convinced me to pay the extra money to fly first-class, Jonathan. I mean, it was only forty-five dollars more than the allowance the Navy gave us," Michael said.

"Michael, how did we live through it?"

"I don't know. What I do know, however, is that you helped me get through it. I don't know how I would have done it without you," Michael said. "What a lot of fuckin' shit they put us through."

"Yeah. Those drill instructors were a bunch of vicious, fuckin' sadists. Christ, it was awful," Jonathan affirmed. "It's lucky for the both of us that the company commander took a liking to you and made you company clerk. It gave both of us some special privileges."

They flew in silence for a while. Michael watched the landscape below change as they climbed. While he was home during this leave he wanted Jonathan to visit. To say that Michael was fond of Jonathan was an understatement. He felt on top of the world sitting next to Jonathan. Maybe it was the fact that he was headed home, at last.

"Are you going to visit me in Mellon, Jonathan? I'd like to see you."

"Yes, I will. I have your number. I'll call you when I get home. I like you a lot and don't want to lose contact with you, and I want to see the barn, if you have one." Jonathan chuckled and stretched out in his seat. "Now I'm going to finish my screwdriver and sleep. I'm sleep-deprived."

"Okay. No barn, though. Just six chickens and a chicken coop. I'll drink one of these and maybe I'll doze, too."

The vibrations of the engines and propellers made Michael think he was sitting inside a giant electric razor. Michael was thinking of his family and their dog, Butterball. How good it will be to get home! He hadn't told them what flight he would be on; just that he would be home this evening. The Manhattan, a cheap one, probably one-third sweet vermouth and two-thirds of some inferior whiskey, however badly it tasted, was warming. He began to feel a little high.

From daydreaming about a future that included spending time with Jonathan, he went into reminiscing. He remembered his first day at school. How he hated leaving home. He missed his mother. He missed his house, his kitchen, Teddy, his garden. The school was full of noisy kids. He hated noise. Individually, and in small groups, he liked his classmates. He avoided the crowded schoolyard and, in particular, the crowded basement where all the kids were packed during inclement weather. When it was basement time, he hid in a stall in the bathroom. The school bus was noisy, too. The kids screamed and yelled, tossing books and lunch boxes back and forth. He tried to sit near the driver, and he avoided sitting near Rosa, who preferred that he did so, so she could sit with her friends. He always tried to save a seat for John Walker, his friend, who got on later. Mrs. Manganaro told Michael not to play with John Walker because his mother was divorced, but Michael played with him anyway in the schoolyard and on the bus. Some days he would play at John's house, too, which was fun since John's mother worked and didn't get home until late. He lied to his mother, and said he was playing kick ball in the schoolyard. Fat chance. He didn't like lying to his mother, but he liked playing with John more. So it didn't matter.

His mind went to happy times on Maiden Lane. The Thanksgiving and Christmas holidays were great. He and Rosa loved Christmas. They always put up the tree together on Christmas Eve and always ran out of lights, bulbs, or ornaments, or tinsel. His father, Anthony Manganaro, made many trips in the car to Main Street to Ray's Hardware Store to get anything they ran out of. When Rosa started to drive, she and Michael went to Ray's. It was a Christmas tradition. Rosa would throw the tinsel on in clumps, and Michael would take the clumps off and put the tinsel back on, a strand at a time. A lot of good-natured teasing surfaced at the annual tree decorating. There was always a nice feeling in the bungalow on Christmas Eve. Louisa put a tempting cold-cut buffet in the dining room with potato salad and various breads, and homemade cake and cookies. Before TV, they always listened to Bing Crosby records and after TV, watching the Tiny Tim movie became a tradition. In the years that Michael sang solos at midnight Mass, Rosa, an alto, would sing in the choir. Those were good times. He remembered putting up the colored lights on the porch in the freezing cold without finger covers (Rosa used to laugh at him when he called gloves finger covers), so he could hold the nails and hammer them in. After every three or so feet, they would go inside to have some hot chocolate, but if no one were around, they would take some of Louisa's Ruby Red Port from her closet stash.

On a daily basis, Rosa and Michael seldom saw each other at school, and at home the only time they spent together was at supper. They did, however, go on family outings together. Every summer, they took day trips to Jordan Lake about thirty-five miles from their home. Anthony would fill up the old ice chest at Miller's Icehouse at the crack of dawn and then drive home to pick everyone up. The lake had about forty scattered campsites, and he liked to arrive early enough, so the car could be driven right up to a site, so that they wouldn't have to cart all the stuff they brought to the site. The ice chest would be full of chicken parts, hamburgers, hotdogs, peaches, plums, tomatoes and usually a thick steak for supper. They brought a case of soda and a case of beer. They took home the beverages they didn't use, but the food always got used up. Rosa and Michael enjoyed each other on these trips. They took long walks in the wilderness down along the old brook and sometimes into the rolling hills above the lake. Their father was a swimmer and a diver. Louisa, Rosa and Michael were afraid of the water and just got pleasure keeping cool by wading or using the old inner tube in the roped off shallow section of the late. Once in a while, Mr. and Mrs. Gruber, who were neighbors and owners of Gruber's, and their daughter, Maureen, joined them. Rosa didn't have a good time then. She thought Maureen was lusting after Michael, and she was right.

Michael loved movies. He was hoping someday to get Jonathan as interested in them as he was. Jonathan. Jonathan. He couldn't stop thinking about him, but after all, how could he, when he was sitting right next to him. Michael couldn't remember at first how his addiction to movies started. Then he did. He remembered. When he was eleven, he used to deliver show cards, a monthly calendar of movies to be shown at the Mellon Movie Palace, to his selected route and, in turn, received a pass to go to as many shows as he could in a month. The movie's double features were changed four times a week. He went often, and since he did this for about two years, he was able to see many current and many old movies, as well. He became a real movie buff. Sometimes, Rosa would join him. The manager liked Rosa, so when he was there he let her in for free. Michael loved Rosa and her company.

It was at one of these movies that he met Gary Plotsky. Gary Plotsky went to St. John's Catholic School, and Michael went to Mellon Junior High. Gary delivered show cards, too, and wanted to become a friend of Michael's. At first, Michael didn't want to be Gary's friend because Gary was a little overweight and had a slight accent. One Sunday afternoon Gary asked, "Can I sit with you today for the Rock Hudson movie?"

Michael replied, "Not unless you pay me a nickel."

Gary walked away, and Michael felt sorry that he had been unkind. He was going to look for Gary and apologize when Gary returned and unceremoniously handed a nickel to Michael. They went to the movies together for weeks, and Michael and Gary became the closest of friends. But every time they got together, whether it was for pizza, bowling or church, Gary had Michael's nickel ready. During boot camp, when Michael had a fever and was nursing an infected shoulder from a blister from carrying that make-believe rifle, mail call brought a letter from Gary. When Michael saw that a nickel was Scotch taped to the letter he felt better, and the contents of the letter really cheered him up.

Michael and Gary were inseparable through the remainder of junior high and high school. Halfway through high school Gary flunked out of Catholic school because he was unable to pass Latin and went to Mellon High, and he was in some of Michael's classes. They spend many, many hours on "The Rock," a monument that they had adopted deep in the forest, accessible only by foot. Trials, tribulations, rejections, plans for the future, and, of course, sex were all subjects for "The Rock" discussions. "The Rock" seemed even to help relieve occasional depression.

Gary's letter to Michael closed with, "While you're home, let's bundle up and visit 'The Rock.'"

The same stewardess appeared next to Jonathan. She was exceptionally pretty with medium length blond hair, and she looked great in the airline outfit.

"You guys look great in those snappy uniforms. Are you going home on leave?" she asked, leaning slightly toward Jonathan, thrusting her ample breasts, which were pressed against her starched, white blouse, almost into his face.

"Yes," Jonathan said, smiling his big smile. "You look terrific, too. We're going back to New York City. I live in Manhattan, and my friend, Michael, lives about ninety miles out of town. Are you from the City?"

Christ, Michael thought, can't you hear that accent? Sounds like she's from the bayou.

"No. I'm from Houma, Louisiana, but I fly in and out of the New York area airports so often, that I share an apartment in Howard Beach on Long Island with three girls and two guys. It's great for layovers and for when we're on reserve," she said.

"But with two guys?" Jonathan inquired.

She laughed. "They're interested in each other, if you know what I mean."

"Can I call you?" Jonathan asked.

"Yes." She gave Jonathan her phone number on a beverage napkin and then headed for the cockpit. He put the napkin in his pocket.

Michael cringed. "Jonathan, you're such a flirt."

"Maybe. But I may be able to help her out."

"What do you mean?"

Janice, the stewardess, turned and came back to their row.

"I forgot to take your food orders."

"No problem. I'll take the chicken," Jonathan said.

"And I'll have the lamb," Michael added.

"Thanks. See you guys later."

After she walked away, Jonathan said, "Looks like she really needs it."

"What?"

"Seven good inches."

"I'm about to be sick," Michael said in disbelief.

Chapter 2

Michael was in his own bed. His head was on his own pillow. He was awake now staring at the water crack in the ceiling, the same crack that seemed to reappear during any major rainfall regardless of his father's efforts to repair the roof. He had gotten so used to the crack that he missed it during his time away at boot camp. Last night when he had gotten home, Rosa and his mother and father were waiting for him. Butterball, too. Everybody was happy that he was home, and they marveled at the physical changes in him. He had put on about twenty-five pounds of muscle. Michael was thrilled to be home at last for a thirty-day leave, and he was so excited that he had one of his favorite drinks, a Manhattan, to calm down. Then he had another and another. He really didn't remember any more about last night, other than being tired and going to bed early to enjoy sleeping in his own bed.

Michael got out of bed and shut the window. It was getting too cold now to keep the window fully open. He must have forgotten to close it last night, or maybe he had forgotten how cold it usually got the week before Thanksgiving.

He walked over to the mirror on top of the bureau and tilted it, so he could see his entire body. In boot camp the only mirrors available were the small ones in the latrine attached to the bulkhead over the sinks, which the recruits used primarily for shaving. He stood there nude. Those painful hours of exercise and calisthenics certainly had paid off. The hours of pushing that fuckin' piece paid off, too. And all that endless marching had made his legs and back strong and improved his posture. The pushups and sit-ups didn't hurt either. And whoever would have thought that someone who was afraid of water at Atlantic City in June would have become an expert swimmer in only sixteen weeks at the Ramapo Naval Training Center? Christ, he thought, you really have changed. He admired his upper-body development, his shoulders, his biceps and triceps, and particularly his pecs, and his thirty-inch waist. He had never been in such good physical shape. He ran his fingers over his chest and arms, and then he turned sideways, so he could see his muscled back and shoulders. All his life he had wanted to look like this and finally, he thought, he looked super, except, of course, for the hair, but that, indeed, would grow back.

He had a lot to do during his time home.

"Michael, it's almost ten," he heard his mother say from outside his door. "Your father and sister left for work hours ago. Would you like me to make some breakfast for you?"

"Thanks, Mom. I'll be out in a minute."

"What do you want?"

"Orange juice, coffee and maybe some bacon and eggs."

"Coming right up."

He stood before the mirror. Damn, you do look great.

His mother was a good cook, except for eggs. Either the yolks broke, or the eggs turned crunchy around the edges with black stuff on the bottom. He always wondered how she could make some of the best dishes he had ever eaten and still crucify eggs. He should have asked for French toast. She made that taste as if it had floated down from heaven. Maybe he should ask for that tomorrow.

He put on a bathrobe and sat down at his desk. It felt peculiar sitting in a bathrobe instead of skivvies. He was going to have to get used to a lot of things now that he was home again; particularly he was going to have to get used to refraining from using his newly acquired, vulgar vocabulary. Fuckin'a man, he was going to have to watch it.

He lit a Lucky Strike and took a long drag. There was someone on his mind that he wanted to think about. Jonathan Taylor. He wanted to think about him all the time. He even liked the way his name sounded in his mind—Jonathan Taylor. He wanted to get together with him during their leave. But now, he just had to think.

Jonathan Taylor's friendship had been important to him all through boot camp, and he cherished the hours they spent together. Jonathan was definitely a ray of sunshine in an otherwise bleak, depressing, oppressive atmosphere. He was gentle, thoughtful and kind in a harsh, callous environment. He was special. Michael felt that his friendship with Jonathan would last a lifetime.

He liked Jonathan from the moment they met at the gedunk truck on a Sunday afternoon. Michael bought a brownie and a bag of chips, and

Jonathan bought some chocolate covered donuts. They sat on the grass between the barracks and ate gedunk.

Michael, being the company clerk, was fortunate enough to have a small office on the second floor of the company's barracks next to the Company Commander's office. He liked to retreat to the office after his evening swimming lesson. After Jonathan finished his duties he would visit with Michael in his office for his remaining days of boot camp. Michael didn't have duties such as watches because of his function as company clerk, and because he sang as soloist for the Blue Jackets' Choir on Sundays.

Jonathan was six-feet with blond hair and weighed about 165 pounds. He had very expressive, big blue eyes, and he used them to emphasize his conversations. Sometimes Michael thought he looked like Troy Donohue with Bette Davis eyes.

Michael learned that he came from a very wealthy family who lived in a high-rise apartment on the East Side of Manhattan, and that his father was Jonathan Anthony Taylor, Chairman and President of Taylor Oil, a company with substantial oil wells pumping non-stop in Oklahoma and Texas. Jonathan had gone to a very exclusive military high school and had attended Brown University for several semesters before joining the Navy. Jonathan never explained why he enlisted instead of getting into some officer candidate-training program. Michael guessed that he didn't need the money and probably didn't want to make the six-year commitment in the reserves. Maybe it was because he wore glasses sometimes, and perhaps one of the requirements for OCS was 20/20 vision. Who knows?

Michael did know that he was very attracted to Jonathan. He liked the way he looked, the way he talked, the way he laughed. Michael couldn't keep his eyes off Jonathan except by resolute determination to do so, so others wouldn't notice. Even so, several times the company commander came into the company clerk's office for one reason or other to check on Michael and Jonathan to make sure all was well. While they never discussed it, never planned it, they both would shower each evening at about the same time. Michael felt a great deal of pleasure seeing Jonathan soap up and shower, but inevitably Jonathan would start getting an erection, and Michael would flee lest others detect the sexual vibration between the two.

The phone rang twice, and Michael heard his mother pick it up in the kitchen.

"Hello," Michael heard her say. "Yes. He's here. Let me tell him you're calling."

He heard his mother's footsteps coming to his door. She knocked twice and said, "Michael it's for you. It's Jonathan. Jonathan Taylor."

"Thanks, Mom."

Michael picked up the extension in his room.

"Hi, Jonathan. How's everything going?"

"Fine, Michael. I'm glad you're home. Nobody was here last night when I got home. I guess they forgot I was coming. My father and his wife are on holiday for a few days and Adele, our housekeeper, isn't exactly sure when they'll be returning. I tried to call my mother, and her answering service told me she was away, too. Some homecoming. How was it at your place? Were they surprised to see the hunk the Navy made out of the skinny weakling I met just sixteen weeks ago?"

Michael laughed. "Yeah, they were. I was happy to see my mom and dad and Rosa, and they sure seemed happy to see me, but the best greeting came from my dog. It feels so queer being home, though. We all got a little drunk last night, but I'm sorry that you didn't have a group waiting for you. You should have come home with me. I told you that."

"Yeah. I should have. But, if the invitation's still open, I'd like to visit."

Michael's heart beat faster. "When? You know you're always welcome, but I have to warn you, we're simple folk, small house, no servants."

"Michael, stop being so apologetic. I want to see you, and I'd love to meet your mother and father and Rosa. I've heard so much about them. I could come later today, if that's okay and if you'll tell me how to get there."

"Of course it's okay. You can come for dinner, but you have to bring your uniform to wear. My dad's crazy about his son wearing the uniform, and I thought it would be nice if you did, too. As far as getting here, just take NYCN Transit from Grand Central to Poughkeepsie. The trains travel regularly today. Call and let me know which train you'll be on, and I'll pick you up. Bring what you need, so you can stay over. I'd love to see you, and I must tell you, I miss you already even though I only saw you yesterday."

"Great. I'll call you as soon as I know. Talk to you later."

"I can't wait to see you, buddy. Bye."

Michael's mother announced that breakfast was ready.

"I'll be right there, Mom."

He went into the kitchen and realized that not much had changed. The black stove was still there. There was a small fire in it. His mother kept the coffeepot on the back of it all day to keep it warm. She loved her coffee and drank about ten cups a day.

"Where's Butterball?"

"She's out back playing. If she knew you were up she'd be in here in a second. She kept going into your room this morning, checking on you. I guess she couldn't figure out why you weren't getting up. She missed you while you were gone, and she went into your room several times a day looking for you during your absence. God, we had her a long time. Since you found her, remember?"

"I didn't find her, Mom. She found me. That was the night that Drew and I were sleeping, or rather, camping in the backyard, and this mangy dog came into the tent and ate my sandwich."

"I was proud of you, Michael, when you took her down into the cellar and cleaned her up. You brought her up here to dry her by the stove and then you fed her and asked if she could stay for a while. Well, she's still here."

Breakfast was great. Eggs just right. Maybe she took an Eggs 101 class or something. His mother had a lot of questions about the Navy, and he did the best he could to provide all the answers.

"Who's Jonathan Taylor?" she quizzed.

"Ma, he's my best friend from boot camp. I invited him to dinner tonight."

"Michael, you should have asked me, but, of course, it's alright. What does he like to eat?"

"Could you make lasagna? Your lasagna is terrific, and I know he'd love it. I'll go to the store and get you anything you need. He'll be calling me later to let me know what train he'll be on. He lives in Manhattan."

"He's coming all the way from Manhattan to have my lasagna? I'll have to make a good batch. Your father will be glad to know that you made a new friend so early in the Navy. Is he cute? Will Rosa like him? Is he Catholic, not that it matters?"

"Ma!"

"I was just kidding. You know that."

"He's really good looking and rich, Ma. And his father is president of a pretty big oil company. The main office for the company is in New York, but most of its oil comes from Texas and Oklahoma where its refining and manufacturing plants are."

"Well, I hope he likes us, Michael," Louisa said.

Jonathan called and said he would be on the 4:10. That only gave Michael a few hours to get ready. He showered, shaved and put on some dungarees and a flannel shirt. He picked up the car keys and drove off to the A&P to pick up some mozzarella and ricotta that his mother needed for supper, picked up some wine at the Main Street Winery, and then he walked across the street to The Flower Shop to pick up some mums.

When he got home he looked around the living room. The place looked nice. Clean. Homey. There were two sets of bay windows with white tie-backed curtains looking out over Maiden Lane. There was a fireplace on the opposite side from the windows. The walls were covered with gray wallpaper with large flower arrangements on it. There were two royal blue club chairs and one dark gray sofa. There were several end tables and one coffee table that Michael particularly liked with a blue mirror top. Mrs. Manganaro loved art deco blue glass pieces and there were several around the room. She also liked to crochet, and two of her afghans were on the club chairs. There was a Steinway baby grand piano in the far corner of the room that Mrs. Manganaro had inherited from a deceased neighbor for whom she had done many favors. There was a new Dumont television settled in the center of one of the bay windows, and there was a closed sewing machine in a mahogany table in the other set of bay windows. The room looked nice; maybe not what Jonathan was probably used to, but nice. Michael went around the room and picked up the newspapers and magazines that were scattered and put them in the basket under the piano. He arranged the mums in the vase on the coffee table, but the arrangement looked a little sparse, so he went into the garden, and all he could find were some lingering greens, which he cut to fill in the arrangement. He also found a lone pumpkin that he brought in.

"You never made such a fuss for any of your other friends," observed Louisa.

"Well Jonathan is…oh, I don't know, Ma. I just want the place to look as homey and welcoming as I told him it was."

"You're not ashamed of your home are you?"

"Good God, no."

"Maybe I should put on something else," she said as she ran her hand down the sleeve of her dress.

Michael noticed her discomfort and offered, "I'm proud of you and the nice home you have always made for us, but if you would be more comfortable changing, go ahead, but I love you just the way you are. It's time I went to pick him up. See you later."

He went over to the sofa where he had thrown his coat and was about to leave, but he turned around and walked over to this mother, who was standing between the dining room and the living room. He kissed her impulsively and said, "I missed you, Mom."

"I missed you, too."

"Should I stop at Gruber's and pick up some cake or something?"

"Michael, that would be a good idea. See if they have that apricot crumb cake or strawberry shortcake, and if they don't have either of those, get a butter cake, you know the one, with the holes on top and brown sugar. Do you need any money?"

"No, thanks, Mom."

It didn't take Michael too long to drive to the station. The train pulled in, and Jonathan came onto the platform. He was carrying a garment bag and a small gym bag. He was wearing tan chinos and an expensive red cashmere sweater and cordovan penny loafers. He looked fabulous.

Michael ran up the platform steps and shook Jonathan's hand as he took his garment bag. He said, "How great to see you. And you look so special in civvies, without your Navy clothes. The car's over there parked under those trees."

"You look good, too, Michael."

The walked over to the car, a '58 blue Buick Rivera convertible.

"Michael, nice car. Is it yours?"

"Yes. Or almost. It was my uncle's and he died last year. He left it to my grandparents and they're both too old to drive, and they were going to sell it. But then they decided to sort of half give it to me and half I pay them one hundred dollars a month for a year. I think it's a pretty good deal for both them and me."

"Wow. So do I. How many miles do you get?"

"Not too many, I'm afraid. It's a V8, 300 horsepower, so I get about 7 around town and about 11 or 12 on the highway. I'm going to be stationed initially in Norfolk, and I plan on driving down. That way I'll find out how she handles on a long trip."

"I got my orders when we left yesterday, and I'm going to Norfolk, too. I'm going to be on the *U.S.S. Lake Erie.*"

"No shit. I'm going to be on the *U.S.S. Weehawken.* Maybe we'll be near each other."

"Wouldn't that be terrific?"

They both smiled. Jonathan opened the window and took in several deep breaths of air. It smelled good. Fresh air. Fresh, country, civilian air.

They drove through Saddlebrook and past several horse farms. Jonathan had his hands folded on his lap. Michael noticed that he must have gotten a manicure earlier in the day. He had nice hands, but they were unlike hands Michael was used to. Nobody in the country had his nails manicured. They passed the largest estate in the area, and Michael pointed it out to Jonathan. "That's the Balmoral Estate, Balmoral Hills. Willington Balmoral owns most of the land on both sides of this road."

"My father knows him. He's on the board of the Metro-Tri-State Opera with my father, as well as on the board of Taylor Oil."

"Oh." Michael didn't know what to say. For the moment he felt like a country bumpkin. He remained quiet until they were almost home.

Jonathan was watching Michael as he drove. He was a careful driver. Jonathan could tell that right away. But, Michael's serious look caused him concern. Had he said something wrong? Maybe he shouldn't talk about his father anymore.

They drove down Main Street, and Michael pulled up in front of Gruber's.

"I have to stop in here and pick up our dessert. Come on in with me, Jonathan."

"Sure."

They went into Gruber's, and Maureen Gruber was behind the counter. She was 18 and all through school, even since the second grade, she'd had a crush on Michael. When she saw him come in, her light German face blushed a deep crimson.

"Michael, Michael," she squealed. "You're home. You look just wonderful. Look what they did to you. And who's this?"

"Maureen, it's good to see you. You look well. How are you?" "Fine."

"This is my friend, Jonathan. We went through boot camp together. Jonathan, this is my old buddy, Maureen Gruber. We went all through school together."

"How do you do, Maureen?"

"I'm good. And you?"

"I'm well, thank you. And I'm pleased to meet an old friend of Michael's."

"Welcome to Gruber's," she said as she stared at Jonathan. She thought he looked a little like Tab Hunter, but maybe more like Troy Donahue.

"Maureen, can we have that strawberry shortcake in the refrigerator?"

"Actually that was supposed to be for someone's birthday today, and they never came to pick it up. Let me take it in the back and have them change the greeting from 'Happy Birthday' to 'Welcome Home—Michael and Jonathan'." She disappeared into the back room.

They both laughed. They were going to have a good time together even in these strange civilian circumstances. Michael felt like he was on a different planet from the Ramapo Naval Training Center. He never noticed that Jonathan talked a little differently. *How do you do?* Maybe that's the way they greet others in Manhattan. A little more formal than here. I wonder how they talk down south in Norfolk? Maureen came back in.

"It's fixed. Do you like it?"

"It's great, Maureen. Thanks very much," Michael said appreciatively.

She put the cake in a white box and tied it with white string.

"How much?"

"It's on the house, just to welcome you home. It's really great to see you and to meet you, Jonathan. Stop in again soon. Are you going to sing for us on Sunday, now that you're home?"

"You know, Maureen, I hadn't thought about it, but now that you mention it, maybe I should."

"It really would be a treat for all of us. You could wear your uniform. The *Mellon Press* could take your picture."

Now it was Michael's turn to blush. "Maybe. Thank you very much for the cake. I really appreciate it. Please say hello to your mother and father for me. We have to get going, Maureen. Good to see you. Bye."

"Goodbye, Maureen. I'm glad to have met you," Jonathan said with a big smile and a wink.

They left the little bakery and its wonderful aroma and got back in the car. They continued the ride home.

Jonathan said, "Did you ever get into her pants?"

"No, Jonathan, and I wouldn't tell you if I did," Michael said.

"Sorry. I didn't mean to get so personal. It's just that I feel so close to you that I forgot that we've never discussed sex or anything."

"No offense taken, buddy. Maybe tonight we can talk about some stuff that I have on my mind. We'll see."

As Michael drove down the narrow country road home, he realized how nice Jonathan smelled. The fragrance was delicate, definitely not after-shave. It was warm, soft, and woodsy. Jonathan must be getting warm, causing the fragrance to evaporate from his body and through his wool sweater into the cool air in the car. Michael also realized that Jonathan was sitting a little closer than most passengers would. He was less than a foot away from Michael, and Michael could actually feel the heat from Jonathan's body, particularly from his thigh, which was even closer than the rest of him. Michael wiped some small beads of perspiration from his upper lip, hoping Jonathan didn't notice. He opened his window a crack. He was anxious, having a panic attack.

Michael did not want to be a queer. The very thought that he might be a faggot made him want to vomit. The main reason he forced himself to successfully complete boot camp was to prove to everyone, particularly his father, that he was an all-American, butch-boy-next-door. Nothing sexual happened between Michael and Jonathan in boot camp. Michael wasn't aware that fear alone had made certain that nothing happened between them. He remembered Jonathan sitting across from him in that small office in his skivvies, ever so nonchalantly, casually touching his crotch and starring at Michael with those big, sad doe eyes.

The penalties for homosexual activity in 1960 armed forces of the United States were severe; the least of which were a dishonorable discharge and, more probably, a long prison term for sodomy. Faggots and cocksuckers did not belong in the Navy, but in prison, or, after discharged in disgrace more often than not, they brought their sinful lives to a close at the end of a rope, overdosing on drugs, slitting wrists, and other fatal acts. The hour-long compulsory attendance session on unauthorized sexual activity they were forced to endure during boot camp was included in the same session as venereal diseases. The first slide presentation concluded with prison inmates in an unnamed penal institution incarcerated for their perversions, and the second showed hospitalized individuals rotting away from all types of secondary conditions resulting from untreated sexually transmitted diseases, mainly gonorrhea and syphilis. It featured a woman, who had gone insane due to syphilis, chained to the wall and lying in a puddle in a psychiatric asylum. Recruits were told to strictly obey "off limits" warnings, particularly as they designated those establishments known to be frequented by homosexuals. They were told to be aware of the actions of their fellow sailors and to turn in anyone they had suspected was a homosexual to superiors. There was no question how the military, society in general, and God felt about deviation. Homosexuals were scum and should, if possible, be eliminated and those homosexuals who practiced their evil should be tortured. Sexual activity between unmarried heterosexuals was, for some unexplained reason, not only condoned, but also encouraged as long as condoms were used and medical attention sought as necessary. During their first and only six-hour leave from the training center the Catholic

Navy chaplain along with a medical officer in a captain's uniform gave out condoms at the gate as the recruits left the base. Nothing, however tempting or inviting, was going to happen between Michael and Jonathan while they were subject to the Uniform Code of Military Justice.

Michael remembered that he had felt the same way right then driving in the car as he had when Jonathan would slowly spread his legs and let his hand slide to rest on his upper thigh, while letting his thumb press against his testicles when they were at the training center. Michael wasn't sure what was going on then, and he wasn't sure now. Michael asked himself: Was Jonathan a faggot? A queer? Was he a cocksucker? Why did he ask me about getting into Maureen's pants? And what about flirting with Janice on the plane? What was going on? Was he making fun of me? Was he one of the set-ups that led you on and then turned you in? He had heard about them. Maybe he was one of those who would do something with you and then, feeling intense remorse, confess to a priest, or Navy chaplain, or Commanding Officer. Maybe he talked a lot and would confide in some other guy who would blow the whistle on the both of them. Jonathan was a bomb ready to explode. For all his physical beauty and desirability, Jonathan was trouble.

They were home. His father's car was in the driveway, pulled all the way forward to leave room for Michael. Michael parked right behind the green-and-tan '54 Chevy.

"We're home. That's my father's car. Learned to drive in it," Michael announced as he reached into the back of the car for Jonathan's bags.

"I learned to drive at a driving school in Manhattan. I wish my father had taught me. But we didn't have a car, and my father was always too busy anyway."

"I don't know about that. I mean having your father teach you. My dad and I didn't speak for days after each lesson."

Jonathan laughed, "I guess you're right. Particularly with my father, the perfectionist."

"Jonathan, you could have driven up here if you had a car."

"I do have a car, Michael. My father bought it for me for my twenty-first birthday last May."

"What kind?"

"A Jag."

"You're kidding."

"Nope. A green one with cream colored leather interior."

"Sounds great."

"Why didn't you drive up then?"

"Because the car's in the garage at my building. Has been for a few months."

"Is something wrong with it?"

"No. With me."

"What's that?"

"Lost my license for six months for speeding."

"You'd really be lost up here without a driver's license."

"Well, I miss it, too. But in the city it's not all that important."

"Oh."

"Can I give you a hand?"

"Sure. I've got your bags. Could you bring in the cake? I just can't tell you how happy I am to have you here."

Jonathan replied, "If only you knew how good it feels to be wanted. You know, I've been so rushed getting to the train and all, I forgot to get a gift for your mother."

Michael thought about what Jonathan had just said, as they got out of the car and started walking toward the house. "We're very casual about stuff like that up here. No one expects guests or company to bring anything, but if they do bring something, like a dessert or casserole, everyone appreciates it and enjoys. As a matter of fact, I'm sure mom is going to insist on giving you a care package of food to take home when you leave tomorrow."

"Actually, that would be nice. Other than Navy chow, I never get home cooking. Adele, our housekeeper, doesn't cook, and we all eat out."

Butterball, the eighty-percent Cocker Spaniel, came bouncing across the yard through the leaves to greet them. She was a light tan, over-weight mixed breed, looking almost exactly like a Cocker Spaniel, but not quite. Her ears were half the length of a regular Spaniel's. Michael never could imagine what kind of dog represented the twenty-percent. She was happy as she jumped up on Michael for his usual hug.

Next, she jumped up on Jonathan. Startled, he jumped back. "Does he bite?"

Michael put his arm around Jonathan and said, "Of course not. *She* doesn't bite. You're not used to pets, are you?"

"No, I'm afraid not, Michael," he said as he sat down on the cool ground covered with brown leaves. "What's her name?"

"Butterball."

"How fitting," he laughed. "Here, Butterball. Come here, girl," he called.

Butterball, who was running around in circles, ran back to Jonathan and put both her front paws on Jonathan's thighs. Jonathan put his head next to the dog's, and gave her a hug just as Michael had done. Butterball licked his ear.

"Michael, I think she likes me."

"She's not the only one."

Chapter 3

Michael was sure that his mother and father would like Jonathan, but wasn't sure about Rosa. She liked tough, blue-collar men. Those were the guys she liked to go out with. The educated, refined need not apply. She liked to talk about baseball, football, rock-n-roll and Elvis. She loved to bowl and do carpentry. She didn't enjoy classical music, except for Catholic Church music, despised opera and loathed the ballet. She thought tennis was for rich faggots, and ballroom dancing was for queers. She did love sailors though, and perhaps she wouldn't notice Jonathan's manicured fingernails and his cultured speech pattern when he was wearing his uniform.

Things were out of his hands now. However, he silently prayed, as they entered the house on Maiden Lane, that they would all like each other just in case his fantasy became reality. He had never felt like this in his entire life.

Chapter 4

It was about 5 p.m. when they entered the house. Butterball followed them in. Anthony Manganaro was sitting on the sofa looking through the *Mellon Press* and was listening to the evening news on one of the two channels they were able to get. He immediately got up when they came in.

"Mike, you got back fast. Your mother said you were going to stop for some cake," he said. He reached out his hand to Jonathan and greeted, "You must be Jonathan."

"Yes, Sir. I'm very happy to meet you, Mr. Manganaro," he said sharply as he shook Mr. Manganaro's hand firmly.

"I'm happy to meet you. Mike wrote about you in his letters, and we were hoping that you'd come up someday. Please make yourself at home."

"Thank you. Michael spoke to me about you, Mr. Manganaro, and about his mother and Rosa, I think, about every day. What's that wonderful smell?"

"That would be," Michael offered, "lasagna baking in the oven."

"Wow! It smells great."

"Let's go to my room, so you can put your stuff in there."

"Okay."

They left the living room and went through the dining room to Michael's bedroom.

"This is my room, and you're welcome to share it," Michael said as he handed the bags to Jonathan and took the cake box and put it on the bed. Actually, you're my first sleepover guest. You can use the desk as a dresser; some of the drawers are empty, and there's plenty of room in the closet. The bathroom's across the hall. And we only have one. When we first moved here when I was about three, we had an outhouse. My dad put in the bathroom with my mother's help. He also put in running

21

water from the well out back, so my mom didn't have to carry barrels from the pump. I'll show you the pump later. It's still there."

Jonathan was astonished. He never thought about where water came from other than from the faucet. When he hung his dress uniform in the closet, he noticed that the closet smelled like Michael. He never realized that Michael had such a distinct odor, but he did. Jonathan lingered at the closet for a moment and took a deep breath. The fragrance was earthy and sexy with a top-note of Ivory soap. He wanted to make love to Michael as soon as he could, but under the circumstances he wasn't sure he was going to be able to. He knew Michael was terrified, in the closet, and almost as frightened as he himself had been, when he had his first real grownup sexual adventure with the ballet dancer from the Metro-Tri-State Opera whom his father brought home. Stanley, that dancer, was older, built beautifully and very experienced. He took time to explain what being a homosexual was and to put Jonathan at ease. Perhaps Jonathan could do that with Michael, too. But he had to really handle it well. Michael loved the Navy so much, or so pretended, that he might frighten easily and panic. If that happened, he could be trouble.

"We can change later. But first let's go into the kitchen, so you can meet my mother."

"Sure."

When Michael saw his mother in the kitchen, he smiled when he noticed she had changed into her favorite "I Love Lucy" dress. It was a simple dress with long sleeves and a big, full shirt made out of taffeta, which made it make a rusting sound as she walked. It was her only dressy dress.

"Ma, I'd like you to meet Jonathan. Jonathan, my mother."

Jonathan extended his hand and shook Louisa's hand gently. She pulled him closer to her and kissed him on his cheek. He kissed her back.

"Mrs. Manganaro, I'm so glad to meet you. Michael tells me you're a wonderful cook. There were so many nights at camp that we talked about all the wonderful food you made, and it made both of us home-sick."

"Well you're here now, and I hope I don't disappoint you," she said looking him directly in his eyes. They were the most beautiful eyes she had ever seen. She was embarrassed because when she hugged him and felt his muscular body next to hers, she felt an attraction that she had never felt for anyone other than her husband. For shame. She blushed.

Jonathan said, "What smells so good? Is it your lasagna?"

"I hope so," she said. "Would you like something to drink?"

"No thanks," Jonathan said.

Michael asked, "When is dinner going to be ready? Jonathan and I are going to get changed into our uniforms for dinner. Dad said he wanted to share his first meal with his son in uniform."

"Dinner should be ready in about fifteen minutes," she said. "Maureen called. There's a choir rehearsal tonight, and Mrs. Rhine would like you to go if you can. It's at seven-thirty. She would like you to sing *Panis Angelicus* for communion on Sunday at the eleven o'clock High Mass, and she'd like to run over it with you."

"How could I? Does she know I have company?"

"The whole town knows. It seems Jonathan made quite an impression on Maureen, and Mrs. Rhine said you should bring him, and that she would run through your stuff first, and you wouldn't have to stay for the entire rehearsal." Michael looked at Jonathan inquisitively.

Jonathan said, "You don't have to ask me. I'd love to hear you sing in person. The only way I heard you in boot camp was over the radio with the Blue Jackets' Choir. I wanted to go a number of times, but I always had some watch or duty or something."

"Great. I'll call her back right now. We'll go after supper, and we'll be dressed in our uniforms. We'll look great, and it'll be fun."

Louisa liked seeing Michael standing next to Jonathan. They looked good together. Sort of like brothers. But she didn't know what she felt. Michael was good looking, talented and her son, but Jonathan was like a real life model for a toothpaste commercial.

They went back into Michael's bedroom to change.

"Shouldn't you lock the door?" Jonathan asked.

"Yeah. I guess so." Michael turned the lock.

Michael turned on the desk lamp and the large lamp on the double dresser. He made a quick call to Maureen to let her know they were going to the rehearsal. Then Michael got his dress uniform out of the closet and laid it on the bed with his scarf, which still had to be rolled and tied. His shoes were already spit-shined and were waiting under the bed.

Jonathan took out his garments, also and put them on the bed.

Michael took off his dungarees and shirt and sat down on the bed. He was wearing his authorized skivvies, white T-shirt and white boxer shorts stenciled with his name and serial number. Jonathan took off his sweater, folded it and put it in a desk drawer.

"Michael, I've been waiting for months to be alone with you like this."

"I know. Me, too."

"Michael, I really like you," he said softly, as he touched him on the shoulder.

"I know," he said as he watched Jonathan remove his chinos. He saw that Jonathan was getting half a hard-on, and the only thing he could think to say was, "Jonathan, you're wearing jockey shorts, and that's not authorized."

"I'm not in uniform yet, and I'm not on duty."

Michael heard his father walk past his door on his way to the kitchen. Michael felt his heart beating in his chest, and his forehead was covered with sweat. Jonathan's erect member had escaped the top of his shorts and was rigidly standing against his stomach. Michael saw a drop of pre-cum on the tip of Jonathan's penis, and he felt as if he were going to faint.

Jonathan saw the visible signs of panic in Michael and said, "Michael, come on. Hurry up and get dressed for dinner. Don't let this bother you," he said as he stuck his penis back into his shorts. "I always get horny when I change clothes, particularly when I'm starving."

"Sure. I'll be dressed in two minutes." Michael stood up, and they both got dressed.

Just as they were about to leave the room, Jonathan said, "Have you ever been kissed by a man and kissed him back?"

"No."

"I don't mean right now, but later before we hit the sack, would you like us to see what it feels like to kiss each other?"

"Yes." Michael unlocked the door.

Chapter 5

Anthony and Louisa Manganaro were seated at the dining room table when Michael and Jonathan came in. The table was covered with food: black and green olives, celery, red peppers, bread, butter, olive oil and wine vinegar in beautiful decanters, a roasted chicken encrusted in herbs, a large bottle of red table wine and a large baking dish of steaming hot lasagna. There was also a large wooden bowl of salad with cucumbers and plum tomatoes liberally dressed with garlic, oil and vinegar. Jonathan thought the smell in the room was fabulous, not at all like the aroma-free restaurants he frequented in New York City prior to joining the Navy. Michael's mother and father faced each other from the ends of the table, and Jonathan and Michael were seated together next to each other on the side of the table nearest the wall.

"Where's Rosa?" Michael inquired.

"She's working late," Louisa said. "They're running trial balances at the bank. They do that around the middle of the quarter, getting ready for interest period posting at the end of the quarter, the last three business days of December. She puts in a lot of overtime since she was promoted to supervisor."

"She was always good with math," her father said, "and she enjoys going to Manhattan every Monday and Tuesday evening to attend the American Institute of Banking. She got herself a little *Spitfire,* so she could go back and forth."

Michael said, "I didn't get to see that car yet. It must have been parked in the street last night when I got in and gone by the time I woke up this morning."

"Probably," Anthony said. "She uses it all the time. Uses it for work, too."

Michael asked, "What color is it?"

"Fire engine red," Anthony said. "I thought it was a little too dangerous to drive such a small car, but she insisted, and you know how stubborn she is, so I resigned myself to not thinking about her whizzing down the highway."

Mrs. Manganaro asked, "Jonathan, would you please say grace for us?"

Michael was shocked; he didn't know anything about Jonathan's religious background.

Jonathan began, "Father in heaven, we ask for Your very special blessing this evening for all of us gathered at this home and for those not here with us who are part of our lives. We thank You for this food and all the things You provide for us so bountifully. We ask that You watch over each of us and guide us to do Your will, so that we may enjoy eternity with You. We ask this in the name of Your Son, Jesus. Amen."

"Amen."

Michael was stunned, speechless.

"Thank you, Jonathan. That was lovely," Mrs. Manganaro said. "Jonathan, help yourself, please."

They all passed the food, and Louisa served each some lasagna from the baking dish in the center of the table.

"You both look handsome," she said.

"Thank you, Ma."

"Thank you, Mrs. Manganaro."

Michael's father said, "Michael, we had the piano tuned for you in case you wanted to play when you came home."

"Thanks. I appreciate it."

Jonathan was enjoying his food. The lasagna was truly the best he'd ever had. He sipped his wine and that was good, also. He felt the warmth of this family and wanted to very much be a part of it. Fantasizing, he thought how wonderful it would be if he and Michael could be joined somehow in a long, meaningful relationship, and that he could be a part of this family.

There was some cheerful laughter, and Michael could sense that Jonathan was accepted as part of the group. It made him feel good. It had been easier without Rosa. It worked out well that she had to stay at work. Michael was thinking about kissing Jonathan later and was sure it would be okay. Kissing probably didn't mean that you were queer. But he did want to talk to Jonathan about his fear that he might be a homosexual and to see what Jonathan thought. Did he dare trust him? He wanted to find out more about him. He took a drink of his wine. Only one glass. One glass relaxed him, but more than one would cause him to sing slightly flat. He was happy. It felt good to be home. His parents were gracious people, and Jonathan, God bless him, was an absolute delight. Why didn't Jonathan's parents like him? How could people be so cruel? Michael was in no hurry to meet them.

After they finished eating, Michael said, "Ma, thanks for the meal. It was great. Why don't you and Dad go sit in the living room and watch TV? Jonathan and I will put on the coffee and do the dishes. We'll bring the coffee and cake in there later."

His father said, "That sounds like a plan to me."

"No argument from me," Louisa said as she rose from the table. "Thank you."

After Mr. and Mrs. Manganaro left the room, Michael said, "We'd better take our jumpers off before we do the dishes, so they don't get messed up."

They took them off and put them on the bed in Michael's room. They then cleared the table of dishes and took them into the kitchen.

Michael said, "When my mother asked you to say grace, I was ready to rescue you. I didn't know if you believed in God or anything."

"So I surprised you?"

"Frankly, yes. Very pleasantly, however. Do you go to church now?"

"Yes and I always have. I just don't believe in all the dogma, particularly as it relates to sexual activity, masturbation, and things like birth control, priestly celibacy. And sometime soon a law will be passed allowing abortion, and I'm not sure how I feel about that. But I did go to an all-boys' Catholic grammar school, and I believed in most of the Church's teachings until I started to be sexually aware. Then I started to question a lot. One of the kids I went to school with told me how to jerk off. His name was Sonny. He was tall and skinny with black hair and a year or so older than everyone else in the class. He was considered the class stud since word was out that he was screwing one of the girls from St. Mary's Academy. He told me about masturbating in such detail that just hearing about it made me get excited. Then he took me up to the roof of his apartment building and gave me a demonstration. I couldn't believe that I enjoyed watching Sonny do it, but I did. Very much so. I watched him spray the tar roof. He asked me if I wanted to try it, but I told him I would wait until I got home. So I went home and tried it night after night. Nothing. Finally, one night it happened. It was the most exciting, wonderful sensation that I had ever experienced, and from that night forward, I knew that the priests and brothers were crazy. They had to have tried it, and once having felt that feeling and not wanting to experience it time and again, meant that they were truly nuts. There was absolutely nothing wrong with this. And since that day, I have done it on a daily basis and very often more than once a day. Thank you, Sonny!"

"I'm so glad to hear you say that because I remember my first time. I was in my bed, the same bed you'll be sharing with me later, and came for the first time. I felt this delightful burning sensation, which was at once both thrilling and almost painful. I felt like my insides came out of my chest, and I felt like I was going down a roller coaster. It was dark, and I didn't know exactly what had happened. I got up in the dark and locked the door. Then turned on the lamp and examined myself. There were drops of white stuff, sort of like egg whites, all over my chest and some was on my lips. This must be it, I thought. Cum. Sperm. I rubbed it off my lips with my hand and smelled it. It smelled like shrimp to me." He laughed. "Then I licked some of it off my hand, and it tasted like shrimp, too. My first thought after that was 'Me big and strong like Tarzan. Now I, too, could be a baby maker.'"

Jonathan chimed, "I thought I was the only one who tasted it."

They finished the dishes and took the freshly perked coffee and strawberry shortcake to the living room and put the cups and other things on the blue mirror top of the coffee table and joined Michael's mother and father. They were sitting on the sofa, and Butterball was between them.

Chapter 6

St. John's Roman Catholic Church was located on Main Street, two blocks up from Gruber's. The church and school took up one half of a village block, and the rectory and the convent took up the other half. The church and school were completed in 1951, and the convent the following year. The rectory was built in the late 1800's as a private residence for a plantation owner. During the Depression it was purchased by the Church and used as an orphanage until World War II, when it was converted to a rectory. It was a three-story, wood building with porches running around the entire first floor and halfway around the second floor. When Michael had reason to go inside the rectory, he was overwhelmed by its beauty. All the rooms had rich mahogany woodwork and high ceilings. Some had stained glass windows and fireplaces. They were furnished with antiques and beautiful Persian carpets. The walls of the two reception rooms, which were on the first floor on each side of the entrance hall, were covered with exquisite paintings and tapestries. Both of those rooms had huge fireplaces and lead crystal chandeliers.

Father Duffy sometimes would invite Michael to coffee when Michael played the organ or sang at the 7 a.m. Mass on Sundays. Father Duffy was a down-to-earth guy and always had his Sunday breakfast in the kitchen, which was in the basement below the dining room. You had to go through it to get from the church to the rectory without going outside. Agnes, the housekeeper, always had donuts and coffee for Father Duffy and sent breakfast up to the other priests on the dumbwaiter.

The church was large, but long and narrow. It was modern, without extensive decorations, except for the statues of Mary and Joseph in the front and the crucifix hanging over the altar. There were candles, both the nickel and quarter kinds, in front of the statues and wooden carved Stations of the Cross fastened strategically around the church. The windows were stained, but not very attractively. Some of the glass pieces were colored throughout, and other panels were painted. One could scrape the paint off the windows down to the clear glass with one's fingernails. Maybe when it was time to install the windows, Michael had always thought, the construction budget was running low. The church could seat one thousand, and at many Masses the place would be packed to capacity. The inside stucco walls were painted beige. The floor was slate. The pews were walnut and were polished weekly by the custodian, Joe Russo.

The church had received a large gift from Willington Balmoral in 1946, as a tribute to all the service men and women from the area who lost their lives in the war. It was a new Aroura Tanner pipe organ. Mr. Balmoral wasn't a Catholic, but he helped the church often and served on various church committees. He was generous to all the churches in the Poughkeepsie area, but had a special relationship with St. John's. He and the pastor had been friends since childhood. He was truly appreciative of all the church did for the community. Mr. Balmoral, because of his connection with the Metro-Tri-State Opera, often invited soloists to be guests at St. John's for Christmas and Easter. And because so many people liked to sing with the celebrities on the holidays, the volunteer choir was large and quite good. The church was fortunate to have Mrs. Rhine, Mellon's favorite music teacher, as the organist and choir director. Most of the people in the choir had been singing with the group for years. Michael had been singing with the St. John's Choir since he was eleven and had been soloing there since he was fifteen, when his voice had settled in as a baritone. Michael had often played the organ when Mrs. Rhine was away, but his repertoire was limited.

It was 7:15 p.m. when Jonathan and Michael left the house. Michael had his sheet music under his arm. They got into the car. Michael realized that the front porch lights were on. He was glad Jonathan didn't sit too close when he got in the car. He started the engine and drove down the street headed for the main road. It would only be a few minutes to get to St. John's. As soon as he shifted, he extended his hand to Jonathan's hand and held it for a minute.

"I'm so happy you're here, Jonathan."

Jonathan squeezed Michael's hand and said, "Why don't you pull over, up in one of those spaces for just a minute."

"Sure." Michael said as he drove the car into a small clearing off the main shoulder. He stopped the car and turned to Jonathan, who was now almost right beside him with his left arm over the back of Michael's seat. He slid his arm down onto Michael's shoulder and put his right hand on the inside of Michael's right thigh. Jonathan kissed Michael with his mouth closed and held Michael to him tightly. Michael trembled, but didn't pull away. He closed his eyes. Jonathan stopped kissing for a few seconds and then covered Michael's lips with his own with his lips slightly parted. He let his tongue caress Michael's upper lip until Michael moaned and opened his mouth. Jonathan slid his tongue into Michael's mouth.

Michael returned Jonathan's kisses with eager passion. He had been waiting a long time for this. Michael put his hand on Jonathan's and guided it to his crotch, so he could feel how hard he was. Maybe this was better than talking. Michael noticed that the windows of the car had fogged up, and he leaned back for a moment to catch his breath.

"Jonathan, I never want this to stop."

"Do you think I do? But we do have to talk about stuff in general. And I want you to know you can trust me. You really can. I promise." He felt Michael's penis pressing against the front panel of his bell-bottoms. "I'm in love with you, Michael, but it's seven-thirty, and we're already late."

"Wow. I'm trembling all over. Let me catch my breath."

Michael turned on the defroster for a minute and opened a window. He was wondering what would happen next and was relieved when Jonathan spoke.

"Michael, whatever you decide, I want you to know that I'll support you, and I promise you that whatever we talk about, or whatever we do shall remain just between us."

"I understand," Michael said. But he wasn't sure that he did.

"Is that St. John's?"

"Yes."

Michael pulled into the parking lot. Michael turned on the dome light and looked at his face in the rear view mirror. Well there were no big, red *Homo* or *Faggot* stamps on his forehead. He turned and looked at Jonathan, "Does it show?"

"Oh, Michael. Don't be silly. Forget about it now. When we get back to your house you can make a pitcher of those Manhattans that you love, and we can have a few drinks, a smoke, relax and talk until tomorrow. You'll see; it will be okay. Trust me."

"Thanks."

They went into the church through the side door and up the two flights of stairs to the choir loft. The practice had begun. They had just started singing the *Credo* when Michael and Jonathan entered the choir loft and quietly found seats near the door. When they were around midpoint in the piece, the choir stopped singing and Mrs. Rhine played a soft interlude. This interlude, Michael recognized, was the accompaniment for his solo. Mrs. Rhine stopped playing when she spotted Michael and Jonathan in the corner.

"Hi, Guys," she welcomed. "Michael, we never do *Missa Stella Maris* without you. We need you for all the baritone solos. We're up to your part in the *Credo* now. Do you have the music?"

He shook his head, "No."

"Clarice, please give him your copy, and for now look on with someone. Michael, we reserved a seat for you next to the console and a seat for Jonathan next to you. Come on over. We'll do the introductions at break, so that we will have covered all your stuff, in case you have someplace to go. Allison, please give Jonathan your music, so he can follow. Thanks."

Michael and Jonathan found their seats. Michael found his place in the music and showed Jonathan where they were.

Mrs. Rhine lifted both her hands up in the air until everyone was quiet and said, "Take it from # 46 where the chorus is ending with '*descéndit de coelis.*' I'll give you your notes, starting with the basses." She gave them the notes on the organ, as they hummed along.

They sang solemnly. Michael stood up and then began to sing, "*Et in carnátus est de Spíritu Santo.*" Jonathan began to get goose bumps when Michael began a little more strongly, telling the story, "*ex Mária Vírgine.*" Then the hair stood up on his neck.

The choir loft was lit only with rude fluorescent tubes hidden behind the beams that held up the roof. Jonathan stared into the blackness in the cavern of the church and saw only the candles flickering at the front. Michael sang angelically, and Jonathan had to hold back tears. There were no sounds other than those of the organ and Michael, and the occasional tap, tap, tap of Mrs. Rhine's foot on the pedals.

Michael finished the solo, sat down, and continued singing the *Credo* with the choir. Michael looked at Jonathan, and he thought he detected misty eyes. He said nothing. He quietly faced toward the front of the church and looked into the darkness as he continued singing.

Mrs. Rhine congratulated them, "That was really good. I don't think we have to go over it again."

Everyone was readjusting their music when Clarice asked, "Are we going to go over the *Sanctus, Benedictus* and *Agnus Dei* tonight?"

"No," Mrs. Rhine said. "We pretty much have those down pat. We'll just run over them on Sunday in the cafeteria before Mass. But now I want you all to put your music down and to relax. I want to run through *Panis Angelicus* with Michael. Okay with you, Michael?"

"Yes, Ma'am. I brought my music with me."

"Good. I'm going to play the full introduction, very slowly, as I'm sure César intended," she said.

Michael always got a kick out of how she would refer to composers by their first names, as if she would be meeting them after rehearsal for coffee at the Mellon Diner. Actually, César Auguste Frank, the Belgium-French composer and organist, was one of her favorite composers and *Panis Angelicus* was her favorite piece by him. And it was perfect for Michael's voice. It was slow, dramatic and had many rests built in. It was more operatic than not, and a real "show off" piece. Michael would do it well.

She began to play the organ using the swell and great keyboards with soft stops, flutes and strings, and heavy pedal stops to emphasize the sustained bass notes that set the mood for the entrance of the solo voice. Jonathan, having heard the piece before, many times, could listen to the introduction and anticipate the voice entrance. He just knew when Michael would begin. And he was right.

Michael began singing. For the first time, Jonathan saw how nervous Michael was. His body was vibrating, and his hands shook the sheet music he was holding. His legs were also moving inside his bell-bottoms. Why was he so nervous? He sounded fabulous. He sounded so good, in fact, that Jonathan had to bite the inside of his cheek, so he wouldn't cry. Michael's voice filled the large, empty church, and as Michael stopped singing at each rest, Jonathan could hear a small echo. It was exciting to hear. Jonathan had gone to a lot of Metro-Tri-State Opera performances, and although he hadn't learned to like opera that much, he did get to appreciate the quality of good singing. And Michael could sing with the best of them. He wasn't just good; he was superb. No wonder they all wanted him to sing when he came home. What a treat to have someone who could sing like Michael in your own community.

Michael and Mrs. Rhine held the last note until they stopped together. There was silence for about three seconds before the choir members broke into applause. Michael, already seated, smiled humbly and stood up halfway and bowed.

Jonathan whispered into Michael's ear, "You were fuckin' wonderful!"

"Thanks."

Mrs. Rhine made some generic announcements and called a fifteen-minute break.

Michael introduced Jonathan to the group, and in general he had a pleasant time. Maureen was there, and she helped with the introductions. Bruce Rollins was there, too, and he followed the three of them as they circulated around the choir loft saying hello to everyone. He thought Jonathan looked very tempting.

Michael and Jonathan were both eager to leave and head to the house on Maiden Lane.

Chapter 7

Louisa and Anthony were sitting on the sofa when Michael and Jonathan left. Anthony was eating a second piece of cake and enjoying another cup of coffee. Louisa was preparing to take the dishes to the kitchen.

"The kids turned out great," Anthony said. "I can't believe the change in Michael. He left here a skinny kid and came back a man."

"He's still a kid," Louisa said, "even though he looks like a man. They must have made him exercise like crazy."

"Well, he seems a little different to me. More determined or something. I wonder if the company he was in changed his attitude or ideas about anything."

"I don't think so. He always did whatever he wanted to do. Thought whatever he wanted to think. Remember how many times he got in trouble in school for daring to be different? Remember when he got beaten up for being the only boy in home economics class? Did that stop him from going? Not even when the Poughkeepsie gang members flushed his head in the toilet. What you're really saying is that the Navy has physically made him more like the son you always wanted instead of the one who would rather make curtains on the sewing machine than adjust a carburetor. And the way he looks now, he looks more the carburetor type. Am I right, or am I wrong?"

He took a deep breath and exhaled loudly. "You're right, of course. I never was comfortable telling the guys at the shop that my son won the first prize in the apple pie contest at the Poughkeepsie Annual Fair."

"Of course, I'm right. You never liked his friend, Gary, either. You said it wasn't healthy that they should spend so much time together. That they should take all those long walks in the mountains. You even hated the fact that he didn't date in high school like you wanted him to. You would have had him on some sports team instead of being the editor of the school newspaper, starring in the senior play, singing in the church choir and being a straight "A" student."

"I never said anything like that."

"No. You didn't have to. But I could feel it, and if I could feel it, I'm sure he could, too."

"How so?"

"Well, for example, every time his cousin James did something spectacular during one of his high school football games—which was almost every week—you would show him the newspaper and talk about it constantly. 'James did it again. Isn't he the greatest? Aunt Rosemarie and Uncle John are so proud of him.' And on and on. How do you think that made him feel?"

"Why didn't you say something?"

"I didn't know what to say. Anytime I said anything about your family, particularly about your dear sister, Rosemarie, you pouted for days."

"I didn't realize I was doing that," Anthony said.

"How many times did you hear Michael sing?"

"Hardly ever. You know I always went to the 6 a.m. Mass and he always sang at the 11 o'clock."

"Well I know it hurt him. He told me so. In any case, what did you think of Jonathan?" Louisa asked.

"Seems like a nice guy. A little older than Michael, I think."

"I think he's very good-looking and very nice. Michael seems to have found a special friend in Jonathan, a friend that he has always wanted. I mean he always had friends, but Jonathan seems to be the special one. I just hope that Jonathan doesn't hurt Michael."

Anthony picked up the cups and saucers and began to follow Louisa out of the room as he said, "Some of the special things that I have always loved about Michael were his sensitivity and kindness, like when he took care of Butterball, and when he sat up all night applying the hot compresses to Rosa's face when she had that skin infection that almost turned into blood poisoning. Often though, I thought, these two virtues might cause him pain. He was always so vulnerable. But Jonathan seems okay. I did wonder, however, why he didn't mention anything about his family."

"Probably because they're rich, and he didn't want to make us self-conscious."

"What do you mean rich?"

Louisa continued, "His father is president of Taylor Oil; that's what I mean."

"Wow. Not small potatoes."

Butterball woke up, stretched, and followed them out of the room.

The telephone in the kitchen was ringing.

"Hello," Mr. Manganaro said, as he picked up the receiver.

"Hi. It's Gary. Is Michael home?"

"Hi, Gary. He came in last night, but he's out at choir rehearsal now. He should be home later. I'll have him call you when he gets in."

"That's great. I'm looking forward to talking to him. How long is he going to be home for?"

"I believe he said thirty days. But I'm not sure. How are things going with you? Just because Michael isn't around much anymore doesn't mean you have to be a stranger. I miss you and so does Louisa."

"Why thank you. I got a new job with Equality Life. I'm learning some new computer stuff. I like it, and it's more money than I was making in Poughkeepsie, but I have to commute to Manhattan every day."

"Wow. That's some commute."

"Actually, I'm getting used to it. I do a lot of reading on the train. There are all kinds of training manuals that I'm studying about computers. It seems that in the future everyone will be using computers. Would you believe that at a meeting last week one of the leaders was saying that in ten or fifteen years we'll be able to get cash from machines by using a card and a code of some sort without tellers? Doesn't seem possible, does it?"

"No. Wait until I mention it to Rosa."

"Thanks again for letting Michael know I called."

"You're welcome." Mr. Manganaro hung up.

Louisa was putting dishes in the sink. She started to rinse them.

"That was Gary."

"I heard. That was the nicest you ever were to him."

"Well, we've known him since Michael met him in junior high school, and I guess he makes me feel comfortable."

"And Jonathan doesn't?"

"I didn't say that."

"What else did he say?"

"He told me he works in Manhattan now. A lot of people are commuting these days. There just are no good paying jobs up here."

The kitchen door opened. Rosa came in. She greeted, "How'd things go today?"

"Michael's friend, Jonathan, came today and he's staying over. They're at choir rehearsal now," her mother said.

"I know, Ma. I heard at the bank. One of the customer service repre-sentatives, Bruce Rollins, belongs to the choir. He got a call from a friend of his who got a call from Maureen. To make a long story short, he heard that Jonathan was gorgeous, and he wasn't going to miss rehearsal for anything. Bruce, by the way, is the guy I told you about who wears all the beautiful clothing, and who everyone thinks likes guys."

Louisa and Anthony looked at each other.

Chapter 8

Melissa Taylor sat on the edge of her bed. She was depressed to be again at Golden Hill in Connecticut. She had been there over a week, and the worst part of her withdrawal from alcohol was over, but the emotional and psychological pains were very real.

She did, however, find a sense of peace and tranquility in the beauty of the Golden Hill facility, a country estate with a main house and several smaller houses with hundreds of feet of space between them. The grounds were beautifully landscaped. Nothing was fenced in. No one would know that it was a hospital, a top-notch psychiatric hospital at that. Only those with some sort of pedigree could be patients. If you had to be a drunk, or suffering from some psychological disorder, Golden Hill was the place to recover. Her room was on the second floor of the main house and down the hall from the nurses' station. She had a four-poster bed with a lace canopy, a large Queen Anne writing desk, an early American rocking chair and other suitable antique furniture that fit in nicely. The walls were painted a dark forest green. There was also a fireplace that she wasn't allowed to use. The two paneled windows had ecru lace curtains with floral cotton valances and velvet draperies. During her first few days, the rocking chair was used by her "Special." At Golden Hill "Specials" were used to supervise patients during the stabilization process for withdrawal from alcohol and/or drugs, and for the more disturbed individuals, for as long as was necessary. Golden Hill was a psychiatric hospital with no bars on the windows.

She looked at the beautiful flower arrangement on the desk. It was from her ex-husband, Jonathan Anthony. The card that came with the flowers said:

"Missy,

Please get well soon. Don't worry about insurance coverage for the hospitalization; I'll make up whatever they don't cover. Jonathan is coming home in a few days. He said he was coming in before Thanksgiving. Call him. He loves you so. Kindest personal regards,

JAT."

Yes, she would call Jonathan. That was a good idea. She went down to the main floor where the pay phones were. At Golden Hill you needed permission from the head nurse prior to making phone calls. The hospital didn't want patients being upset by calls from or to family members, friends, employers without a senior staff member aware of it.

"Good evening, Jessica," she said to the head nurse. "I'd like to make a phone call or two. My son should be home from boot camp, and I'd like to say hello."

"You're not supposed to make or receive any calls until you've been here at least ten days, but if you make it real short, so your son knows you're here, you have my blessing. Instead of using the pay phone, please use the phone right here on my desk. This way I can listen in the background and enter the call on your chart."

Melissa said, "That would be great. I appreciate it."

She got the operator and gave her the number of Jonathan's apartment.

Adele answered, "Taylor residence."

"Hello, Adele, It's Missy. How are you?"

"Fine, Mrs. Taylor, thank you. And you?"

"Not that great, Adele, but okay. When my son comes home I'd like to talk to him."

"He came in last night, but today he went to visit a friend that he met at the training center. I have that number if you want to call there. I found it this morning on the refrigerator."

"Please, may I have it?"

She got the number, and with Jessica's permission, made the second call.

"Hello," Louisa said on the phone in the kitchen.

"Hello. I'm Melissa Taylor, Jonathan's mother. I understand that he may be visiting you. May I speak to him?"

"Yes, certainly, but unfortunately, he's gone to choir rehearsal with my son, Michael. I think they should be getting home within the hour. Can I have him call you?"

"Actually, no. I'm in a hospital where phone calls are restricted, so he can't call me. Would you be kind enough to give him a message?"

"Of course."

"Please tell him I'm at Golden Hill. He knows where it is. And that I'm doing fine. Visiting hours are from 3 p.m. to 9 p.m. every day, and that I miss him."

"I'll tell him. I hope you'll be feeling better.

"Thank you very much. Good-bye."

"Good-bye."

She stared out the window at the landscaped gardens. How did I make such a mess of my life? I lost my husband and my son.

Thanksgiving was coming. Another holiday at Golden Hill. Shit!

Chapter 9

Michael and Jonathan left St. John's and headed home.

"Michael, I enjoyed the rehearsal, and your singing really blew me away. I had no idea you were so good. I mean the sound. It was thrilling to listen to," Jonathan said as he took the end paper off a roll of LifeSavers. "Would you like one?"

Michael took one. "Thanks. And thanks for that nice compliment. I was really nervous with you there."

"I saw that. You were actually shaking."

"I know. I know it may sound crazy, but I have never been that nervous before. I wanted so much to please you, and I never felt that way about anybody else. I just cared more about what you thought of my singing, than I would have cared what the Pope thought if I were singing for him."

"Michael, I wanted you to do well. I felt like I was part of you. I felt the vibration of your singing not only in my ears, but also throughout my body. I never felt that way before about anybody either. You know what, Michael? I'm coming back here on Sunday to hear you perform. I mean, you don't have to spend time with me. I'll just come on the train, get a taxi, hear you sing and go back home."

"You will not. I'd love to have you here on Sunday. One of us will pick you up at the station and bring you to church. I'll probably already be there. Then you'll stay for dinner, which is right after church at one. My mother always makes a scrumptious Sunday dinner."

"Sounds good. You don't think your mother will mind?"

"No. Of course, not. She loves to cook, and I'm even going to ask another friend, so you'll get to know him. He's Gary, and we've been best friends for ages."

"Great."

Michael turned on the car radio. Chubby Checker was singing *The Twist*. Michael was thinking about what might happen later. The song ended, and he turned the radio off. They drove quietly for a mile.

"Michael, you're so quiet. What are you thinking about?"

"What am I thinking about? I'm thinking about later. What might happen later. I'm afraid, Jonathan. I know what I feel like doing, and if I do that with you, it definitely means I'm homosexual."

"So," Jonathan said, "I'm one."

"What about Janice on the plane?"

"That was just from years of pretending to be heterosexual. I put on a good show. I've had sex with girls, too, to reinforce my masculine ego that I'm okay. But it doesn't feel natural to me to have sex with females, but with a man, it's a different story. I've had only two homosexual experiences, but I knew the first time, without any doubt, that being with someone of the same gender felt perfectly natural and comfortable, and both of the guys I had sex with were just acquaintances. I can't even imagine how mind-blowing it would be to have sex with someone I cared about like you, Michael."

"Jonathan, I thought about having sex with you since the day we met. I've thought about you every minute of every day. When you kissed me before I thought I was going to come in my pants."

"Michael, can I ask you a question?"

"Yes."

"Did something bad happen to you once with a homosexual?"

Michael was caught by surprise. Nobody had asked him a question like that before. His mind went back to a time when he was fourteen. "Yes, something ugly happened."

Jonathan moved closer to Michael. "I have a feeling that someone, some guy, maybe an authority figure, in the past tried to take advantage of you. Maybe tried to rape you. Am I right?"

"Yes. And I'll tell you about it sometime, but not now. It was so ugly and upsetting that the only person I ever told about it was Gary, the friend you'll meet on Sunday. When it happened I stayed home from school for a week and wouldn't come out of my room. And the guy who did it to me kept calling and leaving messages with my mother and father. They couldn't figure out what was wrong with me, and the guy probably was terrified that I was going to turn him in. I was fourteen and a real basket case. Everything I ate came back up. Gary came over before school, and he came back after school every day. We talked and talked and talked. He convinced me that it was in my best interest back then to keep it to myself, because nobody would believe me, and that speaking out would cause me unbelievable pain. I didn't have any proof, and it would have been my word against his."

"Michael, I'm sorry that that happened to you. And I now, more than I did before, want to meet Gary. He gave you good advice. I'd like to hear the whole story if you ever care to share it with me."

"Thanks, Jonathan. If the three of us get to be alone on Sunday, you and me and Gary, I probably will tell you. Like I said, Gary is the only person in the world who knows about this. He really helped me. He was, and is, a great friend. I hope the two of you get along."

"Me, too. Hey, I see your house, and the Spitfire is in the driveway. You'll have to park in the street. And there's Butterball waiting on the front porch."

Michael pulled the car up to the curb in front of his house. "And now on a lighter note, what did you think of Bruce Rollins?"

Jonathan laughed. "A flaming queen."

"He liked you," Michael said.

"I know, but I think he knew I was taken."

Michael frowned. "You mean it's obvious?"

"Yes. To probably anyone tuned in. Mrs. Rhine knows. Maureen may know, may suspect, but doesn't really think it's possible because she'd take either of us."

"You mean my mother and father might be able to tell?"

"No, not your father. He believes what makes him comfortable, and anything that might happen between us would not make him comfortable. He's not ready yet. But your mother, on the other hand, yes, probably suspects. I can tell that she knows you very well."

"You think?"

"I know."

"Jonathan, my mother and I used to be very close. After my sister went to school, we spent two years together. She taught me to read and cook and garden and stuff like that."

Butterball ran from the porch to greet them, as they got out of the car.

Chapter 10

Some of the choir members went to the Mellon Diner after practice. Others went to John's Pizzeria. John's was next to Ray's Hardware. It was the only place that served beer and wine on Main Street. Their pizza was thin-crusted with a gourmet tomato and basil sauce, oregano and freshly homemade mozzarella. They served better than average Italian food, but the place was always packed for the pizza, particularly on Wednesday, choir rehearsal night, which also happened to be bowling night. Friday night the place was also crowded after the local AA meeting. But the waitresses didn't like to work on Fridays because the checks were smaller with no drinking, and as a result, tips were smaller, too. Also, sober patrons seemed less generous with their money.

Clarice, Maureen, Bruce and Harry found a booth in the back near the double swinging doors of the kitchen. There was a lit candle stuck in an empty Chianti bottle that was covered with different colored wax drippings. On their way in they had passed Gary, Michael's friend, sitting at the circular bar having a beer. They asked him to join them when their pizza came. He promised he would.

Maureen said, "It's good to be inside. It feels warm and cozy. I'm glad they have the fireplace going. I didn't realize it was going to get so nippy."

"Neither did I," Clarice said.

"Now that we're here, are we going to gossip?" asked Bruce raising an eyebrow.

"Bruce, what's up?" Maureen asked.

"In all the years since you've known Michael, did he ever leave rehearsal and not come here? And we saw Gary at the bar alone. Did you ever see Gary out alone, without Michael?"

They shook their heads.

"I thought not," he continued. "I wonder who this Jonathan is. He's a real Gucci boy if ever I saw one."

"What do you mean, Bruce?" Maureen quizzed.

"I think Jonathan is a lavender boy."

Clarice wanted to know, "What's a lavender boy?"

"A faggot," he said. "Plain and simple, a homo."

Harry spoke. "Oh, shut up, Bruce! Speak for yourself. You don't even know Jonathan, and Michael's been our friend for a long, long time."

"Mark my words," Bruce said, mimicking a schoolteacher they all knew.

Their waitress, Theresa Garafolo, arrived and took their drink and pizza order. Shortly after that, Gary came over.

"Pull up a chair," Maureen suggested, "and join us."

"Thanks," Gary said as he got a chair. He sat at the end of the table in the aisle.

Bruce asked, "Where's Michael tonight?"

"I called his house an hour ago, and his father told me he went to choir rehearsal. That's why I'm here. I thought he would come with you guys, and I'd planned to buy him a welcome home beer. Guess I was wrong."

"Then you haven't seen him since he's been home?" Bruce asked.

"No. I suppose he's busy."

"Busy. I should think so," said Bruce. "You haven't met Jonathan then?"

"Who's Jonathan?" Gary asked.

Maureen said, "A friend Michael met in boot camp. He's visiting. He came to choir practice tonight."

Bruce added, "And they sat so close together. They couldn't keep their eyes off each other."

Harry said, "Bruce, you're an asshole and a pervert. You'd go down on either one of them if you could. Gary, Jonathan seemed like a real nice guy. Good-looking, too. He's from New York City, and his family is out of town, so Michael invited him to spend two days in the country. I'm sure as soon as they get settled, you'll meet him. And, Gary, wait until you see Michael. He looks great."

"I left a message with his father. I hope he calls soon. I want an update on all his activities. I miss him."

Maureen felt sorry for Gary. He seemed crushed that Michael had not talked to him since he came home yesterday. He didn't say it, but she was sure it was so. She had known both of them since they became friends, and she was very aware that Gary needed Michael's friendship a great deal. How deeply Michael needed Gary, she didn't know, but she was sure he needed him.

Theresa brought their drinks. "Your pizza will be right out. How are you, Gary? Where's Michael? I heard he's home."

Chapter 11

They went into the house. Rosa was alone in the living room. She stood up when they came in and walked over to Jonathan.

"Hi, Jonathan. I'm Rosa. Heard you were coming, and I'm glad you're here."

"Hi, Rosa. I can't tell you how much I enjoy being here. Your mother and father and Michael have made me feel so welcome. It's good to meet you. I've been looking forward to it. Michael talked about you all the time. I've heard the story about the first time you left him to go to school a dozen times."

"Oh, no! He put you through that?"

"Yes, but I enjoyed it. I don't have any brothers or sisters, so I thoroughly liked his stories. And now that I'm here, I'd like to get your versions of some of the more bizarre ones when you were little kids. Did you make him sit on one end of a seesaw at Clarice's, and then you and Clarice climbed up to the top of her back stoop? Then, and I can't believe this, the both of you jumped on the other end of the seesaw and catapulted Michael into a cherry tree?"

"Oh, God. We did. And the firemen took an hour to get him down."

Michael laughed. "I told you it was true, and you didn't believe me."

"I heard about the candle-making and the fire."

"Michael, you told him that, too?"

"Yes."

"Unbelievable," she said.

Louisa and Anthony came in.

"Welcome back, guys," Anthony said. "How'd things go?"

"Okay," Michael said.

Louisa said, "I have a message for you, Jonathan. Your mother called. She said she was at Golden Hill and said you knew where it was and the visiting hours are from 3 p.m. to 9 p.m. She said she was doing fine and that she misses you, but that she couldn't receive any phone calls."

Jonathan was obviously stunned by the message. "Thank you. May I be excused, please?"

"Of course," Louisa said.

Jonathan left the room and went into Michael's bedroom.

"What's Golden Hill?" Michael asked.

"I don't know," his mother said.

Rosa said, "Apparently, it's not good news. He seemed to be having such a good time, and then all of a sudden he looked miserable."

Michael said, "I'll just let him be alone for a while, then I'll go in and see what the story is."

"Good idea," his father said. "And Gary called you while you were out."

"Oh. He did? I have to get back to him, Dad. But before I do, Mom, can I have Gary and Jonathan here for dinner on Sunday? Jonathan wants to come up on Sunday to hear the choir sing again."

"The choir? He wants to hear you. And, yes, I'd like that. We haven't had roast pork in a long time, and I know Gary likes it. Talk to Jonathan later and find out if he does."

Rosa said, "I love roast pork. Michael, you haven't seen my car yet."

"Hey, let's go out and take a look." He still had his coat on, and Rosa grabbed hers from behind the door. They went out. A neighbor was burning leaves, and the aroma filled the evening air.

Rosa pointed to her car in the driveway.

"This is it, Michael. Nice? Huh?"

"Really neat. I'd like to drive it someday, if you'll let me. But why did you want to get me out of there?"

"Because I know what Golden Hill is."

"You do."

"Yes. It's a psychiatric hospital that specializes in alcohol and drug addiction and depression. The president of the bank's wife went there for electroshock therapy. Jonathan seems very sweet, Michael. I like him. He needs you."

"I don't know what to say."

"Just be there for him. Like you were there for me once, remember?"

"Yes."

"Now go."

"I will, but first I have to call Gary before I forget."

He went back into the house and went straight to the kitchen. He called Gary and found out that he was at John's. He called there and got him on the phone. He apologized for taking so long to call, but said he'd like to get together with Gary on Sunday and invited him to dinner after church. Gary seemed very pleased when he returned to his group at the pizzeria with the news that Michael had called.

Michael went to the door of his room. He took a deep breath. He knocked on the door three times and said, "Jonathan, it's me. May I come in?"

"Yes."

Jonathan was lying on the bed with his clothes on face down into a pillow. Michael took off his coat and jumper. He sat down on the bed next to Jonathan with his back propped up against the headboard. He put his hand on Jonathan's back and said nothing. Jonathan lifted his head from the pillow and his shoulders off the bed. He leaned across Michael and laid his head on Michael's chest. Michael kissed the top of Jonathan's head and put his arm across his back. He held one of Jonathan's hands in his own. Michael could feel Jonathan's tears wetting his T-shirt.

Chapter 12

Michael lay very still as Jonathan slept. He didn't want to wake him. He heard the TV being silenced and the footsteps of his parents passing his room. In the quiet bedroom he listened to Jonathan breathe.

"No, Anthony. Don't open the door."

"I just wanted to make sure they're alright."

She shook her head. "No."

"Right."

Then Michael heard a car start. Sounded like the Spitfire. It was probably Rosa. She was, no doubt, going to the Mellon Diner to get Chesterfields. It was the only business in Mellon that stayed open 24 hours. Michael could tell Jonathan was dreaming by his movements. Jonathan was no longer lying with his head on Michael, but next to him, still fully clothed with the exception of his shoes, which Michael had taken off for him. Finally, Jonathan turned away from Michael and moved toward the wall. Michael got up carefully, trying not to disturb Jonathan.

Michael wanted a cigarette, and decided he would smoke outside on the front porch. He took off his bell-bottoms and put on dungarees and a sweatshirt and went outside. I'll just sit here and wait for Rosa to come back, he thought. He lit up. Maiden Lane was a pretty street. Michael loved living there. He always had. When they first moved in, there were only two small houses on the block, but now there were twelve, six on each side of the street. Maple trees lined the street, and each house had well-maintained front lawns. The Manganaro's house had hedges all around the property with openings for the front walk and driveway. Several of the houses had small picket fences. The night was cool, and Michael could still smell the lingering scent of burnt leaves. None of the houses had lights on. The night was clear, and the stars were brilliantly shining. Just as he was finishing his cigarette, Rosa returned.

When she got out of her car she saw her brother sitting on the stairs of the front porch. She went to him.

"Hey, Little Brother. Are you okay?"

"Yeah."

"And how about Jonathan?"

"He's still sleeping, I hope."

"Must be hard."

"Yeah. Melissa Taylor is Jonathan's mother, but he lives with his father and stepmother. I don't know too much more except that his father divorced his mother when Jonathan was about thirteen, and he was awarded custody of Jonathan. Jonathan told me about his family shortly after I met him at Ramapo. He mentioned that as long as he remembered his mother drank a lot. Crashed cars and stuff. We really didn't get into it. It made me uncomfortable."

"You mean you thought of our own mother's periodic drinking."

"Yes, Rosa. The Ruby Red Port bottle in the closet kept coming to mind."

"Fortunately, for us, Michael, we have always been well cared for and other than brief spells of discomfort, or should I say embarrassment, the Ruby Red hasn't affected us to any great extent."

"We're really lucky, Rosa. I know ma has some things that she obsesses on that cause her to be miserable at times, but she has been a good mother to us and a good wife to dad."

Rosa added, "And when she tells me some of the things that happened to her when she was growing up, no wonder she gets spooked. A couple glasses of wine mellow her out."

"I guess."

"Well, it's just like you with your Manhattans."

"You think?"

"Of course, I think. And I also think you should consider laying off them. I love you, Little Brother, and you're only twenty. Why do you need to drink so often?"

"Who knows? But you're right. I drink more than I should. It embarrasses me that you notice. I'll try to slow down, and we both should lay off these things," he said pointing to the cigarettes in his pocket. "Let's go in in case Jonathan wakes up."

"Michael, remember, nothing escapes me. I used to beat you up when you were little and probably could still today if the Navy hadn't gotten hold of you. I just wanted you to know that you don't look like my little brother anymore. And I'll never say it again, so listen good: I think you look hot."

Michael smiled and put his arm around Rosa, and they went in.

Michael went back into his room. Jonathan was sitting in the chair by the desk.

"You're awake," Michael greeted.

"Yes. Oh, Michael, I'm so, so sorry. I didn't mean to carry on so."

"Hey. I understand." He sat on the bed facing Jonathan. He reached out and took both of Jonathan's hands in his.

"What time is it? My watch stopped. Did I sleep long?"

"It's only a little after midnight."

"I feel like it's been hours. Wow. I do feel better, now, however. Boot camp was so tiring, not having anyone welcome me home and then this. My mother has been to Golden Hill before, but it never ceases to be a shock. The last time she was there it was because she had slit her wrists and almost bled to death before a neighbor found her. If she doesn't get her act together, she might not make it next time."

"How does your father handle it?"

"I think he cares, but with a good deal of detachment these days. I remember when I was younger. I missed my mother after the divorce even though I saw her on holidays and weekends. My father spoke of her to me often and always had nice things to say. He just couldn't deal with her refusal to admit to having a problem and doing something to take care of it. He's a take-charge, face-the-problem-and-deal-with-it, kind of guy. He's a fighter. Mom's a runner. She runs away from stuff into fantasy. He could never relate to that. All these years he paid her bills, paid for her hospitalizations and sent lots of gifts, anything he could do to make her happy, short of reconciliation. When I was looking through some papers to get documentation for my security clearance before we were sworn in, I found a copy of the divorce decree. It was the first time I ever saw it. My mother was only supposed to see me on alternate weekends, but my father allowed her to see me on all weekends, if she were sober and able. He also paid her alimony far in excess of the amount stipulated in the court document. He paid for her tuition for various courses in drama, the arts, literature and things that interested her at NYU. 'Always remember,' he would tell me, 'your mother is a lady. Just because we are no longer married doesn't change the fact that she is your mother and very special, but we unfortunately are not suited to be together. She has problems, but I loved her more than I could tell you, once. She never intended to hurt you, or me, and I will help her as much as I can.'

"As far as how my father feels today, I'm sure he cares a great deal. I'm sure he's been on the phone with the hospital a dozen times to make sure she's set up to receive the best care. To give you an example of how I'm like my mother, I felt that when my father wasn't home to greet me, I sulked. I didn't take any action to remedy the situation. But I could have called him. I'm sure Adele has the number where he is."

"Jonathan, why don't you get his number and call him tomorrow?"

Jonathan was feeling better. "I will. Yes," he replied.

Feeling a release of tension, they both laughed.

"Michael, I owe your parents an apology for leaving so abruptly."

"No, you don't. Later, maybe after you're home, I'll say something. But not now. Not necessary. Your mother's sick, but she's getting better and will fully recover. That's it." He continued, "You know, Jonathan, Connecticut isn't that far from here, just a few minutes. We could drive there tomorrow in time for visiting hours. I could drop you off and you could probably take a NYCN Transit train back to the City. Where's this place?"

"New Canaan."

"There's a NYCN Transit stop there. I saw it on the map at Grand Central once."

"You're right. I remember going over there after school on the train when my father's limo was in the shop.

"Good. Tomorrow we have a plan. Forget the train. First, we'll get up and I'll show you how to feed the chickens. You did express an interest in doing that, and then we'll have a good breakfast. Next we'll take a hike in the woods nearby. We can come home and get cleaned up, and we can head to New Canaan for lunch, and I'll drop you off at Golden Hill.

"That sounds terrific."

"Then we have a plan?"

"We have a plan."

Michael got up from the bed and leaned over Jonathan. Michael put his hands under Jonathan's armpits and lifted him up. When Jonathan was standing he was an inch taller than Michael was. Michael put his arms around Jonathan's neck, and they kissed. Jonathan put his arms around Michael and pulled him close. Jonathan and Michael were immediately, aroused and Jonathan pushed Michael away.

"Michael, weren't you going to mix up some Manhattans once upon a time?"

"Yes. And I will. Right now."

"I'd like to take a quick shower while you do that, okay?"

"Sure."

Chapter 13

Jonathan had finished his shower and was seated in the chair by the desk. He was wearing the terrycloth robe that he'd brought with him. Michael had made an art deco shaker full of Manhattans and put it and the glasses on a tray on the desk. Jonathan was towel drying his head as he sipped his drink. Then Michael went to take a shower.

Michael returned to his room and whispered, "We have to be quiet. Everyone's asleep, but they keep their doors open. I'm closing and locking this one."

"Super."

"I need a drink."

Jonathan poured some of the mixture into a tall cocktail glass and handed it to Michael. Michael drank half of it and didn't say anything for a few minutes. He sat on the edge of his bed and stared at Jonathan's feet. Nice feet. Michael's heart was beating faster than usual; he could feel it. And he was perspiring, and he wasn't sure if the shower he had just taken was too hot and had caused it, or if there were another reason.

Jonathan asked, "Michael, did you ever have a happy sexual experience with a guy?"

"As a kid, you know, we did some stuff in the woods where we all played. The entire group did, so I didn't think anything about it. The last time I enjoyed any sexual stuff with a guy, and that was just mutual touching and butt exploration and admiration, was when I went camping in the backyard with Drew, who had just moved in across the street. It makes me laugh now when I think about it. We didn't even know how to masturbate yet, but we would endure the scorching summer heat, the lumps on the damp ground and the relentless attacks by killer mosquitoes all for a little touching when, without the touching, we could have been comfortable in our own beds. Jonathan, I must tell you, at the time I thought Drew had the most beautiful fanny I ever did see."

"I used to camp out in the backyard, too, behind our townhouse in the city when we were all together before the divorce. I wanted to go to Central Park, but my father wouldn't let me. Probably would have been illegal anyway. But I got into real trouble in the backyard anyway. I took some extension cords from the house and hooked up a lamp in the tent. Unfortunately, I didn't know that shadows of what we were doing inside appeared on the walls of the tent, and, since we were doing pretty much the same things you were doing, butt exploration and related activities, one of our neighbors who was having a barbecue saw the shadows and telephoned my father.

"No, shit!" Michael finished his drink.

"Not good, I tell you. I had to go to therapy for three months, and my father stayed angry with me for a long time. Anytime after that, whenever I did anything to displease him, he'd ask, 'Camping in the backyard again?'"

Jonathan finished his drink and stood up and took off his robe.

Michael loved the way Jonathan looked standing nude in the light of the desk lamp. Michael took off his robe and dropped it on top of Jonathan's on the floor. They stood together with the fronts of their bodies barely touching. Jonathan reached behind himself and turned the lamp off. In the darkness they stood ready for each other, at last.

Michael asked, "Which side of the bed do you want?"

"I don't think it's going to matter," was Jonathan's reply.

Chapter 14

Michael and Jonathan slid under the covers. The sheets were cool against their naked bodies. They both were squeaky clean and smelled like Ivory soap. They lay very close facing one another in the darkness. They were waiting for their eyes to adjust. A small amount of light was coming in the window from the brightly shining moon. It wasn't long before they could see.

"Jonathan, you look nice without clothes," Michael said.

"You look nice, too. Every time I saw you shower at Ramapo I got excited thinking about the possibility that we might someday get together. And quite frankly, I can't believe we're lying in the same bed stark naked," Jonathan chuckled.

"God, I wanted you so. I didn't think I'd feel comfortable with you in bed, much less my bed. But I do. Very comfortable. I'm ecstatic. I fantasized about you every time I jerked off during the last few months. And here we are, and we're talking, but we're not doing anything yet."

"Oh, but we will be," Jonathan said suggestively. "There's no hurry now that we're here. I wanted to have you in boot camp in your little cubbyhole office. But I realized you would never have been agreeable to that, so I patiently waited. The last thing I expected, though, was that I'd fall in love with you, and I have."

Michael smiled. "I'm glad you have because I love you, and I never thought I'd tell you. I thought we'd get together, have a couple 'unauthorized' cheap feels, touch each other and then move on."

Jonathan rolled over on his stomach and leaned over Michael's face supporting himself by leaning on his elbows. "We can start by kissing, touching or anything you want. I have two goals right now. The first is to satisfy you completely, and the second is to have you satisfy me. Talk to me. Tell me what you want."

"I can tell you the truth?"

"Yes, Michael."

"I want you to lie on top of me. I'm dying to know what it would feel like."

Michael was lying on his back, and Jonathan pushed Michael's legs slightly apart. He knelt between Michael's thighs and slowly lay down on him, so that their erect penises were side by side, and Jonathan was supporting his upper torso on his arms and elbows on either side of Michael.

"Well, Michael? Do you like me on top of you, looking down at you?"

"It feels better than anything I've ever dreamed about. I want you so much. Is it okay to talk while we do this?"

"Michael, talking can be the best part. It feels good for me to be in this position on you, so that for a few precious minutes I can be responsible for giving you some real pleasure. And what we're doing, Michael, is having sex."

"Is that so? Then, am I a homosexual yet?"

He made Jonathan laugh. "You big silly man. You, like the rest of us, had your gender preference determined at conception!"

"Yes, I agree with you. In my heart I've always known that."

Jonathan pinned Michael's arms above his head to the bed and caressed his right armpit with his mouth and tongue and then his left. Michael closed his eyes and started to relax. When Jonathan released his arms and kissed him, Michael put his arms around Jonathan's back and pulled him down, tight and close. They kissed passionately, and Jonathan started very slow, rhythmic, pelvic thrusts against Michael. Michael squeezed his buttocks, as he returned each of those thrusts. They moved together.

Jonathan said, "You smell good enough to eat." Jonathan licked Michael's throat, neck and his ears. "And you taste delicious."

Michael moaned softly, "Oh, Jonathan that feels so good. Oh, yes. Don't stop. Oh, please don't stop."

Jonathan put his hands under Michael's back, then over the back of his shoulders and then grabbed them tightly.

Michael clasped his fingers behind Jonathan's back in a vise-like grip.

Jonathan pressed his mouth hard against Michael's mouth and stuck his tongue deeply into Michael's mouth. Jonathan raised his torso off Michael's chest while he increased the speed and intensity of his pelvic thrusts. Michael raised his legs and put them over Jonathan's calves. Jonathan was staring into Michael's eyes and watched as his face muscles tensed up with pleasure and anticipation. Michael began moaning so loudly that Jonathan covered Michael's mouth with one of his hands. He screamed out, but it was muffled, as he exploded with years of pent up passion, shooting projectiles of semen over his body from his navel to his chin. Jonathan lay back down on top of Michael and didn't move while Michael erupted once more, trembling and shaking. He lay there until Michael, who had his arms tightly around his neck, released him and went limp.

"Damn, Michael," Jonathan said, "You almost woke everybody up."

"Oh, Jonathan. That was wonderful. I never knew that it would be so good."

They lay side by side once more.

"Michael, do you have a face cloth or something, so we can clean up, so this stuff doesn't stain the sheets? I assume your mother does the laundry."

"Oh, shit! You're right." Michael jumped up, turned on the light, put on his bathrobe and went to get a face cloth. He returned with a damp one and cleaned Jonathan and himself. "Even rubbing your chest with a wash cloth turns me on. I better go rinse this out. I'll be right back."

Jonathan got up from the bed and poured two drinks. He lit two Lucky Strikes and put one in the ashtray for Michael.

Michael returned, "That's taken care of."

Jonathan was sitting on the floor next to the bed with his drink, lit cigarette and ashtray. Michael took his drink, sat down facing Jonathan and picked up his cigarette.

"Thanks, Jonathan."

"You're welcome. Now you are a full-pledged, practicing homosexual."

"I know," Michael said. "You didn't come yet did you?"

"No, Michael. Not always necessary."

Michael took a deep drag and exhaled a cloud of smoke slowly, "But I want you to."

"I do too, but not just yet."

"I want to do something to you I've never done before."

"And that would be?"

"I want to suck you."

"You want to, do you? Well, I'd like you to, but not tonight. You might have second thoughts about it later, and I don't want that to happen. We both had a long day. We're tired and just really getting to know each other. If you still feel like it, you can do it tomorrow. There are things I'd like to do to you, too, but they can wait until we know each other better and are more sure of what they would mean to us, where we're headed with this, and the consequences we could suffer if anyone found out."

"So you're saying, we should slow down."

"Yes. Exactly."

"I love you, Jonathan."

"I love you, Michael. You have no idea."

They finished their cigarettes, drinks, turned off the light and got back into bed. Jonathan put his hand on Michael's buttocks and felt each cheek and let his hand stop with his finger resting in the crack between them. Michael reached down and let his hand touch Jonathan's pubic hair.

"Good night, Jonathan."

They kissed.

Jonathan said, "Good night, Precious."

Michael really liked the way that sounded.

Sleep came to the young lovers presently.

Chapter 15

Michael woke up first. He opened the window and stuck his head out. Frost covered the hedges and maple trees as well as the Buick, which was in the driveway. By the time he and Jonathan would return from their walk in the woods, the sun would have cleared the frost off the convertible's top. He could see the sun rising over the hills. It was going to be a nice day. A nice day for a drive to Golden Hill. He turned around to look at Jonathan lying nude on his back on top of the covers. Slowly daylight began to fill the room. Cold air rushed in through the window and across Jonathan's body. He felt the cold and woke up.

"Christ, Michael. It's freezing in here," he said as he pulled the blankets he had kicked off during the night over himself.

"I'm sorry, Jonathan. I was just getting some fresh air," he apologized.

Jonathan had his head under the blankets and just groaned an acknowledgment.

Michael offered, "I was just enjoying looking at you in the daylight. You looked really nice. I wanted to kiss your body everywhere."

Jonathan stuck his head out from under the covers and said, "If you're asking permission. Permission granted. But shut the fuckin' window."

Even though Michael wanted to air the room of stale cigarette smoke and let the fresh air in, he did as Jonathan said. He shut the window. He enjoyed doing what Jonathan told him to do. But it was odd for him to listen to anyone.

"Get back in bed, Michael," Jonathan ordered.

"Aye, aye, Sir!" Michael acknowledged with a mock salute. He got under the covers with Jonathan.

They cuddled and embraced, entwining their legs. They were immediately aroused.

"Michael, touch it."

"Oh, man."

"Would you like to taste it?"

He murmured softly, "Yes," but his answer was almost drowned out by the sounds of Butterball scratching on the bottom of the door. Then she barked softly. And then a little louder. She began scratching impatiently.

Jonathan asked, "What time is it, Michael?"

"It's about ten to eight."

"It's late."

"Yeah, for all we have to do."

"Why don't you let Butterball in, Michael?"

"Okay."

Michael opened the door and welcomed his friend, the happy, furry friend who had sought him out all those years ago when he was camping in the backyard.

Butterball jumped on the bed and licked Michael on his face until Michael covered his face with the blanket, then Butterball gave Jonathan the full welcome. She licked his chin, neck, nose, forehead and hair.

"Michael, Butterball's great, but she completely destroyed my mood. Maybe later. I want you to do it."

"I want it so bad."

Chapter 16

Jonathan was waiting outside for Michael, who was still in the house talking to his mother. He was looking forward to, albeit with some anxiety, visiting his mother at Golden Hill. He was looking forward, too, to spending this time with Michael, and therein lay the problem. He had never felt this way before. It wasn't just sex, wanting a cute guy, wanting Michael, and he did want Michael sexually, very much so, but he also wanted to be physically near Michael always. He wanted to be emotionally tuned into Michael and mentally tuned into him as well, always and everywhere. What was this craziness? Just the thought of being dropped off at Golden Hill and having Michael leave him there distressed him. The thought of returning to Manhattan alone for two days until Sunday made him feel forlorn and abandoned.

Jonathan walked over to the blue convertible and got into the front passenger seat to wait for Michael. The inside of the car was surprisingly warm from the sun. He sat back and closed his eyes and felt the warmth from the sun's rays cover his face and shoulders as they came through the windshield. This is just what I've always wanted, dreamed about, so why should it make me so nervous and afraid?

Michael came out of the house, ran across the dead grass and jumped into the Buick into the driver's seat next to Jonathan. "Sorry I took so long. Mom wanted to know all about what to make for Sunday dinner before she left for the store."

"You weren't long, Michael. I enjoyed sitting here for a few minutes in the sun. Felt like being in Puerto Rico. And that was a great breakfast your mother made. I really enjoyed it. I hope you told her."

"Jonathan, you told her yourself, and she was very pleased. She really likes you a lot. I can tell."

Michael started the car and backed out of the driveway.

"I'm glad she does," Jonathan said. "Where are we headed first?"

"Just for a drive through Mellon. I'll point out the high school and stuff like that."

"Cool," Jonathan said, but he wasn't thinking about seeing Mellon, just about never leaving Michael's side.

They drove quietly toward the school. Michael waved to someone he knew at an intersection, and Jonathan enjoyed photographing each of the country houses in his mind as they passed by. Jonathan thought that Norman Rockwell must have been the set designer for this incredible countryside. Each house was different, attractive, and each had well-kept grounds. Smoke was coming from many of the chimneys. One woman came out of the front door of her house, picked up two bottles of milk from the box on her front porch and disappeared back inside the house. The traffic light changed and they continued to the school.

Michael drove slower than usual. He wanted to stretch the day out as long as he could. The last thing in the world he wanted to do was to drop Jonathan off at Golden Hill and leave without him. He would miss him so until Sunday. And then on Sunday he'd never get a chance to be alone with him with all the others around, in church, at home, with Gary. Michael was a little on the shy side and as afraid of rejection as anyone was, but he wanted to, had to, let Jonathan know how he felt.

"Jonathan, what are you going to do when you get home? I mean, suppose nobody's there?"

"Fuck. I don't know. Just hang out, I guess," he said, clearly depressed.

"Well, I'm going to miss you like you wouldn't believe. I don't want you to leave, particularly because you may not have anything to go to. I want you with me. I want you to stay until Sunday."

"Michael, do you really mean it? Because I've been thinking the same thing. I don't care if my father and his wife are home, I really want to be with you."

"And I want to be with you with all my heart."

Jonathan slid over to Michael, and kissed him on the cheek.

"God damn, Jonathan. This is going to be great. We'll be together at least through Sunday. Oh! I don't want you out of my sight. I love you so."

"Me, too. So what's the new plan?"

"How's this? Instead of dropping you off at Golden Hill, I'll drive you to your apartment. I can hang out someplace and wait for you. You do what you have to, get some more clothes and stuff, and then we'll drive up to visit your mother, and I'll find something to do until you're done, and then we go back to Mellon."

Jonathan edited, "That's great, but you can park near my apartment and come in with me. If they're home, you can meet my father and Lillian, and if they're not, I'll just show you around."

Michael took his eyes from the road, which he seldom did, and smiled a big smile at Jonathan.

Since they were no longer headed for the school, they needed to get onto the parkway, and they had passed the entrance to the Taconic a few minutes earlier. Michael made a U-turn and headed back. In no time they were on their way to Manhattan. Michael was looking forward to seeing a Manhattan apartment. Michael had never been in a real apartment. Everybody he knew lived in a house on the ground, except for Richard Schlesinger, who lived in the apartment on the second floor of a two-family house.

The sun was coming into the car strongly from the East across Michael's face from the window on his left. As they got onto the Henry Hudson Parkway, Michael noticed the sun was almost directly overhead. It must have been about noon.

"Michael, hang a left at the Seventy-ninth Street exit."

"Okay. Are we almost there?"

"Yes. But we're on the West Side of town, and we just have to get to the East. During the daytime it shouldn't be too difficult. Gee, it's almost quarter to twelve. We made good time. And, Michael, I was right. You really are a good driver."

"Thanks."

Chapter 17

Michael left his car with the parking attendant and walked outside the garage to Jonathan who was standing on the street waiting for him. They started to walk in the direction that Jonathan indicated. Michael was surprised when Jonathan took Michael's hand in his, but he didn't pull away. They walked about two blocks.

"That's it," Jonathan said as he pointed across the street, squeezed Michael's hand and then released it. He led the way through the traffic. Michael followed.

Michael looked up at the spectacular residential building. Michael, who had come to the city on occasion to see the Christmas Show at Radio City Music Hall or to see a Broadway show, never realized that some of the tall buildings might be residential buildings instead of commercial ones.

As they walked under the dark green canopy, Michael asked, "You don't live in the penthouse, do you, Jonathan?"

"No, Michael, just on the thirty-second floor."

"How many apartments are on that floor?"

"Used to be four, but my father combined them into one. Depending on what room you're in you can see New Jersey, the George Washington Bridge, Queens, Brooklyn, Long Island, the Statue of Liberty."

"How many of you live there?"

"Me and my father and Lillian. That's it."

Michael felt giddy. "Shit, I can't wait to see this."

"Let's go in."

There were two uniformed doormen at the entrance, Kevin Riley and John Riley.

"Good afternoon, Mr. Taylor," said the older doorman.

"Hi, Kevin. And how are you, John," he asked of the younger door-man, Kevin's son.

"Great, Mr. Taylor. Do you have any bags you want me to get?"

"No, thank you, John. I'll be getting more stuff and leaving again soon. But I'll be back on Sunday. Is everything all right? Who's home?"

John's father answered, "Everything's good. No problems. Mr. and Mrs. Taylor are still away. Adele was here earlier, but finished and left about a half-hour ago. Apparently, she didn't know you were coming home."

"Thank you, Kevin. Thank you. This is my friend, Michael."

"How do you do, sir?" Kevin asked while John nodded a greeting as he shook Michael's hand.

"Great. Great. Good to meet you both," Michael said. There was that *How do you do?* again.

"See you later," Jonathan said as he steered Michael to the elevators. "This is our elevator, Michael. It services five floors. It opens right into the foyer of our apartment as long as you have the key."

The door of the elevator opened and Jonathan stepped out leading Michael to follow him by placing his hand behind Michael's arm. The small foyer contained a table against the wall facing the elevator with a large mirror above it. A large bouquet of dried fall flowers in a pewter vase was on the left side of the table and a basket for newspapers and mail was on the right. The basket was empty. Adele had probably already put the mail and newspapers inside the apartment. A small dark brown, velvet loveseat was on the left wall. The door to the apartment was on the right wall and between the table and the door was an enor-mous empty brass shell, like the ones used at every entrance at the Navy Training Center, for umbrellas, etc. The walls were covered with beige-on-beige textured fabric.

"Here goes," Jonathan said as he put his key in the door lock. Jonathan opened the door and stepped into the apartment. He stood beside the open door and bowed and said, "Come in, Michael. Welcome."

As Michael walked into the apartment he was suddenly aware of the strong smell of lemons and furniture polish. He walked into the center of the main hall and dropped his coat that he had been carrying onto the floor. He was looking out the windows at Central Park. "Oh! My God. Jonathan, this is the most beautiful view I've ever seen."

"Really," Jonathan said as he took Michael by the hand and walked him toward the window. "Go right up to the window, Michael, and take a good look. And if you care to later, I'll take you for a walk around the apartment on the terrace. Since this floor is recessed, the terrace completely surrounds the apartment. All the rooms have sliding glass doors onto it. Neat? Huh?"

"Super. Wow! This is absolutely fantastic!"

Jonathan said, "Everyone says that. It is a spectacular view. Even people who live in Manhattan marvel at the view, probably because of the way my dad designed the apartment. He studied architecture in college, as well as art and literature. One of his attributes is that he is into beauty. Churches, landscapes, interior design, even loves the Garden State Parkway and hates the Jersey Turnpike. Anyway, most people put the hall areas inside their apartments without windows, but he arranged all the rooms to be on the outside walls, and of course, they all have windows."

"So that's Central Park from the air."

"Yes it is. Right now most of the trees are bare except for the orange leaves that you see, but in summer it's all so green you can't see those roads or cars or anything and in winter when it snows it looks just like some of the post cards you've seen."

"I bet."

Jonathan walked to the panel on the wall next to he entrance door. He opened the panel to expose the electric switches for the entire floor.

"What are you doing, Jonathan?"

"Adjusting the lighting for the apartment. For example, since I'm going to show you everything, all the rooms, I put the setting on 6 or *All Rooms-Afternoon with Guests*. Of course, you can adjust each room individually to override the main setting. But using the main setting is really convenient. Most of the main settings include the proper lighting for all the artwork throughout the apartment.

Michael walked over to Jonathan and began looking over the typed list on the panel's door. He said, "Suppose we were here alone just watching TV, is there a setting for that, too?"

Jonathan wasn't sure. He read down the list. "Yes! Here it is. Setting 19. *Projection Room, Kitchen, Jonathan's Bedroom, Guest Bedroom SW and Main Corridor.* By the way, Guest Bedroom SW is the one next to mine."

Michael said, "Which means we can watch some TV, get a snack, mix a few drinks, skip down the corridor to the bedroom and then we can fool around."

Jonathan said, "Yes, Precious." He put his arms around Michael and pulled him close. They kissed for a long time until he released Michael.

"But," Jonathan added, "that would be Setting 19 only if my father and Lillian were home, and if they weren't, it would be 18. *Projection Room, Kitchen, Jonathan's Bedroom and Main Corridor.* I want you to be as near to me as possible and as often as possible." Jonathan closed the panel door.

"I'm looking forward to the tour," Michael said blushing a little as he looked around the room and noticed a beautiful painting of a boy carrying a pitchfork walking toward a barn that hung over the dark green sofa. "That's a wonderful painting, Jonathan. And I didn't notice it when I came in."

"That's because it wasn't lit. Now it is."

"I don't know very much about art, but this painting is spectacular!" Michael went up close to examine the signature. "Jonathan, I can't believe it. Is it real?"

Jonathan smiled. "Yes, Michael, it's real. It's an Andrew Wyeth. Andrew Newell Wyeth. We have several more of his around the place. My father really enjoys looking at his work. Most of his pictures are of old buildings, hills and fields from two locations, his boyhood home in Pennsylvania and his summer home in Maine. Dad says they're serene and add a real homey touch to city apartments. I also think he just likes to own some of Wyeth's work because of Wyeth's celebrity status. I understand both President Eisenhower and Soviet leader, Premier Khrushchev, are admirers of his work, and that Mamie Eisenhower has chosen one of his paintings for a public room in the White House. So much for that, but I do like his work, too. If you care to, we can check out some of his work while you're here in the city at our museums."

"I'd like that. I've never been to a museum other than when we went on a class trip to The Museum of Natural History."

"Then it's off to the museums when you come to visit me."

"That especially sounds like something I'd like to do. Is it expensive?"

"No. And that's the part that's hard to understand. One dollar gets you into any museum in the city to see some of the greatest art works in the world and you can stay as long as you want. Actually, some students and the like take sketchpads, and they sit down on the benches or floor and draw."

"That really sounds cool. By the way, how many rooms are there up here?" Michael inquired changing the subject.

Jonathan made a face to show that he was counting. "Nine, plus two guest bedrooms, eleven in all. Also, all four bedrooms have their own bathrooms, and there is a powder room for guests right over there, so guests don't have to go into the bedrooms."

Michael had never been this far off the ground unless he was in an airplane. "What rooms are they?"

"Well, the first is the one we're in, the hall. Then there's the kitchen, which I'm sure you'll like. It's fully stocked, as if anyone were going to cook in there. The caterers sometimes use it when my father has business associates or clients for cocktails or dinner. Of course, there's a dining room. Same story there. We can have thirty-six people for a sit down dinner, but that's never been done. The kitchen is behind that wall, and the dining room is behind the kitchen and takes up the Northwest corner of the floor—gorgeous views of Central Park and New Jersey. The dining room has early morning sun for about a half-hour and no sun until just before sunset. On the other side of this room is the Projection Room, which takes up the whole Northeast corner. In clear weather you can watch planes take off and land at LaGuardia airport. Unfortunately, most of the times we use that room the windows are completely covered with heavy draperies, so the room is dark. There are several televisions in there as well as two 70 millimeter motion picture projectors."

"Jonathan, what's a 70 millimeter motion picture projector?"

"They're the large projectors. Like the ones in the movie theaters. We have regular and Cinemascope screens and the latest stereophonic sound system. On the East Side of the floor we have a library and a music room. Both of these you must see. I can't even describe them. Dad has all the old classics in leather bound volumes in the library and in the music room, besides a great sound system, there is an extensive record collection, everything from Glenn Miller to Bernstein, and lots of photographs of my father with opera stars placed on a Steinway grand piano. Nobody plays. Anyway, you've got to see the music room. Each of the library and music room has its own bar and a good selection of alcoholic beverages. I wanted to have a wine cellar, but Lillian and my father thought it was too pretentious. In the middle of the opposite side of the floor is the sitting room. I love this room. It's very comfortable to sit and relax in. Often I put music on in the music room and listen to it in the sitting room, which is the only room with connecting speakers. It's a nice sunny room in the late afternoon where I like to write letters and think. Lillian decorated it, and I hated it at first, but she really did a good job. Lillian likes to read and sew, and sometimes we spend hours together there hardly speaking. Just being in the same room with Lillian makes me feel settled. The furniture in that room is very similar to the furniture in your home. Some club chairs, footrests and a plaid country sofa. Lillian crocheted a wonderful afghan, and it's on my favorite chair. I feel good there, if that makes any sense."

"Makes a lot of sense. I gather from what you say that you don't dislike Lillian."

"No, Michael. No, I don't. She's okay, and she sure makes my father happy. She even took care of my mother when she was laid up with a broken leg. Actually, she and my mother get along, too. The only thing that makes me uncomfortable is the sex thing. I'm glad they have a room almost a block away from me."

"You mean to say that you like to think they don't have sex together, is that right?"

Jonathan's facial expression made his feelings clear. "Yuck!"

"How do you think they would feel if they knew about our relationship?"

Jonathan said, "Michael, I don't know if my father would kill me first or vomit first. In any case, you'd have time to escape."

Michael laughed. "Just remember, we live in a glass house. Now, please show me the kitchen."

"You got it. Come on."

They went into the kitchen, and Jonathan immediately spotted Adele's handwriting on a large note stuck with cherry magnets to the refrigerator door. It said simply, "Call your father." It had the telephone number on.

"Hey, Michael. Here's a note from Adele to call my father."

"So call him, and after you call him, I'll call my mother and let her know our plans."

Since the number was probably a hotel, Jonathan had the operator make a person-to-person call for him.

"This is Jonathan Taylor," his father told the operator.

"Here is your party, sir," the operator said to Jonathan, who was waiting patiently on the phone in the kitchen.

"Hello," his father answered.

"Hi! It's me."

"Where are you?"

"Home."

"Home? You said in your letter that you would be coming home the Tuesday before Thanksgiving. We expected you next week, next Tuesday."

"No wonder no one was here. I did say that, but I meant the Tuesday, a week before Thanksgiving," Jonathan said as he looked toward Michael.

Michael frowned and shook his head.

"Jonathan, what are you doing with yourself all alone?"

"Actually, Dad, I spent yesterday with a friend I'd met in boot camp, and he's with me now. We're going to drive up to New Canaan, so I can visit Mom, and then I'm going to stay with him and his family through Sunday. His name is Michael, and he's singing on Sunday at St. John's. You know the church in Mellon that Willington Balmoral gets the Metro soloists for the holidays. It's right near Poughkeepsie."

"Well it's good to hear that you're busy and have some good company. We'll be home on Monday, so I won't worry about your getting into trouble. I'm glad you're going to visit your mother. Be sure to say hello for me. I hope to meet Michael sometime during your leave."

"You will, Dad. It's so great to talk to you. Is Lillian there?"

"Yes. Right here. Lillian, Jonathan wants to talk to you." He handed the phone to Lillian, who had already removed her earring.

"Hey, Jonathan!"

"Lillian, how's everything going? Where are you guys?"

"Everything is going well, and we're fine as usual here at the Fontainebleau down here in Miami. I wanted to get a tan, so I'd look good for you when you got home."

Jonathan smiled and said, "You always look good to me, Lillian. I'm taking my friend Michael on a tour of the place here, and I can't wait to show him our room."

"The room you used to hate," she laughed.

"I was hoping that you'd forget that some day."

"I won't. But I'm glad you have company until we get back. Your father was mouthing your conversation with me as he spoke to you."

"Of course. Well, I miss you both and I'm looking forward to next week when you get back. I have to get back to Michael. Oh, Michael, by the way, is a neighbor of the Balmorals."

Michael looked at Jonathan with disbelief covering his face.

"Goodbye now. See you next week," Jonathan said as he hung up.

"Jonathan!"

"Well, you *are* neighbors."

"You're a piece of work," Michael said as he kissed Jonathan on his lips.

Jonathan took Michael's hand and asked, "How do you like the kitchen?"

"What's not to like?" Michael asked as he looked around. The room had the same view as the main hall, and he noticed a table and three chairs outside on the terrace. A large butcher-block table was in the center of the long, rectangular room with cabinets underneath it and four stools placed at the end of the twelve-foot table near the windows and glass doors. Against the west wall was a seven-burner commercial gas stove with an aluminum hood over it with built-in exhaust fans. Two ovens were on one side of the stove and a gigantic refrigerator-freezer on the other.

"Jonathan, do you mind if I take a look in the refrigerator?"

"No, go ahead."

Michael opened the door of the refrigerator and was amazed that it was full of food. "My God, Jonathan," he said, "there's enough food in here to feed the whole company for a day including mid-rats."

"Yeah. Adele always gets stocked up from Silverstein's when guests are coming, and I guess I qualify for guest-hood since I've been gone so long. I guess Adele went shopping this morning when she realized I was probably going to be home today. I told her Tuesday when I came in that I was going to be home for thirty days. It's lunchtime. Would you like something to eat? I know I'm hungry."

"Me, too."

"Take out what you want. There's always turkey, roast beef, salami and stuff. There should be rye bread and French bread in the breadbox on the counter next to the sink if I'm not mistaken. Make yourself at home. Put whatever you want on the table, and I'll get plates, glasses, knives and forks. You should find some ice tea and milk, if that's okay. There's probably beer, too."

"No beer for me. I'm driving. I see some tomatoes and lettuce and potato salad."

In a few minutes the table was set and loaded with food from one of the best delicatessens in Manhattan. Michael put a large pitcher of iced tea on the butcher-block table. Perched on stools at the end of the table, they sat quietly, wolfing down hearty sandwiches quickly. Neither of them had realized how hungry they were, probably from the drive down to the city and the exhilaration they were experiencing from their developing friendship and from the intensity of feelings that were overwhelming them. They finished their lunch with some éclairs from Gino's Pastry Shop in Little Italy.

Michael leaned against the back of the stool with his hand on his abdomen and sighed, "I'm stuffed. That was great. And those éclairs really hit he spot."

"It was good. Silverstein's is one of the best places around here to get prepared food. Everybody uses them to cater their parties and business functions. The stuff is always fresh. Not particularly fancy, but good quality. For really elegant occasions, my father calls them "BS" affairs, most people use the exotic caterers on the "A" list. But for your good, all-purpose, hungry crowd, everybody uses Silverstein's. And Gino's bakery in Little Italy is the best place for homemade Italian cookies, pastries and cakes. It's not really that far from here. We should stop and get some pastries to take home to your parents before we leave today."

"They would love that. And no wonder I love you, Jonathan."

"And your mother won't love either one of us if you forget to call her, Michael."

"Damn. I knew I forgot something. May I use the phone?"

"Of course. You can use the one on the wall right next to the fridge."

Michael dialed the 914 number, and Louisa answered.

"Ma, it's me."

"Hey, where are you?"

"I'm with Jonathan in the city. At his house. We drove down."

"You haven't driven to the city in a couple of years. You always said there was no place to park."

"It's okay. We parked in a garage. We're in Jonathan's apartment right now. We just had lunch."

"Good. Where did you eat?"

"At Jonathan's. In the kitchen."

"His apartment has a kitchen? I always pictured people who lived in expensive New York apartments eating out all the time in fancy restaurants, and that their apartments were more like hotel suites with room service. Like in the movies."

"Well this apartment is like a gigantic house in the sky, which I'll tell you about when I get home, but it does have a kitchen."

"I can't wait to hear about it when you get home. What time are you coming home anyway?"

"Well, we're going to New Canaan in a little while, and then I'd like to bring Jonathan home and have him stay with us until Sunday, if that's okay with you."

"Of course, it's okay. Should I fix up the sofa in the living room for him?"

"No, it's not necessary, Mom. He can stay with me in my room like last night," Michael answered his mother. Just saying it made him feel warm. The recollection of Jonathan's delicate manly fragrance seemed to fill his nostrils.

"That's fine with me, as long as you both get a good night's sleep."

"Great, Mom."

"Also, call Maureen when you get back. She wants to do something with you tomorrow night."

"Okay, Mom." Michael hung up the phone and smiled at Jonathan. He spread his arms in welcome as he said, "It's all set."

Jonathan accepted Michael's outreached greeting and hugged him tightly around his back. He ran the tips of his fingers up and down Michael's back along his spinal cord. Michael was beginning to get hard; Jonathan could feel it. They both were. They kissed pressing their bodies together softly, swaying and rocking.

Jonathan stepped back sliding his hands from Michael's back, over his shoulders and down his arms until he held Michael's hands in his own. "If we don't stop this," he said, "we'll never get to visit my mother."

"I know," Michael grinned.

"If we climb into bed, we'll never get there."

"What about the tour of the apartment?"

"I'll give you the tour some other time."

"Shit, Jonathan, I'm so fuckin' hard and horny. I want you so much."

"And I want you. And we're going to have each other tonight, at your house, in your bed. I want you. I want you to explore every inch of me that you care to, and I want to do the same to you."

They kissed again, teasing each other's tongues. They embraced eagerly until Michael broke away and said, "Oh, Jonathan. I need a cold shower."

"Come outside with me for a few minutes and look at the skaters on the rink in the park."

"Good idea."

They stood outside on the terrace and viewed the spectacular panorama below. The skaters looked like a Currier and Ives painting. Their sexual longings were somewhat suppressed by the cold, and when they went back into the apartment, Michael noticed what a mess the kitchen table was in.

"Jonathan, can you give me a hand cleaning up the table?"

Jonathan shook his head, "Don't overdo it, Michael. Just put the unused food back in the refrigerator. There's waxed paper and stuff over the counter. Adele will clean up the rest."

"Jonathan, you're so lazy."

"No, Michael. The lady needs the job. We make a mess. She cleans. It's the way of the world."

Chapter 18

Jonathan packed some clothes for the weekend and left a note for Adele on the refrigerator door with Michael's phone number on it as he had done yesterday morning, letting her know when his father and Lillian would be home.

They left the apartment and drove down to Little Italy headed for Gino's. They got there rather quickly driving down Fifth Avenue and through Washington Square. Jonathan guided Michael through the city streets until they reached Mulberry Street. Michael found a parking space a few doors down from the pastry shop in front of Mario's Restaurant. Michael peered into the small shops that lined the street as they walked to Gino's. The windows were full of Italian foodstuffs, and one pasta store had some red and green spaghetti bowls that Michael admired. Michael looked into the coffee shop that was next door to Theresa's Restaurant. It has a variety of antique coffee grinders on display. Jonathan, who was extremely knowledgeable about all areas of the city, gave Michael a running commentary on the area. Little Italy was one of his favorite places to visit.

When they went into Gino's he could smell freshly baked goods filling the store, and Michael recognized the aroma of anise, almond and vanilla. The showcases were filled with assorted, beautifully decorated pastries and cookies.

Jonathan picked out the selection, getting about four of each kind. The salesclerk put the cookies in a box and weighed them. It was almost two pounds.

"Michael, let's get a rum cake, too."

"Okay."

Jonathan asked the girl behind the counter for a rum cake and for six Napoleons and for six éclairs.

"Jonathan," Michael protested, "that's too much. We'll all get fat."

"It's my treat. My thank you for your parents' hospitality."

"Since you put it that way, okay."

When the salesgirl finished and totaled up the purchases Michael was surprised at the cost, how expensive the purchases were, New York City prices, but he decided to remain silent. If Jonathan wanted to do this, it was alright with him.

They got back in the car, and Jonathan put the boxes filled with goodies in the back on the floor securely between his bag and the back seat.

Michael started the car and Jonathan instructed, "Just go down this street until we reach Canal and then turn right. And Michael did. Michael was surprised that as soon as they got on Canal Street they had left Little Italy and were in Chinatown. The traffic was so heavy that Michael had to stop every few feet and he had a chance to look at the stores that were on Canal Street. There were restaurants and grocery stores with large signs in Chinese. Several had rabbits and ducks hanging outside. Michael had never seen that before. They were stopped for a traffic light next to a fish truck that was making a delivery. The smell was overwhelming, and Michael was glad it wasn't August. He secretly rejoiced when the light changed. They turned right again on Sixth Avenue, recently renamed Avenue of the Americas, but the name hadn't caught on yet. Traffic was light. It wasn't long before they were on the Henry Hudson Parkway and were on their way to New Canaan. They didn't talk much during the drive. Each of them was just enjoying being next to each other.

Michael pulled into the long driveway of Golden Hill. It looked more like a luxury resort than a psychiatric hospital, Michael thought. It was a large white Victorian structure with a large front porch and many additions to its sides, and probably to the back, although Michael couldn't see those. The window frames and louvered shutters were painted a dark green. Even though the grass was no longer green and most of the trees were bare, one could easily tell that the grounds were exceptionally well maintained. There were some huge evergreen trees in front of the main entrance. By the size of them Michael knew they must have been old, perhaps a hundred years or so. They looked almost as tall as the tree they used at Rockefeller Center for Christmas.

"Jonathan, do you think it'll be okay if I parked over there?"

"I'm sure."

"Good. I'll wait for you."

"Why don't you come in with me?"

"No. Not today."

"Well I can't leave you just sitting here."

"Sure you can. I don't mind."

"I'll tell you what, I'm going in for a few minutes, and then when I find out what the status is, I'll come out and let you know."

"Good idea. I'll just get into the cookies and stuff in the back."

Jonathan laughed and got out of the car and said before he closed the door, "I'll be right back."

He entered the front door and walked over to the nurse's station. An attractive, red-haired, young woman was on duty. The nurses at Golden Hill didn't wear traditional uniforms, but regular street clothes, nice dresses and suits that would be approved by Katherine Gibbs.

"Hello, I'm Jonathan Taylor, Melissa Taylor's son."

"How do you do, Mr. Taylor? I'm Connie."

"Please call me Jonathan. Mr. Taylor is my father, an old guy who's in his forties." He smiled his smile.

She blushed as she returned that smile like most people did. "Of course, Jonathan."

"How is my mother?"

"She's actually doing very well. She's been here over a week and coming along nicely."

"Is she in her room now?"

"No, but she should be back to Main House soon."

"Back?"

"Yes. She's swimming at the recreation center from two to three and it's about three o'clock now. You can wait in the reception area if you like or go down to the center and meet her and walk back."

"I think I'd better wait in the reception area. I have a friend with me who drove me up. May he come in also?"

"Normally we only allow relatives, and close ones at that, because of our patients desire for privacy, and their guaranteed anonymous participation in the Golden Hill Program, but if he's a friend of your family I'm sure it will be okay. But please ask him to keep the names of any people he may recognize during his visit to himself."

"Yes, certainly," and Jonathan smiled again. Mission accomplished. "Thank you, I'll bring him in."

Jonathan almost ran to the car to pick up Michael.

"Come on, Michael. You're cleared for entry into the crazy house for the rich and famous."

"Are you sure it's a good idea?"

"Yes, I'm sure. Now, come on."

Michael joined Jonathan and headed toward the white-and-green mansion. Once inside the main hall, Jonathan steered Michael to the reception room, which was off the main hall and practically had to push Michael through the door.

To say that the reception room was elegantly furnished was an understatement. The four tall windows were covered with crisply starched white curtains and dark green brocade draperies and pleated valances. Several French eighteenth century chairs were strategically placed throughout the room. A plush green carpet, lighter than the color of the draperies, was installed wall-to-wall and on top of it was an eighteen-foot square Persian carpet. The scones on each of the mahogany wall panels matched the lead crystal chandelier that hung from the ceiling in the middle of the room. Waterford glass ashtrays were on all the tables in the room with sterling silver table lighters and mahogany boxes containing an assortment of cigarettes. There was an enormous bouquet of white gladiolas in a ceramic vase on the table in front of the settee. All other tables had small bouquets of violets and pansies. Michael thought they must have a hothouse on the premises. Maybe they had a garden as therapy. There were a few portraits of people Michael didn't recognize around the room with the exception of one of George Washington by Paul Stuart. He wondered if it were an original, but with this décor, with this splendid décor, it probably was. Shit, this really must be a place for the rich and famous. There was a glass breakfront in which there were a large assortment of liquors and glasses. In a corner there was a secretary opened with stationary with the Golden Hill logo on it. On the desk were several fountain pens next to the paper and a bottle of blue Waterman's ink. Michael heard soft music. It was chamber music that he could not identify, and he looked around in vain for the speakers. Maybe they were behind the sofa or the secretary. Who knows?

They sat on two chairs with a table between them.

"This place is gorgeous," Michael said.

"It is, isn't it? And aren't the flowers beautiful?"

"They sure are."

"When I first came up here I wondered how they always had all these wonderful flowers in all the rooms."

"I was thinking that they might have a greenhouse on the grounds and use gardening as a therapy for the patients," Michael said.

"Damn! You're exactly right. You're a genius. I never thought of that until my mother was working in there one day."

"I'm not a genius, Jonathan, but I grew up growing things. Flowers. Vegetables. Worms in the dirt, butterflies, mosquitoes."

"I suppose our frame of reference is different."

"I guess."

They heard the door open in the vestibule.

Jonathan walked over to the doorway and spotted his mother.

The people entering, as well as his mother, saw him.

"Jonathan!" she exclaimed.

"Ma! How good to see you."

They put their arms around each other. They kissed each other on the lips.

"Mom, I'm so happy that you're okay. When I got home, as soon as I heard that you were here, I wanted to come to see you."

"I'm so glad to see you, Jonathan. And I'm so sorry this has happened to me again."

"Don't worry about it. You're here, and things will get better. I mean this place always helps you, doesn't it?"

"Yes. I love the pampering I get here."

Michael rose from his seat and turned his back on the reunion in the doorway and pretended to study one of the portraits on the wall.

"Ma, a friend came with me. Actually he drove me here. We met in boot camp, and I'm visiting his family in Mellon. Would you like to meet him? He's right here in the reception room."

"Yes, Jonathan. I'd like that very much"

Jonathan led his mother into the room and walked over to Michael. Michael turned to face them.

"Mother, I'd like you to meet my friend, Michael Manganaro. Michael, this is my mother, Mrs. Melissa Taylor."

"Michael," his mother greeted with her hand outstretched, "I am happy to meet you, and I thank you for bringing my son to visit me."

"It's my pleasure to meet you, Mrs. Taylor. I hope you're feeling better."

"Yes. Thank you. I'm feeling much better."

The beauty of Jonathan's mother stunned Michael. She had those same eyes. Eyes just like Jonathan's, and she had the same smile. Jonathan looked just like her. Michael had previously thought that Jonathan must have looked like his father, but now he could see that he strongly resembled Mrs. Taylor.

"Ma, so how's everything?"

"Great. Your father has helped a lot. He's made sure that the insurance is covering most of my stay, so I don't have to worry about anything. And he sent the most beautiful flowers."

"He asked about you earlier this afternoon when I spoke to him, and he asked me to say hello."

"How nice. He still takes care of me. I am grateful for that. Where is he?"

"He's in Florida with Lillian."

"He always did like the warm climate. The sun. Getting a tan. And Lillian, how is she?"

"Dad and Lillian are both fine, Mom."

"I'm glad. Why don't you and Michael come to my room and visit for a while. I want to take my coat off and get out of my sweat suit and get comfortable."

"Sure. Come on, Michael."

They followed Melissa down the corridor that was on the other side of the reception room and followed her to her room.

"Let me change. Make yourselves comfortable," Melissa Taylor said as she picked up some clothes from the chair and went into the bathroom.

Michael looked around the room after she left. The room was exquisite. The furniture was not what he would have expected in a hospital room. He loved the four-poster bed with the lace canopy and the Queen Anne writing desk. The room was restful and quietly recuperative.

Mrs. Taylor reentered the room. She was wearing a white dress and had put on a touch of makeup. She looked like a movie star. And a young one at that. Michael was shocked. He thought she was one of the most attractive women he had ever seen. Michael wondered how old she was. She didn't even look like she was thirty-five. Maybe she had Jonathan when she was a teenager.

"So, what are you handsome guys up to?" she asked.

"A lot, Mom. I'm visiting Michael's family in Mellon, which is located near Poughkeepsie. We went to the apartment this morning, and some day soon Michael's going to let me drive his car."

"Oh, God, Michael, you trust him?"

"Yes, I do, at least I will when his license is reinstated."

They laughed, and some of the tension of visiting someone in an institution like this was lifted. When Michael was growing up, people in "insane asylums" were nuts, plain and simple. When he used to explore the woods near a county asylum, he knew that people referred to those in that institution as nuts who would never get out. Sometimes you could hear the screams from within. There were no facilities like this that he was aware of where people with different mental problems would be helped. This woman would get out.

Michael immediately liked this woman. She seemed very special. He wasn't sure why he liked her so much. She did look a lot like Jonathan, but more than her physical appearance, she had something he couldn't put his finger on, and something that just seemed wholesome. Michael sensed that he and this lady had something in common.

Melissa stared at Michael for a moment and said, "You know, seeing the two of you together is quite interesting. I mean you look so similar in ways. Like you were brothers or something. And it's quite clear to me that you have grown very fond of each other in a very short time." To herself, she thought, if they're not lovers now, they will be soon.

She returned to the dressing room to finish dressing. She also knew her son well and always knew that he had a competitive mean streak. She hoped a nice kid like Michael could handle it and that it would not hurt him too much. Jonathan, Jr. was the apple who didn't fall a far distance from his father's tree. And she liked his father a lot, and still wasn't jealous of Lillian who seemed a little more pragmatic. Lillian could handle his indiscretions better than she ever could. Perhaps because Lillian was older when she married Jonathan than she had been, and because she was an executive with heavy business savvy, not the least of which was having street smarts. When she had married him, herself, she was eighteen, a former high school beauty queen. Jonathan was a driven man, bent on making his first million. And she knew he would. Many millions. It was interesting how her thoughts ran that day. For instance, because during her marriage all Jonathan's investments were in his business and securities, she was only entitled to what the court awarded to her and none of his property, and since she had been deemed an unfit mother, she didn't get custody of Jonathan the amount she received wasn't very much. But he did give her more than the court decreed and for that she was grateful. Lillian, on the other hand, made him buy an expensive apartment, a large country house in Seaside Heights, New Jersey, and lots of, not necessarily expensive, but quality jewelry. The community property laws would favor her with a large settlement to which she would be entitled if they ever divorced. She remembered days when she was so exhausted from caring for Jonathan and their pretentious, too-large townhouse that she couldn't attend some of his business functions. Jonathan went alone without complaint and when he returned he didn't hide lipstick, powder, or perfume on his clothes. She imagined Lillian didn't miss a business function, and that at the first appearance of any residual stains of a female liaison on him at any time, she, in her best Gucci outfit, would be in her lawyer's office at daybreak. Still, she liked her. She was good for him. He was not in control of their marriage; Lillian held at least a fifty-percent interest. He would have a lot to lose if he didn't control his outside interest in women.

She came out of the dressing room and joined the two handsome men.

"Hey, Guys, can I take you for a tour of the grounds? I'm allowed to go out alone now."

"Sure." They responded together.

As they were leaving they ran into Mrs. Taylor's attending physician, Dr. Jared Franklin. Mrs. Taylor introduced him to Jonathan and Michael. When he realized that Jonathan was only going to be in town for such a short time and that he might not get another chance to visit his mother, Dr. Franklin gave Mrs. Taylor permission to leave the grounds for two-and-a-half hours to have dinner in town as long as she was accompanied by her son. Consequently, after the tour of the grounds they headed to downtown New Canaan.

They had a very nice dinner. Michael had a good time, and he knew Mrs. Taylor did, too. He also knew that Jonathan was glowing with the success of the visit.

Chapter 19

He felt good in his new, gray wool suit. Losing fifteen pounds during his recent two-week army reserve stint at Ft. Jenkins helped. He hated the exercise, and he couldn't eat the slop they called chow. His shoes were nice and shiny. Once a week he treated himself to a shine. It was seventy-five cents well spent. Gary had a good day at work. One of those days when nothing went wrong. He liked his hours at the insurance company, 8 a.m. to 4 p.m., that enabled him to get the early 4:10 p.m. train home each night if he didn't have to stay late. He got on the train at Grand Central tonight and it was only half-full. Since this was the Thursday before Thanksgiving week many commuters had already left the city for vacations that would include the Thanksgiving holiday. He got a good seat with no one near him, so he could concentrate on reading his Bemco Manual. Yesterday, the train was crowded and he could not comfortably read. Not only that, but there was a major distraction.

Yesterday, the only seat he could find was next to an elderly woman who was sleeping. He faced two other passengers who were in the seat where you traveled backwards. At least he was facing forward. He liked that. People were standing in the aisle, and he felt claustrophobic. He felt squashed in and wasn't even able to open his briefcase, so that he could get out anything to read. A fat woman standing in the aisle was rubbing her belly against his shoulder. The stench of her toilet water gagged him. With any luck at all she would get off at 125th Street. And God was good. She did get off and many of the standees got off, too. The sleeping elderly woman woke up and got off, as well, and Gary moved into the window seat.

He noticed that the two other passengers across from him were very attractive men. He tried not to stare. He glanced at them only occasionally and looked out the window the rest of the time. He was glad that he moved to the seat next to the window. The man sitting in the window seat across from him was either in his late twenties or early thirties. He was wearing an expensive, three piece, gray pinstriped suit, and a white French-cuffed shirt with gold cufflinks. His tie was obviously expensive. Bright, nail enamel red. He appeared to be more elegant than the other people riding this train were. Most guys his age with good jobs these days wore button-down shirts, not fancy French cuffs. His left hand was on his thigh, and Gary noticed a gold wedding ring. His right hand rested on his right thigh near his crouch.

Gary watched as the man in the suit moved his thigh against the other passenger who looked like a college student, who was wearing tan chinos and a red sweater. The college guy moved his thigh away from the advancing temptation of the thigh in the suit. Damn, Gary thought, both of these guys are gorgeous. He thought about Michael who was always horny. He would have liked both of them. There were so many things he would like to think about that happened during their years of friendship. But he'd think about that later. What was happening across from his held his interest. The suit man moved his leg further toward the student and, instead of moving away, the student moved his leg toward the suit man and obviously was pressing against the man's leg.

The man said, "Do you take this train often? I've never seen you before."

"No. I'm just going to visit a friend in Mellon."

"Ah. If you're ever up this way again, why don't you call me?" He reached into his breast pocket and pulled out a business card and gave it to the student.

"Thank you, Sir." He said as he took the card, looked at it and placed it in his pocket. "I'll do that."

"That would be great. I have to get off at the next station. I do hope you'll call."

"I will."

The man in the expensive suit got up when the train was pulling into the station. Gary could see the erection in his trousers. The man turned his back to Gary and let the front of his hips pass closely to the student's face. He said, "I want to hear from you."

"You will. For sure."

The man left.

Gary wanted to say something to the younger man, but he wasn't sure what he could say. Maybe he should say that he lived in Mellon, too, but that would have let the stranger know that he had observed what had taken place, and that he had heard the conversation.

The train continued until they were almost to Poughkeepsie. Gary finally decided to say something.

"I'm glad the train isn't so crowded now," Gary offered to the stranger.

"Me, too. I can't believe that people put themselves through this every day. What a drag."

"It's not so bad, once you get used to it."

"I guess so, but it's not for me."

The train pulled into the Poughkeepsie station.

Gary stood up, and so did his remaining travel companion from the other seat. He was sorry that he hadn't spoken more to that handsome young stranger, but he followed him off the train, hoping that they might speak on the platform, but, unfortunately, the guy walked quickly south, and Gary had to walk north to the side of the station where he had parked his car. He had wanted to follow the cute stranger, but he felt too shy. Oh, well.

But that was yesterday and today was Thursday. He was looking forward to seeing Michael on Sunday. He hadn't seen him for months. He missed visiting the Manganaro house. Many of his most peaceful moments during his turbulent puberty years were spent in the kitchen of that house on Maiden Lane and in Michael's bedroom. He remembered the hours and hours of talking. Talking about everything from religion to school to sex. Gary came from a large family, four brothers and two sisters. Spending time at the Manganaro's was indeed peaceful. He couldn't ever get used to the fact that at the dinner table they talked one at a time, but at his house everyone spoke simultaneously. He chuckled to himself as he thought of all the well-spent nickels.

Chapter 20

Michael closed the door behind him and locked it. It had been a long day, and he was glad to be home at last alone with Jonathan. Michael turned on the desk lamp and the overhead light and then sat on the edge of the bed. He watched Jonathan pull his red cashmere sweater over his head and pull his arms out of the sleeves.

"Michael, remember the days when we had hair and used to worry about messing it when we put sweaters on or took them off?" Jonathan said as he stared at himself in the mirror and rubbed his hand over he shaved scalp.

"Yeah, I do. I wonder how long it's going to take to grow back."

"I don't think it'll take too long. I hope not anyway. I remember the first time I saw you in the barracks with your beautiful blond hair, Michael. I think it was the first thing I noticed about you."

Michael said, "I noticed your hair, too. I remember thinking that I wanted to talk to you then, but I was too shy to ask anything. I thought you were the nicest looking guy I'd ever seen. I never thought in a million years that you would like me."

Jonathan sat down next to Michael and said, "The incredible thing is that I thought the same thing when I first saw you. I remember that you were struggling with the paint stenciling your clothes. You didn't see me that day because I was two tables behind you."

"I saw you, but I immediately felt the incredible desire that I was ashamed of, and I was afraid if you knew what I was thinking, or saw me staring, you'd kick the shit out of me."

"Me?" Jonathan smiled his smile.

Michael looked into Jonathan's eyes and said, "Yes."

Jonathan said, "Let's light those candles and turn out these bright lights. Okay?"

"Sure. There are matches over there next to the ashtray."

"Great. I'll do it." Jonathan walked around the bed to the desk and lit four votive candles and placed one on each night table next to the bed, one on the desk and one of the windowsills. Then he turned the desk lamp off. "Michael, do you mind if I turn the radio on?"

"No. It's tuned into the Top 40's station if that's okay." Jonathan turned the knob on the small, tabletop, brown RCA radio and turned the volume down fairly low. Mark Dinning was singing *Teen Angel.*"

"Good." Jonathan walked around the bed and flicked the light switch off for the overhead light before he rejoined Michael on the bed. "That's better, isn't it?"

"Yes. I'm glad everyone went to bed early. They should be sound asleep now."

"Michael, would you like to undress me?

"Yes." Michael reached for the button on Jonathan's shirt.

"No, Michael. Shoes first."

Michael knelt down between Jonathan's legs and took each of his loafers off. He looked up at Jonathan. And then he pressed his face onto Jonathan's upper thigh.

"That feels nice, Michael."

Michael felt the warmth of Jonathan's body as well as his hard penis against his cheek. He managed to take off Jonathan's socks without lifting his cheek from the pulsating member inside Jonathan's chinos. He unbuckled Jonathan's belt and pulled down the zipper. Jonathan raised his hips off the bed, so that Michael could slide his pants down. Michael removed the chinos and put them behind him. He put his hands on Jonathan's thighs and licked the bulge that was before him in Jonathan's white jockey shorts. Jonathan moaned. Michael turned the elastic trim of the shorts back to expose the head of Jonathan's penis. He put his mouth on it, enjoying hearing Jonathan's sounds of appreciative pleasure. He slowly removed the jockey shorts and began doing what he had fantasized about since puberty.

Jonathan took off his shirt and tossed it on top of his chinos. Michael continued eagerly. Like a hungry puppy, Jonathan thought.

"Slower, Michael, slower. Easy. I don't want to come yet."

Michael slowed his movements, and Jonathan guided them with his hands behind Michael's head. Jonathan placed his hands under Michael's arms and lifted him, so that he could kiss him. And he kissed him harder than he had ever done.

"Now let me take your clothes off," Jonathan said as he quickly removed Michael's shoes, dungarees and sweatshirt. He pulled the bedspread and blankets down to the bottom of the bed. He kissed Michael again and lowered him onto the bed. He removed Michael's socks.

"Michael, why don't you roll onto your stomach, so I can give you a massage? Your shoulder muscles seem tight."

"Sure. I've never had a massage."

"Well there's always a first time. I know you'll enjoy it. I brought some baby oil with me. Do you have a beach towel or something to put on the bed?"

"I have an old camping blanket in the top of that closet," Michael said as he pointed to it.

"I'll get it, Michael. You don't have to get up."

Jonathan found the blanket and spread it on the other side of the bed and said, "Move onto the blanket, on your stomach, so I don't get any of the oil on the sheets."

Michael moved across the bed and onto the blanket.

Jonathan said, "And now for the unveiling. I have to remove your shorts, so I don't get any oil on them either." He slid his hands from the top of the back of Michael's thighs up and under his shorts over the cheeks of Michael's butt and then pulled them off slowly. Michael lifted his hips off the bed, so Jonathan could get the shorts over his erect penis. The white flesh of Michael's butt was exposed. Jonathan sat next to Michael on the edge of the bed on the worn-out, gray army blanket with his thigh against Michael's side. Michael looked vulnerable and enticing lying on his stomach and Jonathan said, "Spread your legs apart just a little, so I have access to all of you."

Michael did so, and Jonathan saw that the tip of Michael's erect penis was crushed against the blanket, and Jonathan could not resist the temptation to kiss Michael's tailbone. Then let his tongue slip between the top two inches of the crack between Michael's cheeks, and then he kissed the head of his penis. Jonathan smelled the fragrance emanating from Michael's private areas, those areas that are privy only to people allowed access. The fuzz on Michael's butt tickled his tongue. He was enjoying thoughts of what he would do one day, and one day very soon, to reap the full pleasure from that most precious, statue-like butt. He placed his left hand on Michael's lower back, as he picked up the bottle of baby oil from the floor.

Michael thoroughly enjoyed having Jonathan at his side. His body felt terrific next to his back. The hairs on Jonathan's leg felt tantalizing next to the side of his body. When Jonathan had kissed his tailbone, Michael closed his eyes and hoped he would continue and move further down. He almost came when Jonathan's tongue did proceed. Michael didn't know for sure what he wanted to happen, but he was sure that he wanted Jonathan to touch him down there. He wished he could say it out loud, but say what? To tell Jonathan that he would like his tongue tickling his anus? Jonathan would just think he was a pervert. A pig. Maybe he should just keep his mouth shut, after all this was just a massage.

Jonathan dribbled some oil onto Michael's back and began massaging his shoulders. His hands pressed deeply into the muscles on Michael's back and shoulders.

"Let me know if this is too strong, Michael."

"No. It's just great."

Jonathan massaged Michael's shoulders and his neck.

"Don't anticipate what I'm going to do to you, Michael. Just relax. Let your arms go limp."

"Yes," Michael said almost inaudibly.

He then took each of Michael's arms and massaged them one at a time and included each hand and each finger. He worked his hands slowly down the left side of Michael's back, and then he worked on the right side.

"Oh, that feels so good."

"It's supposed to."

Jonathan then put both his hands on his back and worked on Michael's entire back with long strokes from top to bottom. The sight of Michael lying on the bed was more beautiful than any sight Jonathan had seen. What a pleasure it was to just look at him! He let his fingers gently knead the top of Michael's buttocks and said, "Now for your feet."

"My feet?" Michael asked, clearly disappointed with the direction the hands would go.

"Yes, your feet."

Jonathan stood at the end of the bed and lifted Michael's left leg and examined his foot. "All that marching in those lousy boots gave you a lot of calluses. But I'll take care of that."

He squirted a large amount of oil into the palm of his hand and began to rub the underside of Michael's foot. He pressed his thumb heavily on the bottom of his foot in a rotating motion until he could feel Michael relax. And then rubbed the rough calluses on his heel.

"Jonathan, that feels heavenly."

Jonathan took each toe and rubbed the oil gently into each one. He gently put Michael's left leg down on the bed and started with his right.

"You're not snoring on me, are you, Michael? Don't you fall asleep."

Michael laughed. "I'm not sleeping. Just enjoying. I never had this done to me before."

"You'll get used to it. I plan to take care of you, Precious, always."

"Do you mean that?"

"Yes. Yes, I do. Always, Precious."

Michael loved being called that, and he just moaned with pleasure.

"I like when you call me that, Jonathan."

"When we're alone it's okay, but when others are around how about if I give you a second nickname, *Press*, and only you and I will know what it means."

"I like that. Press. Yes, that's good. I'll have to come up with one for you, too. And I will."

"I'm sure of it."

"I love you so, Jonathan Taylor."

"Precious, I am now going to work on your legs."

"Super."

Chapter 21

Friday was a clear, beautiful, crisp day and Michael was still glowing from the joy he experienced the night before. He had never felt the happiness he had known as when he was with Jonathan. Just before Michael fell asleep, he prayed that they would always be together. He felt sad that he wouldn't be able to share his happiness with anyone else, except, of course, with Gary. He'd have to get Gary alone somehow, but with Jonathan around he didn't know how that would be possible. However, it might be possible to get Jonathan involved in something, maybe washing the car, so he could call Gary in private on the phone and share this with him. After all, this is what they dreamed about for each of them, particularly in all their talks on the rock.

Michael was happy. He had never thought that he would feel the way he felt about Jonathan, the way just being with Jonathan made him feel. It was good. Jonathan could do no wrong. He was everything that Michael had dreamed about. Fantasized about. Michael thought, if I were a girl, I'd want to have his children.

Chapter 22

Friday started out great, but Michael left Jonathan alone with Louisa for just a few minutes, and, in only a short time, Jonathan agreed with her suggestion that he and Michael should go out with some local girls that night. Maureen called Michael later and suggested they see a movie. In front of his mother and at Jonathan's urging, Michael felt that he had no choice but to say yes. Michael hated the idea of spending time at a drive-in on a double date with girls instead of being someplace with Jonathan, alone, preferably in his bed. Jonathan had told Michael that it would be in their own best interests to "butch it up" as he phrased it, but Michael didn't buy it. He was pissed.

Jonathan didn't say anything. Michael just pouted. The car sped along the road to Maureen's house, where they would pick up the girls. The radio was silent. Jonathan felt sorry that he had gone along with Michael's mother's suggestion that they double date. Michael meant the world to him and he had alienated him. He knew that Michael was mad as hell at him and that hurt. There was a barrier between them now and it really sucked. He wanted Michael. He wanted Michael's lips on his. He wanted to feel Michael's hands on his body, his neck, his shoulders. The silence was making him feel like jumping out of the car, getting a taxi to the train, boarding NYCN Transit headed to the city, crawling into bed and pulling the covers over his head and forgetting he had ever met Michael Manganaro. Fuck it. It was the pits.

Michael felt a burning in his nose, that feeling you get before you were going to sneeze. He felt his eyes moisten and that made him sniff back hard. He did that twice. He was not going to cry in front of Jonathan, his fuckin' friend, the stud. "Oh, shit! This sucks," he almost said out loud.

Jonathan had to break through the barrier. He spoke. "Michael, I was wrong to commit us to this without discussing it with you first. I'm sorry. I really am. Please forgive me. Please, Precious, please."

Michael wanted to continue to pout, to say something biting, bitchy, unkind. He wanted to punish Jonathan for his cruelty, but he couldn't. He began to relax. Jonathan's tone was conciliatory, contrite and sexy and besides he called him Precious. He began to feel warmer. After all, it would only be a few hours and he'd have Jonathan all to himself. Just thinking about laying his face upon Jonathan's lap and smelling his aroma was soothing. And he would like to see this movie, *The Fly*, again, anyway. It was funny, and he was fond of Maureen. What the hell. He reached over and touched Jonathan's hand and said, "I love you and that's all there is to it. You're more important to me than anything in the world. I forgive you. With all my heart I love you. And, besides, you were right, we probably should 'butch it up.' Cop a feel or two."

Michael could see Jonathan smiling in the semi-darkness of the car as Jonathan said, "Yeah, buddy. Let's pick up the chicks. Got any rubbers?"

Chapter 23

They had picked up the girls, Maureen, who had had a crush on Michael since they were kids, and her friend, Theresa. Maureen was brought up in a Catholic home and went to a Catholic school. She was extremely aware of her sexual desires and careful of her conduct, and careful with the favors she gave to others, particularly offering none unless she liked a person a lot. She adored Michael. Theresa, on the other hand, was high-spirited and loved to party, and was generous and had been known throughout Mellon High School as one of the girls who put out. And, of course, a good-looking guy like Jonathan would definitely score. And that Michael realized meant Jonathan wasn't completely his yet.

Michael and Maureen were seated in the front seat. The movie had just started and Michael took the little heater the Stardust Drive-in provided and hooked it onto the window on the passenger side of the car. Maureen was already snuggled next to him on the front seat with her feet propped on the gearshift casing. He was meticulous about his car and he was annoyed that she put her feet where she did, but he didn't say anything. He really was quite horny tonight and wanted some action and, even though he really wanted some male action, female action was better than nothing at all. He put his arm around her shoulder and she kissed his neck. Because Michael knew that she had lusted after him for years, he was going to get some sexual pleasure from the experience. They had been only on a few casual dates. It was getting warm in the car, so he helped her remove her coat. They kissed. Maureen opened her mouth slightly and let Michael insert his tongue. She loved the way Michael tasted. His long eyelashes tickled her check. She liked feeling his body against hers. She enjoyed feeling him carefully moved his hand from her shoulder to the top of her back. He unzipped the back of her

jumper and unbuttoned her back blouse buttons. Eventually he was able
to touch the back of her brassiere. He felt the warmth of her body pressing against his sweating hand. There, he had it is his grasp, the clip on
her brassiere. He struggled and finally got the clasp opened. Maureen
wasn't a heavy young woman, but she was a little plump with big, heavy
breasts. As soon as the clasp released her breasts fell two inches. Michael
placed his face on top of them and smelled the fragrance, *White
Shoulders*, which she borrowed from her mother. Goddamn it! He was
getting really hard. He wanted to enjoy more of her. But he knew from
past experience that she would only let him touch her breasts quickly
and then she would button up. He decided he would try to get into her
vagina. Never too successful there, but he'd give it a shot. All he could
hope for was getting under her dress, past her girdle, into her panties,
and then if he were lucky, he might be able to maneuver one of his fingers into the warm, moist entry place. He put his hand on her leg. She
resisted a little as his fingers moved up her leg and beyond. She was
beginning to relax and enjoy the warmth of his hands on her leg. She
wanted to let him suspect she was enjoying it, too, so she released her
clamped knees and let her legs spread slightly. She was really getting
excited, and she was getting ready to commit mortal sin, if she hadn't
already done so. She let him in. He was successful. He would keep that
finger unwashed until the morning. The sweet smell of success. Maureen
then vowed that she would have to go to confession the next day.
Michael was just about to accept the blame and apologize, when all of a
sudden Michael felt it happened. He came in his pants. "Oh my God,"
he whispered to himself, "these pants are so fucking light they're going
to stain. Shit. I'll have to wash them out as soon as I get home and see
what happens. Maybe the stains will come out." Maureen knew what
had happened and was secretly proud that Michael reached a climax.
She wanted to put her head in his lap, but didn't dare. Instead she held
his hand in hers and kissed him softly on his neck. No doubt about it,
confession tomorrow.

Michael watched Jonathan in the back seat with Theresa in the rear
view mirror. Lots of kissing and touching. If Jonathan were going to
score, what was taking him so long? Lots of groaning and moaning, too.
A small yelp or two. Laughter, too.

Jonathan and Theresa continued their lovemaking activity even
stronger. The car began to move. Michael and Maureen moved down
into the front seat, so none of their friends could see them as the car

started rocking, and the windows fogged up. The next time Michael looked in the mirror he saw Jonathan's bare buttocks contracting.

Theresa screamed, "Oh, yes! Yes! Oh, yes! Don't stop. Don't stop. Oh, my God, don't stop."

Does that feel good, baby? Do you like it hard?"

"Yes. Yes. Yes. Jesus fuckin' Christ! Fuck me. FUCK ME!" She screamed out loud.

Michael felt queasy. It almost sounded like Jonathan was hurting Theresa, but they both seemed to be enjoying it.

The activity stopped. The sound of the silence filled the Buick. Michael held his breath.

Jonathan spoke, "That was good, baby. You know how to satisfy a man."

Theresa just cooed, and she helped Jonathan wipe the wetness from his pubic hairs, testicles and penis with her handkerchief, which had a multi-colored-crocheted edge. All ladies used fancy handkerchiefs, her mother had always reminded. Theresa never left home without one. She buried her head in his pubic hair and kissed the tip, and then the shaft of his penis. Then she was thrilled to help her man to pull up his shorts and his pants.

Jonathan spoke again as Theresa was getting dressed, "Let's blow this joint and get some burgers."

The movie wasn't over, but they left anyway.

After they ate at the Mellon Diner, they dropped off the girls.

Michael was silent and that made Jonathan uncomfortable. Extremely.

Jonathan said, "I thought you told me you liked girls, too."

"But not like that, Jonathan." Michael was visibly upset. He was jealous as hell. Jonathan got laid, and he didn't, and he wanted Jonathan inside of himself, not inside Theresa, the waitress.

"For Christ's sake, pull over, Michael, or you'll get us both killed."

They sat on the shoulder for a few minutes, and Jonathan was at a loss for words. He felt lousy, and he lit the car dome light, so he could find his cigarettes in the back seat, and then he noticed them. The stains. He grabbed Michael's crouch and crushed his balls until Michael cried out.

"You came, too, you phony bastard."

Michael felt embarrassed and then felt like a real hypocrite. He changed his forlorn look into a smile and almost at once laughed. "Oh, fuck. I did. I guess I'm a manipulative phony."

They both laughed and Michael said, "But mine won't get pregnant. Yours could."

"One of the benefits of having *dinero*. Who gives a shit?"

"That doesn't sound exactly right to me, but you are my guest."

"Precious, you're not just my host, you belong to me. You always will and when we get home, I'm going to show you how I really want you to please me, okay?"

"I can't wait."

Chapter 24

When they were safely in Michael's room, Jonathan said, "After tonight, you may always want me."

Michael was eager with anticipation.

"Remember how exciting and pleasant your massage was, but because of the phone calls you got, we didn't finish. Well, I want to finish tonight."

Michael remembered the massage. It was truly great. They undressed, looking at each other strangely, like they had never seen each other without clothes.

"Hey, Michael, after the chicks we better shower."

"Yeah, and wash yourself real good, Stud-boy."

"And you, Precious, better use the fingernail brush. You told me your fingers got into some very dark, disgusting places."

"Jonathan, let me make sure everyone's asleep."

"Why?"

"Because I want to shower with you."

"Cool," was Jonathan's happy response.

Michael checked his parents' room. They were both out cold. He peeked into his sister's room. She was fast asleep with Butterball snoring at her feet.

Michael went back to his room. "Let's go, man. It's hit the shower time."

"Alright!"

They enjoyed soaping each other and caressing their bodies. They kissed and were rinsing when the water began to get cool, then almost freezing. They jumped out of the bathtub, and Michael offered Jonathan a towel.

Michael said, "We only have one water heater in the basement, and everybody else probably took showers, too."

"In an apartment house you never run out of hot water. Sometimes I stand in the shower for a half-hour. Never gave it much thought."

"Well, up here we have to. Not only are we conservative with hot water, but with water in general because it comes from a well out back."

"I see," Jonathan said not really understanding conserving anything.

Later, they were lying next to each other when Jonathan said, "Turn over on your stomach, Michael."

Michael turned over and enjoyed doing what he was told to do, and Jonathan stood up and walked to the bottom of the bed and started stroking Michael's legs. Then he massaged his butt. Oh, it feels so good, thought Michael, and Jonathan's hands got rougher, more demanding. But that felt good, too, just on the comfortable side of painful.

"Now I'm going to loosen you up."

"Really?"

Jonathan put one of his fingers into Michael's anus and probed the warm inside of Michael's body. He slowly massaged his prostate. Michael moaned.

"Do you like what I'm doing to you?"

"Oh, yes."

Jonathan asked, "Michael, can I put another one in?"

"Yes," Michael said, "but is it going to hurt?"

"It's supposed to hurt a little. But the burning sensation will stop. Trust me. It gets you ready for later."

"Later?"

"Yes, later when I put it in."

"You mean you're going to try to put that big thing inside of me."

"Yes."

"Oh, no. It'll never fit, and it'll hurt like hell.

"Trust me, it won't hurt for very long, and you're going to love it."

Michael lay quietly with his eyes closed for a minute before he said, "Okay, I'm ready for the second finger."

"Here goes. Now it's going to sting. But I'll be gentle. And if it hurts too much, I'll take it out. Okay?"

"Yeah."

Jonathan inserted another finger.

"Ouch," Michael exclaimed into the mattress.

Jonathan removed his fingers.

"Jonathan, let me catch my breath. I'm really nervous about this, but I want you to try it again."

"Anything you say."

"Try once again, please."

This time Jonathan put more lotion on his fingers and was even gentler as he entered Michael more slowly.

"Actually, Jonathan, I like it. Keep doing it."

"Tell me when you're ready for the tip."

"Never."

"But you will be."

Jonathan kept on massaging Michael's anus with his fingers going in and out and turning slightly each time they entered. When Jonathan felt Michael's muscles contract and release, he knew he was beginning to relax and to enjoy his probing.

Finally, Michael whispered, "Okay, Jonathan just try putting the head in, but only the tip, when you're ready."

Jonathan kissed the white cheeks of Michael's buttocks and massaged them. He kissed the top of the back of his thighs as well as the inside of them, as he slowly spread his legs and laid down on top of Michael with the tip of his penis pressed into the crack between Michael's butt. He gently applied pressure on Michael's anus. Then stopped. Then pressure. Each time a little harder. When he felt Michael was ready, he slowly put the tip of his penis into Michael.

"Take it out."

And Jonathan removed it quickly. He continued massaging Michael's butt with one hand, and he put more lotion on the tip of his penis with the other.

"Please. I want you inside of me."

"I want to be."

"Try again," Michael said.

Jonathan entered his lover again.

"Eek," Michael yelled, "but don't take it out. Leave it in until I get used to it, but don't move. Please just stay still."

And Jonathan did just that.

"I'm ready for more. Real slow."

Slowly, inch-by-inch, Jonathan inserted his entire manhood into Michael. When he had completely inserted his penis, he stopped all movement.

"Give me a little more."

"It's all in."

Michael reached down to feel it and was surprised to discover the whole thing was in there.

"Jonathan, you're completely inside me. This is so fuckin' intimate. Your body is inside mine," he said in almost disbelief because there was no longer any pain.

"I know, and it feels fantastic. I feel like we belong to each other."

"Would you like to start moving in and out of me?"

"Yes. I would like that very much."

"Please fuck me, Jonathan. I want you so."

Jonathan began thrusting his penis into Michael. Slowly at first, then faster and harder. Michael enjoyed feeling the pressure of Jonathan inside him. Each penetration made his own penis harder. He liked hearing Jonathan's testicles slap against his butt. It wasn't long before they both came, and Michael was shocked that it was such a real pleasure. How exhilarating. How satisfying.

"You better wear a pair of shorts to bed tonight," Jonathan said. "Sometimes there may be a little bleeding the first time."

"Jonathan, I really liked doing it. I mean it felt good having you take charge, and in a strange way, I sort of felt wanted, that you liked me a lot."

"Actually, I do like you a lot. I love you, and you will get used to it. Because that's the way I'm going to take you every day of our lives together, understand, Precious?"

"And tomorrow's my turn. I want to feel how it feels to be inside you."

"It's a deal. I want to feel you inside me."

Michael lay next to Jonathan that night, and a tear ran down his cheek. I really love him. This intimacy. This is what it's all about.

Good Night My Love was playing softly on the radio.

Chapter 25

Anthony and Louisa left the house early that Saturday morning to do some much needed, major grocery shopping. It was their monthly trip. They were going to the largest supermarket in the area, which was about ten miles outside of Mellon. Right next to the supermarket was a huge farmer's market that sold everything from produce to hardware and dry goods. Anthony loved going through the farmer's market and often bought things they would never use, like old 78 records. When they finished shopping the back seat of the car, as well as the trunk, would be filled with bags.

Michael hated helping to put away the stuff they came home with, so he conveniently always tried to be absent when they returned from their excursions, and this day was no exception. He was just waking up when he heard two car doors slam, and the engine start. He knew they were on their way.

Jonathan was just waking up, too.

"Jonathan, my father and mother just left on one of their monthly shopping trips."

"You mean, we're alone?"

"No. Not really. Rosa is probably still sleeping."

"Let's get ready and have breakfast in town at the diner, okay?"

"Sure."

There was a knock on the door.

"Rosa?" Michael asked.

"Yes. Are you guys decent?"

"We're still under the covers."

"Can I come in for a minute?"

"Of course, Rosa," Michael replied.

Rosa came into the bedroom.

"Good morning, Jonathan, Michael," she said. She was dressed and ready to go out.

"Michael, I don't want to be here when they get home with all the stuff they always buy, so I thought I'd asked you guys if I could treat you to breakfast at the diner. I would really like that. We haven't had too much time together."

"What do you say, Jonathan?"

"I personally would enjoy that a lot."

"Then the answer is yes. We'll be ready in a half-hour. Is that okay?"

"Yes. While you're getting ready, I'll take my car for gas and a wash."

Jonathan said, "I saw your Spitfire outside. Cool car. I bet you look real cute driving it."

"Thanks, Jonathan. You're a sweetheart."

She couldn't keep her eyes off Jonathan's handsome face and his broad, naked shoulders. He's most likely nude under those covers, she thought, and she noticed that Michael didn't have his undershirt on as he usually did when he went to bed. For as long as she could remember he wore an undershirt to bed. They are both naked, she thought. The door opened and Butterball ran into the room when she realized where Rosa had gone and jumped onto the bed. She landed between Michael and Jonathan, and she caused the blankets to shift, so that Rosa could see the entire right side of Jonathan's body. He was naked. She was sorry she couldn't see more. God, he was a good-looking guy. But she suspected he was into guys. She had always suspected that Michael was different and into guys, too, and now her suspicions were confirmed. He probably did like guys more than girls. Two guys didn't just sleep in the same bed without clothes unless they were enjoying each other. She wasn't sure how she felt about it, but she would think about it later.

"I'll be back in thirty minutes. I'll blow the horn. We can all squeeze into my car. We're all skinny enough," she said as she smiled. She left the room.

"She knows, Michael. She does."

"You think?"

"Yes. She noticed that I wasn't wearing any clothes when Butterball jumped on the bed."

"Well, I'll talk to her later and find out. She won't say anything, I'm sure. She's been one of my best friends since we were little."

"You're lucky to have such a lovely family. Rosa is real nice."

"Yeah, but I'm not sure about how she feels about us. We better get ready; she'll be back before we know it. Why don't you shower first, Jonathan? I have to make a call."

"Okay." He picked up his things and headed for the bathroom.

Michael looked through some mail on his dresser and then called Gary.

"Hey, Gary. It's me."

"I know. How are you?"

"Great. Super. I have something to tell you. It's a surprise, and something we've been talking about for years."

"I think I can guess."

"You can?"

"Yeah. I put two and two together, and I think I know. I remembered how you acted when you had a crush on Brian Little in high school. I thought about that Wednesday when you didn't come to John's after choir rehearsal and why you didn't call me as soon as you got home. And the choir members were talking about the friend you have visiting you from New York. They said he was good-looking, and then it hit me like a ton of bricks. You're in love, aren't you, Michael?"

"Yes. You always did know what was happening with me. Sometimes before I knew myself. Yes, I am."

"That's really something. I sent you off to the Navy to become a man, and you fall in love with one instead. This country is going down," he laughed. "So, I understand his name is Jonathan."

"Correct. Jonathan Taylor. He's everything I always dreamed about, Gary. You'll like him."

"Okay, when do we meet?"

"Sunday after church. He's staying for dinner, and you'll be here."

"I'm looking forward to it. I am a little jealous. I though we'd have some time together when you were home."

"We will, Gary. He's only staying until Sunday afternoon, and then he's headed back to the city."

"Are you going to drive him?"

"I think I'll just take him to the station. Once he gets off the train at Grand Central he's almost home."

"Great, then we can spend Sunday evening together. I want to hear all about him and about your experiences in boot camp. Must have been hell. I also want to fill you in on all that's been happening here, and we can watch Alfred Hitchcock with your mother and father like old times. I miss doing that. Are you singing something special on Sunday?"

"The normal Mass solos and *Panis Angelicus.*"

"Oh, Michael, I love that. I'll come to that Mass to hear you. Maybe my sister, Sophia, will come, too. She loves to hear you sing. She said the best part of her wedding was your singing."

"I'd like to see her again. She's working on the third kid, no?"

"Yeah. The third one is almost ready to pop. She's due in about two weeks. She can hardly walk. That hunk of a husband she married, the guy I always had the hots for, has literally kept her barefoot and pregnant."

"Okay, then we'll see you on Sunday. Sit in your usual place please, so I can see you."

"You bet."

"Got to go. I hear the water's off. He's getting out of the shower, and I have to get ready, too. Rosa's taking us to breakfast at the diner. It's shopping day for the parents, and you know what that's like when they get home."

Gary laughed. "Burned twice. Believe me, I know."

Michael laughed, too.

Gary asked, "Did anything happen between you? I mean sexually?"

"Yes."

"Goddamn. I want to hear all about it."

"And you will. Goodbye for now, Gary. See you in church."

"Goodbye, Michael. Love you. Maybe I shouldn't say that anymore. I'm looking forward to tomorrow. And I'll have a nickel."

"Hey, I can't tell you how happy your nickel made me feel when it arrived in your letter to me in boot camp. You're a very special friend. And I hope you'll be my friend for the rest of my life."

"Me, too, Michael."

Jonathan came back, and Michael went into the bathroom for his shower.

They were both ready when Rosa blew the horn. They headed for the Mellon Diner. Rosa could sense the closeness that had developed between her brother and Jonathan. She knew instinctively that a real bonding had occurred. She loved her brother deeply and wanted to let him know how she wouldn't mind if this was what he wanted. She felt remorse and regret for all the unkind things she had said about ballet dancers and faggots in the past. Here she was in her Spitfire squashed together with the two best-looking guys in Mellon, and they liked each other. Mind-blowing, she thought.

Rosa was able to park in an empty space near the entry steps. They went inside and took the only booth available, next to the cashier. Their waitress, an older woman with bleached blond hair with pencils stuck into her bun, took their orders. Michael looked around the diner to see if there was anyone there that they knew. No one. Their orders arrived.

Just as they were beginning to enjoy breakfast, Michael saw Mrs. Rhine come in. She was buying the morning papers from the cashier. She saw Michael and walked over to the booth.

"Michael, it's good to see you again. Good morning. Hello, Rosa. Good to see you, too, Jonathan."

They all greeted Mrs. Rhine and asked her if she would join them.

"I wish I could, but I have to get to church for a quick run through with a guest soloist who will be singing with us on Sunday. I was going to call you later and tell you about it."

"Guest soloist?" Michael asked.

"Yes. She just debuted at the Metro-Tri-State Opera, and she is a guest of the Balmorals for the weekend. Mr. Balmoral called me last night and asked if it would be okay if she joined us on Sunday. When he told me about her singing career, I asked him if she would sing a solo for us. We haven't had a guest since Easter. Can you believe that?"

"That's great. Who is it?"

"Helene Theofanus. She has toured extensively in Europe, and this will be her third time singing in the United States. She sang three weeks ago at the Metro as Alisa, a mezzo-soprano, in *Lucia Di Lammermoor*. And last week she recorded a Christmas album at St. Cecelia's Cathedral in Newark with the Boys Choir of New Jersey. It's going to be released in time for Christmas. I think she said the first week of December. I understand she's terrific. I hope I don't make any mistakes."

"What's she going to sing?"

"Gounod's *Ave Maria* for offertory."

"Wow," Rosa said. "I'll get to hear my wonderful brother and someone famous, too."

Michael said, "Mrs. Rhine, now I'm more nervous than I was before."

"Oh, Michael. You'll be fine. I'm the one who should be nervous."

Jonathan said, "You play really well, Mrs. Rhine. Nothing to worry about. I met Mrs. Theofanus in Paris last year with my father at the Paris Opera. She was appearing in Georges Bizet's *Carmen*. She sang beautifully and acted superbly as well. She was absolutely charming, and I understand from my dad that she was a real pleasure to work with."

"You know Helene Theofanus?" Mrs. Rhine asked.

"Only from a quick backstage meeting. My father is on the board of the Metro with Mr. Balmoral."

"It certainly is a small world," Mrs. Rhine said.

"Sure is," Michael said.

"She's supposed to meet me here, so we could pick up some coffee to take to church for our run-through. You know how cold it is there when they don't put on the heat."

A few of the customers sitting at the counter turned to look at the elegant stranger who had just come into the diner. Mellon residents weren't used to seeing such striking beauty. She was tall and wore a real leopard coat with a matching hat. She wore black patent leather, platform, high-heeled shoes with open heals and toes. She had long, black hair, and her makeup was exquisitely applied. Jonathan recognized her at once. It was Mrs. Theofanus. Jonathan rose from the table and went over to greet her.

"Dame Helene Theofanus, how do you do? I'm Jonathan Taylor. You know my father, Jonathan Anthony Taylor. He introduced us in Paris."

"*Oui*. I remember. You are the gentlemen with the pretty blue eyes. How could I not remember you? How do you do?"

"I enjoyed your interpretation of Carmen very much that night. You ignited the audience with your passionate recitatives, and the audience went crazy when you sang the *Habanera*. Your dressing room was so full that night that I didn't get a chance to get a word in edgewise. We all just loved hearing you," Jonathan said.

"Bless you, Jonathan. I'm glad you're a fan. I'm glad so many young people are enjoying opera these days."

Jonathan offered his arm to her and led her to the booth where Michael and Rosa were seated and where Mrs. Rhine was standing. He introduced her to them and asked the waitress if she could get another chair.

Rosa, Michael and Jonathan finished their breakfast while Dame Helene Theofanus and Mrs. Rhine had coffee.

Michael was proud of Jonathan. He knew about so many things that were foreign to Michael. He was so glad they met. Thank God he decided to join the Navy. He wouldn't have met Jonathan if he hadn't, and now his life was beginning to move forward in the direction that he wanted it to go.

Mrs. Rhine reminded Michael that the *Mellon Press* was going to be in church to take his picture.

"I'd like that," Michael said, "but I think they should take a picture of the entire choir with our guest. It's not often that we have celebrities joining us."

"That's a great idea, Michael. Mrs. Theofanus, would you be kind enough to join us for a photograph?"

"I would be honored. Delighted. Thank you for including me."

"That's great," said Mrs. Rhine as they prepared to leave.

"I understand that a reporter from a Newark paper will be in the congregation, too. He called me this morning with some questions about my Christmas album, and when he told me he would be reviewing my recording for their magazine for next week, I invited him to come up to hear me in person. Tomorrow."

"How exciting," Rosa added.

"I need the names and addresses of all the choir members, Mrs. Rhine, so that I can send everyone a complimentary record."

"Right after we finish."

Chapter 26

Theresa was combing her long brunette hair in her room when the phone rang.

"Hello," she said as she picked up the receiver.

"Hi, Theresa, it's Maureen. I had to call you and talk about last night."

Theresa chuckled. "I figured I'd hear from you."

"How's it going?"

"Good. I had a real good time."

"I could tell."

Theresa laughed. "You seemed to be having a good time, too."

"Not as good as you had. I heard you, not that I was eavesdropping, of course. God, you made a lot of noise. I hope no one outside the car could hear you!"

"How could they? All the windows were closed in Michael's car and in everyone else's."

"I guess I'm paranoid."

"Guess so."

"I didn't think, I mean, I've heard, and we've talked about your having sex, going all the way, but I didn't know you did it on the first date."

"Usually, I don't, Maureen, but I wasn't going to miss an opportunity like that. He was drop-dead gorgeous and, of course, since I really hadn't had any since August, I really wanted it. And I really wanted it with him."

"He is gorgeous! I've never done it, but Jonathan is really something. Did he use protection?"

"No."

"Are you serious? Weren't you afraid of getting pregnant?"

"Not really. You said he was rich and that his father was someone important."

"I'm not sure how rich. I mean, I just heard gossip that he was friends with the Balmorals, and that his father is head of a large oil company."

"Well?"

"What difference does it make?"

"Well, I really don't care if he made me pregnant. I'd certainly make some money if he did. Maybe I could stop working in the pizza place for a while. And the kid would certainly be beautiful! God, I almost wish I could have a baby by him."

"You're only eighteen. Why would you want that?"

"Well, who do you think I could find here, a country kid or a gas station mechanic? No, I want more. Much, much more."

"You just found out that you won that scholarship to Tulane that you applied for last year. Don't you want to go?"

"Sure I do, but the scholarship doesn't pay for everything. That's why I work all the shifts I do. I think I have enough money for the first year at this point. My parents can't help. My father's been out of work for six months with his bad back. I don't know how much money he'll get from NYCN Transit for the accident. After all, it was their fault, but it might take years. I can't count on that."

"I didn't know that things were that way for you. I thought your parents had money, living in that big house on Second Avenue and all. I'm headed for the State University myself. Not expensive. But you? I mean, Tulane is a famous school, and even the traveling there would be expensive."

"I want to get as far away from here as I can. You know my rep. I'd like to get a fresh start down in Louisiana. Maybe I could find a rich, beautiful, blond stud, southern man down there."

"All you ever think about is men."

"God bless them."

"Anyway, Theresa, last night was the first time I ever seriously considered going all the way outside of marriage."

"Why, Maureen! I thought you didn't believe in it. That it was a sin almost as bad as murder."

"I may have changed my mind."

"May have?"

"Yeah, you made it sound too good to be true. I want to know what it feels like."

"I thought you were saving yourself for Michael. That's all you talked about since the sixth grade."

"I was, but..." Maureen said and stopped talking for a minute.

"But, what?" Theresa asked.

"Well, I would love to get married, and if he asked me, I would say yes immediately. I'd jump at the chance. I want him so much. He's the only guy I've ever wanted. I play with myself before I fall asleep every night thinking about how much I want him."

"Well, Maureen, why don't you tell him? Now's your chance. He's home for a while."

"Theresa, I couldn't. That would be a sin."

"What?"

"He has to want me, too, and I'm not sure that he does. If he did, he'd force me. I would like that, and then I wouldn't have to feel guilty. I still want to marry him, and I don't think that that would be possible if I did it willingly with him first."

"I love you, my friend, but I think you are *nuts.*"

"He's so religious. I remember when he was an altar boy when we were young and all. And his family. They're so Italian and old fashioned. I don't think having sex with him would be a good idea, that's all."

"Are you thinking what I think your thinking?"

"Yes. Maybe I should try it with someone else first and see."

"Like I said, you're nuts. And if you were thinking about Jonathan our friendship would be over. You're pissing me off, because I think that's what you're thinking, isn't it?"

"I'm sorry. I wasn't thinking seriously about it. Just daydreaming. You enjoyed him so."

"I did. I have to get to work in a few minutes, but you better scale down your daydreams to a manageable size. Realistic ones. Stick to Michael, and we can be the greatest of pals. Go after Jonathan, and you're dead meat. Understand?"

"Yes."

"Good. I like your comprehension of this."

"I had another thought. A really upsetting one, though."

"And, what was that?"

"Do you think? Oh, forget it."

"Jonathan's not a homo, if that's what you're thinking."

"No, not really, but Michael and Jonathan seem to like each other a lot."

"Who wouldn't like Jonathan for Christ's sake, Maureen?" Theresa laughed merrily, as she thought about Jonathan's performance in the car. She said, "Maureen, there must be two of you, because one of you alone couldn't think up anything that stupid!"

"Bye. Have a good day, Theresa."

Chapter 27

Breakfast took longer than they expected, and Rosa had to go to work. Michael called a Mellon taxi. Michael and Jonathan got into the back seat. On the way home Jonathan reached into his pocket and pulled out the business card the stranger on the train had given him.

Addison Konklin
Commercial Real Estate Sales and Management
Stamford, Connecticut
203-444-1987

Damn, he thought, that guy had been hot. Jonathan was starting to get hard just remembering how nice it felt to have that muscular thigh pressing against his, and how equally terrific it felt to return the pressure. He put the card back into his pocket. Maybe, if he could find an excuse to get a few minutes of privacy, he'd check him out. Better yet, it might be better to call next week. Jonathan had his coat on his lap, and so did Michael. Jonathan reached under Michael's coat and guided his hand to his excited member.

"Michael, I just wanted you to know, and to feel, how much I'm enjoying myself visiting you."

Michael pulled his hand back and said, "I'm glad." He blushed and looked deeply into Jonathan's eyes and said, "I'm very glad." His heart was pounding. He moved away from Jonathan toward the door and looked out the window.

Jonathan wondered why Michael moved away. Because they were in a taxi? Maybe I shouldn't have done that? Maybe he could read my mind. No. But one thing is for sure; I'm going to throw that card away as soon I have a minute. Michael is the best thing that's happened to me, and I think I was about to screw that up. Asshole. Damn. That's the kind of stuff my father did to my mother. Just fuckin' stupid. I want Michael, and I want him to be a part of my life for a good long time.

"I made another mistake, Press."

"I know, but it's okay. Just please be a little more careful, we're back in Kansas now."

Chapter 28

They were in Michael's bed. Jonathan fell asleep soon after their active lovemaking concluded. Michael was lying on his back with Jonathan's arm across his chest and his leg over one of Michael's. Jonathan was breathing peacefully against Michael's shoulder.

Michael had never known such sheer joy. This was what he had dreamt about all his life. When his body was inside Jonathan, he was beside himself with pleasure. When he exploded and deposited his semen inside Jonathan, he was in ecstasy, and he wanted to experience that feeling again and again until the end of time.

He just lay in the bed thinking about how good life was now with his own special person. This was the first time he remembered not being nervous about singing the next day. With Jonathan beside him he could do anything, anything at all. After about an hour, Michael, too, fell asleep.

They slept in each other's arms under the heavy quilt. The window was open a crack, and a cold breeze blew the curtains apart and continued across the bed.

Chapter 29

The sun was shining brightly on Sunday morning. It blinded Rosa as she drove east along Main Street in Mellon on the way to church. She watched Michael nervously reviewing his music, as if it were new to him. He really looks nice in his uniform. They were using his car, and he had asked her to drive. He hated to eat or drive before performing. Jonathan was sitting in the back seat. He was wearing his uniform, too. Rosa sensed that they loved each other.

Jonathan was looking at the back of Michael's neck. Too bad Rosa was there. He would have liked to kiss it if he could. Oh well, might not have a chance to do that for a long time. Today after church they were going to meet up with Gary. He had an uneasy feeling about meeting him. Stop it, he silently told himself. You're jealous of someone you haven't even met yet.

St. John's was only a block away.

"I'll let you and Jonathan out by the side entrance, and I'll try to find a parking space nearby. I hope I won't be too late; I don't want to miss anything," Rosa said as she pulled off Main Street onto Maple. "I'll make a U-turn and let you out right at the side door."

"You're swell, Rosa," Michael said as he reached toward Rosa and kissed her cheek. He was always especially loving when he was nervous.

"Break a leg, Michael," she said as she pulled the car to the curb.

"See you later," Jonathan said to Rosa as he got out of the car and put on his white cap, slightly more slanted than was authorized.

Michael dropped a few pieces of music as he got out of the car, and Jonathan helped him pick them up.

"Michael, you're going to be great," Jonathan said as he patted Michael's back.

"Thanks, Jonathan. I appreciate the confidence you have in me. Here goes," he said as he led the way into St. John's

They went into the church and up the stairs into the choir loft.

Two large gardenia plants with abundant white flowers and glossy, deep green leaves were on top of the organ console. Their heavy fragrance filled the choir loft. Michael also saw several of the same plants almost a block away on the altar. Mrs. Rhine told him they came from the Mellon Florist for this special occasion. She suspected Mr. Balmoral was the donor.

Sun streamed through the stained glass windows along the east side of the church. No lights were lit yet. Just candles. The superintendent usually lit the beautiful chandeliers that hung over the pews on either side of the church as soon as he heard the organ playing the prelude. And that usually began when the church was half-full.

Today it was completely full, and it was only quarter to eleven. Word had gotten out that Michael was going to be singing, and that alone would have filled St. John's, but with Dame Helene Theofanus also scheduled to sing, people were beginning to stand in the aisles along the east and west walls.

Mrs. Rhine started to play Mozart's *Ave Verum Corpus.* All twelve chandeliers were lighted. The church even had heat today. You could not only feel it, but also smell it.

The choir had just finished running over some things in the school cafeteria and was now in place in the choir loft.

Michael and Jonathan took their seats next to the console. Michael was beginning to perspire. He could feel his boxers getting damp and sticking to him. He turned on the small fan that was on the floor next to the kneeler and positioned it, so that it would blow directly on him when he was singing. Michael tried to calm himself by looking down at the backs of people he recognized in the congregation. He saw Gary who turned around and gave him a small wave. He saw Theresa sitting way up front. Good, he thought, I'm going to think impure thoughts, and that will keep my mind off my nervousness. He sat back and took a deep breath. He'd never done it with a girl, and it probably was better than masturbating. No wonder Jonathan liked to do it. God, to have a girl scream like that, to be able to give such pleasure must make you feel like King Kong, or King of the Hill, or Super Stud, or something. Maybe I could be a Super Breeder. It must feel nice and warm inside a vagina. Fingers like it there. He let his mind drift. How come I'm not attracted to Gary at all? We're best friends? And Gary is cute. And I've known him forever. But Jonathan, whom I've only known for a couple of months,

I'm crazy about. I'd have Jonathan in any way I could. Sticking it into Theresa wouldn't be bad either. I'd love to make her scream.

He stopped daydreaming when he saw his mother and father arrive. They turned around and smiled at him and let the ushers show them to their reserved seats in the first pew on St. Joseph's side of the church.

Jonathan was looking down at the people in the congregation. There are really nice looking people here. A lot more young people were here as opposed to Manhattan. Most of the people seem to be Polish and Italian. When he went to church in Manhattan he noticed that there weren't many young people, but lots of older folks getting ready to check out. Depressing.

Jonathan saw the guy, who had sat across from him on the train coming up here, turn around and wave to Michael. He'd ask Michael about that later. Jonathan winked at Michael and mouthed a very tiny kiss. It was exactly 11 a.m., and the priests entered the sanctuary from the sacristy with bells ringing and the Mass began.

The choir sang the Mass parts very well, and Mrs. Theofanus fit in equally as if she were just another singer. She did not overpower the other sopranos, but blended in. Michael did the solo parts of the Mass more than adequately. He knew he did well, and it was strange, indeed, for him to appreciate his own performance. He felt good with Jonathan so close by him in this sun-filled house of God. The music, the fragrance of the flowers, the smell of incense and candles, the sight of the handsomely dressed congregation, all of it was exciting. What a morning. And the best part was being right next to this guy Jonathan. Michael wanted every inch of him to be his.

When Dame Helene Theofanus sang *Ave Maria*, there was not a cough to be heard in the church. Her rich voice vibrated Jonathan's very being, and he could feel the tension she created in the congregation as well. He could hear some pocketbooks being opened as ladies took out handkerchiefs for their sniffles.

The only distractions came from the two photographers who were in the choir loft. They were constantly moving about taking pictures. The many flashes from the bulbs in their cameras made Michael see colored spots. One photographer was from the *Mellon Press* and the other from *The Newark Tribune*.

The Mass proceeded without a hitch. When they got to the *Agnus Dei*, Michael knew his time was only two minutes away. When the choir sang *Dona nobis pacem*, he stood and took several deep breaths.

When the time came, Michael and Mrs. Rhine nodded to each other that each was ready. As soon as Mrs. Rhine started the introduction to *Panis Angelicus,* Jonathan touched Michael's hand lightly and left the choir loft. He walked down the stairs and went into the main sanctuary to join the communion line. The line was long, and it was moving slowly.

Jonathan realized that many people were looking at him and, of course, he liked the attention. People always stared at him, but with his Navy uniform on he looked even more striking. When Michael began singing Jonathan felt a warm, comfortable sensation within his body. Precious, you can really sing! Jonathan saw several people in the pews turn around toward the rear of the church to get a look at the singer. Some people on the communion line turned to check out Michael, too. The spotlight has been redirected, Jonathan thought. I'd better get used to it because I know, Precious, you're going to be big someday, and I'm going to be at your side.

Michael's voice filled St. John's, *"Pauper, Pauper, servus et húmilis."* Jonathan felt the hairs on the back of his neck tingle.

The organ interlude between the two parts of the piece was just beginning when Jonathan noticed Theresa in the end of one of the pews he would pass in a minute. She looked at his crotch and then deeply into his eyes. She parted her lips slightly and caressed them with her tongue, and, then she closed her mouth and continued looking directly into his eyes. Since no one was looking at him now, he returned the gesture, and then he looked reverently at the slate floor with his hands folded in front of his abdomen in pretended prayer as he walked past her.

Jonathan reached the altar and knelt on the red velvet cushion. He said, "Amen," and received the Host. He made the Sign of the Cross, stood up and started his journey back to the choir loft via the west aisle. Michael finished his solo. Jonathan recognized Mr. Balmoral and nodded a respectful hello and said very quietly, "Hello, sir." Mr. Balmoral smiled and squeezed his wife's arm, so she would recognize Jonathan. She did, and she smiled. Then Jonathan also noticed that the Balmorals were sitting next to Mr. and Mrs. Manganaro, who were kneeling. Mrs. Rhine was playing some soft music as most of the congregation said post communion prayers.

Jonathan continued walking toward the rear of the church and went up the stairs into the choir loft. It wasn't long before the congregation was dismissed. Mrs. Rhine played Henry Purcell's *Trumpet Tune* as the congregation filed out.

Mrs. Theofanus was putting on her coat and getting ready to leave when Jonathan went over to her and said, "You and my friend have made my day. You sang splendidly, and I loved hearing you."

"Thank you, Jonathan. And your friend, Jonathan, was superb. I've never heard a young person sing like that. Let's go to him. I want to tell him so."

They walked over to Michael.

"Michael, Mrs. Theofanus would like to say something to you."

"Yes, Mrs. Theofanus? I wish I could have paid more attention to your singing, but I was so nervous with you here about my own singing that your *Ave Maria* sort of went by too fast."

She laughed. "I've had that same experience many, many times. I've even missed entrances because of it. But I did want to tell you that you sounded like an angel, very professional, and that I hope you continue studying music and working with that fine instrument God has blessed you with."

"Thank you very much. I appreciate it," Michael said as he gave her a warm hug, stepped back, and shook her hand. "Thank you for the compliment and for caring to join us."

"It was a real joy for me. Now I must go down and find Mr. and Mrs. Balmoral."

Jonathan thought that Michael was really special. Warm and kind. And gentle. And sincere.

Chapter 30

Gary looked up into the choir loft as he leaving Mass. He was hoping to get Michael's attention, but was unable to do so. Michael was busy talking to some people. He saw another sailor in uniform besides Michael. He must be Jonathan. The sailor looked down into the congregation, but didn't see Gary. Gary realized that that sailor was the same cute guy he thought was a college student on the train coming to Poughkeepsie last Wednesday. Shit. He needed a drink.

Gary had to walk west on Main Street to retrieve his car. He was feeling jumpy and extremely nervous, and he wasn't entirely sure why, but since he only felt that way on Sunday mornings, it might be partly due to his excessive drinking on Saturday nights. And today he felt worse than usual. He never drank heavily until Michael abandoned him last August. Something was wrong here, and he thought he'd better check it out, but he wasn't sure exactly what to do, or to whom he should talk. Just as he was going to get into his car he realized that he was only a half block from John's, and it was after 12 o'clock, so they'd be open. Why not, he thought. I'll just go in for a Bud.

He went into John's. There were three people at the bar of the pizzeria whom he recognized, but didn't know. The bartender, Mario, was Theresa's uncle.

"What brings you in so early, Gary?" Mario inquired. "Michael's home."

"We're all going to Michael's for dinner, and we didn't make plans to meet any place in particular. When everybody came out of church, I couldn't even get near Michael, so I thought I'd kill some time and not be the first one to get to the house."

"What can I get you?"

"A Bud, please."

Mario reached under the bar into the wash bucket that was filled with ice and assorted cans of beer. He took out a Bud.

"Here you go."

Gary put a dollar on the bar and Mario gave him two quarters change.

Michael hated the stale smell of the place. Cigarette smoke and sour beer. But his need for the comfort and sedation from a beer blinded him to the ugliness of this place in the early afternoon. Even though there was bright sunshine outside, it was dark and dingy in John's. No fireplaces were lit. Nothing was cooking in the kitchen. Most of the lights were out, and the tables were bare except for the chairs that were stacked on top of them.

Gary poured his beer into the tall frosted glass. He drank half of it, and he could almost immediately feel the sedation that his body experienced from the alcohol. He began to relax. He had enjoyed hearing Michael sing. He was sorry his sister wasn't able to go to the Mass. She was getting too close to the delivery date, and her doctor thought she should stay close to home. Gary thought the guest soloist was great. He would love to hear her sing *O Holy Night* for midnight Mass.

Gary was feeling left out. He wasn't sure how he was going to act this afternoon. He wanted to see Michael, Mr. and Mrs. Manganaro and Rosa and the Butterball, too, but he just wished Jonathan weren't around. He was spoiling everything. Fuck. He had so looked forward to Michael's return. Michael never mentioned Jonathan in any of his letters. This was not the kind of surprise he had expected.

Michael had been the only person he ever really cared about. He had expected to spend more of the month with him. Gary had even planned to take a week's vacation just to stay in Mellon to be with Michael while he was home. Share good times with him. He finished his beer. He was feeling a little better now.

"Another one, please."

"You bet."

As he drank his second beer be felt even better, a lot better. He temporarily forgot his anger toward Michael. He realized that Michael was probably happier than he had ever been.

Maybe things would work out. Who knows?

His skin burned as he had a shocking thought. Had he been in love with Michael all these years? But because they were both afraid of it, nothing ever happened? He decided to get control of himself. He'd have to. He wanted Michael always to be his friend and no matter what the circumstances were, he would adjust. He had been looking forward to visiting Michael's house for months, and he was determined that one blond, handsome, blue-eyed faggot from New York City was not going to spoil that. And he wasn't even going to let on that he knew Jonathan had been flirting on the train big time.

He left the bar and headed for Maiden Lane.

Chapter 31

It was almost one o'clock when Gary pulled up behind Rosa's car, which was parked in the street. Michael's car and his father's Chevy were in the driveway. Butterball was lying in the sun on the side porch. She liked the warmth of the sun on her back on these cold afternoons. When she saw Gary she leaped up and ran toward him barking happily.

"Hey, girl! How've you been? You looking after things for old Ga?" Gary ruffled her coat and kissed her on her head as he played with both of her ears. He knelt down on the frozen soil, holding Butterball's head tightly against his stomach as he took a deep breath. It's good to be back here, he thought. Gary lifted his head and surveyed the bungalow that he had so grown to love over the years. The front door opened. Jonathan came out and walked rapidly toward Gary.

"You must be Gary," he said, his hand outstretched as he approached him.

"Yeah. That's me," Gary said as he shook Jonathan's hand robustly. "And you must be Jonathan. Michael told me about you on the phone."

"Well, I'm glad to finally meet you. Michael talked about you quite a bit in boot camp. The rock and stuff like that."

"He did?"

"Sure. He told me that you've been best friends for a long, long time. I wish I knew him as well as you do, but we only met in boot camp."

Either the booze was having its desired effect, or this Jonathan guy was a real charmer. Probably both. Gary took a long, hard look at Jonathan. Handsome was an understatement. His uniform fit him as if it were tailor made. As Gary looked down to his trousers he could see the outline of his penis pressing against the front flap of his bell-bottoms. He had looked super on the train, but today he looked even more attractive in this Navy costume.

Jonathan stepped beside Gary and put his arm around Gary's shoulder. Gary could feel the warmth of his hand through his coat. Gary put his arm around Jonathan's waist, and they walked side by side like old buddies.

"Michael's inside waiting for you, but he's up to his elbows in some sort of potato dumpling dough!"

Gary smiled, "Doesn't surprise me one bit. He really likes to cook. Always has. I can smell the food way out here."

Gary enjoyed walking next to Jonathan.

Jonathan looked at Gary inquisitively and asked, "Weren't you on NYCN Transit on Wednesday coming from the city? The 4:10?"

"Yes. When I saw you standing next to Michael this morning in the choir loft, I realized that I had seen you before. Had I known you were a friend of Michael's, I wouldn't have been so shy."

"When I saw you sitting across from me on the train I wondered if you looked anything like the Gary I heard so much about. Isn't that strange?"

"Yeah! Quite a coincidence, too. Since Michael's in the kitchen, let's go around the back, Jonathan. Never got used to using the front door."

"Sure. Let's."

Gary decided that he would never mention the other hot stranger from the train. He turned his head and looked into Jonathan's eyes and smiled and said, "Michael is in love with you, isn't he, Jonathan?"

"Yes, Gary. He is."

"Well then, I have to adopt you, too, into our friendship."

"That's kind of you, Gary, and since I know how fond of him you are, I want you to know that I love him, too. After we met here, home on leave, I realized that I wanted him in my life always."

"Anyone else know?"

"Not really."

"Hmm."

They went into the steamy kitchen. Michael was molding the potato dumplings into balls and placing them on waxed paper on the table. Michael wiped sweat from his upper lip with the back of his flour-covered hand.

"Hey, Michael. Long time no see. You look fabulous and you sang terrific, too. Sophia will die when I tell her how well you sang. Damn."

"You're a sight for sore eyes, Gary. I'm so glad you could come."

"Me, too."

"And I'm glad you two met."

Jonathan smiled his smile and said, "Michael, love, we actually met on the train coming up here. But neither of us knew that we were connected through you."

Michael laughed. "Did you talk to each other?"

"Yep," Gary said. "And I must admit I was trying to flirt with the good-looking cutie sitting across from me. I've become a lot more brazen since I've been working in the city."

"Well," Michael observed, "you two seem to hit if off, and I'm glad."

Gary slipped a nickel into Michael's hand.

Jonathan put his arms around Michael and Gary and said, "It's time for a group hug!"

"I don't want to get flour on you guys. I'm done here. Let me wash off."

Gary cleaned himself off in the kitchen sink.

"Now, we only have to boil these suckers about fifteen minutes before everything else is ready for dinner. Come on, let's go into my room for a few minutes before we eat. I want to change into something more comfortable and I'm sure Jonathan does too. These damn uniforms are so hard to keep clean."

Chapter 32

Willington was in his study reading. His wife, Jennifer, in their second-floor bedroom, was dressing for cocktails. Helene Theofanus was looking over some old sheet music in the library. The phone rang in the study, and Willington answered it. He had been talking for a few minutes when, even though she was upstairs, Jenny thought she detected alarm in his voice. She walked rapidly down the long staircase and stood outside the study door.

"Don't worry, Lillian. I will find him and have him call you," Willington Balmoral said. "You take care of yourself. Don't worry about a thing. I'll help in any way I can."

Jennifer Balmoral walked into the study and was standing beside her husband, as he hung up the phone.

"I have to find Jonathan, Jenny."

"Is it something serious, Bill? I heard you from our room. You sounded awful."

"A disaster, Jenny. Any idea how we can find Jonathan?"

"He was staying with the young man who sang this morning. The sailor he introduced us to. I can't remember his name. There were so many people talking at once outside the church."

"That's it. I'll call Mrs. Rhine, she'll know."

Helene Theofanus came into the room. "Is something wrong?"

"Yes, Helene. I have to find Jonathan. We know he was staying with the sailor who sang this morning."

"Oh, yes. His name was Michael Manganaro, I think."

"More than likely he lives in Mellon, Bill. We could look him up in the book."

"Maybe we should. In any case, I probably shouldn't call Mrs. Rhine. However, I probably should call Father Duffy."

"Bill, tell me what's wrong."

"Sit down, please. Both of you."

Mrs. Theofanus and Mrs. Balmoral sat next to each other on the green brocade covered sofa near the fireplace. Willington poured three brandies from the crystal decanter on the coffee table and gave one to each of the women and sat across from them on the other sofa. He took a sip of his brandy.

"I was just talking to Lillian Taylor. She called from her hospital bed in Miami. There's been an accident."

Jenny asked, "Is she all right?"

"Not exactly all right, but she should recover. There was an automobile accident a few hours ago. It seems she remembered a phone conversation with her stepson the other day. He mentioned that he was staying with a friend up here who was to sing at a local church, and that we were neighbors."

"Well, we can find him easily enough."

"But there's more. While Jonathan and Lillian were driving their rented car across Collins Avenue another driver ran a red light and crashed into their car."

"Oh, my God!" Jenny said.

Mr. Balmoral took another sip of his brandy.

"Tell me, Bill. What's the hard part? What's wrong?"

"Jonathan Taylor was pronounced dead on arrival at the hospital. Lillian is in intensive care."

"My, God! Oh, Bill. I'm so sorry. He's one of your best friends. You have to find his son."

"How do I tell a son that his father passed away?"

Mrs. Theofanus offered, "You certainly wouldn't want to do it on the phone, Bill."

"You're right," Jenny said. "I think, as you suggested, you should call Father Duffy. Ask his advice."

"You're both right. That's the thing to do."

Mrs. Balmoral got up and walked over to her husband, sat down and put her arm around his shoulder.

"Whew. You're shaking like a leaf, Bill. Finish your drink first, and then call him."

"Yes, Jenny."

Mrs. Theofanus rose and said, "If you'll excuse me, I'll go into the kitchen and help Mary Alice to make us some tea."

"Thanks," Jenny said.

Chapter 33

Father Duffy, St. John's Pastor, was having coffee and apple strudel in the kitchen of the rectory when the call came from Mr. Balmoral. He had been listening with concern ever since the housekeeper had handed him the receiver.

"This is really something, Bill. What started out to be such a happy day has turned into such a sad one. I just don't know what to say. Of course, we have to find the boy and tell him as soon as possible. In person would be best. I know the family he is staying with. Wonderful people. I've known Mr. and Mrs. Manganaro since they came to Mellon when they were first married. Their son is a great guy. Everyone loves him."

"What do you suggest, Duff?"

"Would you like me to join you? We could go over to their house and tell the young man in person. I don't know him, of course, but you do, and maybe I could think of an easy way to break it to him."

"Solid idea, Father."

"Would you like to go right now?"

"Yes, I think we should."

"I tell you what. I'll call first and let them know we're coming."

"What will you tell them?"

"That we have something very important and urgent to tell Jonathan."

"Okay. Sounds good to me."

"Do you want to pick me up in your car? Or do you want me to pick you up?"

"I think I don't feel like driving at the moment, but Jason, my driver, is still here. I kept him here today to drive Mrs. Theofanus around. I think I will ask him to drive us."

"Good. I'll make the call and will wait for you to pick me up."

"Fine. Thanks, Duff. I'll be there in ten."

131

Chapter 34

Sunday was a great success. Louisa, Anthony, Rosa, Michael, Jonathan and Gary enjoyed each other. The conversation at the dinner table was lively, filled with laughter. The house was filled with happiness. Michael was home. Gary was here again, and Jonathan was a welcomed new member of the household. Louisa turned on the lights, as it was beginning to get dark out. It was definitely time for coffee and desert.

Rosa said, "You're a great cook, Mom, but one of the problems with that is, that I eat too much." And Rosa meant it. She was wearing dark colors these days to hide an extra twenty pounds, and on Sundays she always wore her "buffet pants" with the expandable elastic waistband.

Louisa rose from the table. "Thank you, Rosa. I'm going to put on the coffee while the guys go into the living room. Will you help me, Rosa?"

"Sure, Mom."

As she was leaving the dining room Louisa said, "I can't wait to try the tempting pastries that Jonathan brought for us."

"Me, neither," Gary said. "I feel so loved in this house, Michael. And the food is terrific. I missed all of you."

Anthony let out a big laugh. "You're always welcome here, Gary. We missed you. And, Jonathan, I can't wait to taste those pastries either. I'm sure they're better than anything we get from Gruber's."

The phone rang.

"I'll get it," Rosa said, as she headed for the kitchen.

"Hello."

"Hi. Is this Rosa?"

"Yes."

"This is Father Duffy, Rosa. Is your father there?"

"Yes, Father. I'll get him for you." She put the phone down on the counter and went into the dining room. "Dad, it's Father Duffy. For you."

"I don't want to drive that bus again to the senior Christmas party like last year. Did you tell him that?"

"Be serious, Dad."

Anthony followed Rosa into the kitchen. Rosa knew that something was wrong.

"Hello. This in Tony Manganaro, Father. What can I do for you?

"Something has happened. Something serious, Tony. Mr. Balmoral called me, and we have to speak with Jonathan. I think he's staying with you, isn't he?"

"Yes, he is. What happened?"

"We have to tell him in person, Tony. We'd like to come over as soon as we can. Say in about a half-hour? Is that okay?"

"Sure, but what's the matter?"

"We have something important and urgent to tell Jonathan. But until we get there, please just say that we are coming over."

"Sure. You are certainly welcome."

"Thanks."

"See you soon."

Anthony Manganaro went back into the dining room, as Rosa and Louisa were clearing the table.

"Mike, why don't you and Jonathan and Gary to come with me into the living room, while your mother and sister clear the table. Maybe you could play the piano for us, Mike. Father Duffy and Mr. Balmoral are coming over."

"Why?" Michael asked.

"They have to talk about something."

"Probably," Jonathan said, "to ask me to encourage my father to get you some musical scholarship or something, Michael."

Michael laughed out loud.

Anthony Manganaro said, "I'll be back in a minute." He left to go to his bedroom to get his high blood pressure medicine. He was feeling dizzy.

Rosa kept quite. Something was seriously wrong. Father Duffy was usually extremely jovial and friendly. Had something not been wrong, he would have complimented Michael's singing that morning.

Louisa came out of the kitchen drying her hands on a kitchen towel. "Did I hear you right, Anthony?"

"Yes."

"Willington Balmoral is coming to our house?"

Chapter 35

Lillian Taylor was on the phone when the doctor and the young intern went into her room. She covered the mouthpiece with her hand as she said, "May I have a few more minutes, please? I'm notifying next of kin right now. I want to make sure I finish these few calls before I go under the anesthesia."

"Of course," said the doctor. "We'll come back." And they left.

"Well, initially, the only way I could think of to reach Jonathan was through a friend he had with him in New York at our apartment. I tried our apartment, but Adele never stays that late. Jonathan had told us he would be staying with his friend someplace near Poughkeepsie, and, that his friend was a neighbor of the Balmorals. So I called Willington, and he said he would find him for me."

"Well that was a good idea, Lillian. Shows that you pay attention when people tell you things."

"Well, I tell you, Missy, I've been in some pain, and they gave me something for it. I was a little fuzzy, but then I remembered his father saying Jonathan met Michael in boot camp, and that he would be staying with him over the weekend, but that en route to wherever Michael lives, Jonathan intended to drive to New Canaan to say hello to you. So I realized that you were probably at Golden Hill, and then I remembered Jonathan's sending you flowers over the phone. I hope you don't mind that I called you, but a personal visit is not in the cards for me at the moment. Not for a few days or weeks, I think."

"Oh, Lillian, I appreciate your reaching me very much. I'd rather know what happened from you, instead of from someone I don't know. How very terrible for you. But I don't want Jonathan to find out about his father from strangers either. I have his number. I mean where's he staying. Will you tell him?"

"Are you sure that's what you want, Missy?"

"Yes. And do it as soon as possible please. You have to help him, you know. He's going to have to make the funeral arrangements by himself. Not easy for a 21-year old without a family member to do it with. I'm laid up here; you're there. I wonder, Lillian, if his new friend will give him a hand? He seemed like a great guy. Anyway, please call him. I know he'd rather hear it from you. I have a feeling he'll call me as soon as he finds out." She gave Lillian the Manganaros' number.

"Okay, Missy. It won't be easy, but I'll do it. For my husband, for you, for Jonathan, and, of course, for myself. You're right, too, Missy. He should find out from family. We're going to have to stick together now."

"I know, Lillian. I am very sorry. About everything. I hope you're feeling better real soon. Thank you so much for letting me know. I'll pray for your speedy recovery. Goodbye, now. Take care."

Chapter 36

Michael was playing *My Prayer* on the piano with Jonathan at his side when the phone in the kitchen rang.

"It's for you, Jonathan," Rosa yelled from the kitchen. "It's Lillian."

Jonathan said, "Be right back, Michael."

Rosa and her mother left the kitchen, when Jonathan picked up the phone call. They joined the others in the living room.

Lillian and Jonathan spoke for about fifteen minutes. Then Jonathan put down the receiver on the cradle, sat down at the kitchen table and cried.

Butterball sat by his feet. He cried. When he realized that Butterball's head was on his foot, he stopped crying and blew his nose. He reached down and touched the dog's head.

They all sat silently in the living room. Quietly. Something was wrong, and they all sensed it. They heard footsteps on the front porch.

Anthony got up and opened the door.

Father Duffy and Mr. Balmoral were standing on the porch.

"Father. Mr. Balmoral. I didn't expect to be seeing you so soon after just meeting you this morning. Please come in."

"How do you do, Mr. Manganaro?" Willington said and extended his hand.

Michael thought, he talks just like Jonathan. *How do you do?*

They both came in.

Louisa, Michael, Rosa and Gary stood up to greet them, Father Duffy and the rich man from Hill House, as his home was known by the residents of this lower middle-class community.

"Nice to see you again, Mrs. Manganaro. I wish it were under more pleasant circumstances."

Louisa looked puzzled, as did the others in the room.

Jonathan appeared in the doorway between the dining room and the living room. Everyone in the room was looking at him. Butterball was there standing next to him.

His eyes were bloodshot, but he was no longer crying. He was in shock, but appeared to be composed.

"I'm glad I'm not alone at a time like this. I'm here with the best friend I've ever had, and his family. And one loving, fuzzy, animal friend, too." He reached down and petted Butterball."

Anthony and Louisa looked puzzled.

Jonathan sniffed and cleared his throat. "I've just spoken to Lillian, my father's wife, and she told me. She's in the hospital, pretty badly hurt. My father died this afternoon."

Michael went over to Jonathan, and put his arms around Jonathan's shoulder, "I'm sorry, Jonathan."

"Thanks, Michael, I want to talk to you about all this, but first I want to thank these kind people for coming. Mr. Balmoral, Lillian told me when she called you, you said you were going to find me for her. And you did. I certainly appreciate your effort. After she spoke to you she remembered where my mother was, and then she called her, too. Michael and I just paid my mother a visit the other day, and she had the telephone number here."

"We came over to ask you to call Lillian and to tell you this about this tragedy as soon as possible. Lillian asked me to."

"I really appreciate that. You both were very kind to do it and go so far out of your way."

Louisa said, "Why don't you all have a seat? Make yourselves comfortable."

"Thanks, Mrs. Manganaro," Willington said. He sat in one of the club chairs by the bay windows. Father Duffy sat on the piano bench.

"Actually, I could use a seat myself," Jonathan said as he sat on the sofa. Michael sat next to him, and their thighs touched.

Gary, who had known Father Duffy all his life, said, "Father, may I share your bench."

"Of course, Gary."

"Jonathan, I'm so sorry for everything," Louisa said as she stood next to him with her hand on his shoulder.

Anthony's eyes were misty as he offered, "Jonathan, can I get you anything? Maybe a drink?"

"You know what I'd like? Some hot coffee and maybe even something to munch on. My stomach feels a little queasy."

"I'll get you something," Louisa said. "Anyone else like coffee or anything?"

Several heads nodded yes.

"Rosa, please give me a hand in the kitchen," Louisa said as she put her hand on Rosa's back and steered her through the dining room.

"Thanks, Mom, for getting me out of that room. So depressing."

"They'll all feel better after coffee."

Mr. Balmoral sat forward in his chair toward Jonathan. "Jonathan, I want you to know that I'll help in any way I can. You'll be really busy during the next few days attending to a myriad of details. What do you plan on doing first?"

"Well tomorrow I want to call Lillian and get her preliminary thoughts on bringing my father back to New York for the funeral. I want to call her the first thing in the morning and then fly down and see her later in the day."

"Sounds good. After you get her thoughts you'll have a much better idea how to proceed."

"I know that I'll have to get in touch with Patrick Connelly, my father's attorney, to get probate proceedings started as soon as possible. That will probably be my second call. Lillian told me last night that no matter how distressed or sad I felt during this time that I must do what I have to do, to marshal and protect the assets, particularly making sure our family interest in Taylor Oil remains, just that, our family interest. She told me that my father had named both of us, Lillian and myself, co-executors."

"Then you really are going to have your hands full."

"I know, sir. She told me to make sure I also got the Will out of father's desk and then to get in touch with his accountant, Stephen Brasso. She said the taxes on the estate were going to be phenomenal, and that he should get working on anything to help us as soon as possible."

"Lillian has a good head on her shoulders. You're lucky to have her in the family. She'll be a great help to you, Jonathan. You may need the Will when you visit the funeral director to make the plans. Also, may I make a practical suggestion?"

"Yes, sir. Of course."

"Have you any joint accounts with your father?"

"Yes. We have a rather large one at The New York City Savings Bank."

"Do you have a checking account in your own name?"

"Yes, at the Chemical Agricultural Bank."

"Good. Tomorrow as soon as the banks open, go to the savings bank and withdraw most of the balance of the joint account. Get a check to yourself and deposit it into your checking account at Chemical. Don't mention that your father died. They don't need to know that yet, because once the banks find out that your father died, all accounts with his name on them will be tied up until taxes are paid and tax waivers are issued. That may take time, and you may need some funds liquid in the weeks ahead. Of course, Jonathan, if you ever run into a problem in that area, I'm here."

"Thanks, sir. That is a great, practical suggestion. And at 9 a.m. sharp Michael and I will be at the savings bank with bankbook in hand."

Michael listened to this and was secretly surprised. He wants me with him, he thought.

"Mr. Balmoral. I appreciate your support. I have to call my mother, too. She must be upset."

"Jonathan, you also may wish to consider asking for a hardship discharge from the Navy, because you are the only surviving child to run your father's businesses."

"Do you think?"

Mr. Balmoral nodded.

Jonathan hadn't even thought about that.

Louisa and Rosa returned with a steaming coffeepot, cups, saucers, spoons and a tray of assorted pastries.

"How do I begin that discharge procedure, Mr. Balmoral?"

"I'm not sure at this point, Jonathan, but I have a friend or two in the Senate, and one in the Department of Defense. I'll find out for you as soon as I can and get back to you."

"Thank you."

Chapter 37

Michael lay next to Jonathan. They were both awake. Michael pulled up the covers.

"Jonathan, I don't have any idea what you're feeling, or what you're going through."

"Michael, you're a sweetheart. And I do want you to know a secret."

"What's that, Jonathan?"

"I'm not sure what I'm feeling, either."

"Am I supposed to ask, or just be quiet? This is strange to me."

"Just be you, Michael."

"Okay."

"I'm sad that he died like this."

"But?"

"But, he was the world's biggest pain in the ass. I don't think he ever really liked me."

"He must have liked you, and he trusted you, too. If he didn't, he wouldn't have made you one of the executors of his estate."

"Yeah. I guess."

"You know I'm right, Jonathan."

"Yes, Michael."

They held hands under the covers.

"Michael, have all the drinks you had with dinner worn off?"

"Yes. Jonathan. Why?"

"Because it's almost one in the morning, and we're not accomplishing anything just lying here."

"I like being with you, Jonathan. You know that."

"Sure, but I mean, we could be on our way to Manhattan."

"We?"

"Oh, Michael, I forgot to ask you. Will you spend the next couple of days with me?"

"Yes. I'd like to do that very much."

Jonathan leaned over Michael and let his tongue slip between Michael's lips, softly, gently, as he began to cry.

Chapter 38

When Michael woke up, he saw that Jonathan was already dressed, looking out the window. "What time is it, Jonathan?" Michael asked yawning.

"It's almost 6:15."

"I'm getting up right now."

"Your mother and father were up real early. I heard them, so I went to the kitchen. We had breakfast. I really like your parents, Michael."

"Thanks, Jonathan, I'm glad you like them. I better get a move on; we have to get going to the city."

"I told them that you were going to spend the week with me, and they agreed that it was a good idea."

"That's good."

"I'm sorry that my phone call probably woke you up. I was just talking to my mother. She wants to leave Golden Hill and help me."

"Would that be a good idea?"

"Not sure, but Dr. Franklin said he thought it might be good for her, as long as she has company. When I spoke to him, I promised to get her to AA meetings in the city. He told me there are hundreds. One of her problems, Michael, is that she has never had any responsibilities in recent years that she enjoyed. So who knows? He also told me that if it doesn't work out, there would always be room for her at Golden Hill."

"When can she leave?"

"We can pick her up later on our way to the city. I hope you don't mind driving. We may need your car this week."

"No problem. I love to drive, and I and my car are at your disposal." He got out of bed and walked behind Jonathan, put his arms around his waist and softly kissed the back of his neck.

Michael took a quick shower. He ate a bacon-and-egg sandwich while he was shaving. He had two glasses of orange juice as he got dressed. It wasn't long before they were on the road. And they did pick up Melissa Taylor one hour later and headed to Manhattan.

Michael was driving, and Jonathan was sitting next to him in the front seat. Jonathan turned around and spoke to his mother who was in the back seat, "Mom, you can stay in one of the guestrooms as long as you like. Michael will be staying in my room with me."

"That sounds like a good idea to me," Missy said as she closed her eyes for a minute. Yes. They are lovers. There are two guestrooms, and Michael isn't assigned to one of them. Jonathan has found a sweetheart of a guy. He is lucky. God bless his conceited, young ass.

No one spoke for a while, as Michael drove toward Manhattan in the rush hour traffic.

"Are you going to call Lillian when you get home, Jonathan?" Missy asked.

"Yes. As soon as I get in."

"Please make sure my visiting is okay with her."

"Sure, Mom. But you know it is."

Michael spoke. "Jonathan, you have so many people to call. So many things to do."

"And one of those things I want to tend to, is seeing if Adele can work full-time for the next couple of weeks."

It wasn't long before they arrived at the apartment, and Missy was unpacking her bags in the guestroom, and Michael and Jonathan were in the library behind his father's desk. Jonathan opened one of the side drawers, and located a dozen or so bankbooks held together by a fat rubber band. He took the rubber band off and looked through them.

"Michael, this is it, the joint account."

"Great. You should do what Mr. Balmoral suggested right way. Do you want me to come with you?"

"Yes. But first, I'd like you to get settled in our room."

"Okay."

"Let me show you the way."

"Don't you have to start making all the calls you have to make?"

"Sure, but I have a phone in my room. I think it would be good for you to hear them, so you'll know what is going on. I really need your help."

"Fine. Anything you say."

When Michael followed Jonathan into the bedroom, he was immediately drawn to the windows. He could see the Empire State Building and the Statue of Liberty. "What a spectacular view!" he exclaimed.

"Wait till you see it at night," Jonathan said as he walked next to Michael and took his hand in his.

"That's the East River, and that's the Hudson," he said, as he pointed to each. He began to cry again.

Michael guided Jonathan to the bed. They sat on it, and Michael held Jonathan in his arms, as Jonathan shook, trembled and cried.

Chapter 39

Jonathan and Michael sat quietly for a long time on the bed just holding hands. They heard Missy coming down the corridor headed for their room. She stood at the door, and then knocked and said, "May I come in?"

"Sure, Mom," Jonathan replied.

"I'm unpacked," Missy said as she entered. "Have you called Lillian yet?"

"Not yet, Mom. We have to go to the bank first. Then I'll call."

Just then, they heard a click in the front door latch, and they walked into the hall. Adele came in carrying here usual bags of paraphernalia.

"Adele, how good to see you," Jonathan said.

"Hello, Adele," Missy greeted, as they hugged each other.

Jonathan put his hand on Michael's shoulder and guided him toward Adele. "Adele, this is my friend, Michael. My Michael."

"How do you do, Michael? I just wish we were meeting under more pleasant circumstances."

"I do, too, Adele," Michael said. "I'm glad to meet you because Jonathan has told me many nice things about you."

"Thanks, Michael. Everyone, I'm sorry to hear about Mr. Taylor's passing. So very sorry. And about Mrs. Taylor? How is she, Jonathan?"

"I'll find out later. I have to call her in about an hour."

"Thanks for your kindness, Adele," Missy said.

Jonathan rubbed his chin and asked, "Adele, for the next month or two, can you come everyday and maybe even stay overnight? We have the extra guest room, and we could sure use your help. Michael and Missy are going to stay with me for a while. I don't know how long mom will be in the hospital in Florida. I'll find out more about that tonight when we both get together."

Missy had never heard Jonathan refer to Lillian as "mom." And, for some reason she didn't understand, she didn't mind at all. Lillian had done a great job leading Jonathan through his teen years, something she had to admit to herself that she would not have been able to do successfully. It was the first time Michael heard Jonathan refer to Lillian so intimately and, consequently, he realized how very fond he must be of his father's second wife.

"Jonathan, I'm sure I can, but I'd like to make a few phone calls to find replacements for jobs that I had lined up.

"Thanks, Adele, that would be just fine."

"Jonathan, if you'll excuse me, I'll go into the kitchen and put on a pot of coffee and make a few calls."

Adele was able to make the arrangements, and she then served Missy, Jonathan and Michael coffee in the bright, sunny music room.

Adele said, "The phones should start ringing very soon. Mr. Taylor's photograph is on the front page of the *Globe*. It's almost ten. Do you want to take calls, or do you want me to take messages?"

"Oh, please take messages. But I do want to talk to Mr. Connelly, Mr. Brasso and, of course, dad's secretary, Barbara Greenfeld. Use your judgment, Adele. Mom, could you help answer some of the calls, too? That would help a lot. You could use dad's desk in the library. He has all the phone lines on his desk."

"I'll be glad to help."

For obvious reasons, the young men excused themselves and headed out to The New York City Savings Bank, where Jonathan wanted to make a withdrawal of $9,900. The teller verified his signature, asked some test questions because of the size of the withdrawal, and had him sign a second time on the reverse side of the ticket. Her supervisor verified his signature, too, and initialed his approval next to the second signature. The supervisor even suggested a passbook loan to save the interest. Jonathan declined. When the supervisor countersigned the check, Jonathan and Michael left the savings bank, headed to the Chemical Agricultural Bank, and promptly deposited it.

On their way back to the apartment Jonathan said, "Michael, I want you with me in Florida during this trip."

"Sure, I want to be with you, too, Jonathan. I love you more than you'll ever know."

Chapter 40

The aircraft sped down the runway of Newark airport with its propellers roaring until it was airborne. Michael watched the industrial
cities of New Jersey below shrinking as they climbed. By the time they
were approaching their cruising altitude, he couldn't see anything below
except the sun sparkling on the Atlantic Ocean, and the seemingly endless
New Jersey shoreline. It was early afternoon, and the sun was streaming
in his window. Jonathan hadn't said anything since they boarded the
plane, and he appeared to be in deep thought. Michael decided not to
interrupt those thoughts. He knew that Jonathan had enough to think
about. Within a day his life had been turned upside down.

Jonathan turned to Michael. He smiled and said, "Do you realize that
last Monday we were still at Ramapo, anticipating our freedom the next
day?"

"Yes, I sure do."

"Remember how we were looking forward to flying home together?"

"Yes. How could I forget?"

"Well, we've been there, done that. And now here we are on a plane
again. It seems like years since last Tuesday."

"All I know, Jonathan, is that a week ago I felt that I was thinking
such strange thoughts about you, that I thought I was going out of my
mind. I was terrified. I really thought I was crazy. And now, in spite of
the tragedy you are going though, I'm feeling more comfortable than I've
ever felt in my life. I feel needed, and wanted, and feeling wonderful to
be with you, and part of your life."

Jonathan squeezed Michael's hand. "I'm glad you're by my side,
Michael. I don't know what I would have done if you had rejected me. I
need you now more than ever. I need your support, and the kindness
you've shown me since the first day we met."

"Well, I'm glad I'm able to be here, Jonathan. You're one of the nicest things God has given me."

"Thanks. I feel the same way about you."

"Jonathan, let's get some rest for a while before they start serving food and stuff."

"Good idea."

They pushed their seats back, and Jonathan punched Michael's shoulder hard.

"Ouch!"

"Have a good nap, Precious."

"You prick."

Jonathan chuckled softly. Michael liked to hear that; it felt comforting.

Michael said, "I'm happy to be with you whatever the circumstances are."

They both fell asleep.

Chapter 41

Lillian had been feeling better as each hour passed since she had spoken with Jonathan that morning. During the day, she had also spoken to Adele and Willington Balmoral. They were both going to be very helpful in the days ahead. She was pleased that Jonathan was coming to Miami that afternoon. It would be good to see him, and it would also be good to meet his friend, Michael. Bill Balmoral had said he was a very polite, nice young man, and that he came from a fine family. He told her of their meeting the night before.

She had spoken to Missy about an hour ago. She knew that Missy was staying at their apartment, and she was grateful for that. Missy was a good person, and she was, after all, Jonathan's mother. She'd be a terrific help. Maybe it wouldn't be necessary to hire a full-time nurse as long as Missy was there. She decided to think about that later. Missy had spoken about Michael. She said he was one of the nicest friends that Jonathan ever had. She suggested, ever so tactfully, that she thought their relationship was more than a friendship, that it probably was a love thing. It was the first time since the accident that Lillian smiled. She wasn't surprised. It would have pissed off Jonathan Anthony, the dominator, to no end to have his son with a boyfriend. Anyway, that was one thing she wouldn't have to deal with now.

She was particularly pleased that she had not been as seriously injured, as they first thought. She didn't have any internal injuries that they could detect, and she'd probably be able to leave the hospital tomorrow. It wasn't necessary to have her in intensive care any longer, but since they planned on discharging her in the morning, they decided to leave her there for one more night's observation.

She was sitting up in her bed collecting her thoughts. She took a few deep breaths and stared out the window at the ocean. She was on too high a floor and too far from the window to see any of the beach below, but she did see a large passenger liner headed south. It was so close to shore that she assumed it had probably just left Ft. Lauderdale and was headed to the Caribbean.

She was going to discuss the funeral plans with Jonathan when he came in. She was sure he was up to doing his part. He was going to do a lot of growing up in the months ahead.

Yesterday, when she arrived at the hospital, she regained consciousness and signed some documents authorizing her care and identifying her deceased husband. She also made some necessary phone calls, notwithstanding the disapproval of the doctors. Patients in intensive care weren't permitted to have telephones in their rooms, but Mrs. Jonathan Taylor insisted. She ordered them to put one in, and so they did.

She had some visitors from the Miami Police Department, too. They asked her about the accident and told her there were several witnesses, three of whom had pulled her and her husband out of the car, when the car that hit them burst into flames. The driver and passenger of the other vehicle were killed. The police gave her the names, addresses and telephone numbers of the three good Samaritans. She intended to thank them personally later in the day. Maybe Jonathan could help her with that. It was hard doing everything with one hand. Tiresome, too.

The only flowers that were in her room were from the auto rental company, the Fontainebleau and Jonathan. The arrangements from the car company and hotel were elegant and beautiful, but Jonathan's arrangement of tiny yellow roses and very small white orchids was understated and truly pretty. Jonathan didn't know much about flowers. She wondered if his friend had helped him tell the florist what to send. She leaned back and buzzed the nurse to lower her bed. The nurse was there in a minute and helped arrange the sheets and pillow and lowered the back of the bed to make Mrs. Taylor more comfortable. She closed her eyes after the nurse left.

What a wonderful vacation they had been having. It had been like a second honeymoon. It wasn't often that they could spend so much time together. She was just as busy as her husband had been with her position at the advertising agency. One of the things she loved so about Jonathan was his ability to make friends and his ability to enjoy himself. It was fun to play with him. He knew how to do so many things. He swam well, played tennis fairly well, golfed poorly, but he was always smiling. People were drawn to him everywhere they went. She reached for the tissues next to her bed. She realized that she had been sobbing for almost half an hour.

The last time she had held him in her arms was on Saturday night, while they were dancing to *Moonlight Serenade.* What a great night it had been. When they got back to the hotel, she was looking forward to a romantic lovemaking night. She was in the shower, and Jonathan Anthony took his clothes off and threw them over a chair and laid down on the bed. He had fallen asleep. When she came out of the shower and saw him sleeping soundly, she didn't wake him. She just kissed him and pulled the covers over him. How she wished she had awakened him. It was too late now. Nothing could change that. Lillian was not into regrets.

She quickly blew her nose and wiped her eyes when she heard the knock on the door. They're probably coming to take my vitals again or draw some more blood.

"Come in."

"Lillian! How nice to see you," Jonathan exclaimed, as he entered the room followed by Michael.

"Hi, Jonathan. Come here, sweetheart, and give me a kiss."

Jonathan walked over to her and kissed her on the cheek.

"Oh, Jonathan, I'm so glad you're here," she said, as she reached out for his hand and held it.

Jonathan noticed that she still looked pretty, even with the bandage around her head. He saw her left arm and hand in a cast.

"I was so worried about you, Lillian. I'm sorry about your husband."

"And I'm sorry about your father, Jonathan. Very sorry."

They both broke into tears for a moment and offered each other a tissue.

"Your flowers are right here next to my bed. What good taste you have."

Lillian was looking toward Michael, who had remained near the door. Michael was almost going to leave, when Jonathan realized that Lillian was looking at him.

"Oh, Lillian, may I present my friend, Michael Manganaro."

"Mr. Manganaro, how do you do?" Lillian greeted.

"Very well thanks, Mrs. Taylor. How do you do?" Michael said and surprised himself at his formality.

"I'm okay, but I've been better. I can't believe I'm meeting one of Jonathan's friends looking like this. Please don't be scared. I know I must look like Halloween or something." She managed a small laugh. "Please pull up some chairs, guys. Did you help Jonathan pick out the flowers?"

"Yes, he did, Lillian. How did you know?"

"Just had a hunch."

As they pulled up the side chairs, Jonathan said, "Well, how are you really?"

"Not as bad as I look. No internal injuries." She pulled the sheets sideways to expose the huge cast on the left leg."

"I have a concussion," she said pointed to her head, "and a broken leg in two places, as well as a broken wrist in several places and four broken fingers. They operated on me last night. I have several pins in my wrist. I understand they took some bone from my hip to use in my wrist."

"You're very luck to be alive."

"I know. We had just finished shopping at the mall where I had purchased several dresses and thirty yards of fabric for some new curtains and slipcovers I intend to make for the sitting room. I put the packages between your father, who was driving, and me."

"Can you tell me what happened?"

"Well, we were turning crossing Collins Avenue when this vehicle slammed into your father's side of the car. That's the last thing I remember clearly."

"Lillian, I'm so sorry."

"Thank you. I'm sure it was the packages of soft materials between us that saved my life. My leg crashed into the gearshift, I think, and I sort of remember the pain in my hand as it hit the steering wheel. But then I blacked out."

"Are you in pain now?"

"Not too much. They're giving me something. Makes me a little depressed and giddy at the same time."

"How long will you be here?"

"I'm expecting to get out tomorrow. I want to go home and do what has to be done. Your father would not have approved of my lounging about here in Miami without him."

"Tomorrow?"

"Yes."

"Well, I guess you have a plan then."

"Always do. But I want to bounce my ideas off you, and I'll need your help to carry them out."

"Anything you say, Lillian."

"I hope you brought some notepaper and a pen."

"I didn't, but you did, didn't you, Michael?"

"Yes, Jonathan. Right here."

"He's great, Lillian, very efficient. Was our company clerk in boot camp."

"He may be very efficient, but I also heard from Mrs. Theofanus, that he was also a wonderful singer."

"She mentioned me?" Michael asked, surprised.

"Yes she did. And I want you to know, Michael, that if you're going to be part of this family, you'll have to work like the dickens to keep up with us. We have a lot to do in the days ahead."

"I'll do anything I can," Michael offered. He was surprised at her directness.

"Jonathan, are you ready to assume your responsibilities as head of Taylor Oil?"

"I haven't given it much thought."

"But you must, and you will, but more about that later. We have the matter of getting your father back to New York and the funeral to plan."

Jonathan turned to Michael. "I told you, Lillian is very much like my father. Things to do. Do them, and move on."

"If I were up and walking around, I would have had this all done by now, but I need your help."

"Shoot."

Michael moved closer to the bottom of the bed with his notebook and pen handy, so he could take notes.

"Well first, Thursday is Thanksgiving. I would like your father to be buried on Friday. That way any of his friends who have the day off and are in town can attend. I have spoken to Mr. Balmoral, and he is making all the arrangements for a 10 a.m. High Mass at St. Stephen's where your father liked to go to church when he had the chance. Your father bought a plot in a cemetery in New Jersey where his parents are buried. I believe the deed to that is in your father's papers along with his Last Will and Testament. You'll have to get that out."

"Yes, I've seen it. I'll get it out as soon as I get home."

"Mr. Balmoral is taking care of the flowers for the church and the music."

"So I don't have to do anything about the church?"

"No, with one exception."

"Which is?"

"You have to get Michael to help us with the music."

"Sure. Michael, will you help with the music?"

"Of course, Jonathan. You know I will."

"Great, Jonathan, you did your first job well," Lillian said. "And thanks, Michael for agreeing to help."

Michael was looking puzzled. "What is it that you want me to do?"

"Sing," Lillian said. "Just sing. Mrs. Theofanus recommended you highly, and since you and Jonathan have become such great friends, I didn't think you'd mind."

"I don't mind at all. I'll be happy to help in any way I can, but I didn't even know Mr. Taylor."

"Doesn't matter," Lillian said. "You're in love with his son, aren't you?"

Jonathan and Michael looked at each other. They were speechless.

"Look, I live in a glass house, and I have no stones. Excuse my abruptness, but are you, or aren't you?"

"Yes." Michael said, and Lillian watched the way he looked at Jonathan.

"I'm glad. I love him, too. Jonathan, how do you feel about Michael?"

"I love him dearly, Lillian. I do. I was thinking about telling you in our room in a long, long conversation. Not here in a hospital."

"Well, I give you my blessing. The only bone I have to pick with you, Jonathan, is that you let Missy know before me!"

Jonathan said, "Missy knows?"

"She suspects. She's a smart lady, too, Jonathan. You don't give her enough credit at times, you know. She told me today on the phone. Does anyone else know?"

Recovering, Michael said, "Only my friend, Gary. He's the only one I told."

"Good. Invite him to the Mass, Michael, because you're going to have a big part in it."

"Sure, but please explain."

"When I asked Mr. Balmoral about the music for the Mass, he suggested I talk to Mrs. Theofanus about it. He told me he was getting about half of the Metro's chorus, and half of their orchestra to perform for the service. It seems that since Mr. Taylor was the prime negotiator for the pay increases they got last year that averted the planned strike, and because of the support he has always provided the company, they would perform as a special tribute to him for his funeral Mass."

"Sounds impressive," Michael said in awe.

Jonathan agreed, "Sounds impressive to me, too, Lillian."

"He even got Mr. Timothy Flanagan, the Metro's organist, to play."

"Sounds great to me, Mrs. Taylor. I'm the world's greatest page-turner."

Lillian laughed. "We want you to do a lot more than turning pages, Michael, and please call me Lillian."

"Lillian."

Lillian coughed and asked for a tissue.

"Lillian, what do you want me to sing?"

"Dame Theofanus suggested that Faure's *Requiem* was the music we should use, and she told me that since it was scored for chorus, soprano and baritone soloist, organ and instruments, you would be the best choice for the baritone soloist."

"Wow. I can't believe that. She only heard me once."

"Apparently, once was all she needed to hear."

"I'm shocked."

"Well don't be," Jonathan said. "I want you to do it."

Lillian asked, "Do you know the work, Michael?"

"Yes. We sang it at St. John's last year for Bishop O'Brien's funeral, but I didn't do the solos. We had someone from the Metro do that."

"Well, now it's your turn. That is, if you are still willing."

"I don't know if I'll have the time to rehearse."

"You have the time. On Thursday, Mrs. Theofanus has invited you to her apartment on Central Park West to rehearse with her at ten in the morning until you are finished."

"To rehearse with her?"

"Game?"

"Sure."

"Could you guys go and get me some coffee from the machine in the lobby? They only give me decaf in here, and I hate decaf. Get yourselves some, too, because we are about to have a long meeting."

"Sure. We'll be right back."

"I have plenty of change if you need it."

"No thanks, Lillian. We have plenty, also."

The young men left the room.

Lillian liked him. Michael seemed to be exactly what Jonathan needed. A nurse came in and took her blood pressure and her pulse. She noted it on her chart and left.

As Michael and Jonathan were walking down the corridor, returning with the coffee, Jonathan said, "Well, Michael, why are you so quiet?"

"I'm just a little surprised. Lillian took me by surprise, that's all."

"She has a way of doing that. That's probably why she is such a good executive at the ad agency. She's not afraid of the truth."

"Well, at least she approves of me and us. I guess that's a good thing."

"Yes, Michael. It is. You'll get to like her; I promise."

"I like her already, but she's not what I expected. I suppose I thought I'd find an injured woman feeling hopeless and helpless."

Jonathan laughed out loud. "Helpless? Lillian? Never."

A passing nurse reminded him to keep his voice down.

"Sorry."

Lillian was putting on lipstick with her right hand.

"Welcome back. I did this without a mirror."

Michael handed her a coffee and said, "You did just fine. You look terrific."

"Thanks, Michael. Now, why don't the two of you have seats?"

Jonathan pulled the chairs closer together and said, "Tell us your plan. Michael will take notes."

"Okay. First, I want you to telephone the funeral home on Amsterdam Avenue. You know the one. Stokes and Stokes. Tell them to get in touch with the hospital here and make arrangements, whatever they have to do, to fly Mr. Taylor home tomorrow, and to have visiting scheduled for Wednesday from 2 to 5, and 7 to 9. The same for Thursday. Tell them about the funeral Mass at St. Stephen's on Friday. Tell them you will be flying home on Tuesday and make an appointment for Tuesday evening to pick out the casket and finalize all the details. Pick out clothes for your father to wear and take them with you. All his clothes that he left at the hotel, I'm donating to Good Will."

"I can do that. But if we fly home tomorrow, how will you get home?"

"I have to go by train. I can't fly with my injuries. I'd like Michael to accompany me, if that's okay."

"Sure, that's okay with me, Lillian," Michael said.

"The hospital is arranging a full-time nurse to travel with me to New York, and she'll be staying with us through Friday. When you leave here tonight, Jonathan, order plane tickets for yourself, and three private compartments on the express train to New York for us. They should be adjoining if possible. To make things a little easier, I'm going to give you your father's wallet to take home. You can use his American Express card. And I want you to start keeping track of any money you lay out for expenses, because the estate will reimburse you later. Since we're the co-executors, we'll have to talk about a lot of things with Mr. Connelly and Mr. Brasso."

"Sure."

"You can stop by tomorrow with Michael with the tickets, which you should pick up the first thing in the morning. I think the train leaves about 11 a.m. and gets into Penn Station on Wednesday at approximately 1 p.m. Have a limousine waiting for me when I get there. You should pick me up tomorrow about 10, and you and Michael and I can head to the train. Then you can use the car to take yourself to the airport. After you get reservations, call me to let me know the correct departure and arrival times."

"Of course, we'll meet you when the train arrives at Penn Station. I'll have dad's usual driver pick us up. I know the train station must have a wheelchair we could use to get you to the car."

"I'm sure they do and your father's driver was a good idea. Jonathan, if he doesn't have holiday plans, I'd like him to remain with us for the rest of the week."

"And if he does have plans?"

"Rent a commercial limousine for the rest of the week. Your father's secretary probably could give you the name of a reliable service Taylor uses."

"You got it."

"Also, I'll need a wheelchair for use at home, and I've already asked Missy to get me one."

"Sure."

"When you're on the telephone tomorrow, tell Adele and Missy the plan. Also, Make appointments for Thursday morning for Mr. Connelly at 9 and for Mr. Brasso at 10. I'd like Mr. Connelly to remain with us when we meet with Mr. Brasso. So let him know that, and tell Mr. Brasso that he'll be there."

"I just hope they're not out of town for the holiday."

"I don't think they will be, but if they are, arrange it for Monday, or whenever they get back. We have to get the Will probated at once, so that we can receive our papers, so we can function. It is very important to Taylor Oil that we retain control."

"No problem. I'll call the both of them and arrange the meetings."

"Jonathan, together you and I are going to own 62.2 percent of the company's common stock. I know the details of the Will. Your father discussed his plans with me in detail. There are two members on the Board of Directors who weren't fond of your father and tried to undermine his efforts. I'm sure they are hoping that the taxes we'll have to pay will force us to sell a large portion of our stock. But we are not going to let that happen."

"Lillian, I'm completely in the dark here. I don't have a lot of money to pay taxes."

"You will have after we work out all the details, but don't worry about it now." She smiled wearily and turned to Michael.

"Michael, are you sure you don't mind escorting this invalid back home?"

"No, I do not mind in the least. It will be a pleasure, Lillian. I'll take good care of you."

"Thanks, Michael," Lillian said. "I'll call Missy because we probably won't be available for the first visiting hours at Stokes. She should receive the visitors for us."

"I'm sure she'll fill in for us," Jonathan said.

"Also, Jonathan, and this is very important. You must get the name of the public relations guy at Taylor from Miss Greenfeld. Talk to him before you leave in the morning. I want an obituary run in Wednesday's *The New York Times*, mentioning the visiting hours of the wake and the Mass on Friday. End it by saying family and friends will be received at the Taylor's home immediately after the burial for rest and a repast. Michael, do you want me to repeat that because it is important?"

"No, thank you. Not necessary. I've got it," Michael said, as he continued writing as rapidly as he could.

"Should it run on Thursday and Friday, as well?"

"Good thinking. Yes it should, but just remove the visiting hours from Friday's."

"I have it all down, Lillian," Michael offered.

"What kind of repast?" Jonathan queried.

"Good question, Jonathan. I want the people who were kind enough to spend their morning and lunchtime with us to have a chance to relax and get a drink and something to eat. Not festive, mind you, but somber and restful. Call Anthony's on East Sixty-third Street. Tell them I want a substantial buffet lunch ready for 150 people for 1:30 p.m. You pick the foods. Real china. The works. Three open bars, which we can set up in the front foyer. Black-tie waiters, servers and bartenders. Good linen and glass wear. Hire a pianist and violinist to play some quiet classical selections from 1:30 to 3:30. Oh, stuff like Handel's *Water Music*. Let the musicians pick the music, but tell them we want it soft and dignified. Call Juilliard. It's in your father's address book. I think he has several students listed who could use some extra money. They should be in black-tie or black dresses."

"I'll get all this done. I don't foresee any problems."

"Jonathan, that's good to hear. I'm leaving it all up to you. You do all the things we talked about, and I'll be very happy and relieved. Michael, you take care of Jonathan tonight and get me safely home on the train. Then on Thursday, work your tail off with Mrs. Theofanus and sing like an angel on Friday."

"What's your phone number here in case we have any questions?"

Lillian gave them the phone number and gave Jonathan his father's wallet from her pocketbook. "Jonathan, your father just cashed about five hundred dollars worth of traveler's checks. Split whatever money is in the wallet between you, so you both have money in your pockets."

Jonathan kissed her on the lips, and Michael kissed her on the cheek. While he was doing that, she squeezed his hand and smiled.

Lillian Taylor was sleeping before Jonathan and Michael left her room.

Chapter 42

Gary looked at his watch first and then at the clock on the wall. It was fifteen minutes to four. Almost time to pack up. He asked the operator for an outside line then dialed the 914 area code and the number.

"Hello," Louise Manganaro said.

"Hi, Mrs. Manganaro, it's Gary."

"Hi, Gary."

"I just called to thank you for a wonderful meal yesterday. I really enjoyed everything. You're a great cook."

"Thanks, Gary. You're always welcome at our table; you know that. We really enjoyed having you. It's been a long time since you've been over. I'm sorry the day ended so sadly. Poor young man. Both his mother and his stepmother in hospitals at the same time, and his father killed."

"His mother's in a hospital, too?"

"Yes. I'll tell you about that sometime, or maybe Michael will. Michael's, by the way, on his way to Florida right now with Jonathan, and Rosa will be on her way to the city soon for A.I.B., that she told you about yesterday. Anthony gets home about five-thirty, and we usually eat around six. Tonight it will be just Anthony and me. We're having leftovers today from yesterday. Gary, would you like to join us for supper?"

"You bet. I'd love to. I'll see you as soon after six as possible. The train gets in at 5:59 p.m. I'll drive right over. Should I bring anything?"

"Nothing. Just yourself."

"Okay. Bye, now."

Gary hung up. He loved going to Michael's house even if Michael wasn't home. Everything about the place reminded him of Michael. He began straightening his desk. He used the men's room and then left for Grand Central. He was hoping the train wouldn't be too crowded today. He thought that because it was Thanksgiving week a lot of people might have taken the week off. The trains had been almost empty since last

Thursday. When he got to the platform, he realized he was right. It was almost time to leave, and the train was half full. He walked rapidly to the second car, which on this line was the bar car. He felt he needed a drink. He had been feeling that way a lot. Particularly, since last night when he got home, because after dinner yesterday the day definitely went downhill. He missed Michael. Damn Jonathan. Damn. Fuck!

He ordered a sidecar from the bartender-waiter. There was a man standing alone at a nearby tall table reading a newspaper. Gary took his drink and put it on the table across from the man. "May I join you?"

The man put his paper down and said, "Of course. Delighted to have company."

Gary realized it was the same guy who had sat next to Jonathan last week. The guy was gorgeous and beautifully dressed. Gary could feel his heart beat faster and his face warming up. The man was about two inches taller than he was. He didn't notice that last week. He was wearing a fragrance that Gary didn't recognize, but it smelled woodsy and clean. He liked it. Gary was so strongly attracted to him, he wanted to touch him. The guy took a sip from his glass. It looked like he was having a highball. He smiled at Gary.

The man said, "I've seen you on this train before, but never in the bar car."

"I hardly ever come in here. Usually, it's too crowded. It's hard enough just getting a seat," Gary answered.

"I know what you mean. But Thanksgiving week is a very popular vacation time for 'breeders;' I think and that's probably why it's so empty."

Gary hadn't heard that expression, 'breeders,' before and guessed that it meant heterosexual baby-makers.

"You're not a breeder then?" Gary asked with a big, nervous smile.

"Not yet! But, I am married. No kids, though. My wife has gone to visit kinfolk this week in her hometown, Raceland, Louisiana. So I have the whole week to play."

Gary couldn't believe that he himself said, "Would you by any chance need a playmate?"

The man put his elbow on the table and his closed hand against the side of his face. He smiled at Gary. His eyes twinkled, as he looked Gary over from his wingtips to his flat top and then to his eyes.

"My name is Addison, Addison Konklin. I live in Oak Valley, but I have a business in Stamford and I'm trying to set up one office in the city by sometime early in January."

"I live in Mellon, right next to Oak Valley. I used to drive to the Oak Valley station, but the parking lots were always full, so now I drive to Poughkeepsie. My name is Gary Plotsky, by the way."

"How do you do, Gary? It's a pleasure to meet you," Addison said. He raised his eyebrows and asked, "How old are you, Gary?"

"Twenty."

"Nice. I'm a little older than you. Do you like to play with older guys?"

"I've never played with older guys."

"Do you think it might be fun to explore that?"

Gary started to perspire, as Addison rubbed his thigh against his.

"Yes. I want to play with you, Addison."

"Is tonight good for you?"

"Not tonight, unfortunately, because I have plans for dinner, but tomorrow would be great."

"Fine. Take the train to Stamford tomorrow, and meet me at Giovanni's right on the main street across from the station. Take the one that gets in about 6 p.m. I'll dine you and wine you, and then I'll show you my office. I usually stay over in the office when my wife's away. You're welcome to stay, too, if you'd like, and I do think you will, but in case things don't work out, I'll drop you off at your home."

"Sounds super to me," Gary said, as he realized he was so nervous he had already finished his drink.

Addison pointed to the bartender and to Gary's empty glass and put a twenty-dollar bill on the table. The bartender walked over with another drink and change when he saw the twenty. Gary thanked Addison and sipped his drink. It tasted great.

Addison knew he had a virgin in his grasp and that really turned him on. He wanted him almost as much as he wanted the blond guy who sat next to him last week. If all went well maybe it could be more than a one-night stand.

When the trained pulled into Oak Valley, they shook hands, and Addison got off. When Gary got off at the next stop, Poughkeepsie, Gary was still shaking a little and found it hard to believe that he had a date with Addison. He had his first date. He'd put it on his calendar, if he had a calendar. He didn't have the foggiest idea of what to do on a date with a guy, but he knew that if Michael were here, Michael would tell him to go ahead and try it. Go for it. Go to Stamford and see what happens. At least he'd probably get a good Italian meal. Some good wine. Damn. He wished he could talk to Michael.

It only took him a few minutes to get to the Manganaros. He went in through the kitchen door and was just in time to help Mrs. Manganaro carry the hot food into the dining room. Mr. Manganaro was already seated at the table.

"Sit down, Gary," Mr. Manganaro said, "Make yourself at home."

"Thank you. It's nice to be here."

"Before you came in, me and Louisa were talking about going to see *Elmer Gantry* after supper. Would you like to come with us?"

"I'd like that very much."

"Good. We miss Rosa and Michael, in particular, and your company would help us feel loved again," Anthony laughed.

Louisa put her hand on Gary's and said, "Seems so strange to us that Michael would come home on leave and then leave for Florida."

"I guess they've become better friends than Michael and me."

Louisa immediately felt sorry she had said what she had. "It's not that way, Gary. I'm sure it's just the circumstances."

Anthony looked at Louisa and Gary, but said nothing.

"What the heck. It gives me the opportunity to know you both better, and I've heard good things about the movie."

Louisa said grace.

Chapter 43

After the meeting with Lillian, Michael and Jonathan went back to the hotel. They closed the door to their room, and they started to undress without speaking. Michael walked over to the sliding glass doors, opened them, and walked onto the terrace. He looked out over the ocean and took a few deep breaths of the salty air.

He called back into the room. "Jonathan, come on out for a minute. It's beautiful out here, and the sun is about to set."

Jonathan pulled his pants back up and went outside. "Yes, Michael, it is beautiful."

"Are you hungry, Jonathan?" Michael asked.

"Starved."

"Why don't we eat out here on the terrace? I can call room service while you make your phone calls."

"Great idea, Precious. Do it, but remember, I'm a meat and potato kind of guy."

"You got it," Michael said, as he used the phone in the sitting room and called room service.

"And get us a bottle of champagne. I sure could use a drink."

Michael ordered prime ribs, baked potatoes with extra sour cream, garlic bread, and tossed green salad, New York cheesecake, champagne, and espresso.

Jonathan started making the phone calls he promised Lillian he would make and made the reservations for the trip home

Michael tried to call home to give his parents an update, but didn't get an answer. They either took a ride in the car to the Dairy Queen, or went to a movie. They probably felt lonely with Rosa at school and me out of town, he thought. He took a shower. He had just finished as a knock on the door announced the food's arrival. Jonathan had just finished a cigarette. They had the food taken to the terrace.

"This is great, Michael, you know how to please your man," Jonathan said, as he surveyed the table full of food.

Michael laughed as the waiter opened the champagne. Michael gave him a good tip, and he disappeared.

They sat down at the table facing each other.

"Jonathan?" Michael asked as he raised his glass, "Is it appropriate at a time like this to make a toast?"

"Yes, it is. Anything we do together is appropriate."

"Okay then, I wish you the very best going forward with all your new responsibilities and a speedy recovery for Lillian."

"Thank you, Michael." Jonathan raised his glass, too, and continued, "And may you and I have a very happy life together, Precious."

"Thank you. Do you really mean that you want me forever, like being married?"

"Yes. Till death do us part."

"Well, what do I say, I do?"

"Only if you want to."

"I want to."

Jonathan removed his signet ring from his finger, leaned across the table and put it on Michael's finger. Michael felt lightheaded and he blushed. Jonathan kissed Michael on his forehead.

"Oh, Jonathan. You really mean it," Michael said looking into Jonathan eyes.

"Yes. Now let's dig in. I'm starved."

Michael felt like he was living some kind of incredible fantasy. He felt as though he belonged to Jonathan at last, and Jonathan belonged to him.

After they ate for a few minutes Jonathan said, "You know, Michael, together we are going to accomplish great things. With Lillian's guidance I'm going to become very wealthy for my lifetime, Michael, not just a flash-in-the-pan millionaire."

"I am sure."

"And, Michael, you should become a professional singer. I can help you, both with money, contacts and emotional support."

"Wouldn't that be great? But I'm not sure I'm good enough."

"You will be with the right training. Even while you're in the Navy, I'm sure we can get you started."

"I can't believe you would do that for me."

"Not for you, Michael, for us. I want my significant other to be famous. And I'll never miss an opening."

"Jonathan, I never really believed that you'd be planning a life with me."

"Believe it, because it's begun."

They finished eating, and both felt stuffed.

"Jonathan, let's take a walk on the beach. I've never taken a walk on the beach in the dark, or with someone I loved before."

"Me neither, and practically speaking, we should work off all this food!"

They took a walk on the beach holding hands. They picked up some shells. Jonathan kissed Michael in the moonlight. Michael thought it felt nice to squish his toes in the damp sand. He felt like making love to Jonathan on the beach, but that would be messy.

"I love you, Mr. Manganaro."

"And I love you, Mr. Taylor of Taylor Oil."

They laughed and slowly walked back to the hotel.

The maid had removed the dishes and had turned down the bed. Moonlight was streaming in the windows.

Jonathan said, "I better take a shower."

"No. I want you now just the way you are. Take your clothes off please and just get into bed."

They undressed each other as they kissed passionately. Michael pushed Jonathan down onto his stomach on the bed. He knelt between Jonathan's legs and massaged his butt. He lay down on top of Jonathan kissing his shoulders and licking his upper back with the tip of his tongue. Jonathan hadn't showered since morning and, after the long flight, the meeting with Lillian, and the walk on the beach, he had an enticing workout body aroma. The smell and taste of his beloved excited Michael, and made him want to be inside Jonathan, and he wasted no time. He had been waiting for this since Sunday morning. He wanted to please Jonathan. To make him feel better. To let him know how much he wanted him. He entered Jonathan without a lubricant except for some of his own saliva. He moved more forcefully than he had in the past and penetrated him more deeply. Jonathan's moans let him know he was achieving his objective. He pounded Jonathan into the bed.

"Oh, my God, Michael, give it to me. Hard, Michael!"

And Michael moved more rapidly, until he couldn't hold back. He didn't want to hold back. Jonathan felt the contractions in Michael's penis. Michael exploded inside his lover and lay still inside him until his erection subsided, and his penis slipped out. He moved off Jonathan and lay beside him.

Michael stared at the ceiling, and Jonathan just enjoyed looking at Michael beside him in the rays of moonlight coming in the bedroom window.

"Jonathan, please sit on my chest and face me."

And Jonathan did.

"Move up, Jonathan. I want it," Michael said, as he put the second pillow under his head.

Jonathan rubbed his penis across Michael's face and across his lips teasing him. Michael inhaled the raunchy smells from Jonathan's groin.

"You want it? How much do you want it?"

Michael did not speak, but answered by taking Jonathan into his mouth. He let his tongue let Jonathan know how much he wanted it. He enjoyed Jonathan's salty taste. The well-groomed Jonathan Taylor, who was always immaculately clean, today smelled like a laborer, and that excited Michael. It was good, Michael thought, to hear Jonathan moan again. Jonathan rose up on his knees and went deeper into Michael's mouth. Jonathan put his hands on the back of the headboard to support himself.

"Michael, this is how I want you; let me know if you mind."

Michael released Jonathan long enough to say, "I want it like this, too. And I want to taste all of you."

Michael could see Jonathan smile in the semi-darkness.

Jonathan was enjoying this and was just aggressive enough to be temporarily dominant without causing discomfort to Michael, or causing him to gag. Now it was his turn to please Michael, and he moved swiftly until he filled Michael's mouth with two days of pungent ejaculatory fluid.

They lay side by side facing each other breathing heavily until their hearts stopped pounding. Finally, holding hands, they kissed with tongues teasing each other.

"Hmmm, Michael, have you been eating shrimp?"

They fell asleep in each other's arms, both longing to be held. They slept well that night.

Chapter 44

Gary felt good. Tonight was going to be his night. Addison was exactly the type of guy he had been looking for. He ate a long lunch and bought an expensive French cuff shirt, some good quality cufflinks and a red silk tie on Madison Avenue and got a haircut and manicure, his first, in a fine salon not too far from his office. He looked great today, and he knew it. I can't wait, he thought. Tonight it's going to happen. Just before returning to his office he also picked up some new white briefs and T-shirts.

Gary watched the clock all afternoon. He couldn't keep his attention on his work. He couldn't concentrate on anything except for Addison. Finally at 3:30, he went to the men's room and put on clean underwear and his new shirt and tie. He was ready. He really looked sharp. Very cosmopolitan. The old dependent Gary from Mellon seemed like a memory. It was funny, he thought, how he kept thinking about Michael. This was the first thing he did on his own without Michael. Michael always got the ideas, made the plans, bought the tickets, and arranged the dates. Over all the years of their friendship, he had always enjoyed turning over his social life to Michael. He did enjoy himself, however, and didn't have to worry about a thing, but today at last he was on his own. Actually, he started yesterday. He couldn't believe that he had said, "I want to play with you, Addison."

He was ready at last. He looked at himself in the bathroom mirror. He was tall and good-looking, very Slavic. His curly, light brown hair added to his youthful attractiveness.

He wanted Addison to want him as much as he wanted Addison. He asked himself, "What the hell took you so long, you asshole?" He knew that the answer to his questions was that he had secretly hoped that the first time would be with Michael, maybe under the stadium steps behind the school. Well, he was determined to enjoy himself tonight, in spite of being dumped by Michael. From this day forward life was going to be different. He understood, it seemed all at once, that Michael would be his friend, but nothing more, and that was that.

He said good night to his co-workers and headed toward Grand Central. He got on the train and made a decision not to drink. He had been drinking much too much lately, and that had not made him happy. He wanted to deal with this experience sober. He had some butterflies in his stomach, but that was okay, too.

The train pulled into the station, and he got off and spotted Giovanni's at once. He pulled up the collar on his overcoat and headed to the restaurant. He took a couple of deep breaths before he opened the door and went it. Addison was sitting in a booth in the rear. He walked quickly toward him. Addison stood up. Gary approached the table.

"May I check your coat, sir?" the young woman asked.

"Please. Thank you," said Gary sounding mature and experienced. "How do you do, Addison?" he said as he extended his hand.

"Good evening, Gary. I'm really well tonight. I've been looking forward to seeing you," he said standing and shook Gary's hand. "How have you been?"

"Well, thanks. I've been looking forward to our meeting as well."

"Please be seated."

"Thank you."

"Gary, I can't believe how nice you look. I'm impressed."

"Thank you."

"Would you like something to drink, Gary?"

"Perhaps a cup of coffee." Gary noticed that Addison wasn't drinking anything alcoholic.

"Great. I'll join you."

"I'm a little hungry and quite frankly, I am really looking forward to seeing your office and spending some time alone with you."

"I was hoping you would be."

"May I make a suggestion?"

"Of course."

"Could we get some food to take out to your office, so we could be alone?"

"I think it's a great suggestion. I was afraid you'd be shy and maybe that you would have had too much to drink."

"Not tonight. This is my first time, and I want to enjoy every single minute of it."

Addison smiled pleasantly. What a nice surprise, he thought. He looked at Gary closely. He had obviously put some real effort into his appearance for the occasion, and Addison was flattered.

"How about if I order for us and we take off? My car's parked two doors down."

"Fine. I love everything."

The office was on Walnut Street. It was nicely furnished like a living room with three desks and a sofa in front of a fireplace that was already lit. Addison locked the door when they were inside.

"Please make yourself comfortable and at home, Gary. I'll put some more wood on the fire," Addison said.

Gary sat down on the sofa and watched Addison take off his jacket and put it with his coat on the wall behind the door. Gary couldn't help but notice the muscular definition of Addison's back. When Addison knelt before the fireplace, Gary checked out his butt. Gary was getting excited. He walked over to the fireplace, and when Addison stood up he put his arms around Addison's waist, and Addison turned toward him. Gary looked up into Addison's eyes and parted his lips. He welcomed the passionate kiss that followed. Addison took him by the hand and led him to the sofa.

"Gary, you surprise me."

"How so? Have I done something wrong?"

"No. Not at all."

Gary opened the buttons on Addison's shirt, and Addison removed his tie. Addison helped Gary undress, too. In minutes they were both nude.

"Gary, the sofa opens to a very comfortable bed. Shall I open it?"

"It's about time," Gary laughed.

Addison opened the bed and turned off the light. The room was dark save for the flickering fire.

They got under the covers, and Gary positioned himself half way on top of Addison and began kissing him. Gary felt Addison's hand running up and down his back and slowly over his buttocks. As Gary continued to kiss Addison he reached down and felt Addison's hard penis. He squeezed it and stoked it while Addison touched him, too.

"Gary, I never thought we'd be in bed so soon. I thought you were hungry."

"I am hungry. Hungry for you since the first time I saw you on the train a week ago. I want you to show me everything you think I should know. I'm a quick study."

"You're a brazen little hussy, Gary, and I love it."

"You feel so good. I love to touch you and taste you. I want to lick you all over, exploring every crevice. You are the most attractive guy I've ever seen naked."

"You're a hot little number yourself," Addison laughed.

They never did get to eat, and they didn't fall asleep until three in the morning. Addison was a great lover, and Gary enjoyed every minute of their lovemaking. They talked a lot, too.

Gary woke up before Addison and noticed that the coffee machine in the corner was the same type as the one in his office, so he put the coffee on. He put some more wood on the fire. He went into the men's room and rinsed out his mouth and combed his hair. He went back into the main room. He enjoyed walking around this strange office naked. The coffee was finished, and the aroma filled the room, and Addison became aware of it.

"Gary, did you make coffee?"

"Yes."

"That was nice of you," Addison said as he sat up in the sofa bed. "Don't you have to get ready for work?"

"I probably forgot to mention it, but I have today off. It's a half-day anyway and nobody works."

"The office here is closed today, as it is every Wednesday, but we're open on Saturdays."

"Do you want to do it again? I know I do."

"You astound me, Gary. Please bring me a cup of coffee. Just a little milk."

"Sure."

Gary carried both their coffees over to the bed and sat down next to Addison. Gary smiled suggestively and looked deeply into Addison's eyes.

"I like you a lot, Mr. Konklin."

"You're very attractive, Gary. I'll never forget last night. And thanks for the coffee. Would it surprise you to know that as soon as I have a few more sips of this coffee, I'll want to make love to you again?"

"It wouldn't surprise me one bit. And I'm hard as a rock, and I can see that you are, also, under this sheet."

Gary moved the sheet and blanket and found the throbbing penis. He put it into his mouth, and let it go down his throat. He continued slowly going up and down on Addison.

"Faster, Gary, faster."

When their lovemaking was over, and Gary was getting ready to leave, Addison said, "I want to see you again, Gary. Would you like that?"

Gary replied, "I'll come to you anytime you want me."

Chapter 45

It was Friday. It had come quickly, so quickly that Michael couldn't believe it. He looked at his watch. It was 9:30 in the morning, and the funeral was at 10:30. He had decided to walk to St. Stephen's by himself, while the close family members went to pay final respects at Stokes and Stokes for the casket closing. He needed the time alone to focus, and he didn't want to see the casket closing anyway. He was nervous enough. He thought the walk through Central Park would do him good. Besides it had started to snow during the early morning hours, and it was still coming down. The city was empty and serene this day after Thanksgiving, and there was no traffic, only an occasional taxi. All the trees and foliage in the park were covered with a good dusting of snow.

He clutched his music to his side and silently prayed that everything would go well. He thought about the events of the past week that brought him to this point in his life.

Michael thought about the last night he and Jonathan spent together in Miami. Michael thought it was the most passionate love session they had had, since they began exploring each other. It would be nice to always remember that night. And that was the night he got his ring.

The snow began coming down harder when he was in the middle of the park.

He felt good wearing the suit and coat that Jonathan had loaned him for this day. He hadn't brought any suits with him.

Time seemed to be flying. The trip home on the train with Lillian on Tuesday and Wednesday seemed long ago. The trip itself had been a good experience. She was one of the smartest people he had ever met. When she wasn't writing on the yellow pad, she engaged him in lively conversation. She allowed her sense of humor to come through her emotional and physical pain. Clearly, she approved of his relationship with

Jonathan. The time flew and she even asked him to read to her because she had trouble holding her book with her injured hand. He had enjoyed doing that for her.

She was not a woman to be pitied. She was vibrant, full of life. He wondered what their relationship would be like if he and Jonathan remained committed to each other.

He arrived at St. Stephen's and found his way to the choir loft in the rear of the gothic structure. The only other person up there was the organist. Michael introduced himself and found out that it was indeed Timothy Flanagan from the Metro-Tri-State Opera. Mr. Flanagan showed him to his seat, which was one of the two armchairs, with red brocade upholstery facing forward three feet from the railing. Flowers were being placed everywhere, and the altar was literally covered with white gladiolas. Several people were vacuuming, and ushers in formal morning dress were placing memorial programs in the pews. Several others were lighting the tall candles attached to the end of each of the pews. Michael estimated that there must have been 200 of them. Each one of the tall candleholders was wrapped in dark, green fern. In front of the massive church, several pews were tied off with white ribbons for all the dignitaries who were expected to attend. Even though there was no sun, Michael admired the stained glass windows that sparkled from the light reflected off the snow. Several altar boys were in front of the church getting prepared. Michael could smell that the incense had already been ignited.

A dozen security personnel were checking for explosive devices, etc. The governors of New York, New Jersey, Connecticut, as well as the mayors of New York City, Newark, Secaucus, Weehawken and Westport were expected. Twenty or so heads of Fortune 500 Companies, who were friends of Jonathan Anthony or of the members of the board of Taylor Oil, were coming as well. Willington Balmoral was expected to give the first eulogy, and Jonathan Taylor the second.

Michael sat back in his chair and tried to relax. He extended the fingers of his left hand and admired the gold ring with the initials *JT*. Just looking at it made him feel very special. The men and women from the opera filed in behind him and took their seats in the choir loft. The musicians took their places with their instruments to their seats on the left side of the loft. Mr. Flanagan sounded an "A" on the organ, and the string instruments began to tune their instruments.

Michael opened the program that had been placed on his seat, and he was surprised to see his name listed next to Dame Helene Theofanus as a guest soloist. He thought over how pleasant spending Thanksgiving morning with Mrs. Theofanus had been. She really helped him a great deal, particularly with his difficult solo in the *Offertory* of Fauré's *Requiem*. They had practiced for several hours until Mrs. Theofanus announced that they were done. She took him to lunch at the Plaza, and he enjoyed that greatly. They got to sit at a corner table that looked out onto Fifth Avenue and Central Park. When Mrs. Theofanus asked for the check, the waiter told her that luncheon had been paid for by the management, and he wished her a nice day. Michael was looking forward to her arrival this morning. Her presence would make him feel more comfortable, more confident.

Michael had called his mother and father, at Lillian's insistence, and invited them to the Mass. Since heavy snow was expected up in their area, they weren't sure if they would be able to make it.

All the candles were now lit, and the inside of St. Stephen's looked magical, not funereal. All the service personnel had disappeared, and guests started to arrive quickly. Michael had never seen so many beautiful fur coats. People arrived, and the ushers seated them behind the white ribbons. A governor surrounded by bodyguards arrived. Michael didn't know which one it was because he didn't get a good look at his face, but Michael thought it might be Governor Richards of New York.

Michael arranged his music and put it on the floor under his chair. He was looking down the center aisle when he saw Anthony and Louisa arrive. They turned around and spotted Michael. His father smiled and gave a small wave. So did his mother. An usher guided them behind the white ribbons, too. There were still twenty minutes to go before the start of the Mass.

Someone put a hand on Michael's shoulder and said, "Well, are you ready, Michael?" It was Dame Theofanus.

"Good morning. Yes, now that you're here."

He started to rise, and she pushed him back. "Sit, Michael, sit." She took off her coat and draped it over the railing. She sat down next to Michael.

"Michael, you look terrified. Let me see you smile."

Michael couldn't help himself. He smiled and reached out and touched her hand. She was good for him.

"Remember, Michael, watch the conductor, keep an eye on the music, and don't worry about what you sound like. It's too late for that during a performance. You worked on that during rehearsal. The most important thing to remember when you are singing with an orchestra and other singers is the tempo the conductor is setting. And take your time."

"Thanks, Dame Theofanus. I'll remember."

"And I'll be seated right beside you all morning. I will not let you get into trouble."

The organist turned on some switches that lit the choir loft's sixteen small chandeliers. All the music stands had lights above the music, and they lit simultaneously. Michael took his music from under this chair and placed it on the stand. He hadn't even seen the stand there before it was lit.

Mr. Flanagan began playing some music that Michael didn't recognize. The organist was only playing the pedals for the first 16 measures and gradually added notes from the five keyboards. Just as the piece was coming to a close a small red light went on, on the telephone on the console. Michael had never seen a telephone on an organ console before. Mr. Flanagan picked up the receiver and spoke to someone. He looked over at Mrs. Theofanus and Michael and then to someone in the orchestra. Michael was wondering what was up. It was 10:29 a.m.

Mr. Flanagan got up and walked over to the orchestra and spoke to the cellist. Then he walked over to Mrs. Theofanus and Michael.

"Helene, Mr. Manganaro, the funeral party is going to be about ten minutes late because of a street closing due to the snow. The family has asked that you sing together Schubert's *Ave Maria* during the delay. I have the music, but only one copy. Can you stand behind me and look over my shoulder?"

"Yes," Helene said. "Okay, Michael?"

"Yes, of course," Michael said.

"What key would you like?"

"I think *G* would be most comfortable for both of us, Timothy," Dame Theofanus said as she looked at Michael to see if he concurred. He nodded.

Mr. Flanagan went back to the console, and Mrs. Theofanus stood up, took off her gloves and straightened her dress. She guided Michael directly behind Timothy, and she stood next to Michael with their bodies touching. Michael began to tremble a little when the cellist began playing during the introduction. Mrs. Theofanus reached down and held his hand. Michael was afraid to start and waited for a fraction of a second until Dame Theofanus began, but then he was fine. They sang together nicely, and there were times when Michael realized that she held back her volume ever so slightly, so that he could more easily be heard. When he realized this, he didn't soften his singing to follow her lead, but continued singing strongly. They smiled at each other during the second portion of the piece still holding hands. As the end of the third portion was approaching, Mrs. Theofanus turned Michael to face her. Michael immediately knew that she was going to do something unusual, and that he was to follow her. And she did. She dramatically slowed down and took some unwritten grace notes in the final *Ave Maria* and held the last note longer than written. Michael followed superbly.

During their song, Lillian, Jonathan and Missy had been seated.

When Helene and Michael finished singing they sat down. Michael took out a handkerchief and removed beads of sweat from his forehead.

Mrs. Theofanus patted his arm. "Good job," she whispered, "particularly since we didn't go over it."

"Thanks."

The phone light lit again. Mr. Flanagan answered and said to Mrs. Theofanus, "They're ready."

She stood up and began chanting in Latin words that Michael knew meant, "Grant them eternal rest, O Lord, and let perpetual light shine upon them."

The pallbearers rolled the casket into position in front of the altar between the first few pews. The altar boys rang the bells, and the celebrants entered the nave of St. Stephen's from the sacristy.

Father Fitzpatrick greeted the congregation. "Good morning, Mrs. Jonathan Anthony Taylor, Mr. Jonathan Taylor and Mrs. Melissa Taylor, Ladies and Gentlemen. The Taylor family and St. Stephen's welcomes you here this morning to participate in Mass for our dearly departed Christian brother, Jonathan Anthony Taylor. There are programs in your pews to help you follow along this morning because everything will be in Latin with the exception of the two eulogies, one by Mr. Willington Balmoral and the other by Mr. Jonathan Taylor. Because Mr. Taylor was such a great supporter of music and the arts, we are being blessed this morning with a gift from the Metro-Tri-State Opera and Orchestra and from soloists Dame Helene Theofanus and Mr. Michael Anthony Manganaro. They are providing our liturgical music. Gabriel Fauré wrote the main portions of the Mass music this morning."

Father Fitzpatrick chanted, "*Requiem aeternam dona eis, Domine, et lux perpetua luceat eis.*" He and the altar boys took seats on the altar.

The choir stood. The organist pressed the pedals for the solo note for four beats, and the solemn singing began

While the choir was singing the *Introit* and *Kyrie,* the church filled to capacity, and the ushers were opening folding chairs for people standing in the aisles. Michael didn't notice because he was intent on following the conductor. The *Offertory* began with the organ introduction, and then singing by the altos and tenors. Michael joined the basses when they began immediately before his solo, so he wouldn't start cold. The basses, altos and tenors ended, and there was a small interlude introducing the baritone solo. Michael took a deep breath at the beginning of the last measure and began softly and sweetly, "*Hostias et preces tibi, Domine...*"

Mr. Balmoral gave a moving eulogy. It sounded like the formal obituary that appeared in the newspaper, but anyone who was sensitive could tell that he cared a great deal about his deceased friend.

Jonathan stood on the pulpit. Michael could hardly see him from the choir loft, but he could hear him clearly. "I am sad today that I have lost my father, as is my father's wife, Lillian, that she lost her husband, and that his former wife, my mother, is very sad that she lost her dearest friend. And I am sure that you are sad, too, for losing one of your friends and/or business associates. While we all have lost a great deal, we have so much that my dad gave to all of us to take with us going forward with our lives. He touched so many people in his short life. We will miss him, but we will remember all he has given to us. My family and I," he said looking first at Lillian and then Missy, "are thankful to each of you for coming this morning. We are more thankful than you'll ever know to Metro-Tri-State Opera and Orchestra and to Dame Theofanus and Mr. Manganaro for this appropriate music this morning. My dad would have felt honored. Please join us this afternoon at the conclusion of the cemetery ceremony at our home to share some thoughts about my dad and for some luncheon. Our address is on the back of the program. Dad, I know, is pleased that you all came." Jonathan took his seat between Lillian and Missy.

The choir sang *Sanctus*, and Dame Theofanus sang *Pie Jesu*. Her singing made Jonathan's eyes tear and his nose run. He reached over to Lillian and rested his hand on her cast. She put her other hand on top of his. Missy handed him a tissue. He blew his nose, sat up straight, and regained his composure.

After the *Agnus Dei* by Michael C. Burris was finished, the congregation went to receive communion. Michael watched the congregation. He didn't go.

Mr. Flanagan played a medley of well-known Catholic hymns from a hymnal he found in the organ bench. The hymns reminded everyone who had been brought up as Catholics about childhood. Michael smiled to himself, "The only thing we're missing is Bing Crosby."

Lillian looked at the altar and at the flowers. The candles on all the pews were elegant and needed on a day like this. Everything at Stokes and Stokes had been elegant, too. Jonathan even had coffee and small cakes available in the lounge downstairs to make guests comfortable. He had chosen everything with extremely good taste. How glad she was that she let him do everything on his own. She hadn't even seen the memorial program until she got hers in her pew. As a matter of fact, she didn't even know that one existed. She wondered where he got the idea. Michael was too busy with his music, and he hadn't mentioned it. It must have been Missy. That's what she was so busy doing with Stokes and Stokes, the newspaper, Mr. Flanagan and the printer on the phone. Bless her! She intended to put the program in her cedar chest and keep it always. A tear ran down her cheek as she thought how much she would miss him. How much indeed. But she caught herself before she burst into full tears. God has sent me the person he loved the most—his son. And his son came with a significant other, whom she suspected was more special than anyone could have predicted for Jonathan. And then there was Missy. She was special in many ways, but unfortunately, very few people ever saw beyond her beauty.

When the church service was ended, Mrs. Theofanus and Michael were standing outside.

"Michael, you better find Jonathan," Mrs. Theofanus said as she moved up on the steps to look over the heads of those gathered in front of the church. She spotted the Taylors getting in a limousine waiting at the curb. "There they are. You should go with them, Michael. I'm going with the Balmorals.

"You're right. I'm on my way. Thank you for everything. You helped me a lot, and I appreciate it. I'll see you later at the apartment. You are coming, aren't you?

"You're welcome, Michael, and I will be there."

Michael's parents were on their way out of the church looking for Michael, but the car with the Taylor family and Michael had already left.

Mr. and Mrs. Balmoral were standing with Mrs. Theofanus. They waved to Louisa and Anthony. Louisa and Anthony went over to Mr. and Mrs. Balmoral.

"Are you going to join us at the cemetery? Did you drive from Mellon?"

"Yes, we did, but I don't know my way around New Jersey and with this snow, I thought we would just head back home."

"You're welcome to join us. We have plenty of room. Our driver is from New Jersey. We'll drop you off later where you parked your car, or at the Taylor apartment," Mrs. Balmoral invited.

"Anthony, I'd like to," Louisa said.

"Sure," Anthony agreed.

Louisa was dying to talk to Mrs. Theofanus. She was feeling that maybe Michael could get the chance she never had. The fact that the Taylors wanted him to sing with these wonderful professionals made her think that one day he might become one of them.

Everyone was silent as the car headed down Ninth Avenue toward the Lincoln Tunnel. They were in New Jersey when Jenny spoke, "You're going to miss him a lot, aren't you, Bill?"

"Yes. He was one of a kind."

"I've only met him a few times myself, but everyone has always spoken so highly of him, I felt like I've known him, too," Mrs. Theofanus said.

"You would have loved him. Not only was he an honest, kind guy, but also everything he touched turned into gold. He did several favors for me in the past, and I hope I'll be able to repay him by helping Lillian and Jonathan," Willington said. "By the way, Helene, you were wonderful this morning. I've never heard you sing better."

"Thank you."

"The *Ave Maria* you did together brought tears to so many eyes. And that young man you sang with was splendid," Mrs. Balmoral said. "He is your son, isn't he, Mr. and Mrs. Manganaro?"

"Yes."

"Thank you, Jenny. He came over to my place yesterday to practice. He really has a beautiful voice. I hope he can continue his musical education. It was a real pleasure singing with him. He's completely unaffected. Doesn't think he's as good as he is, and that's refreshing," Dame Theofanus said.

Louisa said, "He's a little shy. He would rather be part of a group than stand out. I'm surprised he agreed to sing this morning, but if Jonathan asked him I can understand. He's always been the type of person who would go through any discomfort for someone he cares about. I appreciate your taking the time to coach my son, Mrs. Theofanus. It was very nice of you. The music this morning was very uplifting. The voices of the choir members blended smoothly. Your singing with my son was very special, Mrs. Theofanus. It is something I will remember always."

"Thank you. It was my pleasure. I hope to be able to sing with him in the future at a happier occasion. And I think he is going to have to learn to enjoy standing out, because I have the strongest feeling that the world will one-day know Michael Anthony Manganaro. I do so feel it."

Louisa bit her lip. This is what she had wanted to hear. She hoped Dame Theofanus was right.

Their car had been following the Taylor's car, which had just pulled over onto the shoulder of the roadway before entering the New Jersey Turnpike South. Max, the driver of the lead car, came back to the driver of the Balmoral car and told him that the hearse and seven flower cars would be going on first, and that the automobile procession would take a slightly longer route, so that Stokes and Stokes would have time to set up the burial site.

Jonathan was sitting next to Lillian in the first car. He was thinking about his father. "Oh, Lillian, Lillian, I feel so fuckin' awful," he managed to get out before he burst into tears. He laid his head on her lap and cried.

"I know, Johnny. I know." Tears ran down her face and Michael noticed her mascara running with them.

Missy was sitting on the other side of Lillian, and she had been sobbing ever since Ninth Avenue in Manhattan.

Michael was seated facing the others, and he couldn't understand why, but he began crying, too.

Chapter 46

The caterers were loading rinsed dishes and silverware into plastic carriers in the reception hall. There were two four-foot high stacks of rented gear as well as two stacks of folding chairs waiting for the truck. The waiters were busy picking up ashtrays and collecting table clothes and napkins, which were scattered everywhere, including the bathrooms. Now they were making the final exploration for glasses.

Adele was on her hands and knees trying to get a Merlot stain out of the beige carpet with seltzer and a big, old terry cloth bath towel.

Jonathan and Michael, both dressed in heavy winter coats, hats and gloves, came in from the foyer where they had cleaned their feet on the carpet provided for that purpose. "We're back," announced a red-faced Jonathan.

"Well, how did it go? Did you get them out?" Lillian inquired.

"Yes, but let me tell you, it was not the easiest thing to do," Jonathan explained.

"The snow plow really crammed them in," Michael added.

Lillian continued, "Well I'm sure glad my stepson and stepson-in-law were here to help. The building usually has four people on duty, two doormen, a handyman and a superintendent, or an assistant super, but because of the holiday weekend, they only had one doorman on duty, which would have been fine if it hadn't snowed. So, I'm glad you guys were here."

"Well, we got everybody out and on their way. We even helped shovel out some guest of Dr. Orsini, too. You know, the famous plastic surgeon on the seventh floor."

"Well, I'm glad you made friends with him. Never know when I'll need a favor. What do you think, Missy?" she asked stretching her neck and making faces.

"Not just yet, but he's so young, he should still be around when we need him."

Jonathan and Michael threw their coats, hats and gloves on Jonathan's bed and went back to the library. Adele, Missy and Lillian were seated in the center of the room in a small semi-circle on randomly placed chairs. Michael and Jonathan pulled up chairs facing them.

Lillian kicked off her shoe. "God, that feels good."

"Would anyone like something to drink?" Michael asked, beginning to feel at home at *Taylorville,* as he had nicknamed the apartment, standing up and walking to the bar.

"Bless you, Michael. How about a tumbler of champagne?"

Michael held up a highball glass.

"No, Michael. The water tumbler. I'm very thirsty and could really use a big drink."

Michael smiled and slowly filled a tumbler, so it wouldn't foam up and run over.

"Can I have a scotch and soda, Michael?" Adele asked.

"Ginger ale for me," Missy said.

"I'll help you, Michael. I particularly want to watch you make us some Manhattans."

They all began to relax and sipped their drinks. Each was exhausted, emotionally and physically.

"I want to thank you for your help today. It was some day. Jonathan, you did a swell job with everything. I didn't have to worry about a thing. When I first came out of the fog that I was in at the hospital, thinking about arranging the funeral and getting your father back home, making plans for the church and the cemetery overwhelmed me. I couldn't figure out how to manage. Then I thought of you. You could do it, and, Jonathan, you did. You did a spectacular job. I am pleased. Only one thing spooked me, and that was when I saw what you had chosen for your father to wear."

"What?"

"Well, you picked the nicest suit in your dad's closet."

"And?" Jonathan encouraged.

"Well, it wasn't his suit. It was the suit he had made for you for your Christmas present. He wanted you to try it on while you were home on leave in case it needed any alterations."

"Well, he did have great taste. It was the most beautiful suit in the closet."

"That it was, Jonathan, and the most expensive. He kept bringing samples of fabrics home for me to look at. When Mr. Luizza, the tailor, came to pay his respects, he recognized the suit and mentioned it to me. When I told him what had happened, he said he was honored that you had chosen his suit for your father, and that you should stop by his shop and chose another fabric, and he would replace the suit in time for Christmas as a gift to us."

"Gee, Lillian, that's really sweet of him. I'll stop by in the next day or so."

"I thought the reception here this afternoon went very well. You chose a great combination of foods, Jonathan. I understand from Bruno of Anthony's that we had 183 people, not including us. He told me he'll be sending the bill next week, and that he's reducing his per person charge by $2 because the guests consumed much less alcohol than at the usual affairs that he services."

"He mentioned that to me, too, Lillian. Sounds good," Jonathan said.

"And, Missy, I can't thank you enough for that wonderful keepsake program. How did you ever come up with it?"

"Well, Lillian, I've worked on a lot of souvenir journals and programs for charity functions, so when I called St. Stephen's and was told that they routinely only prepare a folded 8-1/2 by 11 inch sheet for funeral Masses for the congregation, I went into action. The printer that Taylor Oil uses did it for us at no cost. It really wasn't that difficult to put it together. I'm so glad you liked it."

"Liked it? I loved it."

Jonathan said, "Mom, you did a swell job." He walked over to his mother and kissed her.

"Thanks, Jonathan."

Lillian sat up straight in her mobile chair. "And now we have Michael."

Michael smiled and looked at Lillian. She smiled back. A special bond had developed between them during the long train trip home from Miami.

"Michael, you sang so very nicely. You helped ease some of the pain I was feeling. Your music came from your heart, and if I could feel it, I'm sure that the others could feel it as well. I don't think any of the guests who came this afternoon failed to mention you except your parents, but they were busy receiving compliments on your behalf from everyone they met. You really did a fine job. I'm glad we twisted your arm."

"Thank you, Lillian. I was scared to death, but I did the best I could."

"Michael, you were the best," Missy said. "I hope you pursue music as a career."

"Mom, that's what Dame Theofanus said," offered Jonathan. "I thought you were wonderful, Michael. We all thank you."

"Thanks. But the next time I sing, I want it to be on a happy function like midnight Mass on Christmas."

Lillian laughed. "I think we can all identify with your feeling about that."

"Lillian," Adele said, "I'm going to be headed home to my family in a few minutes to spend the weekend at home. But I'll see you bright and early on Monday morning."

"That's good, Adele. I appreciate your holding this place together and for answering hundreds of phone calls. Thank you very much. I suppose the subways are empty on a night like this, but Max could drive you if you like."

"No, thanks. The subways are safer in this type of weather, and I'm sure Max would like to get home to visit his family, too."

"You know, I've been so tied up, I completely forgot to let him know that we won't need him for the weekend. Does anyone need Max before Monday?"

They shook their heads.

"Missy, Madeline, the nice nurse the hospital in Florida sent with me, is resting. Poor thing is pooped taking care of this cranky invalid. Could you take me down the elevator to the garage? I want to thank Max in person."

"Sure, Lillian. Do you need a coat?"

"No, it's really all inside."

"Is Madeline still going to go back tomorrow?" Missy asked.

"No, maybe I forgot to mention it, but she is going to stay until Monday morning."

Lillian finished her champagne.

Jonathan said, "Since Thanksgiving passed us this year, I thought we all need a little bit of fun. I hope I'm not suggesting something disrespectful or inappropriate..."

"You could never suggest something disrespectful, Jonathan," Missy interrupted.

"And I agree," Lillian concurred. "What did you have in mind?"

"First, I called to make sure we could get tickets, if you cared to go."

"Go where?" Michael asked.

"The Christmas Show at Radio City Music Hall. They're holding six seats for us for the 10 o'clock show tomorrow morning."

"Jonathan, what a wonderful idea! Not something everyone would think appropriate for a widow in mourning, but under our circumstances, I think it is a great thought. I'd love to go."

"I'm glad. I thought that since Madeline was going to be here until Monday, she'd like to go, too. They give special seating for wheelchair people in the front," Jonathan laughed. "Might as well capitalize on your position."

Lillian laughed, "Your father always said when the world gives you lemons, make lemonade."

"Mom, Michael, are you game?"

"Count me in," Missy said and turned to Michael and said, "And, of course, this cute young man has no choice." Michael lowered his head and smiled at Missy, and turned toward Jonathan nodding his head in approval.

Lillian said, "Okay, that's five of us. Adele won't be in town. You said you had six seats reserved."

"Oh, I forgot the surprise, which along with your wheels will assure us of terrific seats."

Michael asked, "Which is?"

"During lunch this afternoon, I asked Mrs. Theofanus if she had ever been to the Christmas Show. When I told her my plan and invited her, she said she would love to go, and that it would be one of the highlights of her visit to the United States."

Lillian was clearly pleased. He is going to be a mover and shaker just like his father. She was beginning to see Jonathan Anthony in Jonathan. She could almost read his mind. He expects to spend his life with Michael, and he's laying the groundwork for Michael's success. And he was subtle, just like JAT. And there was another thing she observed just today that reminded her of her husband. He sprang back quickly from unhappiness and defeat. Just this morning he was crying in her lap, and this afternoon he was working on a new level. He was doing something good for each of them. He's helping all of us and setting up Michael's future and his own. She hadn't even noticed it before, but he had been "working the room" for the last two hours. He greeted everyone and brought special people, whom he thought might be useful in the future, over to meet her as if she were a reigning monarch on a throne, instead of an injured widow in a wheelchair. She also became aware that Jonathan, for the first time, referred to her, and introduced her, as his second mom. She loved being thought of like that and being addressed as his second mom pleased her, but she realized that he would personally get more mileage out of that than calling her Lillian, my stepmother, or my father's wife. She even heard him say to a senator and his wife, "That was my buddy from boot camp singing. He's a great guy. Would you believe he came all the way from Mellon to Miami to help me escort my second mom home? After all she'd been through, I couldn't just let her travel home with only a nurse, who was a stranger, after all. It's one of the reasons Mr. Balmoral thought I should ask for a release from active duty in the Navy at this time. There are just so many family matters to tend to." Yes, she thought, he knows what he's doing. Not a word without thought. Not a word misspent. Which reminded her about a conversation she had with Governor Richards earlier. He said that as soon as Willington Balmoral got in touch with himself and the Senator, they both got letters off immediately to the Department of Defense and the Department of the Navy. She must remember to tell Jonathan later.

"Jonathan," Lillian said, "I love the Christmas Show idea. We'll go to the show at 10, and I'll treat everyone to a belated Thanksgiving lunch at Sardi's. Then, Jonathan, why don't you and Michael go to Mellon and enjoy the weekend? The next business meeting isn't until Tuesday morning at 10 a.m. at Taylor Oil."

"Michael," Jonathan asked, "am I invited?"

"Yes, of course. What a great time we'll have. I'll call my mother as soon as we get back to our room."

"Great. Now I'm tired and want to rest. I didn't have anything planned for dinner. Maybe you'll want to go out. If not, there's plenty of food left over."

"We may just take a walk. We can walk Adele to the subway. The sidewalks still have a lot of ice."

Adele said, "I'd appreciate that."

"Mom, why don't you come, too?"

"I will, but first I want to take Lillian down to the garage to speak to Max. We'll be right back."

When they came back from the garage, Michael, Jonathan, Missy and Adele dressed for the outdoors.

Missy said, "I'm off, Lillian, with our two young men."

"Goodnight. Walk safely. See you in the morning. Maybe Michael will whip up something great for us for breakfast."

Missy helped Lillian into her room, and then they all left.

Lillian sat down at her dressing table and kissed the photograph of Jonathan Anthony. "I told you he was a great kid, and now he will be a great man. I know that you wouldn't approve of Michael, but, trust me, it's good for him."

She turned off the lamp and managed to crawl into bed. She cried into her pillow.

Chapter 47

It took the Manganaros a long time to drive from the city to Mellon. The traffic was heavy, and it was slowed by several areas of rubbernecking at minor fender benders. There were no serious accidents that they observed, probably because no one could go over thirty miles per hour. The snow was still coming down when they reached Maiden Lane. As they approached their home, they could see the red Spitfire in the forward part of the driveway.

"Louisa, I want to pull up behind Rosa, but I first want to shovel the driveway behind her car, so we can both get out later, or tomorrow if we have to."

"Good idea. The good shovel should be in the garage. I'll go in and put on some fresh coffee and start some supper."

"Thanks, Louisa."

Rosa heard them pull up, and she came out all bundled up. Anthony opened the garage door and took out the sturdy black shovel.

"Hi, Ma, Dad. The snow's been coming down all afternoon. I shoveled the driveway once already. Let me give you a hand, Dad."

"Thanks, Rosa."

"Hi, sweetie. I am going in to put on some coffee and start supper. Would you like some meatloaf? It'll be done in time for *Playhouse 120*."

Rosa walked up to her father and said, "Where have you guys been? You've been gone since 7:30 this morning, and it's close to 8:00 p.m. now."

"Your mother, I'm sure, will fill you in on all the details over supper, but in a nutshell, we heard your brother, you know the one, Michael, sing at the funeral. He was very, very good. We're going to lose him someday, if we haven't already."

"What do you mean 'lose him?' You haven't lost him and you're not going to."

"Rosa, he's moving in a different circle these days. I thought he'd meet some regular guys when he went into the Navy, maybe invite them home during his leave, hang out, have a few beers, watch footfall."

"Well, Dad, he did meet someone nice, Jonathan."

"Gees, Rosa. That's the problem. Jonathan and his folks are not like us. No way. They are loaded. Their apartment is six times as big as our house."

"There's nothing wrong with having money, Daddy. Jonathan seems very well-educated and very sweet."

"Sweet. Shit. Be careful of the car's tires with that sharp shovel."

"Yeah, Dad."

"Sweet. Michael seems completely taken in by their lifestyle, the glamour and stuff. And he sticks next to Jonathan like they were Siamese twins."

Rosa thought about seeing them together in bed last Saturday morning. So I won't have a sister-in-law by Michael, but a super rich, good-looking brother-in-law. That would be okay, too.

Rosa said, "Dad, are you a wee bit jealous?"

"No! And I don't want to talk about it anymore."

"Okay."

They continued with the snow removal.

"And, Rosa, would you believe that Governor Richards was there with his wife? We met them. He told your mother that he expected to see and hear Michael within the next ten years at the Metro-Tri-State Opera. Phony bastard!"

"Dad, I've never heard you curse before except for the time the zoning commission wanted to stop us from having our six chickens."

"I'm sorry, Rosa. I'm tired from all the driving in the snow and the funeral and the cemetery thing. It was heavy duty. And the reception at their home was very elegant, and I suppose I felt out of place. But it really was good, and everybody treated us nicely. Jonathan's stepmother and his mother went out of their way to make us feel comfortable. I guess it's just me. I work on the assembly line for God's sake, and Governor Richards has his arm around Michael's shoulder telling him he's going to be internationally famous one day. Your mother loved it. She ate it up."

"Well, I'm glad she had a good time."

"Oh, and Rosa, the man from Hill House, Mr. Willington Balmoral, took us in his limousine to the cemetery and back. I enjoyed the ride. He and his wife were down-to-earth people. That surprised me. They were particularly nice to your mother. Oh, and by the way, Jenny, his wife, says you helped her at the bank last week and that you were very gracious."

"Well that's nice to hear," she said as she surveyed the driveway. "I think we're done. Let's go in. I forgot my finger covers."

"Finger covers! Sometimes you even talk just like that silly ass brother of yours. Finger covers."

"I love him, Dad, no matter what."

"Even if…"

"Yes, even if."

Anthony pulled his car into the cleared space on the driveway, and they went inside. Louisa was busy in the kitchen. Anthony and Rosa put their wet clothes over the back of the chairs near the fireplace. Rose had kept a good fire going all afternoon. She had been snuggled under one of their mother's afghans reading Grace Metalious' *Peyton Place*. She decided to read it when she had some privacy. Louisa thought the book was trash, pure and simple. But Michael had read it, and thought it was great and gave it to his sister. He put paper clips on the good parts in case she didn't get to read the whole thing. Norman was a wimp, and even though she wasn't into rich guys, she thought that Rodney Harrington was one hot stud. She flushed when she got to the parked car incident at the dance with Betty and Rodney. Whew!

Anthony was in the kitchen warming himself by the coal stove.

"Louisa, do you think we lost Michael?"

Louisa frowned as the phone rang. Anthony picked it up.

"Hello?"

"Dad, did you get home safe?"

"Yes, Mike, but it took a long time. We just got home a little while ago. Rosa helped me shovel the driveway. Your mother is making supper."

"I'm glad you got home all right. Thanks for coming today. I felt so much more comfortable when I saw you and mom walk down the aisle."

"You sang good, Michael. The whole group sang good. I enjoyed it. Your mother did, too, very much, needless to say. The cemetery thing was depressing. The beautiful flowers and the snow softened the reality that someone was going to be buried in the ground forever."

"I know what you mean, Dad, and I felt the same way."

"I'm proud of you. You looked classy standing with his family."

"I'm glad you came."

"Your mother was beside herself when she heard from Mrs. Theofanus that you would really be a top-notch performer someday."

"Dad, she always says nice things. We're getting ready for bed. Dad, did you like their apartment? What did you think of our room?"

"The place was nicer than anything I've seen in the movies, and it's nice that you can share Jonathan's room. The view is spectacular."

"We're all going to the Christmas Show tomorrow morning, then to lunch, and if it's okay with you, Jonathan and I would like to come home to Mellon through Monday afternoon to spend some time with you guys."

"Home? Here? Of course, it's all right. Louisa, Michael and Jonathan are coming home tomorrow afternoon to spend some time with us. Is that okay?"

"Anthony, give me the phone. Michael, we miss you a lot even though we actually spent most of the day together. We want you home, here. I want Jonathan here, as well. I like him very much. So does your father. I'll get your room ready with its wonderful view of the driveway."

"Ma!"

"See you tomorrow. Enjoy the show, and please thank Lillian for her hospitality."

"Bye, Ma."

Rosa came into the kitchen. "I overheard. They're coming home."

"Yes," Louisa said.

"I'm glad," Rosa said.

"Looks like I was wrong before, Rosa. Doesn't look like we lost him at all. We just gained another son."

"Yeah. Right."

Chapter 48

Michael and Jonathan went back to their room. Michael dialed home and turned off the light when his father answered. He was standing near the glass doors in the dark room looking about over the sparkling lights of the city. The Empire State Building looked like a tall jewel. He had removed all his clothes except for his boxer shorts and placed them over a chair by the table. Jonathan came up behind him and put his hands on Michael's hips, as Michael spoke to his father. Jonathan knelt behind him and kissed each cheek of his butt through his shorts. He slid the shorts down over Michael's legs, and Michael stepped out of them.

After Michael said, "Bye, Dad," he turned facing Jonathan, who was kneeling before him.

"They are really looking forward to our visit tomorrow. They like you, Jonathan. I knew they would."

"I'm looking forward to being back there, particularly after this week in the city," Jonathan said as be buried his face into Michael's pubic hair. The phone rang.

"Hello," Michael answered.

"Hi, Michael. It's Gary. I got your number from your mother last Monday when I had dinner at your house."

"You did? That's nice."

"Yeah. I helped fill in the hole that you and Rosa left. We went to the movies after supper. I had a nice time."

"I'm glad you did. I miss you Gary. There's so much I want to talk to you about. I wish you would have come to the Mass this morning."

"I did come. You sounded terrific. I know that you are going to make it some day. I always felt that you would."

"I didn't know that you were there. I didn't see you."

"Of course, you didn't. You were so professionally busy singing with the Metro-Tri-State, you didn't have time to say hello to your old friend, who was waving his young ass off down in the pit trying to get your attention."

"Oh. I'm sorry, Gary. I really was busy concentrating on my music today. It was the biggest musical moment in my life."

"I know, Mike. I'm just teasing. I saw you leaving with the family, and I couldn't get close."

"I'm sorry about that. I'm actually thrilled that you came. Why didn't you come to the apartment?"

"I was with a new friend."

"New friend?"

"Yeah. He was kind enough to drive me down. My car's in the shop."

"Who is he? Never heard about him before."

"His name is Addison. Addison Konklin."

"I mean, is he like a date?"

"More than a date, Michael. More like he likes me sexually."

"Excuse me?"

"He's about ten years older than me, and very experienced."

"Experienced at what, Gary?"

"At pleasing me when me make love."

Michael almost dropped the phone.

"Gary we have to talk. I'll be home tomorrow afternoon. Maybe we could get together over the weekend and talk."

"Sure. I'd like that. I'll call you tomorrow."

"Great, Gary. Thanks for calling. I'll talk to you tomorrow. Bye now."

Michael hung up and walked over to the bed. Jonathan was already comfortably in it.

"Jonathan, that was Gary. He found someone."

"That's nice."

Michael reached over and put his hand on Jonathan's arm. Jonathan turned over with his back to Michael.

"I'm really tired tonight. Exhausted as a matter of fact," Jonathan said softly.

"Okay, good night, Jonathan."

"Good night, Michael."

Ten minutes went by. Michael felt very badly. He made Jonathan unhappy. Michael wanted to fix this. He had to.

"Jonathan, I made a mistake. Please forgive me."

"What mistake?"

"With the long tough week we had together, when we were finally ready to be alone, and get to bed for much needed pleasure and sleep, I took a phone call that could and should have waited. I should have told Gary that I'd call him back tomorrow."

Jonathan rolled over to face Michael.

"Michael, we both had a hard week and you were wonderful to do all the things you did. I over-reacted. Forgive me, Precious. Please. I love you so. I can't stand when you reject me. I feel like your approval is more important than anything in the world to me. I've never experienced anything like this feeling."

"I think I understand because I have very similar feelings. I sometimes feel as if I'm losing my mind. I've never felt like this before. I want you to be so happy. My entire existence revolves around you. I love you so, Jonathan. I didn't mean it. I didn't mean to hurt you at all. Hopefully, I never will."

"I know. I didn't either. Together we'll be a great team, Michael. I know it. I want you always with me, beside me."

"I know, Jonathan, and I think others can tell what we feel for each other. I have a sense that my mother and father are onto us, and I don't think it's going to be as bad as I once thought it would be."

"You know, Michael, I have the same feeling."

"If I turn over on my stomach, would you go back and start over?"

"Yes, if you want me to."

Michael gave Jonathan a quick kiss on his lips, and Michael turned onto his stomach, propped the top of his body up on his elbows, spread his legs just a little and said, "I want you to."

Chapter 49

It was late afternoon, and the sun was already beginning to set behind the mountains when they arrived at the bungalow on Maiden Lane. Jonathan loved the smell of burning wood that permeated the air from the fireplace inside the house. He saw the smoke coming from the chimney on the side of the roof. Michael parked his car on the street behind a huge mound of snow left by the snowplows by the curb in front of the Manganaros' house. Anthony, Rosa and Louisa came out the front door when they heard them arrive. Butterball followed. They stayed on the small path from the front porch to the driveway.

"Welcome home," Rosa shouted as she ran toward them with Butterball at her feet.

"Hiya, Rosa. You look terrific," her brother answered.

"You do, too. I'm glad you're back. And, Jonathan, I'm glad you're here, as well. I missed you, and I've felt sad all week thinking about what you were going through. I'm sorry that your dad died, and last Sunday evening was the most horrible Sunday night I ever remembered. What a shocker! Let me give you a welcome-back hug!"

Jonathan wrapped Rosa tightly in his arms and held her for a while. He kissed her on her cheek and whispered, "Thank you, Rosa. It's been one hell of a week." He squeezed her again and released her.

"I'm happy you've come back with Michael. I feel like I have two little brothers to look after."

"You're a sweetheart."

"My mom and dad told me you have a great apartment in the city. I'd love to see it sometime."

"Michael mentioned that you go to banking college two nights a week. Why don't you come by the apartment one of those nights and check it out? And if you ever need a place to stay overnight, you can use our room, Michael's and mine, and we can sleep in the library or music room on one of the sofa beds."

"So Michael told you about A.I.B."

"What's A.I.B.?"

"The American Institute of Banking."

"I recognize that name now. There was an article recently in the Sunday magazine about their occupying the top two floors of the Woolworth building."

"That's it. Jonathan you know everything."

"Hardly."

"Hello, Mr. and Mrs. Manganaro."

"Glad you made it, Jonathan," Anthony said.

"Me, too, Jonathan. How are things at home?" Louisa asked.

"Actually, after this past week everything should be moving uphill. Things have settled down somewhat, and I can't begin to tell you how happy I am to be here with you today. I missed you and your home this last week. My two moms and I are glad you could join us yesterday. I'm sure Michael was pleased you were there, as well."

"Well, Jonathan, we were glad to give you support." Louisa said, "You're family."

"She's right, Jonathan. But let's take this inside. It's freezing out her. Come on."

Michael was smiling inside and outside, as he listened to the comments of his family and watched their body language. They stood very close to Jonathan, and his father put his arm around his shoulder. For sure, they knew. Michael and Jonathan followed the family in the warmth of the home.

Soon they were all sitting on the living room rug talking. Michael and Jonathan were both on the floor with Butterball between them. Michael was leaning back with his left hand behind him supporting himself.

Louisa said, "That's a lovely ring, Michael. I thought you didn't like to wear a ring."

"You're right, Mom. Normally, I don't."

"Jonathan was wearing a ring just like it last week," Rosa pumped.

"I was. I was wearing it until this morning, as a matter of fact, when Michael here wanted to try it on. And he did," Jonathan laughed, "and it got stuck, and he couldn't get it off. He almost drove us off the Taconic trying. I told him to wait until we got here and use some soap."

Michael was relieved. Bless you, Jonathan. You always know what to say. "Maybe we should do that now. Come on, Jonathan, give me a hand."

Anthony said, "Same thing happened to me when I gained a few pounds a couple years ago. Haven't been able to get my wedding band off since. I'm going down to the cellar to work on the new heating system for the chickens for the winter. We can't keep bringing them into the cellar." Anthony went down the stairs to the basement.

Rosa looked at Louisa. Louisa looked at Rosa.

"It's going to take him a while, Rosa, but he'll come around. Quite frankly, I'm surprised at your reaction."

"I am, too. I'm not shocked or turned-off, or anything negative. I even like the idea a lot. They're perfect for each other, and they look simply yummy side-by-side."

"I need a mother-daughter hug."

They embraced, and they both had tears in their eyes.

"Let's let them know that we know, and that we approve when the time is right," Rosa suggested.

"I think that is a super idea if I ever heard one."

They walked outside the bathroom door and Louisa knocked three times hard.

"We're in here."

"Well, are you decent, or not? Rosa and I have something to tell you," Louisa said.

"Sure, we're decent. Just trying to get the ring off. Come on in."

"Michael, Jonathan, Rosa and I know it's not stuck. I watched your behavior at the reception yesterday. You never left each other for two minutes. You probably didn't even realize it, but you were both constantly touching each other. I love you both. I think I know how strongly you like each other, and I want you to know that."

"And that goes double for me. I have loved you since the days I used to beat you up, Michael, and I am thrilled beyond belief that you met someone in the least likely place—serving your country. And Jonathan, I like you very, very much, and my mother and I welcome you to the family."

They all hugged and kissed until Anthony banged on the door.

"What kind of things are going on in there? I gotta go!"

Louisa pulled the ring off Michael's finger and opened the door.

"Nothing, Anthony. We just got the ring off. It was really stuck." She was holding it in front of Anthony's face between her thumb and index finger. "It almost went down the toilet, but I caught it, or you would have been out in the septic tank with a strainer without finger covers."

Anthony laughed. "It wouldn't be the first time."

Louisa handed the ring back to Michael after Anthony closed the door, and they headed back to the living room.

Louisa looked at the clock on the mantel and said, "Today is one of the few days I haven't been cooking something, and I'm getting hungry. How about you, Rosa?"

"I am getting hungry. How about you guys?" Rosa asked as she turned on the lamps. "It seems to be getting darker earlier and earlier."

"Starving," Michael and Jonathan answered simultaneously. Jonathan put his arm around Michael's waist and said, "How about going to the pizza place on Main Street? My treat."

Louisa said, "I accept. Let me go ask Anthony?" She left the room.

Rosa said, "I love the pizza there."

"And I haven't been there since sometime in August," Michael added. "What made you think of John's?"

"Well, every time we drove past it, it smelled great. And I always saw a lot of people going in and out."

"Food's fabulous," Michael said.

"And everyone from the whole town goes there," Rosa said.

Louis returned. "Anthony's going to stay home and work on the chicken heater, but he wants us to bring him a provolone-and-salami on a hero when we come back."

They put on their coats and were getting ready to leave. Anthony came up from the basement and said, "Have a good time. And don't forget my sandwich." He put a folded twenty-dollar bill into Jonathan's hand and said, "Enjoy the pizza. It's the best. See you all later."

On their way to Main Street, Louisa said, "You know with the stuck ring and all, I forgot to give you your messages, Michael, and I have one for you as well, Jonathan. I put them in my pocketbook. Let me find them. Here. Michael, Maureen, Theresa and Mrs. Rhine called. Gary called, too. Then Mr. Sullivan called to ask you if you would look in on his cabin, particularly since it snowed. He wasn't able to come for Thanksgiving, but hopes to spend Christmas with his family at the cabin. He said if you had time during your leave, he'd like you to check the place out for him. He said that since the roof needed repair, he would really appreciate it if you removed the snow from it to prevent any leaking. He said he would pay you to do it. He'd also like it if you brought wood in from the shed to make sure it was dry when he came on Christmas. I told him I didn't know if you'd have the time."

"Of course, I'll have time. I'll call him when we get back. He doesn't have to pay me. He still thinks I'm fourteen."

"He's a nice man," Louisa said. "Maybe you and Jonathan could check the place out tomorrow."

"Jonathan," Michael asked, "would you like to go for a hike with me tomorrow to Sullivan's cabin. It's way up in the wooded area a little north of here."

"I'd like it a lot. Sounds like fun."

"If you go after church tomorrow, I'll pack you some food. By the time you get there and do what you have to, it may be too dark to come home. You could bring sleeping bags and stay over if you like. It seems to me that you guys could use some time alone after your busy week."

"Sounds romantic to me," Rosa kidded.

"I would like that very much," Jonathan said smiling. "I could use the time to think. And, yes, Michael, I would like to spend some quiet time alone with only you."

"Then we'll do it," Michael said, as he turned left on Main Street.

"And, Jonathan," Louisa continued, "Lillian called. She said there was a letter for you in the Saturday afternoon mail from the Department of Defense. She said she would open it and read it to you if you liked."

"Great."

John's was crowded. Gary was at the bar.

"Hey, Gary," Michael said. "We all came in for pizza. Care to join us?"

"Hi, Michael. Mrs. Manganaro, Rosa, Jonathan. I would, but I'm waiting for Addison. We're going to have a beer, and then Addison is taking me to that expensive French restaurant that just opened on Route 77. I've never had French food before, and Addison assures me that they have the best French cuisine between New York and Montreal."

"Okay, Gary. Call me later, we'll be up until midnight."

"Sure. I'll give you Gary's review of the new place."

They got the last booth available right outside the swinging doors of the kitchen. Theresa was their waitress. She came over as soon as she saw them sit down.

"Hi, folks. Mrs. Manganaro, how nice to have you here. I haven't seen you here in a year."

"Hello, Theresa. These kids of mine don't take me out that often. It feels nice not to have to cook for a change, and better still, not to have to clean up the kitchen. But before I forget, my husband would like a sandwich for us to take home to him. Can I give you that order now, so I don't forget?"

"Sure can. What will it be?"

"A provolone-and-salami on a hero. With vinegar, oil and some oregano. Okay?"

"Yes. And what would you all like tonight?"

Theresa was standing close to Jonathan with her hip against his shoulder.

Jonathan said, "I am glad to see you again, Theresa. You look nice. I think we'd like a large pizza."

"And what would you like on it?"

Rosa said, "Pepperoni."

"And," Michael added, "sausage."

And Louisa said, "And bring us a pitcher of beer."

"No problem," she said as she pushed her hip into Jonathan's arm. "Jonathan, your hair has grown a half-inch since the last time I saw you. You look really swell. I hope to see you again soon."

Theresa left for the kitchen.

Louisa observed the way she had smiled at Jonathan. She had been flirting with Jonathan. I wish she'd leave Michael's friend alone, she thought to herself. She smiled. How silly.

Theresa came back with the beer, glasses, knives, folks, napkins and small plates.

"Here you go. Your pizza will be out in a few minutes." She reached to the waiter's table and got some cheese for their table, both Parmesan and Romano.

"Theresa, you left a message today for me," Michael said.

"Oh, yes, Michael. I just wanted you to relay my condolences to Jonathan. I was devastated to hear about it."

"Thank you very much, Theresa," Jonathan said.

"Thanks, Theresa," Michael said. "We appreciate that."

"Theresa, are you still planning to go to Tulane next September?" Mrs. Manganaro asked.

"I hope so. The only thing that would hold me back now is money. But I have nine full months to get my act together. I have an aunt who lives in Baton Rogue. I may go down early next year and get a job before school and get used to the place."

"Planning ahead like you are is a good thing. I'm sure you'll do fine."

"Thanks. I'll go check on the pie."

Rosa spotted Maureen and Bruce Rollins at a small table in the corner. They waved when they realized she saw them. Rosa waved back.

Chapter 50

When they got home, Jonathan and Michael went into Michael's bedroom. Before he closed the door, Michael said to his family, "We have some phone calls to answer. I hope nobody minds, but we'll have the phone tied up for about a half-hour."

"Go ahead," Louisa said, "and don't forget to call Mr. Sullivan."

"Okay, Mom."

"Yes, Jonathan, I must remember to call Mr. Sullivan. You know, Jonathan, I just thought of something. Mr. Sullivan owns and operates a large gas station in Jersey City, New Jersey. He comes up to the cabin several times a year. He's been doing that for as long as I can recall. But the important thing I remembered is that his station is one of the largest of its kind in the metropolitan area. It's a full-service *TAYLOR OIL.*"

"Well, I remember my father mentioning that station, and it certainly seems to be successful, and that's the bottom line."

"You know, Jonathan, I'm starting to feel intimidated. You're worth millions, and I have five hundred dollars in my savings account."

"You're starting to scare me, Michael. I have never seriously thought of the money before, just that it was available, but I suppose I'm really going to have to make some changes in my life. I don't want to think about it until Monday afternoon when, I am sure, Lillian will be outlining what I should do and say at that important Taylor Oil meeting on Tuesday. Can you promise to keep my money out of our bed tonight and our sleeping bags tomorrow night?"

"Yes. But it is awesome to think about. Are you going to call Lillian first?"

"Sure. May I?" Jonathan asked as he picked up the phone and moved it to the bed. The operator connected him with his New York number.

"Hello," Lillian said.

"Well, hello, Lillian. I got your message. How are you feeling?"

"Jonathan, I can't tell you how much better I am feeling. Going to the show this morning was a real good idea. We still have a strong family. I'm glad you are home now, and that you have Michael in your life. You're lucky, and so am I. We must look beyond our loss and enjoy those things we are fortunate enough to have. Missy is sleeping. She helped me write thank you notes all afternoon. You know, Michael, she's a great record-keeper. She has all our expenses and details in an old note-book. Very neat and easy to understand. When we came back after lunch, I picked up the pile of mail the postman left in our basket in the foyer. Most of it was junk, and then I came across the one from the Defense Department."

"Sounds like we should know what's in it."

"Well, I'm opening it now."

"Great."

"Okay. I'll read it:

Department of Defense
Office of the Secretary
The United States of America
Washington, D.C.

November 23, 1960

Dear Mr. Taylor:

We received two letters on your behalf, one from Governor Richards of New York and one from Senator Goodman. Both letters recommended that your enlistment in The United States Navy be ended as soon as possible with an Honorable Discharge.

We at the Department of Defense and the Department of the Navy are very sorry to hear of your father's passing. We understand the serious responsibilities that you, as the only surviving son in your family, have now to accept. We also realize that those responsibilities will require your full-time attention.

During your stay at The Ramapo Training Center, you received straight 4.0's in all your undertakings. You were an exemplary sailor. We are sure that you would have enjoyed a wonderful experience in the

U.S. Navy, and that you would have made a great contribution to your country in The United States Military.

Enclosed are four forms that must be completed and signed in front of a Notary Public and returned in the envelope provided within 72 hours of your receipt of this letter.

It will take several weeks to process your discharge, but should you not receive it before the due date of your orders to report to your next duty station, please call the Duty Officer of that duty station the day before you are required to report and refer to this letter, a copy of which they have been provided. This will prevent unnecessary complications then and in the future.

If your situation changes in the years to come to allow your full-time participation in The United States Navy, we would recommend your re-enlistment.

We wish you well in all your endeavors, and we ask that you convey to Mrs. Jonathan Anthony Taylor and Mrs. Melissa Turner Taylor our condolences.

You are considered to be in the military on unpaid leave until you are discharged.

Sincerely yours,

Charles W. Skinner
Assistant Secretary of Defense

That's it," Lillian said.

"You mean I just have to fill out those forms, and that's it?"

"Sounds like that to me, Jonathan. I'll fill out what I can for you before you get here, and then you can complete them, and we can get Barbara Greenfeld to notarize them after you sign them in front of her after our meeting on Tuesday. That will get you in under the 72 hours requirement. We can send it back Certified Mail from the main post office on 33rd Street and Eighth Avenue."

"Thanks, Lillian. Now I can really relax. We went out tonight to the best Pizza place I've ever been to. I hope you can come up here someday, so you can taste it. Tomorrow we are going to do some work on a cabin up on the mountain for a friend of the Manganaros. It snowed very heavily here, and we are going to get the snow off the roof and get the wood ready for the owners who will be coming up for Christmas."

"Jonathan, I wish I could see your face. You sound so happy and enthusiastic. I remember when you said only losers did manual labor. I can't believe that you're looking forward to working with your hands."

"I am happy. I feel honored to be working side-by-side with Michael. I like these people a lot, Lillian."

"Believe me, Jonathan, I am a good judge of people, and you are in good hands. Oh, Jonathan, I have to get going. I'm attending an open *AA* meeting with your mother tonight at St. Andrew's. I promised. I have to wake her up, so she can get ready."

"I love you, Lillian. Michael sends his best."

"Good night, sweetheart. And give Michael a kiss for me."

Jonathan hung up the phone.

"Well, Jonathan, are you in, or out, or what?"

"Out, or almost. But I'll tell you about it later. You have phone calls to make before it gets too late."

Jonathan kissed Michael hard and quickly on the mouth. "That's from Lillian."

"Thanks."

"My kisses will come soon enough."

Michael called Mrs. Rhine and bowed out of singing for the next morning. He explained that he had had enough singing for the week, and that he was all sung out, but that he and Jonathan would be down in the congregation enjoying the music. Mrs. Rhine understood and thanked Michael for calling. She got him to agree that if there were any way he could come home for Christmas, he would help with midnight Mass.

Michael called Maureen. She wanted to see him and suggested another double date. He told her he would like to see her, as well, but he explained the work at the cabin, etc. He got off the hook for now.

Chapter 51

"Hi, Maureen. How are you this morning?"

"Great, Theresa. How are you?"

"I'm really swell this morning. My breasts are a little swollen, and my right nipple is very sensitive to touch."

"Maybe you had too much salt."

"I did have Chinese food last night, but before I ate I went to St. John's during confession time to light candles. I lit seven. You know the twenty-five-cent kind. I only had five quarters, but I lit seven anyway. I figured with all the candles I've been lighting over the years, they owed me a discount."

"Why seven, Theresa?"

"Because if in seven days my friend doesn't come to visit again, I'll know I'm in a family way."

"What family? What way?"

"Pregnant, dodo."

"You mean seven days from today?"

"No actually, from yesterday. My last period started Friday, November 4 very late at night. Almost midnight, if I remember correctly, which means, my dear Maureen, that I would have been ovulating starting probably late on the seventeenth and into the eighteenth, and if Jonathan's little sperm soldiers were as aggressive as he was—anyway, Maureen, we'll know this Friday, surely by midnight if my friend cancels the visit. I'm never late. Nevah!"

"You mean you would do all this for what reason, for money?"

"All this and a whole lot more. I want out of this crappy town."

"What would you want to do with the baby?"

"If he wants to pay for it with one of those rich city doctors, I'll have it aborted."

206

"Oh, my God! That's disgusting. It's murder, Theresa, and it's against the law! You could go to jail!"

"Not the way I see it."

"You'll go to hell. Theresa, you'll go to hell."

"Oh, brother! You're more screwed up than I ever thought you were. But don't fret for my eternal life because, if I am pregnant, I expect I would go down south to my aunt's home in Louisiana for a nice long visit and give the kid up for adoption. The last thing that I need is a kid."

"Suppose he wants to do the right thing and marry you?"

"I thought about that. He'd never in a thousand years think of that, but if he did, I'd marry him in a minute. I mean what's not to like? He's great in the sack, good-looking, nice, Catholic and very, very rich, but I'm sure he has other plans for his life that do not include me."

"I can't believe that you are serious about this. I just can't."

"Well, maybe nothing will happen. Maybe nothing has happened, but just in case, I'm all set. And the candles make me feel better."

"Are you going to Mass this morning?"

"Do I ever miss?"

"Nope. I'll see you there."

"Bye, Maureen."

Chapter 52

They woke up about the same time. They had been up late the night before, and it was a great luxury to be able to sleep in this morning. They were under the blankets and Michael had one of his legs over Jonathan's legs.

"Jonathan, it feels so good to be snuggled up with you this morning. We can just enjoy the time together. I'm glad I decided not to sing today. We can spend a leisurely morning together, have a nice quiet breakfast, pack the car for the cabin trip, and then head to church where we can relax. I've never sat with you at Mass in the congregation before."

"That's right. I am looking forward to have you sitting next to me today. Let's sit way up front. I love looking at the artwork on the altar. The crucifix is one of the nicest I've ever seen. We can even walk around and take in the Stations of the Cross. And today I won't be so nervous, because I'll know that you're not coming up to the plate. You'll be with me. Every time you sang, I was more nervous than I think you were."

"Jonathan, your hair is growing. Theresa was right. And now that you're not going back, you can let your hair grow. By Christmas, your hair will be as long and as beautiful as it was when I first saw you."

Jonathan rolled over on top of Michael and pinned his wrists to the bed over his head.

"I'm going to tease you until you're crazy with passion, and then I'm going to stop," he said as he began rubbing his penis against Michael's stomach. He could feel Michael get hard, and he felt Michael's penis sliding up and down the crack of his butt. "You like this, don't you?"

"Yes," Michael said. "You could make me crazy. You really could. I want you so. I always want you."

"Good. That's what I like to hear. I like to hear how much you like all the things I do to you."

They could hear Louisa, Anthony and Rosa setting the table in the dining room. When there was time on Sunday mornings with no nervous soloists, they usually had a big breakfast. Louisa liked to bring out the old waffle iron she got as a wedding present and make her favorite, and everyone else's, recipe. They always had fresh-squeezed orange juice, hickory-smoked breakfast sausage, scrambled eggs with cream cheese, mushrooms and onions. Anthony liked to have red and green peppers sautéed with some Italian hot sausage as well. Louisa used the special coffee she bought on Main Street from Beans and Things instead of the regular coffee she used everyday from the A&P.

"I can smell some wonderful coffee, Michael. Almost as tempting as your smelly armpit. Yum!"

"You are a little pig, and that's partly why I love you."

"Are we supposed to shower and dress before breakfast, or what?"

"Not really. We just go to the dining room in robes and slippers. With only one bathroom, half of us is ready to go out into the world, and the other half is not quite ready. Or we could put on dungarees and sweat-shirts if that would make you more comfortable."

"Yeah, Michael. That definitely would make me feel more comfort-able."

There was a light tap on the door.

"It's me, Louisa. Breakfast is ready whenever you are. If you're decent, I have two cups of piping hot coffee for you, and I'll bring it in and leave it on the desk."

"Thanks, Mom. Please come in."

Louisa went into the bedroom and put the small tray on the desk.

"Good morning, Mrs. Manganaro. Thank you," Jonathan said.

"You're welcome, Jonathan. I'll just open this window a crack and let in some fresh air."

"Good morning, Mom. Thanks."

"Whenever you're ready, come on into the dining room. Dress any way you want to."

As she was leaving the room, she bent over and kissed Michael. She left and closed the door behind her.

Michael reached over to Jonathan and held him in his arms. Michael slowly rubbed his hand up and down Jonathan's back and felt the smoothness of his butt. They kissed.

"Michael, let's have some coffee and join the others. They must be expecting us, or your mother wouldn't have come in with the coffee."

"You're right as usual, Jonathan. Wait till I get you in the cabin. We'll have some real privacy. I can yell as loud as I like, and you won't have to cover my mouth."

"You have the capacity to keep me aroused and excited. Did you know that?"

"Yes," he said and he reached down and felt Jonathan's erection.

"Damn," Jonathan said as he stood up, stepped into his dungarees, forced his stiff penis into the left leg of his dungarees, and zipped them up.

"Jonathan, later you can make me scream out loud. I want you so badly that way."

"It will be nice to be alone with each other, without wondering who might be listening."

"I know. Here I know how thin the walls are, and in *Taylorville* I sometimes feel all of New York can peep into the gigantic windows, even though I know that's not possible because you are so high up nobody could see in, particularly since all the rooms are surrounded by terraces. But it still feels so public."

"We really haven't been alone. Even in Florida, where we had such a lovely intimate experience, I was afraid that a maid or somebody would burst in at any moment."

They had breakfast and packed the car with food, shovels, sleeping bags, blankets, pillows, kerosene, matches, some dry wood and some special lime mix for the outhouse. They put two pairs of boots for the long walk through the snow. Michael put the top down and the passenger seat down, too. That way they were able to put two ladders over the back of the passenger seat and across the back seat. Jonathan would sit in the back seat behind Michael and hold the ladders.

"Michael, I'm going to freeze back here, at least you have the heater in the front."

"It's only about twenty miles. Put a hat on and cover yourself with one of the blankets." Michael laughed. "Candy ass."

They parked near the end of the parking lot of the church, which today was not crowded.

They found seats in the third row on St. Mary's side. They saw Theresa on their way in. She was with her uncle. Michael knelt first and folded his hands. Jonathan knelt right next to him. Their knees touched. Jonathan wondered what Michael was praying about. His own prayer was far from simple. He wanted to be as happy as he was at that moment forever. He wanted his father to be in heaven. He wanted Lillian to completely recover. He wanted to be in Michael's arms until the end of time. Unless it was absolutely necessary, he never wanted to sleep alone again. He knew how difficult it was going to be when Michael went back to the service. Damn it. I guess, he thought, you're not supposed to curse when you're praying. Cool it, or God won't listen. This praying is not supposed to be a negotiation. Dear God, You have something very special to give me. I know it, and I can't fathom what it could be. But please, forgive my selfishness and let me follow Your will. I will take care of those You have put close to me. I promise I will. I'll take care of Your servant, Michael. Even though Your Church has taught us that homosexuality is wrong, I don't believe You would disapprove of me and Michael. I feel that You would want us together. We need each other. You will help him become a great success in the music world. I know he will honor and praise You with his music, with his voice. We need You. You have always helped us, particularly as it related to living with this strong attraction to men we both have had and the courage to live with it. And I thank You for giving me a companion to share the rest of my life with.

Michael felt Jonathan's thigh next to his and didn't move his own away. The sun was streaming in the east windows across the congregation and altar. The different colors were like a rainbow. God must be beauty. Beautiful flowers, music, people, animals. God must love the earth. The mountains surrounding Mellon had to be the work of a divine God who loved beautiful things. The trees that covered the land were magnificent. The Hudson River was probably the most beautiful river in the entire world. The Great Lakes were like treasured jewels. And most of all, the most beautiful thing You created beside Your Son, Jesus, was sitting right beside me, right now. I love him so. Thank You, dear Father in heaven. Thank You very much. I appreciate this gift and will cherish him always. Please keep Your sight on us always. I pray this prayer in the name of Your Son, Jesus. Bye for now. Michael sat back in the pew and blew his nose.

It was nice to sit in the congregation and relax. Michael was so peaceful, that he caught himself almost falling asleep during the homily. The organ sounded much nicer down here. It was full and majestic as Mrs. Rhine played the recessional. She liked to get the people moving. The quicker they got out, the sooner she got to Gruber's before they sold out.

After they left the church, they were on Route 77 headed for the cabin.

"Michael, I'm freezing my fuckin' ass off back here."

Michael was looking in the rear view mirror, and he laughed, looking at Jonathan wrapped up in the old army blanket. The one they used for the massage.

"Michael this isn't funny. I'm fuckin' freezing."

"It's only about three more miles. Get down on the floor behind the seat and hold onto those ladders."

"Okay, but step on it, damn it! I'm freezing."

Michael wasn't sure if Jonathan was mad or joking, or maybe a little of both. Going home they should figure someway to tie the ladders into the trunk. Maybe let them stick out and put red flags on them or something.

"Only one more mile. Hang in there. Hey, there's a donut place right up ahead. I'm going to stop, so we can get some coffee and warm up a little."

"Thanks," he heard the blanket say. There wasn't even a hole in it any longer for Jonathan's face.

"Here we are," Michael told the blanket, as they pulled into the tiny diner.

The cup and saucer on the roof along with the donut were almost as large as the diner. Michael's sunglasses fogged up as soon as he entered the steamy shelter. There were three tiny tables and five stools at the counter. Michael led the blanket to a tiny table. Jonathan let the blanket down around his shoulders and sat down.

"You're a pisser, Michael, and I love you. This was a great idea to let me warm up. You told me we have about a twenty minute walk from where we park the car."

"Yeah, but it's not as bad as it sounds. It should be pretty warm because the snow should be completely covering the ground, and since the sun is so strong, it should be reflecting on the snow and warming the air above it. It won't be so bad. We can pile all the stuff on the ladders and carry them. I only think it will take one trip."

"Michael, I was just thinking a spoiled brat thought."

"And what would that have been?"

"Why the fuck can't we pay someone else to carry this stuff?"

The woman who had been behind the counter came to the table.

"Can I get you some hot coffee and maybe a donut or two? I made them myself this morning. They are nutmeg, cinnamon plain donuts covered with powdered sugar. Not fancy, but real tasty and good."

"I'd like some coffee and a donut."

"Me, too," Jonathan said.

When she came back with the coffee, she asked it they were going to the Sullivan place.

"Yes," Michael said, "How did you know?"

"No one ever comes out this far on a Sunday with ladders sticking out of their car with the top down on a road that only services a few temporary residents like the Sullivans, and the Sullivans are the only ones who didn't get up for Thanksgiving."

"Mr. Sullivan had things to tend to, but he's coming up for Christmas. We are going to get the place ready. Want to get some of the heavy snow off the roof. Check the well, and make sure there aren't any broken windows."

"If you need any help carrying stuff from the road to the cabin, my two boys are home from school until Tuesday. They're in the back watching cartoons."

"Could we ever. I'll pay them gladly."

"Jesse, Sledgeford, come out here," she called out loudly into the back room. Two big strong teenagers came from behind the curtain.

"Yes, Ma?"

"We have two visitors who need help carrying stuff up to the Sullivan cabin. Can you give them a hand?"

"Yes. No problem."

Jonathan took out his wallet and gave each of the young teens a five-dollar bill.

"Wow," Sledgeford said. "You must be rich."

Michael thought, if you only knew.

"Thanks," Jesse said. "We really appreciate the money. We can use it for Christmas. We'll run up ahead of you guys, so you can enjoy your coffee and ma's donuts and warm up. Then drive up to the clearing. We'll carry all your stuff for you. You can enjoy the walk in the fresh snow. I'm sure nobody's been up there since yesterday. Should actually be pretty. Thanks again, Mister. See you up there. Come one, Sledge, let's go."

Michael looked at Jonathan and smiled.

"This is really going to be fun," Jonathan said. "When do you think we'll leave tomorrow, Michael?"

"Probably about 10 a.m., after breakfast."

"That's great, so I can get home to spend some time with Lillian about the Tuesday meeting at Taylor. Maybe Jesse and Sledgeford could meet us at the cabin tomorrow at 10 a.m."

Mrs. Bridgeford, who had been listening said, "They'll be there. You can count on it."

"Super. These donuts are good. Could we take a half-dozen with us?"

"Sure, I'll put them in a tote."

As she was putting the donuts into the bag, she looked at the front page of the *Mellon Press* that was delivered yesterday. "Local Young Man is Baritone Soloist at Funeral of Rich Manhattan Oil Executive." She continued reading. "Jonathan Anthony Taylor, President of Taylor, died after an automobile accident in Miami Beach." Jonathan Anthony Taylor's picture was in an inset, and there was a picture of the singer, Michael Anthony Manganaro standing next to a woman she didn't recognize. There was also a picture of a blond young man standing next to a closed casket, as it was being carried from the huge church. She picked up the coffeepot and the *Mellon Press* and went back to the table.

"Would you like some more hot coffee?"

"Yes, thank you," Jonathan cooed. "It's great coffee. Really hits the spot."

"Would you like some more, too, Mr. Manganaro?"

"How did you know my name?" Michael asked, surprised.

"Your picture was in yesterday's *Mellon Press*. Here, see."

"My parents get this, but we didn't look at it yesterday. Here, look, Jonathan. Yes, more coffee for me, please."

"Then you must be the other person in the picture. Oh, I'm so sorry. Are you the man's son?"

"Yes. I'm Jonathan Taylor."

"Oh, Mr. Taylor, I am so sorry. So sorry indeed."

"Thank you very much."

"This is my friend, Michael Manganaro. He lives in Mellon, and I'm visiting his family."

"It's nice to meet you, Mr. Manganaro. Now that I think of it, I've heard you sing before. You sang at St. John's last Sunday. *Panis Angelicus*, wasn't it?"

"Yes. What a small world!"

"And I bet that pretty girl at the bank is a relative of yours, too. The one who's the supervisor."

"Yes. She is. That's my sister, Rosa."

"Well, I am so glad you stopped in here this morning."

Jonathan was taking out his wallet to pay the bill.

"I couldn't accept any money from you guys. Not at this time. You just go on and finish your coffee. Stop by tomorrow on you way home for another cup. Anyone who sings like you do for the glory of God is always welcome with his friend for a cup of coffee and a donut here in our place. And again, Mr. Taylor, I am sorry about your dad's passing."

They got back in the car and drove onto the road.

"Michael, I can't believe how warm and friendly everyone is up here."

"Well it's different from New York City. That's for sure."

"It's a nice change for me."

"I like it here, but I love New York City," Michael said. "New York is addictive and busy and glamorous. I love the restaurants and the crowds."

"Look over there, the boys are waiting."

Jesse and Sledgeford packed up the ladders and all the supplies and went up the steep hill toward the cabin.

"Michael, did you really expect me to cart all this stuff up this mountain?"

"Yes, Stud-boy. You just got out of boot camp, and you're probably in the best physical shape you've ever been in. Why not?"

"Michael, I'm just kidding. You know that."

"I know. Take these boots and put them on. I'm sure they'll fit. They're a little big for me, but should be just right for you. And I'll wear these. The snow is pretty high in places, over a foot I think with the wind we had yesterday."

"Michael, it's nice up here. It's so quiet. Except for the little donut shop, I haven't seen signs of life for miles."

"It's busier in the warm months."

"I'm ready to go," Jonathan said, as he pulled his wool hat over his ears. "How about you?"

"Ready as I'll ever be. Let's go."

There was a wide expanse of white snow without trees or foliage, and they walked diagonally across it. Jonathan reached down and took a hand full of snow and tasted it.

"It tastes so clean, Michael."

Jonathan bent over again and Michael couldn't resist. He ran up behind Jonathan and threw him down into the snow face first. He jumped onto Jonathan's back and sat on the lower portion of his back and on the top of his butt.

"And now you candy ass sissy from the city, tell me how much you want me. Tell me."

"Let me up," Jonathan struggled. "Let me up!"

Michael twisted one of Jonathan arms behind his back. "Not until you tell me. Tell me how much you want me."

"I want you. I want all of you. I want you to fuck me. I want to have you fuck me real hard. I want you to pound me like you did in Miami."

"Okay, you can get up. Only thing is," Michael laughed, "we'll have to flip a coin, because I want you to do the same thing to me."

Jonathan took Michael's face in his hands and kissed him. Michael was looking into Jonathan eyes, and he noticed his eyebrows were covered with snow.

"We better be careful in case the kids come back."

"Right. The last thing we need is to be convicted of contributing to the delinquency of minors."

When they got to the top of the hill, they could see the cabin. It seemed only a half-mile away. The sun was very low in the sky behind the cabin.

"Let's get a move on. It's almost three o'clock. I want to get the wood inside while it's still light out if we can."

"I agree, Michael," Jonathan said. "What about the snow on the roof?"

"If the snow is very heavy on the roof, and we get a good fire going inside, because of the steep slope of the roof, when the bottom level of the snow melts, the large top layers just slide off. It worked like that a few years ago after a heavy blizzard."

Jonathan said, "You're the expert."

They walked faster as they neared the cabin. It was on the side of the next large hill. There were footsteps in the snow where the boys had been. Michael saw Jesse and Sledgeford walking toward them from the cabin.

"We put everything inside the house. The door was opened. Looks like it blew in during the storm yesterday. There was some snow inside that we swept out for you. Everything seems to be in place. There weren't any other footprints or any other marks in the snow before ours."

"Thanks, Jesse. That was swell of you guys to do that. Will we see you here tomorrow about 10 a.m.?"

"Sure. We'll be here," Jesse said.

"I'll be here," Sledgeford added. "Have a good night. Do you need anything before we go?"

"No thanks. We have everything we need. I'm sure we'll be comfortable. One thing you could do is tell us the weather forecast for tonight and the morning. We were so busy getting ready this morning for church and coming up here we didn't listen."

"Last I heard," Jesse volunteered, "on the radio this morning was that we could be getting a little more snow, and that it was going down into the teens tonight."

Jonathan said, "Thanks, Jesse. That means we better get a move on and get a good fire started. See you both tomorrow."

Michael looked for the padlock that was supposed to be on the door of the cabin. It was nowhere in sight. At least he had the key. Big deal. He'd have to remember to tell Mr. Sullivan that there was no lock after they closed up the place and returned home. If he wanted him to, Michael would buy another lock and come back at a future date and secure the cabin. But that would take up almost a whole day. He got a better idea. On their way home, they would stop at the Donut Diner, give the owner money, and ask if her sons could buy a lock and lock the cabin up that afternoon. That's what they would do. He'd give her his mailing address on Maiden Lane, and she could mail him the key.

They went into the cabin and closed the door. All their gear was in the middle of the room.

"Damn, Michael. It's cold as a witch's tit in here. And it's dark. Snow's covering most of the windows. Let's light some of the lamps and start the fire right away."

"The kerosene is in the big box. Why don't you fill up the lamps? And I'll start the fire pronto. Please hand me the big wood matches. I think they're in the second box."

Jonathan handed them to Michael. Michael knelt in front of the stone fireplace. Ashes remained from the last fire and normally, being the neat, orderly person that he was, Michael would have cleaned out the ashes. He also would have checked to make sure the chimney was clear of debris, but he was cold and wanted a roaring fire going without delay. He rolled up newspapers, layered the kindling and put on some larger pieces of dry wood. He lit the paper in several places and as soon as the fire caught, he would put on some of the larger logs that were stacked against the wall. He sat back on the sofa for a moment. Jonathan had one of the lamps lit. The room began to take on a more welcoming ambience. Jonathan carried the lamp over to the table next to the sofa and set it down and then sat down next to Michael. The kindling was burning. They could feel the heat coming from the fireplace, and the larger wood would be catching soon. Michael knew from the way the flames were dancing up the chimney that there was no obstruction.

"Maybe I should start unpacking the stuff and putting it away," Jonathan suggested.

"Good. Let me know what mom packed for us."

"Well bless your mother."

"What?"

"She packed a fifth of Canadian Club and a small bottle of sweet vermouth. And she even packed a bowl of ice and the shaker from your room with two cocktail glasses. Would you believe it?"

"Yes. Knowing her. I'm putting some more wood on the fire, so we don't freeze to death. We're going to have to make sure the fire lasts through the night, or we'll freeze."

"I'll make us some drinks. I watched you do it at the apartment."

"Thanks, Jonathan."

Jonathan poured the liquor and the wine into that pitcher and stirred it.

Michael put some kerosene in two more lamps and lit them. He filled one that they could use to walk outside later, if they had to use the outhouse.

"Michael, I gathered there is no electricity here. No refrigerator. No TV, no radio. Where's the plumbing? Bathroom?"

Michael laughed. "The pump for water is outside, and so is the toilet. It's called an outhouse. It's way down on the left of the hill almost behind the cabin."

"Oh, my God, I've arrived. I can't figure myself out, Michael. I don't have the basic conveniences, and I'm happier than I've ever been in my entire life. And the only thing I can think of is, that it's because I'm here with you, Precious."

Michael walked up to Jonathan and kissed him.

Jonathan gave Michael a Manhattan and sipped his own.

"What do I do with the food that has to be kept cold?"

"There is a metal box over by the sink that extends outside where you put that stuff. In the warm weather it's filled with large chunks of ice, but I guess with weather expected to be in the teens, we won't have to worry about that tonight."

The room was rustically furnished. On either side of the sofa was a wooden table and between the kitchen and the main room was a large oval wood table covered with oilcloth. There were bunk beds along one wall and a gun rack without guns was near the front door. There was a chest of drawers next to a large trunk against the opposite wall. A bookcase full of old books was next to the cabin door. Red burlap café curtains were on the four windows. A long piece of red burlap fabric was strung across a piece of rope in the corner of the room. Michael thought it probably was a makeshift sort of closet, and he went over and slid the cloth across the rope.

"Jonathan, come over here and look at this."

"Michael, now I've seen everything. Can you believe it?"

"But a great idea for a night like tonight."

The Sullivans had rigged up an indoor toilet, which apparently drained to a cesspool outside and behind the cabin, which was situated on a hill with a sharp incline behind it. The receptacle was situated to insure that any waist material deposited in it didn't pollute the water supply forward of the cabin on the other side of the hill. There were three five-gallon cans filled with ice with a sign above them. "KEEP THESE CANS FILLED WITH WATER!"

"Clever idea, no? Particularly for nights like tonight. I'm going to put this can over near the fireplace to thaw out. It's just slushy, not completely frozen."

"Super."

"Michael, do you think the pump is frozen?"

"No, because I believe the well is deep enough, so it wouldn't freeze. If you care to try it, why don't you take that large milk can in the kitchen and fill it up? I'm sure they must use it for water."

"I will."

Jonathan went outside and pumped and pumped. Finally, after he primed the pump, at Michael's suggestion, the water flowed into the milk can. He carried the can in triumphantly.

"At least we have water."

"And what prompted this sudden desire to have water?"

"I have to take a leak. And I wanted to use our new-found appliance and flush it rather than leaving a tell-tale yellow signature in the snow."

"I knew there had to be a reason." Michael laughed.

The room was beginning to get warm, and Michael wondered if the Manhattan was helping.

"Jonathan, this is the first time we're together without any distractions. Boot camp was a busy place and, except for the few times we spend in that little office and the times we spent in bed, we've never been alone. Even in bed we had the biggest distractions of all, passion and sex."

Jonathan sat down on the sofa. "Does this thing open? If it does, I'd rather sleep here by the fire than in the sleeping bags."

"Let me look." Michael lifted the cushion. "Yes, it does. We'll open it later. I'm glad we brought blankets."

There was a rumbling on the roof that made them both jump.

"What the hell was that?"

They went to the door and opened it. The opening of the doorway was covered.

"Oh, my God, Michael, we're snowed in. We'll never get out, and we'll die here," Jonathan said doing his best Bette Davis imitation.

"Drama. How I love it. Here's your shovel. I have mine. Let's dig. The snow just fell off the front of the cabin's roof. That's all."

In five minutes they had dug a tunnel to the cold evening air. It was dark now and very cold.

"Michael, let's put on some more warm clothes and clean the front of the cabin by the walk and door, so that when the snow finally melts the front of the cabin will be clear."

"You're going to make a good Chairman of the Board, Mr. Taylor. Let's do just that."

It took them about a half-hour to clear the entrance.

"Now, Michael, I am cold and want to go inside."

"Sure, Jonathan, go in and warm up. Mix some more drinks. I want to go to the shed and get extra wood to make sure we don't run out in the middle of the night."

Jonathan went in and hung his heavy coat behind the door and stood in front of the fire warming his hands. Michael filled a wheelbarrow that he found outside the shed with wood and wheeled it through the snow into the cabin and unloaded the wood next to the fireplace. Michael sat down on the sofa for a minute to warm himself.

Jonathan said, "Michael, you're not going to leave that thing in here, are you?"

"No, of course not. I'll take it out in a minute. I'm just defrosting."

"Michael, there is just that little latch on the door. Are there any wild animals up here?"

"Like, what do you mean, Jonathan? Tigers, lions?"

"No, but aren't there bears and stuff like that?"

"Yes, most of them hibernate during the winter, except for the first few cold weeks when they search for food to fill themselves up, so they don't starve during the long winter."

"Oh, that certainly makes me more comfortable. Knock, knock, knock. 'Do you cute young men have any extra food?'"

"Jonathan, if the door seems too fragile for you, we can move the bookcase in front of it and move the bunk beds in front of the bookcase when we're ready to go to bed. While we're awake, up and around, we can fight them off."

"That sounds good to me, at least the part about securing the door before we sleep, but I'm not sure about the fighting-them-off part. But what about the windows?"

"Jonathan, they're covered with snow, and they're not even two feet square. No bear can get through."

"I know, Michael. I'm just not used to roughing it like this."

They sipped their drinks in front of the fire.

"I'll take the wheelbarrow out now."

Jonathan followed him to the door and watched him wheel it to the shed. As he was returning, Jonathan saw a doe look directly at him and then run off into the woods.

"Michael, you did a great job with the fire. It's comfortable and toasty in here now."

"Thanks, Jonathan. What did my mother send for food?"

"Good stuff. A glass baking dish of lasagna, a tomato and lettuce salad, dressing, a loaf of French bread and a bottle of red table wine. And we still have donuts left for dessert."

"I'm getting hungry. How do you think we should heat it?"

"What's that wrought iron thing for? It sort of looks like you could put it over some coals that were hot or something and use it to heat food."

"Hey, Jonathan. I think you're getting the hang of it. Because I'm sure that's exactly what it's for. Let me arrange the wood, so we can put it into the fireplace and heat our lasagna."

"Here's the lasagna. I'll clean off the table and set it. Your mother included some picnic items in the basket, like plates and things. She sure is thoughtful, Michael. I like her a lot."

When he finished, he rejoined Michael in front of the fire. Michael put on a large log.

"Jonathan, I think that large log will last through the night." Michael took Jonathan's hand in his. "What's troubling you, Jonathan?"

"You really have gotten to know me, Michael."

"I know. Anything you'd care to share?"

"Not right now. Maybe later after we've had supper and are in bed. I want to be touching you when we talk. I only feel safe in your arms."

"I think that's a good idea. We can talk later. Like I said before, this is the first time we're together without distractions."

"Can I have one of your cigarettes, Michael?"

"Sure."

They sat quietly as they turned the glass baking dish several times to make sure the lasagna was warm throughout. They both enjoyed the dinner. The food was tasty and filling, and the wine helped pull everything together.

"I don't want to speak of unhappy things in bed, Michael, if we can avoid it. Let's reserve our bed time for raunchy sex and refreshing sleep."

"I think that is a goal that we may work on for the rest of our lives."

"The only thing that's bothering me that I want to talk about now is the shock I'm feeling. All this stuff has happened. Really happened. My father is dead. I know that I have so much to be thankful for, but, shit, Michael, I still feel like that son-of-a-bitch left me. He abandoned me."

"He didn't abandon you, Jonathan."

"Intellectually, I know. I want to yell and scream at someone, and I don't know who. God? But I can't yell at God. Look at all the good things He's done for me. He sent me you, Lillian, your family."

"Jonathan, I don't think you're feeling anything unusual. You're been very brave and have carried on with dignity throughout this ordeal, and, yes, it was an ordeal for all of us. But you were graceful, polite, composed and absolutely charming, helping your mother and Lillian deal with it, too. You should be proud of yourself. I'm glad that you feel comfortable enough with me to share some downtime. You can't be up all the time, especially at a time like this. And if you are feeling any guilt because you've always been a little angry at your father, you didn't in any way, shape or form cause his death."

"Thanks, Michael. I know you're right."

"I am. Now let me help you clean up. Make a garbage bag for the stuff that won't burn, and we'll fill it tomorrow with the ashes from this fire and dispose of it at home. I'm not sure where the garbage cans are out here under all this snow."

It was almost nine o'clock when Michael opened the sofa bed. There were no sheets on it, so he opened the sleeping bags across the mattress and used the blankets they brought for the covers.

"Jonathan, our bed is ready."

"I'll be right there."

The took off their clothes. Michael turned out the kerosene lamps, and then Jonathan reminded him about the door.

"Michael, I know I'm being a pain in the ass, but just suppose a big, black, hungry bear sees the light coming from the cabin, and he's really hungry, and smells the food, and suppose…"

"Okay. Okay. Let's move the bookcase and the bunk beds."

They crawled back into bed when the finished.

"Thanks, Michael."

"Sure. Do you feel better now?"

"I certainly feel better that the door is secured, but I always feel wonderfully wanted and protected when your body is so close to me."

Michael placed his hand on Jonathan's back and pulled him close.

"I love you, Jonathan."

They kissed for a long time. Then they lay silently beside each other and listened to the sounds around them. The fire crackled and a few small pieces of wood crumbled and fell in the fireplace. The wind was whistling through the trees and around the cabin.

"Michael, do you want to fool around?

"I do," Michael said as he turned on his side towards Jonathan.

"Super, because I do," Jonathan turned to Michael and put his hand on the top of Michael's arm.

Michael noticed that, in spite of the smell of the fire, and the damp mustiness of the cabin, Jonathan smelled the same as he did the first time he noticed it in the car driving him to Maiden Lane. Michael touched Jonathan's face with the palm of his hand and his fingertips. He rubbed his thumb over Jonathan's lips very lightly.

"Oh, Michael. It feels so good when you touch me." He kissed Michael's thumb. Michael felt how excited Jonathan was becoming, as Jonathan began to quiver under the blanket. He pressed his thumb into Jonathan's mouth and let him suck it. When he removed his finger from the warmth of Jonathan's mouth, Jonathan kissed his hand. Jonathan took Michael's hand and led it to his own buttocks. Then Jonathan put one of his arms under Michael's body and the other over Michael's side and pulled Michael to him. He held him tightly with both his hands on Michael's back. Michael's fingers began rubbing Jonathan's buttocks and found their way to the most sensitive area where they lingered and massaged it in small circular motions. Michael removed his fingers from Jonathan just long enough to lubricate them. He continued massaging the area while they kissed, and let their tongues explore their mouths.

Michael positioned Jonathan, so that he was lying on his back, and Michael rolled on top of Jonathan. Michael was thrilled to hear Jonathan moaning. He began moaning louder and continuously.

Michael put his tongue into Jonathan's ear, and Jonathan thrust his torso as hard as he could against Michael. As Michael returned the thrust he bit Jonathan on the right side of his neck, and then he bit his shoulder. Jonathan let out a small scream, and Michael realized he really had caused him pain.

"I'm sorry. I'm sorry. I didn't mean it."

"Oh, my God. Don't worry about it and don't stop ravishing me. I love it."

"Jonathan, please turn over onto your stomach." Michael was kneeling in the middle of the bed. While Jonathan was turning, Michael took one of the pillows from the top of the bed and placed it under Jonathan's pelvis. He took care to move Jonathan's erect penis to point toward the bottom of the bed before he settled him onto the pillow. Michael placed his hands on the back of Jonathan's thighs and spread them apart enough, so that he could comfortably remain kneeling behind Jonathan's beautifully proportioned cheeks. He kissed Jonathan's buttocks and let his tongue explore the crack between his cheeks. He moved up and down the crack with his tongue, stopping to occasionally kiss the small fuzzy area at the bottom of Jonathan's back. Then he went down and lifted Jonathan's penis from the pillow and took it into his mouth and massaged it with his lips and tongue. When his mouth left Jonathan's penis he licked his hairy scrotum, each testicle, and then licked the soft flesh above his testicles until he reached Jonathan's most erogenous zone. He massaged this area with his tongue until Jonathan begged him to stop.

"Please, oh, please stop, Michael. I don't want to come like this."

"Okay," Michael said, but it was too late. Jonathan shot wads of semen onto the sleeping bag.

"Oh, my, God!" he screamed as the ejaculations continued.

Michael massaged some of the semen that had landed on the bed onto the top of Jonathan's thighs. He took more of the ejaculated fluid from the sleeping bag, and put it on his penis and entered Jonathan easily.

"Oh, Michael. That feels so nice. Go all the way in. I want to feel you inside of me."

Michael covered Jonathan's body with his own and covered Jonathan's shoulders with his arms. He began moving slowly in and out and enjoyed each thrust forward and each retreat. Jonathan was moaning again and that made him crazy with desire. He extended his arms placing his hands on the bed on either side of Jonathan's shoulders, and he rose above his beloved recipient. He was looking down as the light from the flames danced on Jonathan's white buttocks. He was delighted with the way his stiff member looked going into and out of Jonathan. The harder he pushed it in, the louder Jonathan moaned.

"Give it to me!" Jonathan screamed. "Give it to me hard!"

And Michael did what he was told.

When they were finished, they held each other. They lay side-by-side, breathing heavily and sweating. Michael reached down on the floor and picked up his underpants and wiped the sweat from Jonathan's forehead with them. Then from the cheeks of his face. He kissed Jonathan.

"That was good. Real good," Michael said.

"I have to agree with you there, Precious."

Michael laughed. "But now I feel all sticky."

"There's no place to take a shower," Jonathan observed practically.

"No kidding. I don't care."

"I don't either, but I do have some soap, a face cloth and a towel. And I bet the water in that can that you put by the fire is a little warm by now. I could wash you off, and then you could wash me."

"You know," Michael said, "I like that idea."

It was warm and cozy in the cabin. They laughed and tickled each other while they soaped and rinsed, trying not to drip too much on the old blanket. Then they dried each other with the one big bath towel that they had brought with them. When they were through, Michael got down on the floor and kissed Jonathan's stomach and his navel, and then buried his face into the flesh just above Jonathan's pubic hair.

"I love you, Jonathan. I love you so."

Jonathan got down on his knees, too, and kissed Michael, covering Michael's mouth with his own. He put his arms around Michael's naked body and crushed him to himself.

"I love you, Precious."

They crawled back under the blankets.

"Michael, it feels so good to be with you tonight. I always seem to feel like I'm on vacation when I'm with you."

"I know what you mean. Each time we're together I feel like it's a special, once-in-a-lifetime experience, and I don't want it to end."

There was a rumbling sound overhead.

"Did you hear that, Michael? It sounds like more snow sliding off the roof."

"But this time it sounded like it went behind the cabin, like from right above us."

"I'm so wide awake now, I'd like a drink. How about you?"

"Sure, Jonathan. I think we have some of the wine left. I'd like that, and I could use a cigarette, too."

Michael sat up in bed and put an ashtray between them with some Lucky Strikes and matches. Jonathan poured two glasses of the red wine that remained from dinner and got back into the foldout bed.

"Cheers," Jonathan said as he mouthed a kiss to Michael.

"Cheers," Michael responded as he wiggled his way closer to Jonathan.

"Hey, what's going on here? Are you going to attack me again?" Jonathan laughed as he lit up a cigarette.

"Maybe later, when you're sleeping. That is, if the bear doesn't get you first."

"I guess I'm never going to hear the end of that."

"Nope," Michael said as he took a drink of the Chianti. "You know, Jonathan, you never did tell me something."

"What was that, Michael."

"How you wound up in the Navy?"

"Well, I haven't told you because it's not a part of my life that I'm particularly proud of. That's why."

"I didn't mean to make you uncomfortable, Jonathan. I'm sorry."

"No, it's okay. I suppose I really want you to know. Besides being the patriotic thing to do..."

"You know what I mean, from being a student at Brown to boot camp with the peons."

"Okay. All my life, particularly intensively since puberty, I've felt this incredible attraction to men. I never felt bad about it until shortly before my twenty-first birthday. I began to think that it wasn't going to go away and I could not possibly think of how I could conduct a successful life as a homosexual. I had always thought of having a family. And I knew that's what my father wanted for me, and I never objected to sex with girls. As a matter of fact, I enjoyed getting laid. And I loved to satisfy women. But I always thought about and wanted boys and men more. And my experience in the same sex area was limited as I told you. I wasn't sure how to go about finding, let alone meeting, and hooking up with, people who were like-minded."

"But how did that get you into the Navy?"

"Earlier this year when the weather in the city was getting nice and warm, I went drinking at a local pub on Amsterdam Avenue and got a little high. I took a walk into Central Park where I had heard some cruising took place. I was horny and wanted to find an anonymous partner to have sex with in the bushes. I guess I was drunker than I thought, because I could not stop myself from getting beaten and robbed by two teenage thugs who were members of some gang. I had to testify at a hearing two weeks later after they caught them doing the same thing to someone else. After the hearing, the judge and my father went into the judge's chambers, and I knew they were talking about me. About a month or so went by, and I heard nothing more about the incident. It wasn't until May when I had to appear before the same judge for speeding down the West Side Highway that it was mentioned again. That's when I lost my license. This time when my father and the judge went into the judge's chambers, they asked me to join them. Oh brother, was I in for it. The judge started asking some very personal questions. He asked me if I was having a problem with alcohol. He asked if I had a death wish. Stuff like that. My father asked a few that I won't even repeat. Anyway, I felt like a rat in a trap. While I wasn't arrested for driving while intoxicated, the judge told my father that the officer who gave me the ticket thought he smelt booze on my breath. Shit, man, I had to think fast. I looked around the room and noticed several pictures of people in military uniforms. I saw a picture of the judge in what appeared to be a World War II public relations shoot aboard an aircraft carrier. He was wearing a captain's uniform. And behind the judge on his credenza were pictures of two young men in contemporary Navy enlisted uniforms. The judge asked me if I were having a problem at school. He gave me a chance to talk without putting my foot in my mouth.

"'Judge,' I said, 'I'm in my junior year at Brown, and I'm feeling overwhelmed. I'm almost done with the semester and, quite frankly, I'm exhausted. I've been thinking that as soon as school is through, I'll have my military commitment to fulfill and the thought of one more year of school and several years in the Military as an officer, is mind-blowing. What I'd really like to do is finish the semester and take a leave of absence to follow a dream of mine to become a sailor. It's something I've always secretly wanted to do, but I've been concerned that my father might not approve.'"

"'There is nothing wrong with being an enlisted man, my son. Nothing at all. Why my two sons are enlisted men and they both are on active duty right now. Look,' he said proudly pointing to the picture behind himself."

"Well, Michael, I knew I had him going, or to put it another way, I knew they had me!"

"Wow. You did all that to save face?"

"No. Not to save face. I was being set up for rehab or, worse yet, maybe long-term psychiatric care, or a lobotomy."

"I remember going back to the courtroom and waiting for my father to come out, which he finally did, of course, and he told me that at the end of August of this year I would be in the Navy. And here I am, in the Navy and in your arms. I love you so, Michael. If all the bad shit hadn't happened to me, I might not be here with you right now."

"I realize that. I'm glad you're here with me, but I am sorry that you were so miserable earlier this year. I suppose you were scared like I was."

"Well, it was getting pretty scary for me, Michael. I was drinking a lot more than I know I should have been, and I was obsessing over being a homosexual. My self-esteem was at an all time low. Yeah, things weren't that great."

"Allowing yourself to get into such dangerous situations must have been a nightmare. I mean, you could have been killed by the muggers, or in an automobile accident."

"Michael," Jonathan said, as he held Michael's hand, "it didn't seem important then, but now that you're in my life I want to take good care of myself. If ever I had a reason to live, it's now."

"You better take care of yourself. I'm counting on your not only for my selfish reasons, but also for your mother and Lillian. We are all counting on you. Jonathan, I want to take care of you forever, and I want you by my side supporting and taking care of me. Do we have a plan?"

"We do. Our destinies are intertwined, and it's in our best interests to give each other all that we can."

"I'll give you everything I can. I promise."

"And I'll do the same for you."

They kissed and each of them turned, so their backs and butts were pressed against each other. Jonathan pulled up the blankets.

"Jonathan, it feels good to have your body against mine."

Jonathan jiggled a little in affirmative recognition.

Just before Jonathan feel asleep he said, "You know, Michael, when my trouble started to really cause my father concern last spring, he discussed changing his will with Lillian and she talked him out of it. She really went to bat for me. I hope I don't let either of them down."

"I don't think you will."

No bears attacked during the night.

Chapter 53

They had a delicious Sunday dinner at Giovanni's. Gary let Addison order for him. Everything was good from the mozzarella-and-tomato appetizer to the baked flounder. They shared three things: a small bottle of red table wine, a whipped egg custard for dessert and each other's company. Gary was in a better mood than he had been in for months. He still missed Michael, but Addison was terrific. He was sorry that maybe he wouldn't be able to see Addison again, and that bothered him. After they left the restaurant he didn't speak for quite a while as they walked back to the office through the snow. It was still coming down, but it was light. Just dusting the sidewalks and streets.

When they turned off the main street and out of the streetlights, Addison took Michael's hand.

"It's seems to have gotten colder, Gary."

"That's probably because of the wine and the hot coffee. I was getting a little warm in there."

"Did you enjoy the food?"

"Sure did. It was great."

"You've been quiet the last hour. Is something wrong?"

"No. Not really. Just thinking about us."

"Oh."

Gary said, "I liked going to your church this morning. I've never been to a Presbyterian Church before."

"I'm glad you came. I thought the Mass we went to on Friday was very moving. I've only gone to a Catholic Church once or twice. Was that service very different from a normal service?"

"Not that different. Everything is pretty much the same, except, of course, without the corpse."

"Your friend sang particularly well, don't you think?"

"He did. Michael always sings well. I've been listening to him for years. But on Friday, well, all I can say is that he was terrific. Never heard him sound like that. He may have sounded so good because he is in such good physical shape, or maybe it's because he's in love."

"In love?"

"Yep. With the dead man's son, Jonathan."

"Oh."

"Yes, they're lovers."

"Oh, I see. I thought I recognized him from somewhere."

"Michael?"

"No. The son."

"I think you might have seen him on the train coming up here a week or so ago."

"Could be. Handsome guy. Both of them are."

When they were back in the office, Addison put more wood on the fire.

"Gary, I've really enjoyed the time we spent together this past week."

"Me, too. It's been the nicest week of my life."

"It doesn't have to end."

"But I thought you said your wife was coming back tomorrow."

"She is, Gary, but we could still get together."

"You think?"

"Sure," Addison said as he turned down the blankets on the sofa bed. He enjoyed watching Gary while he took off his own clothes and put them over a chair. He got into bed.

"How often could we get together?" Gary asked.

"Actually, we could be with each other every week if you'd like."

"Addison, I want to be with you as often as you can manage. You know how I feel about you."

"You're very special to me, Gary. I feel the same about you. You've made me very happy since that night in the bar car."

"I love you, Addison," Gary said, as he removed his shorts and got into bed. He pulled the covers up to his chest and sat up next to Addison.

"You smell so good, Gary. Kiss me."

They spent the next few minutes kissing and embracing. The only light in the office was coming from the fireplace. Gary put his head on Addison's chest and playfully licked his nipple.

"Stop that, you horny person."

"Only if you'll tell me when we could be together again."

"Well, I'll tell you, but not to make you stop, only to let you know that I really think we could see one another pretty often. Even though it's only been a short time, you've become a very important part of my life."

"Addison, I can't imagine not seeing you anymore. I just can't. I think about you all the time."

"Gary, you're a sweet guy, but I still want to remind you that I am married."

"Addison, I know that. I know that our time alone will be limited, but any time I spend with you is worth the time I'll spend alone thinking of you."

"Not only are you horny, Gary, but you're a hopeless romantic as well." Addison laughed. "I'd give anything to be with you again. You know that."

"So when?" Gary prodded.

"Well, let's see."

"Addison!" Gary demanded impatiently.

Addison covered Gary's mouth with his.

"Oh, Addison."

"Here's my idea. As I told you, this office is closed on Wednesdays, and I always work catching up when it's quiet here."

"And?"

"Well, I normally stay over on Tuesdays and Wednesdays which works well with my wife's schedule. She plays bridge on Tuesdays at the Westport Country Club and on Wednesdays she works as a volunteer at Holy Name Hospital in the pediatric section. I usually return home on Thursday evening, and we spend an exciting night together grocery shopping."

"Sounds terrific. And I fit in where?"

"Well, my friend, I'm offering you free parking from Tuesday morning through Thursday evening in the parking lot behind this building."

"Meaning I could drive here on Tuesday morning, leave the car here, take the train to New York, and on Thursday evening I could take the train here and then drive home."

"You surely are one of the brightest bulbs on the tree!"

"And now back to us."

"Back to us."

"Stop teasing me, Addison."

"I'm not teasing. Maybe I'm just seeing if I can entice you."

"Entice me already."

"Okay. You could come on Tuesdays and Wednesdays after work and stay over and go to work from here."

"Sounds good. Very good. You mean we could spend two nights together each week."

"Actually, if you came early on Tuesday mornings before everybody got here," Addison suggested, "we could have time for at least a good morning kiss."

"And if you wait for me on Thursday, we could kiss goodbye."

"Maybe more. What do you think?"

"I think I'll have to come up with a story to tell my folks about where I'll be spending those nights."

"Well, isn't it about time you found a girl in the city?"

"Maybe it is about time."

"Yeah. Maybe a girl in the Village, someone on Sullivan Street."

"I like the Village. And, of course, she doesn't have a phone. Real Bohemian."

"You're cooking with petroleum now, Gary."

"And what about my car parked here? Won't your employees wonder about that?"

"Sure. They probably will. But I'll just tell them that the owner is a friend of mine who's attending the Real Estate Institute in New York three days a week, and I said he could park here."

"You mean this is a deal?"

"Yes. I do."

"Aren't we supposed to shake hands on it or something?"

"I have a better idea."

"Yeah?"

"Let's fuck."

Addison slid down on the bed and lay back as Gary moved on top of him. Addison closed his eyes as he felt Gary's muscular body cover his. Addison put his hands on Gary's smooth back, and he welcomed Gary's penetrating tongue.

Chapter 54

Lillian and Missy were sitting quietly in the library at the desk working. They were still in their bathrobes with curlers in their hair. The sun, which had been streaming into the room all morning since they began working, had moved. It was about 11:30 a.m. There were stacks of papers between them, documents provided by Stefano Brasso and Patrick Connelly at their meeting on Thanksgiving morning. Adele brought in coffee on a silver tray and placed in on the edge of the desk.

"Thanks, Adele. We appreciate it," Lillian said as she removed her glasses. "Missy, have you been able to reach all the board members?"

"Yes. They all said they would be happy to meet tomorrow at Taylor's corporate headquarters at 10 a.m. to hear your plans for the future."

"I bet they are. They're probably expecting that I'll be throwing in the towel."

"Probably."

Lillian continued, "I'm expecting a call from Lawrence Raynor. He's the Chairman of Fennimore. I have to fill him in on my plans."

"Lillian, he said he would call you after lunch around 2:30 p.m., if that were okay with you."

"That's super. Thank you. I don't want him to be surprised tomorrow. I'm not sure if he'll be too happy, but I'm sure he'll be supportive, especially since I plan to stay on as a consultant, without pay for at least six months."

"Mr. Brasso and Mr. Connelly are also stopping by later this afternoon after they get through with their court appearance. Mr. Connelly told me that they have many documents for you and Jonathan to sign. He also told me that they were trying to get a court appearance scheduled for the both of you either tomorrow afternoon or on Wednesday. It seems that the executors have to appear personally before the probate judge."

"Seems logical, and that's good. The sooner we get this going, the better I'll feel."

"Mr. Connelly and Mr. Brasso are both coming tomorrow morning to the Taylor meeting, but they have to leave at 11:30 a.m. They have an appointment with people from The Internal Revenue Service and the New York State Income Tax Division to set up a tax escrow accounts for the estate. I think the meeting is taking place in the bank. They'll be opening the safe deposit box. The power of attorney for them to do that is among the papers they will be bringing for you and Jonathan to sign."

"Missy, you are good at this. You've been a real big help. I'm so glad you're here with me, not to mention how much I enjoy your company."

"I am, too. I've learned more about business in a few days with you than I could have learned in two semesters of business school. But when we're done with all this business stuff, we still have to think about getting something for you to wear tomorrow, so you will look terrific. You need a real power outfit. I hate to take the scissors to some of your things, but I'm afraid I'll have to," Missy laughed.

"I'm sure you'll do a great job. I have an old Dior suit that we can experiment with first."

"I was thinking of using one of Jonathan's bulky sports jackets which may fit over your cast. You could wear a dark turtle neck sweater to cover the bruises on your neck."

"That sounds like a good idea! To jazz it up, I can wear my beautiful stone martens over it to make it look a little more feminine and the emerald broach that he gave me for our anniversary."

"You'll look good. Did you want me to be at the meeting?"

"Oh, yes, Missy. Of course. I'm hoping, as well, that you'll join the company to help me. I plan to be there fulltime starting in January with you as my assistant."

"I'd be delighted, but what about Barbara Greenfeld?"

"I hope that she will remain on-board, too, to assist Jonathan. And that reminds me, I want you to get her on the phone for me after I talk to Mr. Raynor. I think it would be a good idea for me to clue her in about my plans, and I also want her to arrange for a meeting at 8:30 a.m. tomorrow with whatever architect Taylor used in the past at the office. I'll need an office for us, and there is a large conference room that is rarely used and could easily be converted to two very comfortable offices for the new president and CEO and her assistant, Melissa Turner Taylor."

"And Mr. Taylor's current office?"

"For our son, Missy. For our son."

"Nice. Real nice, Lillian. I hope you can manage it successfully without too much hassle."

"Nothing in life is hassle-free, but we have Willington Balmoral on our side in case we run into trouble."

Missy poured coffee first for Lillian and then for herself. "Lillian, do you think our son would want this?" She was beginning to enjoy sharing responsibility for Jonathan and at the same time was becoming very fond of Lillian.

"Yes. Yes, I do. He's ready. He'll do a great job. There are many things he can tend to in Texas, Oklahoma, and Louisiana. He loves to travel, and I think he'll be a great salesperson, like his father. There are many meetings in Washington about environmental issues that he can handle very well. God knows I won't be traveling for a while. Have you noticed how well he handles himself in social situations lately?"

"Actually, now that you mention it, I did. I noticed at the reception Friday afternoon. But I thought he was just putting on a show for Michael."

"He may have been, a little. After all, you can see how much he loves him. Why wouldn't he try to put his best foot forward? I think it's a good thing. I think Michael brings out the best in him."

"Now that you put it that way, I must agree. If he had had some debutante on his arm..."

"Exactly. Michael's very proud of Jonathan, and Jonathan's proud of Michael."

"They are good for each other, Lillian. I knew it the day they came to Golden Hill to visit me. I did know it."

"I'm glad you see it. They look good together, and I believe they will enrich each other's lives. I haven't known any homosexuals in long-term relationships, I suppose, because they probably keep that part of their existence hidden. I think it's referred to as 'being in the closet.'"

"Well, if Michael wants to remain in the Navy, he'd better keep his private life secret."

"You're right, and I'm thinking it's time for a little Lillian-to-Son-in-Law talk. They are so young and new at this, I don't believe they realize how obvious they are. I certainly don't want either of them getting hurt."

"Me, neither."

"You know, Missy, since they may very well spend their future together, I also think Jonathan should be replacing his father on the Metro-Tri-State Opera board. He would love that."

"He loves music, and so does Michael."

"Yes. Now you're zoning in, Missy. Let's keep all this in the family."

They both smiled.

"Missy, I believe the By-laws of Taylor Oil are on your side of the desk, and that the List of Directors is also over there someplace. Could you hand them to me please?"

Missy found the documents and handed them to Lillian.

Lillian spent a few minutes looking over the by-laws of Taylor Oil, Inc. and made some notes and underlined some sections with a red pen.

She looked over the alphabetical list of directors as of their last meeting.

Taylor Oil, Inc. List of Directors October 31, 1960

Willington Balmoral
Balmoral Hills
Saddlebrook, New York
Age 59
Land owner, New York, Connecticut, Louisiana
Secretary of the Board, Taylor Oil, Inc.
Stock owned 10.0%

Dr. Anthony Botteri
Grand Central Towers
New York, New York
Age 46
Chief Administrative Officer, Star of the Sea Medical Center
Stock owned 4.8%

Pasquale Botteri
17 Magnolia Drive
Short Hills, New Jersey
Age 47
Chairman and Artistic Director, Metro-Tri-State Opera
President, South Central Gas and Electric
Stock owned 5.0%

Dr. Sean Kennedy
Old Creek Road
Secaucus, New Jersey
Age 51
Chancellor, Board of Education, New York City (Resigning effective 12/31/60 to accept position in the President's Cabinet.)
Stock owned 1.8%

Austin Murphy
12 Basking Lane
Short Hills, New York
Age 49
Executive Vice President, Meridian Drug Stores
Stock owned 6.0%

Jonathan Anthony Taylor
260 Marlboro Place
New York, New York
Age 46
Chairman and President, Taylor Oil, Inc.
Stock owned 50.2%

Lillian Taylor
260 Marlboro Place
New York, New York
Age 34
Executive Vice President, Fennimore, Fennimore and Taylor
Stock owned 11.0%

Remington Williams
260 Marlboro Place
New York, New York
Age 62
President, Amalgamated Corn Bank
Stock owned 5.0%

Outstanding stock owned by others 6.2%

"Missy, this looks like a strong board to me. Have you looked at it?" Lillian asked, as she showed the list to Missy. "I hope everyone chooses to remain. The only two members who might want to leave are Austin Murphy and Dr. Botteri. They both wanted to use Taylor's property and facilities to start a managed health care company. Austin Murphy is Executive Vice President of Meridian Drug Stores and Dr. Botteri is Chief Administrative Officer, Star of the Sea Medical Center. They feel medical care is in for big changes that will affect the way health care is dispensed from hospitals, general practitioners and pharmacies. And I don't think Jonathan wanted that. He felt that that actually might be something that would become a reality in fifteen years and would be a profitable enterprise at that time, but that it was premature in our economic situation now. If the board members remain, we still have to replace Jonathan, obviously, and Sean Kennedy, who's leaving us to join the President's Cabinet in Washington."

"Who will fill the two openings?"

"Well, one will be Jonathan, and I plan to ask the executive committee to recommend someone else prior to our next meeting to fill the Sean Kennedy spot. And, Missy, let me know if you have any ideas."

"Lillian, just the thought of having my little baby on the board of a major corporation makes me feel lightheaded. But I'm sure he'll do a real good job. As far as the other vacancy goes, I will think if there is anyone I know who could serve on the board. Since Mr. Kennedy was an administrative leader and an academician, I may be able to help you. In my years of fundraising, I met a lot of high-level administrators in several institutions in and around the city. I never realized that you and Jonathan had discussed so much business together."

"Well, we did. And I'm so glad we did, or I would have been completely lost now."

"I was so young when we married, I didn't know anything about business."

"Well, from now on you are going to learn. I want to see you holding balance sheets instead of drinks."

"Me, too. Thanks for believing in me, Lillian."

Adele came back into the library. "I'm very hungry, and I'm tired of writing thank-you notes."

"Take a break, Adele," Lillian said. "I'm famished as well. How about you, Missy?"

"Starved."

Adele suggested, "A new restaurant opened down the street—Chinese and it's only a short wheelchair ride away, that's if you'll both get those curlers out of your hair."

Lillian said, "Let's get dressed. We have to be ready for Jonathan and Michael and for Pat and Steve anyway."

They got ready and went to lunch at the China Moon.

Chapter 55

They had fun getting the remainder of the snow off the cabin's roof. Jonathan did a good job chopping wood, particularly since it was the first time he had ever chopped wood, and stacking it in the shed. He was thankful for the calluses he got on his hands in boot camp. Michael enjoyed watching Jonathan work. It turned him on. Jonathan was wearing overalls that Michael let him borrow. Michael couldn't believe that Jonathan didn't own one pair of work clothes. Jonathan found himself looking at Michael at every opportunity. He thought Michael looked sexy in his knitted, red, wool hat, and jeans and lumberjack boots. It didn't take them long to finish up and secure the cabin. Jesse and Sledgeford were right on time. On the way back to Mellon they had the top up on the convertible and had unzipped the rear window. They put the ladders through it and onto the floor in front of the back seats. The ladders stuck out of the back of the car into the air. Michael had secured them tightly, so they would not blow out onto the road. Occasionally, the ladders brushed some low-lying tree branches. They stopped for coffee and donuts at the little diner, and they left money for a new padlock for the cabin. Then they continued to Mellon and dropped off the equipment at Michael's house, took showers and changed clothes.

After lunch they drove to the city. There was little traffic going in their direction on a workday.

Michael and Jonathan arrived at the apartment about three in the afternoon, and when they entered they heard someone playing the piano.

"Must be my mother," Jonathan said. "Certainly isn't Lillian or Adele."

"It sounds nice. I like Broadway show tunes."

"I do, too, Michael. Hopefully, someday you'll star in a Broadway show if you want to."

"I would like to do that! I always fancied being in *Oklahoma* or *My Fair Lady*. Too bad I don't dance."

"You could learn."

"True."

The women were in the music room. Jonathan walked over to Lillian and kissed her and then to Missy and kissed her while she continued playing. He said, "Sounds great, Mom."

"Thanks."

"Take your coats off, and join us for coffee. We just had a super lunch at the China Moon, and we all ate too much. Michael, come here and sit by me," Lillian said from her central position on the sofa. "I missed you guys."

"Hello, Lillian. Hi, Missy. Missed you, too. It's good to be back to my second home," Michael said.

"Well, Michael, I'm glad you feel welcome. Come on. Sit. You, too, Jonathan."

Adele came into the music room carrying flowers. "These just came for you, Jonathan." She handed the large bouquet of cut flowers to him.

"Thanks, Adele," he said as he accepted the flowers and opened the card looking puzzled.

"Who are they from, Jonathan?" Lillian wanted to know.

"From Theresa Garafolo. I went to a movie with her a week or so ago with Michael and his friend, Maureen."

"That's nice," Missy said.

"I wonder how she got our address," Jonathan pondered.

"Maybe we left one of the programs at John's when we went for pizza," Michael suggested. "What does the card say?"

"'Dear Jonathan, I am sorry to hear of your loss. Please give my condolences to your family. I hope we can be together again if that would please you. Kindest personal regards, Theresa.'"

"How often did you see her, Jonathan?" Lillian asked.

"Only once."

"Well, you certainly must have made a good impression, but it does seem a little strange for such a casual acquaintance, and a very young one at that, to send such an elegant bouquet," Lillian observed.

Michael looked directly at Jonathan, and Jonathan returned his look.

"Theresa's a nice girl. She is a waitress at John's, our local pizza place," Michael offered.

"Well, I'll write her a thank-you note later," Jonathan said.

"I'll put them in water for you."

"Thanks, Adele. Then please put them in the main reception area. Then we can all enjoy them."

"I'll be glad to. I set up the tea service on the counter in the kitchen and put out cups, saucers, plates and things on the buffet in the dining room, Lillian, because you said for your meeting you wanted to be able to spread out all your papers."

"Thanks, Adele. Good thinking. You said that you wanted to leave early today, and that you wanted to spend tomorrow with your family. We're in good shape now. Missy's taking good care of me. Would you like to leave soon and get started before the rush hour? It would be fine with me."

"It would be good to get a head start. Thanks, Lillian; I'll be on my way then. I know you'll be at the office all day tomorrow, so I won't worry about you. I do wish you luck, however. I hope you knock their socks off!"

Lillian laughed. "I hope I do. Thanks, Adele. Thanks, for everything."

Adele left, and Lillian reached over and touched Michael's hand. Jonathan watched the warm way she looked at Michael. He could tell that she liked him a lot.

"Jonathan tells me that you're a good cook, Michael, and I haven't had a home-cooked meal in ages. So, what I propose is that after we sign our lives away this afternoon, you guys spend the afternoon together exploring the city a little, and grocery shop for things you need, and then come home, and, you, Michael, can cook for us."

"Lillian, that sounds like fun," Jonathan said.

"And I'd love that," Michael added.

"After dinner, if you guys like, we could watch a movie. We have hundreds to choose from, and Jonathan knows how to operate the large projectors. Just the four of us."

"I've never watched a movie in someone's home before," Michael gushed, clearly excited.

"I haven't either," Missy said.

"Missy, when Jonathan changes the reels, you could help me make some popcorn in the fireplace."

Missy said, "We are going to have fun, and I suspect a real good meal, too."

Shortly, Mr. Brasso and Mr. Connelly arrived and opened their briefcases on the dining room table. The briefcases were full of documents. As they gave each document to Lillian, she explained them carefully to Jonathan before he signed each one. Michael was sitting at the far end of the table reading a book that he had chosen from the library. From what he could gather, Lillian was lending Jonathan a considerable amount of money, so he would have it available to pay his Federal and State taxes in order to retain ownership of the stock in Taylor Oil that his father had bequeathed to him. She even explained some projected financial statements that Mr. Brasso prepared, showing the bottom line results of Lillian's plan to sell most of her stock in Fennimore, Fennimore and Taylor. Along with the several million dollar proceeds of her husband's life insurance policy, which were tax free, the sale of her stock would provide funds to pay her taxes, so that she could retain the Taylor stock she had inherited as well. The main goal of these preliminary undertakings was to be sure Taylor Oil remained under family control. They decided to address what to do with the other assets, mainly some property in Louisiana and Texas, the apartment, the Seaside Heights mansion, varied stock portfolio, some jewelry and a small commercial building on West 23rd Street that, if they decided to keep it, would require extensive and expensive renovation. But first things first. Taylor Oil was Mr. Taylor's biggest project. He had wanted it to continue, and Jonathan and Lillian were determined to carry out his dream.

As Jonathan signed the papers, he noticed his hands were perspiring and trembling, and that sweat was running from under his armpits trickling down his sides. He realized that he was dealing with real money. Millions and millions of dollars. He also realized that Lillian had loved his father deeply, and that she loved him, too. She could have easily taken her share of the stock and continued on with her life without caring about him at all. He had not known that she was such a wealthy women in her own right. Missy, who was sitting next to Jonathan, and who was turning the pages for him to sign on those pages marked with red stickers, looked at him and saw the beads of perspiration above his lip. And she knew what he was thinking. She knew. Without Lillian, they would just have had large sums of money. But with Lillian not only did they have each other, but money, as well, and a reason to pull together. For each one of them life would continue, without Jonathan Anthony Taylor, on roads, that two weeks ago could not have been imagined.

Michael was not reading his book. He was listening, observing and thinking. He loved that beautiful blond stud doing all the signing, and Michael knew that he, indeed, was a homosexual who had found the love of his life, and he himself would one day be famous. He knew that Jonathan would see to it.

All the papers were signed, including the letter Jonathan had to return to the government about his discharge from the Navy.

After the accountant and lawyer left, Jonathan said, "Michael, let's go into

the kitchen, so you can see what we have, and what we don't have. That way we can go shopping and get whatever you need to create a home-cooked dinner to celebrate all this."

"Sure. Let's."

"We can drop off my letter while we're out. I'll show you the main post office in the United States. It's on Eighth Avenue and Thirty-third Street. It's a beautiful building, and the only post office in the country that is always open, twenty-four hours a day, never closes, not even for Christmas."

"God, Jonathan. I love the city. Someday I'm going to call it home."

"You can call it home right now, Michael," he said as he guided Michael into the kitchen and kissed him when they shut the door. He lifted Michael's hand to his lips and kissed it. The hand with the JT ring on it. "I love you so very much, Michael Manganaro-Taylor."

"You are sweet. But I love you just as much, with every breath, every heartbeat."

Michael looked at the complete supplies in the pantry. All the staples were there. The refrigerator was full of anything he might need like milk and butter. The spice rack has every spice Michael had ever used. There were canisters with flour, sugar, coffee, and a decorative wooden chest full of potatoes and onions.

"We won't have to buy much. Maybe some meat and fresh vegetables."

"Great. What do you think you'd like to make for us?"

"How about a large broiled porterhouse steak with homemade French fries made in peanut oil, broccoli with hollandaise sauce and a big lettuce and tomato salad with freshly made garlic cream dressing?"

"Sounds mouth watering. How about dessert?"

"We'll be getting back too late for me to make a homemade dessert, or else I would make you something very special. But I think we should pick up something from the store."

"Well, let's get started."

They put on their coats, scarves and gloves and were on their way out when Lillian asked, "Jonathan, where are you going to take him?"

"Ninth Avenue. Esposito's, that great butcher, and then to some of the Italian stores on the Avenue."

"Nice. Michael, you should enjoy the afternoon. Make him take you for a walk along the Hudson River, if it gets dark. The sight of the New Jersey communities as they turned on their lights is magnificent, almost as nice as it is from the Jersey side looking at Manhattan, as the lights come on."

"I'm really looking forward to it, Lillian. Too bad you're not coming with us."

"Actually, Michael, I'm dying to take a nap, but I couldn't leave the apartment anyway because I have to answer to *Mrs. Taylor Number One,* and she's hell-bent on getting me into something suitable to wear for tomorrow. She thinks I need a power outfit."

"Then you better do what you have to," Michael said with a big smile.

Missy was clearly pleased to be spoken of in such a manner. She was getting very positive strokes from Lillian, and she liked it. She hadn't gotten such nice feedback in many years and, she thought, maybe I'm not such a loser, after all.

"Get the power outfit, Lillian. We're on our way," Jonathan said as they headed out the door.

Lillian took a nap.

Michael and Jonathan held hands as they walked down Ninth Avenue. Michael recognized it as the same area they drove through on their way to the cemetery. He didn't share that with Jonathan.

Near the Port Authority Bus Terminal street vendors were selling Christmas trees. They stopped to look at them.

"Do you think we should get one?" Jonathan asked.

"Yes. I do. I think it would be a good idea, but only after we bought everything else, and we're on our way home. That would be our last stop. You don't think it would be too much to carry, do you?"

"Too much to carry, for sure, but I know Lillian and Missy would love it, and besides, we can get a checker."

"A checker?"

"Yes, a gigantic yellow taxi with passenger room for five obese theater-goers, or two studs with a Christmas tree."

"Great. But, Jonathan, the trees are quite expensive. They want ten dollars for a six-foot tree."

Jonathan lowered his head and turned it sideways toward Michael and frowned. "We're not poverty-stricken like the kids in *A Tree Grows in Brooklyn.*"

Michael had read the book, seen the movie, and understood.

Esposito's meat market overwhelmed Michael with its selection of prime meats. They bought a three-and-a-half pound porterhouse steak and a half-pound of bacon sliced by hand off the slab. Then they went to the greengrocer and picked up vegetables and then stopped at a few other small stores and purchased everything else they wanted, including a small apple pie, which was still warm. An hour later they picked out a balsam fir and hailed a checker. The driver was complaining about getting his car messed up by the tree and its needles until Jonathan gave him a huge tip, two dollars.

"No problem," the driver said as he took them home.

It had gotten quite late, and they didn't have time for a walk along the Hudson River.

When they got home, Lillian and Missy were in the music room listening to the Christmas album Dame Theofanus had sent.

"Hey, you bought a tree!" Lillian exclaimed joyfully as they entered the room.

"Yes," Jonathan said, "and you and Missy and me are going to put it up right here in the music room. Of course, Lillian, you'll be the supervisor, and Michael will prepare dinner. He tells me he needs an hour-and-a-half."

Michael was all smiles as he watched them smelling the tree like little children. "You guys put up a spectacular Christmas tree, and I'll go into the kitchen and get our meal together. We eat at eight-thirty sharp. Is that okay with all of you? When will the tree be ready?"

"Yes, Michael. Eight-thirty is fine, and, if Lillian will tell me where we put the decorations, lights and stand from last year, the tree will be all set up," Jonathan said.

"You know, Jonathan," Lillian said. "In the closet, off the reception area."

Michael took the bags and went into the kitchen.

Jonathan and Missy put up the tree as they continued listening to Dame Theofanus' album. Lillian enjoyed hearing the happy music of the upcoming season with Jonathan and his mother. It so reminded her of her husband. When the second half of the album had finished, so had the initial tree setup. At least it was standing straight in its stand, as straight as they could get it, and the lights were carefully placed on the branches. Jonathan plugged the main plug into the electric socket, and to everyone's amazement all the bulbs lit.

"I'm glad all the lights lit because I just remembered that you're supposed to test them before you put them on the tree."

Michael came into the room, drying his hands on a kitchen towel.

"It looks fabulous!" he said. "I like it."

"Thank you for your appreciation of this monumental accomplishment," Missy said playfully. "But how is dinner coming?"

"Everything is ready. I just have to put the steak into the broiler. It needs about ten minutes on each side. Will you be ready to eat in twenty minutes?"

"Ready? Oh, my God, yes, Michael," Lillian said. "Watching these two put this tree up has me anxious and hungry. They really could make you nuts. You would think they were preparing for a space launch. They did do a fantastic job though, don't you think, Michael?"

"They did. They most certainly did. I'm putting the steak on now. We eat in twenty minutes."

Michael put the steak into the preheated broiler and returned to help with the tree.

The tree looked festive and made the room smell good.

They all sat down to eat in the kitchen. Michael had lit a few candles, and he turned off the overhead lights. The dinner was superb. They enjoyed the prime steak and, in particular, the apple pie that Michael had placed on the back of the range to keep warm.

"Lillian," Jonathan asked, "what kind of movie would you like to see?"

"Oh, I don't care, as long as it's not depressing."

Missy sat up and suggested, "Why not *Miracle on 34th Street*? Do you have it?"

"Yes. Yes we do," Jonathan said, "and I think it's a great choice. Lillian? Michael?"

"I think it would be perfect," Lillian said.

"I love it!" Michael said.

As they continued eating, they all had one thing in common; they all were tired.

"I hope nobody thinks I'm a party pooper, but all of a sudden I feel too tired to watch a movie," Michael said tentatively.

"Bless you, Michael, I feel the same way," Lillian said, "and we have a big day tomorrow."

"I'll gladly take a rain check," Missy said.

"Thank you. Thank you. Thank you," Jonathan said. "The last thing I wanted to do tonight was run the projectors. I'm absolutely wiped out, and I was ashamed to say anything."

"Jonathan, you and Michael really had a hard day. Imagine shoveling snow and chopping wood all morning, then business in the afternoon and, Michael, thank you so much for working so hard in the kitchen. What a day. Missy, you had a busy day, too, on the phone, altering my outfit for tomorrow, working hours on the sewing machine and putting up the tree. I thank you all."

A little later, after they finished the apple pie, Missy said, "Michael, I enjoyed your cooking very much. Thanks. Can I give you help to clean up here?"

"No thanks, Mom. It'll only take a minute," Jonathan said.

"I appreciate the offer, but we'll have it done in no time," Michael said. "I'm glad you enjoyed everything."

"That's an understatement. It was wonderful, Michael. Just terrific. Thank you," Lillian said as she folded her napkin and placed it on the table. "Michael and Jonathan, you're both special, and you belong together. Do you give this young couple your blessing, Missy?"

"Yes. I do."

"Then I give you mine again, too."

"Thanks, Lillian. Thanks, Missy," Michael said with misty eyes.

"Thanks for your support," Jonathan said as he took Michael's hand in his.

"You're welcome. Now it's time to turn in. Don't forget to set your alarm. We have to be at the office by 8 a.m., not a minute later."

Missy helped Lillian leave the kitchen.

They both said good night to Jonathan and Michael.

"Good night, Mom. Lillian. See you tomorrow."

"Good night."

Michael and Jonathan finished working in the kitchen. They turned off the Christmas tree lights and went to their room. Jonathan set the alarm for 6 a.m. They took off their clothes and threw them on a chair and crawled into bed. They were too exhausted to shower. They felt their naked bodies touching. They reached out and caressed each other. They pulled the covers over themselves and kissed. The aromas of the young men blended into the warmth of the bed. They inhaled the security of the fragrance. They fell fast asleep.

Chapter 56

Tuesday was a cold, clear, sunny day in Short Hills, New Jersey. Short Hills was one of the most affluent communities in the metropolitan area and was home to many Fortune 500 senior executives and corporate board members. Pasquale Botteri and Austin Murphy lived only a few blocks from each other, but were only business associates. They had never pursued a friendship, notwithstanding the fact that they both belonged to the Rolling Hills Country Club.

Pasquale Botteri usually didn't use South Central Gas and Electric's limousine often. But he did use it for Taylor Oil meetings in New York and for Metro-Tri-State Opera meetings and functions, which usually involved traveling to New York or Newark. Today was one of those days. He went a few blocks out of his way that morning, as he sometimes did for Taylor Oil, to pick up fellow board member, Austin Murphy. Other than for initial greetings, it wasn't until they were headed north on the Garden State Parkway that they started talking.

"Well, Austin, what do you think we'll learn at this special meeting Lillian called?" Pasquale Botteri asked his companion.

"I suppose she'll share with us how Jonathan Anthony bequeathed his shares of Taylor, and basically how she intends to dispose of them." Austin filled his pipe from a small leather pouch that he took out of his jacket pocket.

"Under New York State Law, she basically is entitled, as his surviving spouse, to receive fifty percent of his assets. I have no idea what his assets are, or what portion of those are Taylor Oil shares. I don't know anything about his financial condition, or liabilities and, quite frankly, it's really none of my business."

Austin struck a wood match on the sole of his shoe and lit his pipe. "Of course not, Pasquale. I just meant that she'll undoubtedly receive a sizable percentage of his stock which, I'm sure, she might want to unload, to pay the enormous tax burden she'll inherit."

Pasquale opened the window a crack, so his associate could smoke. "I know you and my brother, Tony, had grand plans for Taylor to invest in a managed healthcare business, and Jonathan opposed it."

"Well, it's going to come, you know, and Taylor has the land and resources to help make it happen."

"How so?"

"Well, we have space. We have choice space at all our motels and gas stations on the East Coast that could easily include clinics and similar institutions for complete medical care. We have the parking, etc., thanks to Jonathan's environmentally friendly use of space. Individual health care, as we know it, with individual private physicians directing it and insurance coverage as we have it now, is going to change. In the not too distant future, legislation will allow abortions on demand, and we can provide the facilities for it."

"Well, I would definitely be against that for moral reasons, and I don't believe that managed health care will ever come to pass."

"That's what Jonathan thought, but it's going to happen, and we should be ready. If Tony and I would get hold of more stock we could become more influential on the board. Remington Williams would be with us. If we got a large enough block, we could appoint one of us Chairman of the Board."

"Yes, I'm sure that's a possibility, but you'll have to employ a new President because you both have important full-time obligations."

"You're absolutely right. Not only do we have full-time obligations, but we want to draw up and establish a nationwide health care business. Initially, we plan to expand Star of the Sea Medical Center to include about twenty satellite clinics in our immediate area and to begin offering a prescription drug plan to all at deep discounts, scholarshiped by Meridian Drug Stores."

"Well, Austin, let's not project what will take place at the meeting today. The regular and annual meetings of the board don't take place for a few weeks. I'm sure Lillian just wants to give us some idea of what's ahead. I want to hear what she has to say. She's a terrific lady, and I intend to support her in whatever direction she leads."

Austin was disappointed that Pasquale wasn't enthusiastic about his plans. He had been sure that he would have been more supportive of a plan of his brother's. And he was getting pissed. He could feel his neck swelling, and that meant his blood pressure was rising. Damn. He had thought that Pasquale, as President of South Central Gas and Electric, would have picked up a few more shares of stock, in his own best interest, that could have been voted for his and Dr. Botteri's favor.

Amos, the chauffeur, skillfully drove off the Garden State Parkway onto the New Jersey Turnpike. They drove without any further conversation through the Lincoln Tunnel into Manhattan. They came out onto Dyer Avenue and made a right turn onto Thirty-fourth Street. They proceeded to Tenth Avenue where they made a right and continued uptown.

"Pasquale, I didn't mean to be impolite or rude talking about business, but dealing with Jonathan Anthony over the years has really been frustrating to me. It always seemed to me that he was more interested in opera and social functions, than he was about making money."

Pasquale laughed. "Thank God for that, or I might have been out of one of my jobs. But don't make any mistake about it, he was always interested in money, but he also had a great appreciation for the arts and charity, as well. Don't sell him short. He helped all of us in his own way."

"You're right, of course, Pasquale. I didn't mean to be offensive." Austin relaxed and said, "By the way, how are the boys doing?"

"Fine. Real fine. Found them a great nanny."

They headed east on Central Park South and then south on Park Avenue.

Chapter 57

Max parked the limousine in the building garage and decided to read a Perry Mason mystery until two o'clock when he was to pick up the group in front of the building.

Lillian, Missy, Jonathan and Michael were all speeding in the golden elevator with its onyx side panels to the 40th floor of the art deco building. Lillian was thinking about what consequences this morning's meeting might have on Pasquale Botteri. She was hoping that he would stay on, particularly since he was Chairman of the Metro-Tri-State Opera. Taylor needed him and all his connections. He knew everybody and, if Michael chose a professional singing career, he would be a great help indeed. She had felt so sorry for him when he lost his wife to breast cancer earlier in the year, leaving him with two boys to raise. His wife had been only thirty-four when she died, and that was a real tragedy. Pasquale had always treated Lillian kindly, and she would never forget his attention at Stokes and Stokes and at the reception at her home. During the Funeral Mass she noticed tears in his eyes, which she felt were not for the loss of Jonathan Anthony, but from his own loss. He was a friend, and she hoped he would remain so. Her husband had been very fond of Pasquale. Much of their social life in New York City revolved around the opera and the people associated with it. Willington Balmoral thought Pasquale was a great human being. She had heard him say it more than once.

The doors opened, and Jonathan stepped out to hold them open for Lillian and Missy. Michael followed the women. They were in the main reception area of Taylor Oil. It was 7:50 a.m. Barbara Greenfeld heard them arrive and walked out to greet them.

"Good morning, Barbara," Lillian said.

"Good morning, Mrs. Taylor. Good morning everyone," Miss. Greenfeld said as she shook hands.

"Hi, Barbara," Jonathan said.

"Hello, Mr. Taylor. In case anyone wants fresh coffee, I just put it on. It should be done in a minute or two."

"Barbara, you know my mother, Mrs. Melissa Turner Taylor, but you haven't met my friend, Michael. Michael, this is Miss Barbara Greenfeld, my father's assistant. Barbara, this is Michael Manganaro."

"How do you do, Miss. Greenfeld?" Michael greeted, and he was proud of himself. He was learning these formalities.

"How do you do, Mr. Manganaro? It is certainly very nice to meet one of Mr. Taylor's friends."

Ms. Greenfeld opened the thick glass door leading to the executive suite.

"Please follow me. Would you like to have your meeting in Mr. Taylor's office, Mrs. Taylor?"

"Splendid. Yes. Thank you."

They followed Ms. Greenfeld into the large wood paneled office. Nothing had been changed, or moved since Lillian saw it last. Her picture and her husband's were side-by-side on the credenza behind the large walnut desk. There was also a picture of Jonathan Anthony, Jonathan and Missy taken many years ago, when they were working together serving the homeless Thanksgiving dinner at The Church of the Heavenly Rest. After their marriage, Jonathan wanted to put the picture away, but Lillian insisted he leave it where it was. And she was glad that she had done so. Particularly now. She saw how Jonathan, Michael and Missy spotted it.

"Barbara, I do appreciate your kindness in leaving things just the way they were. I'm not going to change anything at this point either."

"Everything is the same as the day Mr. Taylor left. I have processed his mail, however, and I've held those items that I wanted to discuss with you today. I hope that's okay with you."

"More than just okay. It's exactly what I wanted you to do." Lillian noticed a small bouquet of flowers on the desk in front of the sofa. "Where did the flowers come from?"

"I knew you were coming in today, so I picked them up on my way in at Grand Central this morning for you."

"Oh, thank you. That was certainly thoughtful."

"Let me take your coats and put them in the closet."

"Thanks," Lillian said.

Lillian watched Barbara as she handled the coats. Barbara was smartly dressed in a dark blue, wool suit, probably Chanel, with a starched white cotton blouse. She had on one strand of pearls and wore a thin gold wristwatch. She had a ring on her left hand with a large emerald cut sapphire. She wore black, soft leather shoes with a medium heals. She was neat and elegant. She was wearing a fragrance that she recognized as one of those that she had handled for Fennimore. It was *Tweed.* Barbara was a women in her early forties with medium length black hair. Her nail enamel and lipstick matched, and if Lillian wasn't mistaken, it was Revlon's *Fire and Ice.* Looking at Barbara made her suddenly conscious of her own appearance. Missy had done a spectacular job. She felt she looked as good as could be expected in her physical condition, and her stone martens on top of Jonathan's sport jacket looked very smart.

"Let's all be seated, shall we? Jonathan, please sit at your father's desk."

Everyone took seats facing each other around the desk.

"Barbara, may I dictate a short memo to you?"

"Of course." Barbara picked up her steno pad and sat at the corner of the desk next to Lillian.

Lillian began very matter-of-factly, "Please do this in the format you would have used for my husband and address it to Mr. Henry Rayburn with copies to all Taylor Oil officers and staff and with copies to all Members of the Board. I'd like you to do this for me as soon as you can because I want to pass it out at the ten o'clock meeting. And here's the text: Henry, I really appreciate how you, as Executive Vice President of the Company, took charge of Taylor Oil business when my husband was killed. Thank you for staying in contact with me during the period since his death until now. Please do what you have been doing until December 31, 1960. I expect a new management team to be effective on January 1st, 1961, and want you to remain in your position as Executive Vice President at that time. But for now, please keep running the show. I approved your recommendations for year-end bonuses for all and will officially approve them on January 1st. I want the staff to know that under the circumstances, such a large expenditure of funds would not be able to be made without approval of the CEO prior to the Christmas holiday. In addition, I will approve the raises you recommended, as well, sometime in January, but they will be retroactive to December 16, 1960. In the months ahead I expect that many of our officers and employees will be burning some midnight oil to make the transition go smoothly. At the end of the first quarter of next year, I expect to give additional bonuses to all those who are deserving. I will speak to you later about the budget meetings I want held in the latter part of January. Paragraph. Jonathan, my stepson, and I wish all of you a Very Happy and Holy Christmas and a Happy and Prosperous New Year! May the peace of the Lord be with you and your families always. Cordially, Lillian Taylor. That's it, Barbara. Thanks. Now, Missy, can you help me to the second conference room? Jonathan, can you lead the way?"

They left for the other room. Barbara remained behind to type the memo.

"I'll bring the architect to you as soon as he arrives," Barbara called after them.

"Thanks, Barbara."

Lillian looked around the conference room, and it was exactly as she remembered. It measured approximately thirty-two feet by twelve feet with four windows equally spaced along the thirty-two foot external outside wall. The architect arrived, and Lillian outlined her plan to create two offices, one small one where the current entrance door was, which would have one window, and a larger one with three windows and two doors, one of which would go through the dividing wall between the smaller, secretarial office and the larger executive office. She showed him sketches she had made on tracing paper and told him he could take them with him. She explained that most of the work should be done at nights and on weekends, and that it was imperative that these offices be ready by January 1, 1961.

She took the architect to Jonathan Anthony's office and explained that she wanted similar furniture, wall treatment and carpeting, as close as they could get anyway, for the new offices being created in the conference room space.

Barbara finished typing the memo on the Smith-Corona typewriter that she normally used in her office outside Mr. Taylor's. She brought it in to Mrs. Taylor for signature.

Lillian took it from her hand. "Thank you, Barbara. Please have a seat for a minute. We're just concluding our construction meeting, and I want you and everyone else in this room to know exactly what's going on.

Lillian poured herself a drink of water from the carafe on the desk.

"When Mr. Taylor's common stock is transferred to my stepson and me, Barbara, we are going to own 62.2% of the total common stock of the Company. At the Annual Meeting of Stockholders, Jonathan Taylor will be elected to replace his father as Chairman of the Board, and I will

be elected to replace my husband as President and Chief Executive
Officer. This is basically what the ten o'clock meeting is all about."

"Wow! That's great news. I think some of the board members are
going to be surprised."

Lillian smiled. "I think you may be right."

"Do I have a place in the arrangement?" Barbara Greenfeld asked.

"Of course. I'd like you to work with me," Jonathan said, and he
smiled his smile.

She blushed.

"And Missy will work with me, but none of this is going to take place
until January 1st . Only the Board members will know all the details. I
want you, Barbara, to work closely with Henry Rayburn. While I'm at
home, I want you to call me regularly from a phone outside the office,
even if you don't have anything to talk about because I can't call you
with that outdated switchboard. All the operators know who is calling
whom and how often and, of course, they can listen in. No privacy
whatsoever. That's one of the first things I want to get in here, is direct
dialing and do away with the switchboard. The receptionist could direct
calls that come to the main number. I mean it's 1960, not 1940. And
now that I think about it, Barbara, order a decent electric typewriter for
yourself and get one for Missy, too."

"Well, I for one, am glad you're onboard. Welcome."

The architect said he would provide preliminary plans for review in
two days, as well, as a proposal from his company for the construction.
He said that when he came back he would have the requisite books for
furniture, wood paneling, carpeting, paint and electrical fixtures.

"Barbara, you and Jonathan will stay in this suite, and Missy and I
will occupy the new space. Barbara, we are going to remain in the office
until five minutes to ten. Please lock the door for me and use the key and
get us then. In the meantime, please receive our Directors and put them
in the big conference room. When Mr. Brasso and Mr. Connelly arrive
show them to the room and ask them to sit against the rear wall."

"Yes, Mrs. Taylor. The caterer has already set up a breakfast buffet as
usual."

"That's nice. Barbara, after the meeting, Missy, Jonathan and Michael
and I are having lunch at the Cloud Club. Would you like to join us as
my guest?"

"I would. I very much would."

The Directors arrived shortly before ten. They helped themselves to
juice, coffee and tiny pieces of pastry.

Barbara came back into the office at five minutes to ten.

"Thanks, Barbara. Now here's my plan. In four minutes I want to go in. I do not want to allow time for condolences. I saw all these people on Friday. I want to begin immediately. Barbara bring your pad for notes. Missy, I want you beside me at the head of the table. Jonathan, Michael and Barbara, take seats along the wall, please."

Two minutes passed quickly and Mrs. Jonathan Taylor was pushed into the room rapidly by Missy. Those who were seated, stood.

"Good morning." She said. "Please be seated wherever you feel comfortable. I want to begin right away."

"Good morning, Lillian," Willington Balmoral said. "You look very well. I'm glad to see that."

"Thank you."

"Yes, you do. Good morning, Lillian," Dr. Botteri greeted.

"I'll third that. You look very smart," Pasquale Botteri added.

"Thank you. Now I will tell you why we are here this morning. First, I want you to know that I have resigned as Executive Vice President of Fennimore, Fennimore and Taylor effective December 31, 1960." She looked around the room at the faces. Willington smiled ever so slightly. Austin Murphy looked at Pasquale Botteri coldly as if Pasquale knew about this beforehand. Pasquale was pinching his nose with his hand covering his mouth. Lillian was sure he was hiding a smile. Dr. Kennedy opened his eyes wide and sat back in his chair and looked directly into Lillian's eyes. He looked as if he were about to begin some sort of intense interrogation. Remington Williams was looking down at the pad in front of him and began doodling.

"Second, I wanted to remind you that the by-laws of Taylor Oil provide that the Annual Meeting of Stockholders shall be held here at the principal office of the Corporation on the penultimate Thursday of December at two o'clock in the afternoon. That is, of course, Thursday, December 22nd this year. That gives us a little more than three weeks to get ready. And that meeting will be immediately followed by a regular monthly Board of Directors meeting.

"So you see we have two agendas to be prepared. Our current by-laws provide that the number of Directors constituting the entire Board of Directors shall be eight. Because Mr. Taylor is no longer with us we will be seven.

"Missy will you pass out these to all. Thanks. The agenda for the Stockholders Meeting as I see it is being passed out now as well as a memo I dictated this morning.

AGENDA
Annual Stockholders Meeting
December 22, 1960

1. Roll call
2. Proof of notice of meeting
3. Reading of minutes of preceding meeting
4. Report of officers
5. Report of committees
6. Election of Directors
7. Unfinished business
8. New business

"Thank you for looking it over. I am recommending that Jonathan Anthony Taylor's son, Jonathan Taylor, be elected a Director at that meeting effective January 1, 1961, and that he be asked to Chair the Board. I am hoping that that appointment will be unanimously affirmed. And since Dr. Sean Kennedy will be leaving us at the end of this year to become part of the President's Cabinet, I am asking the Membership Committee to search for a replacement and make a recommendation of someone to fill his position on the Board.

"Third, by the time of the Annual Meeting, after transfers of owner-ship are completed, Mr. Taylor's son, Jonathan, and I will own 62.2 per-cent of the common stock of the Corporation. I've have asked our accountant and lawyer, Mr. Stephen Brasso and Mr. Patrick Connelly, to be here today if you had any questions. They are handling the details for us. I think we have a strong Board, and I sincerely hope all of you will remain. If anyone wishes, however, to tender his resignation, I shall reluctantly accept it.

"Fourth, for the regular Board of Directors meeting, we must prepare an agenda for the election of a slate of Corporate officers. I want to re-elect the officers who are in position today. I will be joining Taylor Oil to work full time and agree to serve in the capacity of President and Chief Executive Officer, effective January 1, 1961."

Austin Murphy lit his pipe. His face was all red. His neck was swelling.

Dr. Botteri squirmed in his seat.

Remington Williams said, "Mrs. Taylor are you sure you'll be well enough at that point in time to take on such a responsibility?"

"Yes, Lillian," Dr. Botteri echoed, "are you sure you're ready? This is a real tough job for someone without oil company experience."

"Dr. Botteri," Willington Balmoral said, "Mrs. Taylor was head of Baton Rouge Oil, her father's company, for five years after his death, and was so successful at that, that Taylor Oil acquired it eight years ago in one of our most successful friendly takeovers. It was a very profitable company and increased our bottom line substantially and gave us access to retail outlets in Mississippi, Louisiana and Florida. That certainly must have been prior to your joining the Board."

"And as far as my health is concerned, by January 1st I should be out of this chair and under my own power. In any case, I will entertain thoughts and discussions by Board Members, but I will not tolerate division. Period."

"I didn't know about Baton Rouge Oil. I beg your pardon."

"Apology accepted. Now, I'd like the members to discuss filling Mr. Kennedy's spot with Mrs. Melissa Turner Taylor, who is sitting beside me, over the weeks from now until the next meeting. By that time I hope you will have come up with an eligible candidate. Some of you know Mrs. Taylor, and some of you don't. Therefore, may I present her to all of you now."

Everyone stood up and shook her hand, as she walked around the room.

"Mrs. Taylor knows all the intellectual elite in the City, and I definitely want an academician to fill the spot to be vacated. My husband was very much in favor of helping in all areas of education, particularly in high schools and colleges. He felt strongly that corporations such as Taylor owed that to the communities they called home, and I feel the same way. He even helped legislation get through Congress for increased student loans and other education friendly laws. Mrs. Taylor is joining me as my assistant starting in January, also. In case you didn't notice the resemblance, she is our soon to be Chairman's mother."

The meeting continued until eleven-thirty. The Membership Committee knew what they had to do, and the Secretary of the Board, Willington Balmoral, knew what he had to prepare for the next meeting.

"Thank you all for coming. I'll see you all on the 22nd of December. Maybe I'll be out of this chair. I do want you to know that I appreciate your concern. On the 22nd, Willington, would you be kind enough to Chair that meeting for us, as well as to Chair the regular meeting that follows?"

"Mrs. Taylor, it shall be my pleasure."

Everyone left, it seemed to Lillian, more quickly than they had at past gatherings.

"Missy, can I ask your assistance? I need to use the ladies' room and the door is too narrow, and the wheelchair doesn't fit. It would help me so much if you could just help me inside and then wait for me outside. I'll call when I'm ready to come out."

"Lillian, of course. Someday a law should be passed to make public facilities and office work spaces accessible to all people, even those in wheelchairs."

"Well, Missy, I never thought of that, but I was never disabled before. It's a good thought."

The Cloud Club had a spectacular view, almost as nice as the view from Taylorville. The food was mediocre, but they had delicious Champagne to wash it down. Barbara had a few drinks and made everyone at the table laugh.

"Mrs. Taylor," Barbara said, "I was so excited hearing you speak to those stuffed shirts, who were intent on putting you down, that I almost wet my pants. You really took them by surprise."

Lillian reached over and took Barbara's hand. "That was a sweet thing to say. Thank you."

Chapter 58

Louisa and Anthony had just finished talking to Michael on the phone and were sitting down to supper.

"I can't believe how many things Mike has experienced since August, Louisa. Can you?"

"No. And I just can't picture the meeting he described to us about Taylor Oil this morning. I personally think that that Mrs. Lillian Taylor sounds, well, scary."

"Well, she is going to be heading a big company. It must be a hard job for a man. For a woman, it must be harder. I guess she has to be tough. And Jonathan as Chairman of the Board. It seems to me he's just a few years from delivering groceries on his bike."

"Well, Michael has certainly gotten to see another side of life. And it isn't simple, like here. But I don't believe for one minute that Jonathan Taylor ever delivered groceries on a bike. And if life experience is necessary for success, and if Mrs. Theofanus is right, Michael may be on his way to becoming a great singer."

"Louisa, you shouldn't get your hopes up so high. He still has four years of the Navy to deal with before he can seriously pursue that, if that is what he decides. And what about his friendship? He likes Jonathan more than he has ever liked anyone else, and now Jonathan is going to stay home and Michael's going on to parts unknown. I think he is going to be heartbroken. Very crushed and hurt. I think he is going to be more depressed and lonely than he's ever been when he has to leave Jonathan."

"Why do you say that, Anthony?"

"Because I think our son is in love."

Louisa said, "I know how fond he is of Jonathan, but I think he is probably more infatuated with his position of power and wealth.

Everything is new and exciting. Servants. New York City. That gorgeous apartment. First class travel."

"Well I don't, Louisa. I don't. I think they are homosexuals and that they the are in love. I've been reading up on it. I have a few books down in my workshop."

Louisa knew he was right, but didn't know what to say.

"I know I'm right. The ring episode didn't fool me for one minute. I pretended it did because I wanted to think about it for some time. I wanted to think clearly, and let it sink in. If this is the way Michael is, we have to accept it. I've thought about it before and never said anything. But I do know one thing that is absolutely certain. Michael is one of the kindest people I know, and he couldn't do anything wrong. I don't care what the church says. I will support him."

They heard Rosa's car pull up into the driveway.

She came into the kitchen, just as they were getting ready to eat.

"Hey, you guys. I'm glad I made it in time. I'm starved."

"How did things go at the bank today, Rosa?" Anthony asked.

"Good. Nothing exciting, until I got a phone call from Michael. He had some day. What excitement. It sounded like the meeting at Taylor was from the movies. We had a nice long talk, and he sounded on top of the world. The only thing I detected at the end of the conversation that was a little sad, was that I felt he was getting extremely anxious about going back to the Navy. He said he was going to miss Jonathan and, quite frankly, he's afraid. He seems happier than he's ever been all his life. And I just think, he thinks that his world will fall apart when he separates from Jonathan."

Anthony said, "Rosa, we were just talking about that. Rosa, how would you feel if you found out that your brother liked guys instead of girls?"

"Fine. It really has nothing to do with how I feel. I know it won't be easy for him, but if that's his destiny, he has no choice. They are very much in love. I suspected that they were lovers right away. Anyone can see that. I love him a lot, and if Jonathan is the guy he has chosen, hey, he has my blessing."

"Does he have yours, too, Louisa?"

"Yes, Anthony."

Anthony tossed the salad. Louisa put the remainder of food on the table and sat down. Rosa took off her coat and scarf and put them on an empty chair and sat down, too.

"He has mine, too," Anthony said with tears in his eyes, as he left the table.

The phone rang.

"Hello," Louisa answered.

"Hi, Ma. It's me."

"Well, hello again. We were almost ready to eat, and we were talking about you."

"I just wanted you to know some more good news. Lillian just got back from the doctor, and he says she's healing well, better than expected and that she will be up and around before Christmas. He says she may have to use a crutch or cane for a while, but she should be fine."

"Well that certainly is good news. We're glad to hear it. Your father will be pleased."

"Also, Jonathan and I have a night flight to St. Thomas. We're going to say there until Saturday. Missy and Lillian said they thought we looked a little pale and that we should pick up some rays."

"Sounds wonderful. But how can you afford a trip like that?"

"I can't, but Jonathan can."

"Do you think it's right? I mean to accept such a lavish gift?"

Anthony had returned to the kitchen and was listening.

"Give me the phone, Louisa."

"Your father wants to talk to you," she said as she gave the phone to her husband.

"So, where is this expensive place you're going?"

"St. Thomas."

"Sounds like a fun thing to do. Who's paying?"

"Jonathan is."

"Well, since I never had a partner with money, your mother was always as poor as a church mouse, you shouldn't feel guilty about enjoying Jonathan's good fortune. You should enjoy it."

"You mean that, Dad?"

"Yes, and you have my blessing. Your mother and sister and I finally agreed on one thing. We want you to be happy. Will we be seeing you soon?"

"Yes, on Saturday."

"Oh, by the way, if that ring ever gets stuck again, maybe it's a good sign. Leave it on."

Mr. Manganaro hung up and sat at the table. "Why are you letting the food get cold, Louisa? You always do that."

Louisa went across the table to her husband, and kissed him on the forehead. She hadn't done anything so spontaneous in years.

"Let's eat for heavens sake. I told you I was starved," Rosa said smiling.

Chapter 59

Michael and Jonathan were enjoying every minute of their stay in St. Thomas. The weather was perfect. The temperature was in the 90's. They were staying at Blackbeards's Castle, which was situated on the side of the hill above Charlotte Amalie. It was charming. The grounds were covered with exquisite tropical plants, many of which had fragrant flowers. Neither Michael nor Jonathan knew the names of the plants.

Yesterday, they went to the beach in the morning to start getting a tan. They found a secluded spot and made love in the bright, tropical sunshine. They both were getting sunburned in spite of all the lotion they spread on each other.

In the afternoon, they shopped in town and bought gifts for everyone they knew. Then they took an open taxi back to the hotel. Some of the low-hanging foliage brushed against them, as the jeep-taxi traveled recklessly over the bumpy dirt road up the steep hill.

Today they left shore in a rented sailboat. Michael didn't know a thing about sailing, but he did get a thrill watching Jonathan expertly maneuver the tiny vessel.

"You're good at this, aren't you, Jonathan?" Michael observed.

"I've had lots and lots of practice. We always spent a good portion of summers at our Seaside Heights house. When I first started sailing, I used to practice on the bayside of our property, and later I ventured out into the Atlantic. I had a couple close calls, but after a few years, I got good at it."

"What kind of close calls?"

"Capsized a few times and had to swim back to the beach. Lost two boats."

"That's all? Christ, Jonathan, I hope you don't have any plans of losing this boat!"

"Michael, I'm not fourteen anymore. I have the love of my life with me, the person I want to spend the rest of my life with. And I want that to be for a very long time, many years, not just an afternoon. And besides, I'm about to become Chairman of the Board."

"Whew! That's good news because, like Susan Hayward, *I Want to Live.*"

"Precious, I've watched you become an expert swimmer in boot camp."

"Jonathan! We're so far out, I could never swim back!"

"Precious, you won't have to. I promise."

"I trust you, Stud-boy, but you almost got us caught making love on the beach yesterday. Thank God we finished before those school teachers from Wisconsin discovered our secret place."

"Yeah, those women were funny, though. They hit on us so hard, trying to get us to take them to dinner. It was great that I was so satisfied, or I would have been tempted to fuck one of them."

"Oh, my God! You are a pig!"

"Michael, I have to bury it somewhere."

"Yuck."

Jonathan burst out laughing. "Michael, I was just kidding."

"I know."

The sun was hot.

"Jonathan, want some ice tea?"

"Sure."

The beverage cooled them a little. They ate the boxed lunches the hotel provided and began sailing back to the port.

"Michael, do you know the only thing missing in our relationship?"

"What?"

"A baby. Wouldn't it be great to raise a baby together?"

"My fantasy exactly. But how could we ever manage that?"

"I don't know. Who knows? Maybe one of us could adopt a baby somehow."

"Very unlikely. Single people can't adopt children. The law doesn't permit it, I don't think."

"You're right."

Jonathan offered to give Michael some sailing instructions and Michael declined. Jonathan guided the sailboat toward land. Charlotte Amalie came clearly into view and Michael began to feel safer. They sailed past an aircraft carrier anchored in the harbor. It was the U.S.S.

Boxer, and it seemed gigantic towering above them as they went by in the tiny sailboat.

"What's the matter, Michael? Are you crying?" Jonathan asked sounding alarmed.

Michael wiped his eyes and cleared his throat. "Not really. Just feeling sorry for myself. I'm going to miss you when I go back. I'm going to miss you very, very much."

"Oh, Michael, I'm going to miss you, too, but we'll get together as often as we can manage. You have to remember, Michael, that I have the resources to fly anyplace you are, so we can be together."

"But you'll have so many responsibilities."

"I can manage to work around them. And wherever you are stationed, like in Norfolk, for instance, I can get us an apartment."

"I never thought of it like that."

"Well, Michael, start. We'd be like any other married couple with someone in the military."

"You mean you'd really want just me? And that you'd wait for me even if I went on a long cruise?"

"Yes, of course. I love you. I'll wait for you and promise to give myself only to you always. I thought you understood that."

"I guess my self-esteem isn't as high as I would like it to be. I'm so afraid of losing you. You're the most important person in my life. Since I've never felt this way before, I am scared to death you'll find someone else and dump me."

"Michael, I won't. I want only you."

Jonathan secured the sail and went over to Michael and kissed him tenderly.

"Michael, I love you, and we have the best wishes of both our families behind us. This would not be so if they didn't recognize that we belong together. Just think about it. We have your religious parents, your once-homophobic sister, my dynamic, business-oriented stepmother and my romantic mother pulling for us. Initially, I only expected my mother's understanding and support, but we won them all over. Michael, we are joined. Joined in harmony and love for the rest of our lives. Do you understand?

"Yes, Jonathan. I do. I want only you."

They kissed. A group of sailors on the fantail of the Boxer saw them and several yelled obscene observations and recommendations.

Chapter 60

Maureen was waiting for Theresa to finish work. She was sitting at a booth near the front. Soft music, mostly Christmas carols, was playing over the speaker. That music, in addition to the glass of wine she was sipping, made her feel peaceful. The neon sign, *John's Italian Kitchen,* that was in the front window, cast a cheerful orange light on the tables up front. It made the pine wood paneling take on a holiday sheen. The fireplace was lit and added warmth and spirit to the room, if not real heat. The faint smell of oregano and basil was coming from the kitchen.

She looked at her wristwatch. It wouldn't be long now, and they would be on their way to her house. Tonight was Friday. The night of the great examination. The last food had been served at eleven, and as soon as that table finished, Theresa could clean up and they would be on their way.

She was thinking about Michael. She had heard from Bruce that he was in St. Thomas with Jonathan. She had seen some pictures of St. Thomas in a travel agency ad in a magazine and thought that it was a romantic looking place. It looked like the type of place to go on a honeymoon. Damn, not like they both weren't handsome enough already, now they'll probably come home all tan.

Theresa was spending the night at Gruber's because her parents were having family from Brooklyn visiting, and they were using her room for the night. She didn't want to sleep on the sofa. Theresa had always told Maureen how much she disliked her father's trashy relatives from the pits of the earth, Brooklyn. She had told her that she had to get away from Mellon and those damn relatives from Brooklyn. She had said even the way they talked turned her stomach.

Maureen sat quietly thinking about him. Maybe if she were lucky, he would come home and ask her out. If he did, she'd let him go all the way.

No questions asked. She wouldn't even wear a girdle. Theresa had been explaining exactly how it all felt. Maureen was sure that she hadn't left anything out. Theresa was so descriptive, Maureen thought she could be a great actress. Maybe if we don't go all the way, Maureen thought, he'd let me taste it. Talking with Theresa is beginning to make me crazy, Maureen thought.

Finally, Theresa was ready to leave. It was about a quarter to twelve when they started for Maureen's house on Maple Avenue. Her parents left lights on in the living room when Maureen was out late and that night was no exception. Mr. and Mrs. Gruber usually were in bed early because they always went to the bakery at four in the morning to help the night shift finish baking for the morning rush. Theresa and Maureen went directly to Maureen's room on the second floor.

Maureen and Theresa took their winter coats off and hung them on the coat rack next to the door. She made sure the door was locked.

"Now, Maureen, I have to use the bathroom."

"Well, you know where it is. It's right there."

Maureen removed her shoes and began undressing.

Theresa came out of the bathroom twirling her underpants on her right index finger singing, "I'm in the money. I'm in the money." Theresa tossed her panties to Maureen, who caught them.

"Well?" Theresa asked as she watched Maureen examine them. "Not a spot. Not a fuckin' spot! I told you it would be like that. I'm never late. I've suspected I was pregnant, so I made an appointment with Dr. Giambelli for tomorrow at ten. I told him of my suspicions, and he said he would draw blood for tests, which would give definite results by Tuesday, midday. He said he would telephone me with the results, but I said, in addition, I would visit him later that day to get a written diagnosis."

"Why do you have to have a written diagnosis?"

"For the presentation! Visual evidence is much more effective than hearsay."

"Oh, my God! You're going to go through with it."

"Yes, Maureen, Yes, I am."

"What are you going to do first?"

"If I can, I'll talk to Jonathan, hopefully, tomorrow afternoon. I want to tell him about missing my period and seeing the doctor. I want him to sweat a little before I get the final word. That will double the effect. Then, I don't think it will take too long for this thing to be flushed down the toilet."

Maureen retched. "Please don't talk like that. Please, Theresa."

"Okay. Okay. But I'll have to wait for their offering. I want to see what creative solution they'll come up with."

"You can't prove he's the father."

"And he can't prove he's not. But I can prove that we had intercourse on the evening of November 18th at approximately 9:15 at night. I have at least one witness."

"Why would you need a witness?"

"Well, Maureen, I spoke to the lawyer my father is using to sue the railroad, and he suggested that if I am pregnant, I should have him get depositions of what happened that night from anyone who knew," Theresa said, as she removed her clothes and threw them on the bed.

"You mean I would have to testify in court?"

"No, just make a sworn statement in a lawyer's office."

"What about asking Michael? He was there, too."

"My father's lawyer will get in touch with him if necessary, you know, if Jonathan doesn't play fair. He said the possibility of a scandal for the Taylors would increase if other people began to get involved in this. I mean right now, it's just us, you and me, and the doctor and lawyer, both of whom are bound by confidentiality, but if we have to involve third parties like Michael, who knows where it could take us. I don't think Jonathan would want Michael involved."

"Well, I don't either. But I don't want to do it either."

"You will do it, because it's the right thing to do. If you don't, you'll go to hell!"

Chapter 61

On Saturday when Jonathan and Michael arrived at the apartment from the airport, no one was home. There was a note on the refrigerator door for Jonathan.

"Jonathan, call Theresa. She says it's urgent and that you had her number. We'll be back later this evening. We went to see a play. Love, Lillian."

"Michael, look at this," Jonathan said, handing the note to him.

"I wonder what it's about? Are you going to call?"

"I suppose I have to, to find out what's up."

They went into the bedroom where the early afternoon sun was streaming in. They put their luggage on the bed, and Jonathan picked up the phone. He dialed Theresa's number. There was no answer. He waited for five minutes and called again. Still, no answer.

"No answer?" Michael asked.

"Nope. I'm very curious why she called."

"Me, too. Would you want me to call Maureen and try to find out?"

"Sure. Good idea."

"Okay," Michael said, as he dialed her number, which he knew for years.

"Hello."

"Hi, Maureen. It's Michael."

"Hiya, Michael. Did you just get home from the Caribbean?"

"Yes. We did. We're unpacking as we speak. I plan to be in church tomorrow. How about you?"

"Sure. Singing in the choir is the highlight of my week, unless I spend time with you," Maureen said, as she crossed her fingers and showed them to Theresa.

"Maureen, that's nice to hear."

"Next week," Maureen continued, "*The Apartment* is playing at the drive-in. I would like to go with you and only you. I could bring a nice picnic basket. Fried chicken. Corn bread. We could have a warm supper in the car. Just the two of us. I like how it feels when your eyelash tickles my cheek and your hands explore my body."

"Maureen, the picnic and the movie sound great, and so do the tickling and exploring, but I'm not sure of my schedule for next week. I'm not even home now. I'm here at Jonathan's. But if I can manage it, I'd very much like to be with you."

"Just thinking about being along with you makes me feel warm all over. Just the two of us, Michael. I hope we can go. I'm so glad you called."

"Me, too. Jonathan is here with me. He tried to call Theresa at her house, and he didn't get an answer."

"That's because she's here with me. She probably didn't think to give him this number because she's going home soon. Does he want to talk to her now?"

"Jonathan, Theresa's with Maureen," Michael said, handing the phone to Jonathan.

"Hi, Maureen. It's me, Jonathan."

"I know, Jonathan. You sound as good as you look. Here's Theresa."

"Hi, Jonathan. Did you have a nice vacation?"

"Hi, Theresa. Yeah. We really had a good time. It was great. How have you been? I understand you called."

"I'm glad you enjoyed yourself. I did call, Jonathan. I called because I missed my period and, consequently, went to my doctor today."

"What did he say?"

"That I'm probably pregnant, but we'll know for sure on Tuesday when the result of the blood test comes back."

"And if you are, what do you plan to do?" Jonathan asked.

"We'll, I haven't been with anyone but you since August, so I was hoping you'd help me out somehow."

"I see. You weren't thinking of doing anything dangerous, or illegal, were you? Because I wouldn't help you then."

"Not really. Of course, it entered my mind, but not as a serious option. But, I also do not want the responsibility of raising a kid, Jonathan." She paused for a moment and then continued, "Jonathan, will you help me? My father's lawyer said I should speak to you before I told anyone else. I hope you don't mind."

"You did the right thing, Theresa. Thank you for letting me know about this, so we can deal with it. Just in case you are pregnant, could you come to Manhattan and meet with me and my attorney one day next week? Perhaps, Tuesday evening?"

"Yes. I could."

"You could bring your attorney if you care to."

"I'll come alone, Jonathan. If there are any legal things to be taken care of, your attorney and my attorney can work them out. I'll have the doctor's diagnosis with me. I knew you'd help me, Jonathan. I liked you a lot from the first moment I saw you. If I didn't, I wouldn't be in this jam now. I trust you, Jonathan. I do."

"Theresa, you're swell, and I trust you, too. I believe that you're telling me the truth, and that if you are pregnant, you are pregnant with my child."

"If I am, Jonathan, it is your child. And I'm sure he, or she is beautiful beyond belief, but I thank you for understanding how I feel. I do not want a kid. I'll be hearing from you about the time and place for the meeting, then?"

"Yes. You will."

"Goodbye, Jonathan."

"Bye."

Theresa put the receiver down and put her arms around Maureen.

"Maureen, he is a nice guy. I can tell by what he said that he doesn't want me to abort. I think he wants me to have the baby. Probably wants me to give it up for adoption. That's okay, but wouldn't it be wonderful if he wanted to keep the baby. I'd sign over custody, or whatever I had to do, to give the baby to him."

"Theresa, he'll take care of you financially, I'm sure."

"I know. I know."

Michael was rinsing out his and Jonathan's bathing suits in the bathroom sink. He had been listening to the conversation and didn't know what to say.

"Precious, please come sit with me in the music room."

"Okay."

They walked into the music room.

"I'm going to light a fire. Then I'm going to play some music and mix you a drink. Michael, would you go fill up the ice bucket in the kitchen, while I fix the fire?"

"Sure." Michael took the glass bucket to the kitchen.

Jonathan put on Mrs. Theofanus' album and lit the fire that had already been set. When Michael returned with the ice, Jonathan mixed some Manhattans in a large glass pitcher. He poured the drinks and went over to where Michael was seated on the sofa. He handed a glass to Michael.

"Here's to us, Michael, and our happy life together." They touched glasses and each of them took a sip of their drink.

Jonathan knelt in front of Michael with his hands on Michael's thighs.

"Michael, as soon as I'm done talking to you, I'm going to call Mr. Connelly. As you've heard, Theresa is probably pregnant. While I have the money and connections to terminate that condition, I will not. I'm sure Theresa would prefer that, but I just think it's wrong and illegal. And it is my baby, my child, and I want it."

Michael took Jonathan's hands into his own, asking, "What are you going to do?"

"I want Theresa to carry the pregnancy to term and deliver the baby to me. I will admit paternity, and as the baby's father, I will accept all responsibility to raise the child. I would want Theresa to give up her parental rights."

"Do you think that's possible?"

"Yes. It has to be because that's what I want to happen."

"Aren't you going to get Lillian's input?"

"No, Michael. This is my business, and I know what I want. I want us, you and me, to raise this child. It's mine after all, and what's mine, is yours."

Michael thought Jonathan was getting more attractive with every passing minute. Michael asked, "How can you get her to agree to this?"

"Mr. Connelly is going to have to help me here, but I'm sure we can do it. I don't want to just buy her off with five thousand dollars and have her disappear. I want to help her fulfill her dreams and get started on a new way of life. She can get a good education, and I want to provide her with funds to start off in whatever direction she wants to go. I want, selfishly, for her to have no desire whatsoever to seek the child out in the future. I'm sure Mr. Connelly will come up with a satisfactory plan and payment schedule."

"But I'm going back to the Navy in a week or so. I won't be able to help you."

"Michael, the baby won't be here until next August and you'll only have three more years to go by then. And, who knows, you may be stationed someplace we can all call home."

"I hope so, Jonathan. You make it sound wonderful. I absolutely love the idea. I want it, too."

"Even if we lived here, it would be great. We could hire a full-time nanny and have Lillian and Missy as built-in backup."

"I like it," Michael said. "I do."

"Well, after we get Theresa to agree, we have a long time to make preparations."

"You know, Jonathan, I don't feel so bad about getting ready to go back to the Navy now with this to look forward to. The sooner I get back and do what I have to do, the closer August is."

The phone ran. Michael hadn't realized that the main line rang in all the rooms in the apartment. It was a demanding sound.

"Hello," Jonathan answered.

"Hi, Jonathan. Welcome home. Is Michael there?"

"Sure. Let me put him on. Michael, it's your father."

"Hi, Dad. We just got home a little while ago. We should be home later. Don't hold supper for us. We can eat later or have pizza at John's."

"I called because there's some mail for you. There's a big envelope from the Department of Naval Personnel."

" I wonder what it is. Dad, will you open it for me, please?"

"Okay. There's a large folder, titled 'Michael Anthony Manganaro.' There's a big red stamp on the cover that says 'POLITICAL INFLUENCE.'"

"That's just my personnel file. I think it usually gets sent to the next duty station. I suppose they want me to take it. Is there a letter or anything?"

"Yes. It was still in the envelope. It looks more like a mimeographed form letter."

"What does it say?"

"Let's see. 'Dear Manganaro, Michael Anthony: Your orders to report to the U.S.S. Weehawken on December 17, 1960, have been cancelled. You are to report each workday to the Armed Forces Recruiting Office in New York City to perform general duties as directed from December 19th, 1960 until January 6th, 1961. No government housing is available, but if you require housing, a voucher is enclosed for accommodations at the Waldorf Astoria Hotel on Park Avenue. You will receive food vouchers from the Station when you arrive. You are directed to report for duty on January 9th, 1961 to U.S. Naval Air Station, Toms River, New Jersey to join the Navy Band as Baritone Soloist. A check for a travel advance for one-hundred dollars is enclosed."

"Wait, Dad, let me write this stuff down."

"You don't have to write anything down now. You'll be home later. In a nutshell it means you're home through the holidays, doesn't it?"

"Dad, you're right. Let me tell Jonathan, and we'll see you in a few hours."

Michael hung up and jumped into Jonathan's lap.

"Well, Precious? What's going on? You look like the cat that ate the mouse."

"I'm not going to Norfolk after all. I'm joining the Navy Band as Baritone Soloist on January 9th."

"Michael, they are based near our Seaside Heights house. Right next door in Toms River."

"That's the place. That's where I'm going to be."

"I'm sure there'll be a lot of travel involved, but I'm sure it will be a great experience for you. I'm proud of you, Michael. I really am. You'll get to travel around the world and when you're home in Toms River, we can be together. What a great beginning! We can set up housekeeping in Seaside Heights. Wait till you see how beautiful it is. You're going to love the beach in the nice weather. There is even a boat house on the bayside with a sailboat for me and a rowboat for you."

Michael took a big gulp of his drink. "Jonathan, I'm so fuckin' happy and excited. My heart is pounding."

"Well, you better calm down and don't drink anymore because you're driving us to Mellon later."

"Shit. You're right, but I didn't tell you the best part. Until I report to the Naval Air Station in Toms River, I work at the Armed Forces Recruiting Station in New York City from the 19th of December to January 6th. Regular working hours."

"That's great. You'll be able to have dinner with us on the 22nd after the meeting. And we'll be together for Christmas and New Year's."

They both finished their drinks and went back to the bedroom to put their stuff away.

"Jonathan, are you going to call Mr. Connelly?"

"Yes. Then let's go. I don't want to be here when Lillian comes home. I'll tell her about Theresa later on because I've already made my decision. But I do want to tell her the good news about you."

"Jonathan, come here and kiss me," Michael said.
Jonathan held Michael tightly as they kissed.
"You're crying, Michael."
"Because, I'm so, very, very happy."

Chapter 62

Michael and Rosa left together for Midnight Mass at ten-thirty. Gary stayed with Anthony and Louisa. They planned to leave at eleven-thirty. Addison and his wife were on a cruise to South America for two weeks. Gary knew that one day Addison would leave his wife, so they could be together always. In the meantime, he had to make do.

Jonathan had worked until almost nine at Taylor Oil. He had been compiling a list of questions to be answered at the budget meetings that were scheduled for the second half of January. During the last few weeks, he had gone over all the annual reports of Taylor for the last twenty years, read all their press releases and reviewed the balance sheet as of November 30, 1960. Since December 22nd, when he was officially elected Chairman of the Board, effective January 1st, 1961, he had reviewed all the leases Taylor had with landlords on the East Coast. The timing of the expirations of the leases bothered him. The renewal options also caused him concern. To say that the leases had been haphazardly drawn in favor of the landlords, was an understatement. He wanted to understand the refining and manufacturing operations in Texas, particularly. Lillian had promised to take him on a tour in February with her acting as a guide. She would share with him the wealth of her experience. In the meantime, she had given him a reading list to study. He had filled two legal pads with questions. He was tired, but was looking forward to Midnight Mass and spending the Christmas holiday with Michael.

Max picked him up in front of the building at 9:15. He put his briefcase on the seat next to him and made a decision not to open it, until they returned to the city. He wanted to think for a while and maybe to take a nap, so he wouldn't fall asleep during Mass. This was the second trip Max made today to the Poughkeepsie area. Earlier, he had taken

Lillian and Missy to the Balmorals, so they could spend the holiday with them and Mr. and Mrs. Theofanus. Jonathan was looking forward to hearing Michael sing. Soon, Michael would be singing at important functions for the United States around the world. He might even sing the National Anthem for a space launch, or something like that. He knew the Navy Band was playing for the inauguration, but that Michael wouldn't be member of the Navy Band until after the ceremony and would not be able to participate in the ceremony this time around. Michael was really something. Jonathan felt blessed. He opened the window slightly and lit a cigarette. He remembered a warning that Pat Connelly had given him about meeting Theresa. If he were to run into her, he was to be polite and greet her, but under no circumstances was he to have further conversation, or involvement in any way. If they found themselves at a social function, Jonathan was to leave at once, except, of course, at a church service. She had willingly signed all the necessary documents to insure that he would have sole custody of the child she was carrying, immediately following the child's birth. Theresa was never to see the baby. The documents were signed in front of witnesses and not under duress. The financial arrangements were finalized and could be jeopardized, if Theresa and Jonathan were seen to be having a relationship, or if it looked as if Theresa were in some way being threatened into giving up her parental rights.

Theresa had been more than pleased with the arrangement. All her expenses, including lodging at a fine New Orleans Hotel, meals, entertainment, medical and hospital costs were completely covered and paid for by the father. Theresa signed a document, which said that Jonathan had offered her marriage, but that she declined, and that she preferred not to be married, not to raise a child, but, instead, that she preferred to give sole custody to Jonathan, the child's biological father. Jonathan had been generous, but the details of the financial arrangement were not recorded for obvious reasons. It would not be in Theresa Garafolo's best interests to change her mind. She knew that she'd be back in the house on Second Avenue with the relatives from Brooklyn and a kid that she didn't want, if she backed down. If she held up her part of the bargain, her tuition and expenses were paid for a full four-year stay at Tulane, and she'd have twenty thousand dollars in her pocketbook. Nobody to answer to. No pissed-in diapers. No shit-diapers either. No more pizzas.

St. John's was crowded. There was a live manger scene near the front entrance with local actors and some small animals. Baby Jesus was bundled up in a green snowsuit to which some torn sheets were attached to resemble swaddling clothes. His parents, playing Mary and Joseph, intended to change in the rectory as soon as the Mass started, and then to attend the Mass with their new baby. Everyone stopped to admire the manger on the way into church. The goat was the only problem. She kept trying to escape and run into Main Street. She had to be tied up.

Lillian, Missy, Louisa, Anthony, Willington and Jenny were in the first pew. The Manganaros knelt down to pray. The lights were turned on. Two altar boys were lighting the candles on the altar. The organ started. Mrs. Rhine played *A Christmas Prelude* by John Winston Wright. Then there was a minute of silence.

Jenny reached across her husband and spoke to Anthony. "Mr. Manganaro, we'd love to have you and Mrs. Manganaro join us at our home for a drink after Mass. I expect the young folks will want to go off and do whatever they do, but we would like you to come, please."

"Louisa, I think that would be very nice. Are we able to go?"

"I can't think of anything that I'd like more. Michael, Jonathan and Rosa are on their own. We'd love to come. Thank you."

"That's great," Jenny said. "It will be just Will and me, Mr. and Mrs. Theofanus and Lillian and Missy."

Louisa was thrilled. She was going to be entertained at Hill House by the wealthiest couple in the area. She was going to be in the company of one of the greatest mezzo-sopranos of the day. And most important of all, she was going to spend time with the mother of her son's partner and with his stepmother, as well, who also happened to be the person to become President of an oil company. She was glad she had decided to open Rosa's Christmas present and to wear it tonight. It was a black dress with sequins running across the bodice and down one arm. She was happy with Anthony. Normally, he liked to say home, but to please her, he was going along with this late night invitation. She had no way of knowing then, that over the years ahead, they would travel around the world because of the relationships they would develop with these people.

Jonathan arrived and sat on the end of the pew next to Lillian.

"Hi, Jonathan. I'm glad you made it on time," Lillian said. "And I think you are making some very good decisions. I'm proud of you. And the Seaside Heights house is yours as long as you need it."

The chandeliers were lighted. The ushers passed out the programs, and Louisa read that the first musical selection was *Away in a Manager* and that Michael was the singer. Michael occasionally looked down at the ring on his finger. He felt very comfortable, not as nervous as he had always felt in the past. He felt very complete and loved.

The Mass went quickly. The music was lively and happy, full of joy and hope. The best part, Jonathan thought, was listening to Helene and Michael sing *O Holy Night* together. Jonathan knew that he would hear them sing together often in the years ahead.

0-595-17408-6

Printed in the United States
1264700003B/151-159